Real Life

Also by Kitty Burns Florey

Family Matters
Chez Cordelia
The Garden Path

Real Life

Kitty Burns Florey

William Morrow and Company, Inc.

New York

Copyright © 1986 by Kitty Burns Florey

Library of Congress Cataloging in Publication Data

Florey, Kitty Burns.
Real life.

I. Title.
PS3556.L588R4   1986   813'.54   85-10605
ISBN 0-688-06081-1

Printed in the United States of America

First Edition

1 2 3 4 5 6 7 8 9 10

BOOK DESIGN BY PATRICE FODERO

To Kate,

for invaluable assistance and a million cups of tea,

and with special thanks to

Bob Bechtold
Henry Berliner
Jane Cushman
Lily Forbush
Sara Kane
Karen Kleinerman
Carol Resnick
Richard Russo
Jane Wilson

and to Ken and Natalie

Part One

1

When it became obvious that Dorothea's nephew Hugo was going to be moving in with her, she rummaged through the boxes of junk on her closet shelf and under her bed and finally found what she was looking for: the newspaper clipping about Iris's death. TEEN MOTHER SLAIN IN DRUG DISPUTE. A subheading read BABY SLEEPS THROUGH IT.

Dorrie hadn't thought about Iris in years. The clipping was beige and brittle; the tape where she'd joined the two parts was yellow and had lost its stickum. There was a hazy picture—high school yearbook, probably: black sweater and pearls, and the beautiful smile. That was TEEN MOTHER—Phineas's girl, dead at nineteen. And BABY was Hugo.

She had met Iris twice. The first time, Phineas had brought her over to Dorrie's apartment; Dorrie was just out of college, living in one room in New Haven. She answered the door in her bathrobe. It was Sunday night, *The New York Times* was spread all over the room, and Dorrie was drinking Harveys Bristol Cream.

She hadn't expected Phineas or the teen-age girlfriend she'd been hearing rumors of (her mother called Iris Phineas's chippie). She had half thought, without much hope, that the ring at the door meant the return of Mark, the man she had been in love with for a year, who had left for the West Coast a month before—had imagined finding him on the doorstep, arms outstretched, ready to admit that San Diego was hell, he couldn't live without her, she must marry him instantly.

And there was Phineas with his monkey grin, and beside him a hugely pregnant girl who looked about fifteen and was so absurdly, perfectly beautiful, like a turn-of-the-century china doll in a museum, that she was almost grotesque. Or so Dorrie thought when she opened the door.

She didn't want to offer them her expensive and stingily hoarded sherry, but Phineas picked up the bottle, whistled, and said, with the unamused snicker that preceded nearly everything he uttered, "Will you look at what these bimbos with the college degrees can afford to drink." He took two glasses from the cupboard and poured. "Hot shit," he said, as if it were a toast, and raised his glass to no one in particular.

They stayed half an hour and finished the bottle while Phineas told Dorrie about his job in a car wash. His boss was a jerk, the work was crappy, the pay was piss-poor, and Phineas wasn't going to waste much more of his time in that shit-hole, that was for sure: a prophetic statement, as it turned out. "I thought it was time you met old Iris," Phineas said as they left.

Iris hadn't said a word, just smiled and drank, with one hand resting impersonally on her vast stomach. "Good luck, Iris," Dorrie said at the door, and Iris said, "Oh—thanks," as if she'd just noticed Dorrie's existence. And then she added, politely, with a strained smile, "I'm so glad I finally met you, Dorrie," in a small, squeaky voice that sounded seldom used. On an impulse, Dorrie gave her a quick hug: God, to be put in this predicament by Phinny—the poor girl . . . Her cheek was cool as clay, her stomach harder than a basketball. Her hair smelled of something Dorrie couldn't place right away; it came to her later: marijuana smoke.

Then, on Thanksgiving, Phineas was due for dinner at his parents' house with Iris and the baby. When Dorrie arrived (late on purpose), Phineas was storming around the living room saying, "Jesus Christ," and "Goddamn shit."

"You ought to sign up for a vocabulary-building course, Phinny," Dorrie said, taking off her coat. She kissed her mother, then her father. They were standing together silently by the piano, she in an apron, he holding a teddy bear by one leg, both of them wearing the cowed looks that only Phineas could produce. Iris sat in the wing chair nursing the baby under a tea towel. Dorrie imagined her mother running to get the towel when Iris opened her blouse. Iris wore a flowered shirt, her blond hair was in braids around her head, her eyes were blue and her cheeks pink. If tears hadn't been running down her face she would have looked like a Mary Cassatt madonna.

"Nobody asked for your goddamn opinion, either," Phineas said to Dorrie, then whirled around and said, "Fuck it, goddamn shit, I don't have to take any of this," and headed for the door. Iris buttoned up her shirt—they all had a glimpse of pearly breast, rose-red nipple—and followed him, weeping. Phineas stormed out without another word, but Iris paused in front of Dorrie and held the baby up, a fat pink object with a milky chin who resembled neither her nor Phineas. "Hugo," Iris said, and smiled through the tears. Hugo took one look at his aunt and howled.

"Don't forget Pooh." Dorrie's father offered the bear.

"Oh, Mr. Gilbert," said Iris, her eyes filling again.

"Dad," he said, and his wife chimed in with "And Mom."

"I'm so sorry about this," Iris wailed, and left. Phineas was gunning the motor, Hugo was screaming, and Dorrie's mother, in the doorway, began to sniffle.

"What's he mad at?" Dorrie asked. The car pulled away, and the lull left behind was like the silence after a bombing raid.

"He's on something," her father said. "Again."

"I think they both are," Mrs. Gilbert said through her handkerchief. "Oh, that baby, that poor little thing."

"Is Phineas still planning to marry her?"

"That's what your mother wanted to know."

"That's what started him off, Dorrie," her mother said, weeping. "I don't know where he gets that language. Oh, I don't know, I don't know what to do."

They ate the cold Thanksgiving dinner and tried to cheer up: a familiar scene. Holidays had always keyed Phineas up to his worst pitch, arousing crazily unreal expectations in his parents of happy families at peace around the groaning board. Holidays had never been cause for celebration.

Nor did they improve. By Christmas, Phineas was in jail for selling heroin, and by the Christmas after that Iris was dead.

And Hugo, the pink, bawling baby: Hugo was sent first to Iris's twin sister, Rose, who lived in a country slum with her children—two at that time, but there were four by the time Phineas was dead. When Hugo was eight, Dorrie's parents adopted him. First his grandmother died, then four years later his grandfather. That was when Dorrie inherited Hugo, along with her father's house and his collection of books on Victorian life and literature.

She put the house on the market right away. She felt no connection with it. It was the house of her father's old age, of Hugo's childhood. The repository of her own growing up had already been sold, when her mother died and her father retired and, with Hugo, moved away from the shore and his memories—inland, near Hartford. The new house was in a desirable school district and wasn't hard to sell. Its contents (minus the books), from the rusty bread box and the ancient Hoover to the rolltop desk and her mother's piano, were sold at auction. Then the library—or so Dorrie still called it, although the cartons containing her father's books were still in the attic of the new house, unpacked. She sorted through them for three days, and kept for herself a calf-bound set of

George Eliot, Trollope in the Everyman edition, a few biographies and art books, and (surprise!) a collection of photographs of naked women, c. 1880. She unloaded the rest on a smirking rare-book dealer who handed her a check for three hundred dollars as if he'd put something over on her, so that she racked her memory for days trying to recall what in her father's collection of brittle-paged volumes of literary criticism and history and obscure Victorian novels could have been worth anything. The book dealer's smirk seemed the culmination of something—a lifetime of being cheated?—and it bothered her unreasonably.

She was left with the prospect of Hugo. She took him in because she was all he had. He had no parents, and with his grandfather's death no grandparents—no relatives at all, that anyone knew of. Rose had disappeared—though even Dorrie, who God knows didn't want Hugo herself, couldn't have sent him back to Rose. Dorrie had gone with her parents to retrieve Hugo and had vivid memories of Rose's tumbledown trailer, the stink and the filth, the empty beer bottles, and Rose's vast backside swaying like the padded panniers on an Elizabethan gown. And it had been her father's wish that she be responsible for the boy, if necessary. She had promised—a vow that meant nothing to her. Why should it? Her father had been only sixty-seven on his last birthday, and spry. He liked to boast that he'd never been sick in his life except for Asian flu in 1956. His wife would have knocked on wood and said, "Don't tempt fate," and Martin Gilbert would have replied, "Nonsense," but sure enough fate intervened with a swift, fatal heart attack one spring evening and dropped Hugo into his aunt's life.

He boarded with his friend David Wylie until the school year ended in June, and then David's family delivered him to Dorrie on their way to the Cape. Dorrie didn't like to ask why Hugo couldn't go with them; she rehearsed a dozen ways of offering them money to keep Hugo for the summer and rejected all of them as cold and peculiar sounding. In the end, she could think of no alternative to the delighted smiles, the carefree small talk, the happy wave to the Wylies' departing car. And there was Hugo: short, verging on overweight, looking curiously like old photographs of her father, and grinning at her expectantly.

He arrived nearly bare of possessions. He didn't own a book, didn't have anything resembling a hobby, not even sports equipment. He brought only himself, plus a spare pair of jeans, a suit that had belonged to Dorrie's father and was too long in the leg (Hugo had worn it to the funeral, with sneakers), and a duffel bag full of dirty clothes he expected Dorrie to wash, an assumption that affronted her. She was his legal guardian, his only relative, but she hardly knew the boy, and his presence in her house was disorienting, as if it were a stranger's house she had wandered into. Life seemed impossibly skewed and out of focus with this fat little fourteen-year-old sitting in her favorite chair.

"Why should I wash your dirty clothes for you?" she asked, and the exasperated question emerged so automatically, as if it had been waiting there for its chance to pounce, that she knew exasperation would be one of the motifs of the boy's residence with her. Her heart sank. "Who do you think I am?"

"My surrogate mother," Hugo replied, completely serious.

"The hell I am," she said, and marched him down to the cellar, where the washing machine was.

Dorrie was a potter by trade. At thirty-eight, she made her living by it, and had done so for five years. Not a sumptuous living, but one that supplied her with what she needed. She didn't need much. Just after her brother's death—that had been nearly six years ago—she had bought her house, an old and undistinguished little farmhouse with a pond and an acre of land on a back road in East Latimer, a town tucked next to Rhode Island in the northeast right angle of Connecticut: depressed country, cheap and down at the heels and isolated.

Her friend Rachel Nye suggested Dorrie call the house Erewhon, and addressed her letters that way. Dorrie's last lover, Teddy, after a long drive from Hartford, said (coming up the walk grinning, with a bottle of wine in each hand), "Why didn't you tell me this place was way the hell out in Bumfuck, Egypt?"

She liked its isolation, and took pride in the complicated directions to the place. "What's it near?" people would call up and ask her desperately, pondering the tangle of back roads they were expected to follow. "It's not near anything," Dorrie would say into the phone, laughing, and then, seriously, pretending to be helpful, "Actually it's about halfway between Lemuel Forks and the Marsden River—well, creek really, Marsden Creek—and it's on Little Falls Pond. You can't miss it," and her giggle would spill over.

People did find it, of course. They came to her shop to buy what she made, and they came for lessons in her studio, though she did less teaching now that her things brought more money. And she ventured forth herself, to Providence and Boston, where her pots were sold on consignment in shops, and to the three or four best craft shows in the area. But she preferred, increasingly, to be alone in her little house. She thought of her solitariness as something that had been forced on her at an early age—like piano lessons, or creamed codfish— that she had come to appreciate.

Her moving to the country had been, in part, a defiant tailoring of circumstances to the reality of her life. All right, if no one will love me, I'll retreat from them all; I'll be alone if that's what they want: something like that had buzzed in her mind as she drove the back roads of Connecticut looking at property—along with her natural love of peace and quiet and her growing affection for the dinky, forgotten towns she was getting to know. It took her nearly a year to find the right place. She hadn't much money, and she wanted a view, something beautiful to look at when she raised her eyes from her wheel. She had an image in her mind of serenity, and when she finally found it on Little Falls Pond she had to spend a bit more than she had planned, so that she was in over her head for a year or two, but she got what she wanted.

She bought the place after ten years of teaching in an arts and crafts school in New Haven. Mostly, she had taught women suffering from empty-nest syndromes how to make plant-holders and ashtrays, but she had also helped run the office and organize exhibitions. For this she wasn't paid very well, but she saved every cent she could because, from the time she used to drape a blanket over the clothesline to make a haven for herself and her dolls Junie and Janie, what she had always wanted was a house of her own. All through childhood and for an appalling number of years afterward, it had been an unexamined article of faith that the house would come complete with a husband—would, in fact, be supplied by him as a reward for the inner wonderfulness he would discover under her increasingly thorny and difficult exterior. But at some point when she was approaching thirty, and the men were getting scarcer, didn't seem to notice her at all, and— except for Teddy—left her faster when they did notice her, she became aware that if she wanted a house she had better buy one for herself.

Her shop and studio were downstairs, a large space where once an entrance hall and parlor and kitchen had been. In the front, on white walls, there were plain pine shelves to hold her work, with a hooked rug on the floor and two Shaker rocking chairs Dorrie had made herself, from kits. In back, behind a low partition, were her wheel, worktable, tools, plastic bags full of clay, the blue mug for her tea, a clutter of cans and jars, the old farmhouse sink with its green stains, shelves full of pots and bowls and mugs in various stages. Out back was the little deck, and the salt-kiln shed, and then the pond itself down a stretch of patchy lawn, and the various green of the trees beyond it: her view. Upstairs was her tiny kitchen and the three narrow-windowed, chaotic rooms where she lived, and where every spare corner, every windowsill and tabletop, was crowded with what anyone but Dorrie would have called junk: feathers, photographs, old magazines, ancient mail, bits of clothing, her mother's sketchbooks, and too many pots and mugs and vases (she was her own best customer) that contained everything from flourishing plants to sick plants to buttons and paper clips and bills and dust. And then the cellar, where she kept her kiln, and the washer, and the shelves full of experiments and near-misses and outright flops that nonetheless told her something. She seldom threw anything away.

Dorrie was fond of the orderly elegance of her shop—her mother's side of her—but she loved her private mess more, her father's legacy. Her cluttered rooms could have been the offspring of her father's overstuffed library with its heaps of flyaway student papers and unread scholarly journals mixed up with garden catalogs and newspapers and ashtrays overflowing with pipe ashes and petrified apple cores. "Creative disorder is one thing, Martin, but absolute squalor is something else," his wife used to say when she entered his room, an act she'd performed as seldom as possible. She had said something similar, with her hand on her heart and all her frownlines showing, when she visited Dorrie for the first time, and she'd never gotten used to the chaos. Her infrequent visits had been visibly painful; she'd even implied, in one unguarded moment, that Dorrie's failure to find a man to marry was due to her bad housekeeping. But to Dorrie the mess was sacred; she believed it was an authentic expression of her deepest self that, after years of trying vainly for her mother's kind of order, she had finally given in to, had let herself deserve. The house had its own crazy organization; there was seldom a time she couldn't put her hands on what she needed. And, at the time Phinny's son barged into it, she looked on her wild domestic habits as a vital part of the contentment she had wrestled from the ruin of her life.

Hugo did his load of wash without complaining. He liked being alone in the cool cellar, with its rough stone walls and pleasant clutter of junk, its damp smells of clay and detergent and mildew. He needed to get quietly used to being at his aunt's, to compose himself; saying good-bye to David and his family had hit him harder than he'd expected.

While his clothes slogged around in their suds he examined the pottery collection on the shelves down there: cracked jugs, odd-colored bowls and jars, multicolored shards with numbers painted on them, a series of clay animals with an uneven, bubbly green glaze he found pretty, though he could see it hadn't worked out. He arranged a calf beside its mother, set fat sheep in a row, picked up a tiny cat and put it in his pocket. The washer emptied out suds, filled up, slogged again.

He became restless and went upstairs. His aunt was working on a bowl at her wheel. He stood and watched; she held a wooden implement next to the bowl and as it spun a long coil was sliced off, and a pedestal was created for the bowl to stand on. "Neat," Hugo said.

She turned, smiling her horsey smile. She sure wasn't pretty. She had one of those narrow prune-faces, and she was too thin and bony, though he noticed now that she had nice breasts, for an older woman. She had on cutoff denim shorts and a red T-shirt and no shoes, and her hair was put back with a rubber band. Her legs needed shaving. "How's the wash coming?" she asked.

"It's down there doing its thing."

"It shouldn't take much longer. Then you can hang it out."

He stared at her. "You mean with clothespins and all that?"

"Of course. People don't use dryers on beautiful sunny days."

"On TV they do."

"This is not TV, Hugo."

Something occurred to him. "You don't have a TV."

She laughed. He didn't like her laugh. It was too sudden, and usually too loud for the joke. What was so funny, anyway? "The way you say that," she said. "An accusation. The way you'd say, 'You don't have indoor plumbing.' As if it was serious."

"It is." He hated her.

"Oh, Hugo, for heaven's sake." She turned back to the bowl. Her back was better than her front, at least. He thought he might cry. What was he going to do without Claudette and Tiffany and Prescott and the whole Upton family? It hadn't occurred to him she wouldn't have a television; he hadn't even thought to ask her—that one lousy time she had called him before he arrived. Everyone had a television. The Wylies had three; they even had one in the kitchen so Mrs. Wylie could watch while she made dinner. He looked at the clock on the wall: He had just an hour.

He asked, "How can you not have a TV?"

"It is possible to get along just fine without one, you know."

"Yeah," he said. "Right."

"You can always read a book."

"I don't like to read." She made a noise he couldn't interpret. "You could have taken Grandpa's, at least," he said.

She turned again. He could see she was sick of the conversation, sick of him. He didn't care. She said, "I didn't want Grandpa's. I have one, in fact—a little old black-and-white set somewhere, I think it's in the garage. It's never worked very well out here in the country. I don't have much time for television, Hugo. I go over to the Garners' when there's something I want to see. But you can drag out that old set and try it, if it'll make you happy."

"Can I go and get it now?"

"Hang out the clothes first."

He took a deep breath. He knew tears were threatening behind his eyes. "I watch this program. It's on in an hour. Fifty-eight minutes."

"Do the clothes first, Hugo, or they'll never dry."

He listened. The washer was still making noise. "It's really good," he said.

"What is?"

He knew she would hate his saying it, so he said it anyway. *"Upton's Grove."*

She stared at him. "A soap opera? That's what this program is?"

"All the kids watch it."

"Boys? Watch soaps after school?"

"Some." He and David, at least. He didn't think many other guys did, actually, but he'd never admit it to her. "Most of them do."

"Good Lord, what happened to basketball? What happened to kickball and paper routes? And homework!" She lifted the pot off the wheel and set it on a shelf, then turned to face him. She was so much taller than he that he had to either crane his neck up at her or look straight at her breasts. He looked out the window, at the pond, listening for the washer to stop. "It's time you broke the habit, Hugo. A bright boy like you watching soap operas, for heaven's sake! It's pathetic." Her voice was too high for such a tall person. It went on, "There are plenty of things to do out here, Hugo. There's the pond. I have a little boat, or you could swim. It's kind of weedy, but—" She stopped, thinking. He could tell she was trying to be nice. The washer churned on, then began to make a whining noise. "Or there's a pleasant walk into town, two miles along a very pretty road. You could borrow my bike if you wanted to."

"Who are the Garners?"

"A nice old couple across the pond. You can just see their house through the trees."

He looked. "Do you think they watch *Upton's Grove*?"

"I sincerely doubt it." The washer noise stopped. "There," she said. "The lines are out by the garage, and the clothespins are in a red bag hanging from the post. Bring the basket in when you're done so it doesn't get all buggy."

She looked about to laugh again. She was enjoying his unhappiness, the old biddy—or no, not that exactly. It wasn't a nasty laugh, it was worse than that, as if she thought he was cute or something. "I'm really sort of addicted to it," he said. "I mean, it's not a little thing with me."

"I see that, Hugo," she said, and the amused look changed again to the impatient one. "For the moment, why don't you just get those clothes on the line?"

He hung up the clothes, thinking of Tiffany, who might be having her operation today, though what he really wanted to find out was if Charles Upton would discover that Claudette had taken the necklace and if she could manage to explain why before he did something drastic like call the cops. And there was a new character, that guy Marvin, or Marlin, with the moustache. He'd have to get a new notebook to keep his charts in. He and David had tallied the results from the old one with a calculator, and he'd bequeathed all his material to David as part of his policy of starting everything fresh. Tomorrow he'd go into town and get himself a new notebook, a ruler, a felt-tip marker. For today he'd have to borrow paper from her—if he could get the old set going. What if he couldn't? He looked across the pond, beyond his ratty gray underwear, to the Garners' yellow clapboards. How long would it take to row across the pond? Could you walk around it? he wondered. His fingers fumbled with the clothespins. What if he couldn't see it? The prospect was unimaginable, unbearable.

He found the television set wrapped in a plastic bag in the garage, stuck down in a corner as if it were a moldy flowerpot or something. It wasn't a bad set, wasn't that old. He carted it up to his room, his hole-in-the-wall—which was really what it was, not much more than that, a sort of cavern hollowed out of the end of the living room that must once have been a big closet. Just room for bed and bureau and Hugo. He set the television on the bureau and plugged it in. Static. He turned to channel 8. Static. He clicked the dial through all its paces. Static on all channels. All right, men—stand back. This is a job for the captain.

He worked on each channel in turn, fiddling with the fine tuner, then with the antenna attached to the back of the set.

He pressed down on the top of the housing, tipped the whole thing back at an angle, held the antenna in one hand while he worked the fine tuner with the other—experiments that had coaxed his grandfather's Philco into action before he gave up and bought the Sony. Nothing. He had a quick vision of his grandfather's pink face bent over the set, his fine old fingers on the knobs. Grief overwhelmed him, and he had to bow his head over the bureau, his eyes squeezed shut. The static from the television was giving him a headache; he could hear tantalizing hints of voices behind it, mocking him. For the second time that day he would have liked to cry. Despising himself, he began twiddling knobs. Don't worry, men—hang in there, we're getting it, it's coming, it's coming.

He had never tried to analyze his dependence on *Upton's Grove.* He and his grandfather had begun watching it a couple of years ago. Hugo assumed their addiction was related to their lack of relatives, but he didn't worry about it. So they were loners, bachelors together—widower and orphan. So what? Plenty of people watched soap operas; it didn't mean you were weird or anything. His grandfather was deeply embarrassed by the situation: "Our little vice," he called it, and made Hugo promise not to tell Aunt Dorrie—not that he ever saw Aunt Dorrie, not that he'd tell her if he did.

"At my age I think I'm entitled to a bit of frivolity," his grandfather said to Hugo. At least he wasn't like Harley, Hugo thought. Harley was the aging lecher on *Upton's Grove,* always making a fool of himself with women. But Hugo didn't say that to his grandfather. He said, "I don't think it's that frivolous, Grandpa," and his grandfather laughed.

But it wasn't. It was just life: love, death, birth, murders, operations, those Russian spies, people's little weaknesses. As his grandfather said, "It's not so different from literature, I suppose. It's shallow, of course—that's its limitation. But it's just stories. What people crave are stories, Hugo."

Well, Hugo knew that; it was no big deal. *Upton's Grove* was stories, it was company, and it was something he and his grandfather could do together before he began his home-work and Grandpa started dinner. And it was something to speculate over at dinnertime, trying to second-guess the writers. Grandpa was fantastic at predicting. He knew Tara would be kidnapped two weeks before it happened, and that Prescott would try to kill Tom, and fail. Let's face it, Hugo said to himself. *Upton's Grove* is about the only thing we have in common. But he didn't say that to his grandfather, either.

At the end of half an hour, damp with sweat, he had achieved part of a picture on channel 2 (a snowy man in a raging blizzard croaking out what seemed to be lawn-care tips), and an even snowier, voiceless drama, apparently involving a dog (a tiger? a coyote?) on channel 5. Channel 8, no matter what he did to it, was an undifferentiated sea of light gray dots vibrating against dark gray. Hugo wiped his forehead on his pillowcase. He was hot, his head throbbed, his hands were shaky. We've run into a snag here, men—this calls for drastic action.

He had eight minutes. He ran down the stairs, past the sound of her radio and the whir of the wheel, and out the back door, down to the pond.

The static was like a bad smell drifting across the peaceful afternoon, and Dorrie put on the radio to drown it out. Something baroque, with nervous violins—not her favorite kind of music, but she left it on. She threw another lump of clay on the wheel and centered it: soup bowl number nine; one more and she could take a break. The cold clay revolved between her palms, between her fingers, and she pulled it open, began to shape the bowl, thinking: Hugo. She was aware that she hadn't even begun to comprehend this change in her life. She had expected—what? She'd barely thought about it. "You have the most incredible talent for shutting out real life," Teddy had said to her once, and he had added, "I just wonder what you put in its place." Well, her work. She'd been busy all spring with commissions and the Springfield show, she hadn't had time to prepare for Hugo's coming. And how do you prepare for an unknown quantity, anyhow? If she'd thought of anything these two months, besides plates and bowls and mugs, it had been her father, the same thoughts, the same regrets: who could have known he'd die so young? She had thought there would be years and years, once Hugo left the nest, to make everything up with her father and retrieve the old affectionate closeness that they'd had before Phineas's brat took over her parents' lives.

She removed the bowl and set it gingerly on the table. It wasn't right; there was some kind of imbalance between the lift of the sides and the width of the middle. It would barely do. She had to concentrate. The bowls were part of a commissioned set for a restaurant in Chiswick, her hometown—a trendy vegetarian restaurant by the shore. She had tried for a suggestion of water in the design of the dishes; it would be mostly in the glazing, the wave of blue washing the white, with a greeny-brown band that could suggest, if you wanted it to, a far horizon or the shore: sea colors. But the shape too was part of it; she had devised a low-slung bowl on a wide foot that added up to some sort of natural, unstudied grace, a form that seemed tossed off, a gift of the sea. She didn't articulate it very well, but the proprietors of the place seemed to understand. They liked her designs, at any rate, and the samples she showed them. It was a big job, big enough to pay off the loan for her salt kiln.

She threw another lump on the wheel. The violins were suddenly loud: the static from upstairs had ceased. The back door slammed and she saw Hugo run down across the lawn, ducking under the grayish underwear he had jumbled up on the line. Hell! The child couldn't even work a clothespin; half the things were on the ground. She could just see him between the underpants and shirts, making straight for the pond, and she imagined him throwing himself into the water, floating there dead with weeds in his hair. But he was pulling the boat across the grass to the edge, and she realized he must

be going over to the Garners'. Oh, Lord. She should call Mary
and Ross and tell them that a maniac was about to invade
their sunny little house for the purpose of defiling their television set—that innocent machine, flanked on a shelf by books
and records, that had known only the dignified virtues of *Mas-
terpiece Theatre* and *Live from Lincoln Center*—with the hysterical excesses of *Upton's Grove.*

But she didn't call. Let him fend for himself. Maybe the
Garners would love him. Maybe he could become their pet,
go bird watching with them, get involved in Mary's little theater group. He would have to do something with his days.
Dorrie had imagined him reading away the summer. What
else did kids do, out in the country without friends? She rehearsed a speech in her head: I want to get a couple of things
straight, Hugo. I work very hard. I work in my studio and
in my shop all day, every day. I have to if I'm going to support
myself, much less you. No—leave that out; she had sworn
she wouldn't make him feel a burden. Leave out too the fact
that she liked the long hours of work—that she so preferred
her solitary labor to just about anything else that it was beginning to worry her. Thanks to Teddy, who had kept plugging
away at it. What I'm trying to say, Hugo, is that I won't be
much company. I won't be able to entertain you. You'll have
to . . .

She looked up from the wheel. Hugo was in water to his
knees, pushing the boat back up on the shore. Had he forgotten
the oars? Apparently. Dorrie watched him, amused. The poor
kid would never make it. She tried to imagine his six years
with her father. What had a man whose whole life was books
have made of Hugo's dislike of reading? She and her father
had hardly ever discussed Hugo; Dorrie wasn't interested. Now
that would have to join her list of regrets, that she hadn't
let her father talk about this pathetic boy. She knew only
that he was Phineas's son, that his first eight years had been
spent in turmoil, that her father's absorption in him had been
her own personal sorrow. And then Mrs. Wylie had sent her

his last report card (straight A's, even in English: how could that be?) and had said that Hugo was a nice boy, they were all fond of him, he'd been so good for David—who Dorrie gathered was some kind of misfit. "He has a good appetite," Mrs. Wylie had said. What else? She couldn't remember. Was that all? Smart, nice, overweight, illegitimate, gets along with weirdos? And now she could add his addiction to *Upton's Grove*.

Oh, God, she didn't want Hugo. She gathered the bowl on the wheel back into a lump and dropped it into her pail of slurry. No more today, it was hopeless. She stood up and filled the electric kettle and, waiting for it to boil, looked out the window again. Hugo was in the boat, the oars were in the locks, and he was rowing in a circle. She could see his frantic efforts to control the oars, and the oars skimming the surface futilely. Dig, Hugo, she urged him on. From where she stood he appeared to be crying. She pitied him, then hardened her heart. Tears for a soap opera! The kettle boiled, and she made her tea. When she looked again, the boat was moving unevenly across the water, roughly toward the Garners'. Her heart lifted. She looked at her watch: quarter past. If Ross and Mary were willing to indulge him, he'd see at least part of his ridiculous program.

Sipping her tea, she watched him make his way to the Garners' dock. He stood up in the boat, precariously, and guided himself to shore by hanging on to their metal railing, then climbed out and pulled the boat onto the grass. At least he'd had the sense not to leave it drifting. He disappeared into the Garners' fir grove, and Dorrie finished her tea and went, after all, back to her wheel.

The clay always fascinated her; as if it were her lover, she couldn't keep her hands off it. Even when she was bored with the repetition, or distracted by troubles, or physically worn out, with pain in her lower back and twinges in her forearms, the clay drew her: the magic potential of it, the transformations that could be worked, the clean hollows she saw in her mind and felt between her hands. "It's so fitting that you make empty vessels," Teddy had said during their last hard days. She would have given a lot not to keep recalling Teddy. He was two years gone, and for the first months after the breakup she'd thought of him scarcely at all; she had been filled with the relief of his leaving, the way a tree might feel when its leaves finally dropped. And then the fact of all their time together—four years—began to haunt her. Certain words of his, the facial expressions that went with them, meals they'd eaten while their interminable talks went on, afternoons and evenings in bed—all of this dogged her and added up to a gallery of failure. She couldn't even answer the phone without recalling Teddy. She still, when she couldn't catch herself, greeted the ringing of the phone with a mild curse at the intrusion. "Why curse your phone calls, Dorrie?" Teddy used to scold her. She'd never liked the way he thinned his lips out and clamped them together after one of his earnest pronouncements. "It could be good news," he said. "It could be something positive happening, something exciting—it could be life." Clamp.

"It's usually someone trying to sell me insulation or eternal light bulbs."

"But it's not healthy, the way you automatically reject the outside world."

"It's not healthy for light bulbs to outlive their owners," she said. But when he was in his reforming mood he couldn't be distracted by joking.

"He sounds like your mother," Rachel told Dorrie when she used to complain about Teddy. During the same period, Rachel was separating from and then divorcing her husband, and she and Dorrie spent long hours dissecting their relationships with Teddy and William.

"But he must love me," Dorrie said. "Or he wouldn't spend so much time trying to whack me into shape," though even she could see there was something wrong with her conclusion.

"He loves you the way a missionary loves his flock," Rachel

said. "Is that what you want? To give up your native rites and customs for Teddyism?"

Unlike Teddy, Dorrie could always laugh. In her worst moments, she could be as caustic as Rachel about the tenets of Teddyism. But when she was with him, Dorrie slipped back into the role of disciple with a readiness that dismayed her.

"You're so damned humble," Rachel always said.

"Humility is the cardinal virtue of Teddyism."

"I honestly don't see what you get out of the relationship."

"I get Teddy," Dorrie said, surprised.

She had loved him because he had bright brown eyes, he seemed to know everything, he tanned a beautiful honey-color in the summer, and he had loved her first. And now—it wasn't that she missed him, exactly, after all this time; and it wasn't that she didn't know, even better than she'd known back in those tough times, that they weren't good for each other.

"You're lonely," Rachel said when Dorrie told her that Teddy was often on her mind. "You need a new messiah."

No messiah had presented himself. Dorrie edged close to forty and began to believe that Teddy had been her last chance. She could have pushed it and married him—and should have, she told herself sadly but perhaps without conviction. She did want to be married; wherever she went she saw homely married couples, cozy together, and wished she was like them. She had to comfort Rachel once when, shortly after her divorce, she found a shopping list in the depths of an old purse: PAPER TOWELS, BREAD, TUNA, it said in Rachel's handwriting, and below that, in William's, JELLY, CLEANSER, TEABAGS. "I just miss that," Rachel wept, and Dorrie almost wept too, because she'd never had it to miss, that snug, unthinking conspiracy.

She hadn't had a beau (her father's word) since Teddy walked down the path for the last time. In the mirror she saw her face erode as surely as any vulnerable surface that suffered the seasons. She thought of herself as an old maid, and said the words to herself with a certain cruel pleasure: old maid, spinster, old bat. She plucked gray strands like weeds

from her black thatch of hair. She bought an expensive rejuve-
nating cream called Jolie Jeunesse. She read articles on face-
lifts, and periodically considered one. She pressed her palms
together hard, as if in prayer, to keep the flab from her upper
arms and the droop from her bosom. She could see herself
growing more cantankerous, like Miss LaPorte, the old lady
who had lived next door when she was a child. Dorrie expected
any day to find herself ordering the neighbors' kids off her
property and badgering the police with complaints about a
man looking in her window.

Working at the wheel Dorrie was free from the mirror,
from her collection of regrets and guilts and wishes. In the
studio, she was a person who made empty vessels; filling them
wasn't her business.

Tiffany's operation was postponed. Dr. Wendell couldn't
face operating on someone he used to be in love with, and
Tiffany didn't want anyone else to do it. There was a big
scene between them, and another between Tiffany and Michael,
her husband, so that even though Charles and Claudette
thrashed it out again about the missing necklace (for a moment
he thought Claudette was going to confess!), and Paula and
Gus talked for quite a while about Crystal's baby, it looked
as though Tiffany won out in the air-time category. But of
course he couldn't be sure; he'd missed the whole first half.
There was no point in beginning his record keeping today,
but he did it anyway. He borrowed some paper (pale blue
stationery, with flowers in the corners) from Mrs. Garner,
and a pen, and thank God there was a clock on the shelf
above the television. Tiffany chalked up six whole minutes:
not quite a record, but a respectable showing for a mere half
hour.

Mr. Garner wasn't there; he had gone to Providence, to
the dentist. But Mrs. Garner sat and watched with Hugo. It
was interesting to him that his aunt wasn't unique; here was
another person who had never seen a soap opera, and she

said her husband hadn't either, that she was aware of. "Unless he has a whole secret life," she said, smiling at Hugo as if that was pretty improbable.

"It must be living in the country," he said. This was during the commercials. "I guess you get a little out of touch with things." First they advertised a cake mix, and showed a big chocolate cake, kids snitching slices and then the mother, looking guilty (why?), taking the last one. Then there was a commercial for diet soda. Hugo hated the commercials—most of them, anyway. He hated the ones where some perky mom worried about her family's nutrition, for example, and the ones full of phony girls in bathing suits drinking soda from straws, with close-ups of their big lips.

"I guess we do," Mrs. Garner said, still smiling. She was in her sixties, at least—tiny and pretty with plain white hair, something like the way he remembered his grandmother. "We're really out in the sticks here, you know. I don't suppose there's going to be much for you to do, Hugo."

"It's pretty, though," he said quickly. "The pond and everything. It's a lot nicer than Hartford."

"You like living with your aunt?"

The Diet Pepsi commercial was winding down. The girls all stuck their hips out and shook their hair forward into their faces while they sang the jingle. "I've only been there a day," he said to Mrs. Garner, with caution. "She's real nice, though."

"If only she had a television."

He looked at her gratefully. "That's it," he said. "That's my only complaint. I mean, otherwise—"

Mrs. Garner nodded, and Tiffany appeared, crying. Hugo was glad he didn't have to finish the sentence.

When the show was over, he passed his notes over to Mrs. Garner. "Tiffany used to be just a minor character. Even last summer, she was just this waitress who worked at the club— that's the Grove Club, where everybody always goes for dinner and stuff. Of course, even then she was nice and everybody really liked her, but then she had an affair with Dr. Wendell—

he's Claudette's stepfather? Claudette's the one with the necklace? Anyway, then she started being on all the time. It wasn't
even gradual, which is what surprised me. She went boom!
like that! from two minutes a week to seven or eight minutes
a day, and now—" He shrugged, and indicated the flowered
stationery. "She's definitely a star. See for yourself."

"How long have you been keeping your records, Hugo?"
she asked him.

They were sitting on a kind of enclosed porch, where the
television was—the sun room, Mrs. Garner called it, but she
had pulled the drapes to shut out the light, and it was like
evening in there. Hugo thought he would like to live in that
room, he wondered if he could move in, he would sleep on
the short fat little sofa, he could do chores for them and watch
television.

"What?"

"Your records," Mrs. Garner said. "How far back do they
go?"

"I started the first of this year. January third, to be exact.
I didn't miss a day, even when I had the flu. I was really
sweating, I was throwing up—I felt really awful, but I knew
I'd feel worse if I screwed up my records. And then—" He
stopped. He had been going to say he had managed to see it
even on the Monday his grandfather was buried, that Mrs.
Wylie had insisted he sit down to it with David. "Your life
should go on as normally as possible," she had said. "That
way you'll be able to handle this better." He didn't think he'd
handled it particularly well. David had kept the records that
day. Hugo had watched *Upton's Grove* in tears. One good
thing about David was that you didn't have to hide things
like that from him. Hugo wasn't even sure he'd noticed. "My
friend Dave and I used to do it together."

"I suppose it's educational, in its way."

"My grandfather said it was. He said you don't find all
that many good practical uses for math. Of course, he was
an English professor."

She gave him another glass of apple juice, and then he went outside to mow the lawn. He hauled the mower (a hand mower! first clothespins, then no television, now a hand mower!) out of the garage, thinking what a nice lady Mrs. Garner was. She hadn't hesitated: "Of course you can watch your program!" and led him into the sun room, talking all the way. "You're Dorrie's nephew. Well, she told us you'd be coming, I think. I didn't even know she had a nephew, but of course—and how about a cookie or two? a glass of apple juice? We had some blueberries, but I think—" He liked that kind of chatter; it was just being friendly, you didn't have to listen to it. He was afraid she'd continue it during *Upton's Grove,* but she was silent and attentive, and waited for the commercials to ask him questions. He wondered if he'd made a convert, and the possibility thrilled him.

He mowed an H, filled it in, mowed another. Years ago, his grandfather used to mow the lawn with a hand mower much like this one, old and on its last legs. Wheels, he corrected himself, snickering. Then his grandfather had got an electric mower. He never let Hugo use it, always mowed the lawn himself. Hugo mowed another H. He could look across the pond and see his aunt's house. From here it looked shabby, in need of paint, the yard full of tumbledown sheds. His underwear on the line. He thought of how she had laughed at him and wished he'd leave so she could work in peace. He began to miss his grandfather again. Not even a week ago he'd told himself he was finished with missing him, he was handling it, he was coping, adjusting, accepting—all the things Mrs. Wylie, who was a psychologist, had said he should do. And now it was back, rising in his throat like apple juice—sour but with an undertaste of sweetness that he wished he could just give in to, just huddle in a corner somewhere and cry it out all over again, huddle in the dark sun room or in the room he had shared with David. It was lonelier over there with a blood relative than it had been at the Wylies' house. What a life: a life of missing people. He pondered that for a minute, pleased with his pun, and then he began to list them.

First his mother. He couldn't remember her but he knew he'd missed her because Rose had said he'd cried for a week when she died, and wouldn't eat. Then Rose and his father. He'd been sometimes with one, sometimes with the other, sometimes with both together, so that when his father died and he was taken from Rose there were two of them to miss, not to mention his cousins—the little ones, not Shane and Monty. Then his grandmother in her coffin, looking stuffed, with too much rouge on her cheeks. Then his grandfather, and that was the most recent and hardest because he was older and knew what death was, as Mrs. Wylie put it. He did know what death was: Death is missing people, he thought. If he were the type to write poetry—which he wasn't, except when forced to in English class—he would begin a poem with the line "Life is missing people," and end it with "Death is missing people," and the idea would be that first you stress "missing" and then you stress "people." He wondered how that could be done. A poet would know. David would know.

He came to the end of the lawn, and that distracted him. It had taken practically no time; the lawn wasn't big enough to pay for a half hour of *Upton's Grove*. He put the mower away and was searching for something else to do when Mrs. Garner came out the back door. "You don't have much lawn," Hugo said. "It took me about two minutes."

"Grass is too much trouble to keep up," Mrs. Garner said, smiling. He wondered if it was the same smile she'd had before, if she had kept it on her face while she puttered around the house. "When you get to a certain age," she added. How could she say that and smile at the same time? Hugo couldn't understand how old people, close to death, could stay so cheerful, could take so calmly their loss of strength, their inability to mow a lawn. Well, he would mow the Garners' for them; he would have done it even if they didn't have a television. And he'd weed the garden, shovel the walks, haul wood. He surveyed their property, looking for chores, and was struck by

the prettiness of the place: fir trees making a green-black frieze
for the yellow house, a red umbrella over a white table on
the patio, whole armies of marigolds and some kind of blue
flower, and down a little slope the pond with a willow drooping
into it. He had a sudden mad vision of himself with a girl,
rowing on the pond or sitting in the Garners' dim sun room
eating cookies and watching *Upton's Grove.* Weeding in the
garden together. Even watching his aunt make bowls and mugs.
The girl would say, "I just love things like this," reaching
out one slender finger to touch a rim. He could hear her voice:
"I really like your aunt, Hugo, she's such a character. And
I love this pond. Could you row me across?" Her name would
be—Tiffany? Susannah? Sandra? He had liked a girl named
Sandra in seventh grade. "Where did you get the name Hugo?"
she had asked him once. "It sounds like a made-up name.
What's your real name, Hugo? Or are you a Russian spy?"
All the kids had laughed, because that had been when the
spies were on *Upton's Grove,* and everyone was waiting for
Prescott to catch on before they kidnapped Tara. "What's
your real name, Hugo?" Sandra had asked.

"Hugo Phineas Gilbert," he had made himself reply, for
love.

"Oh, my God," Sandra had said.

"Do you want to come over tomorrow?" Mrs. Garner asked
him. "I don't see why you couldn't come over every afternoon
to watch your program."

His heart was full. He realized that he'd taken it for granted
that he'd come every day. What if she hadn't offered? "Oh,
thanks, Mrs. Garner, thanks so much."

She continued to smile. He wished she wasn't so old; it
seemed wrong to have to feel sorry for such a nice person.
"Tomorrow you'll meet Ross—my husband."

"I'd like to do some more chores. Anything."

"Maybe he can find something for you to do. It's awfully
good of you to offer, Hugo."

"It's the least I can do!"

There was a pause. She stood on the step, looking down at him, puzzled through her smile. "Your parents are dead, Hugo?"

"They've been dead for years," he told her, astonished. It was such an old fact, he hadn't thought there was anyone who didn't know it. "They both died really young. I've been living with my grandfather."

"Oh, I see. Dorrie's father."

"He died in April."

"Yes, I did know that." She reached down one hand and touched his cheek. "And you're what? Twelve?"

"Fourteen," he said, humiliated.

"Of course. You're older than twelve—what am I thinking? I see so few young people. Or at least, young people your age. My grandchildren are two and four."

Jealousy first, then interest. He liked little kids. "I hope I'll get to meet them."

"I'm sure you will." She stood beaming down at him, as if she was waiting for something, and Hugo realized he should go. God, here he was yakking when she probably had to get dinner or something. "Well," he said, and looked across the pond. What a dump. "I'd better get home."

"You'll have to get used to calling it home, won't you?"

It was just what he had been thinking—or nearly. He had been thinking how it made him feel sick, to call his aunt's place home. "I'll see you tomorrow," he said, trying to match her smile.

He could sense her watching him walk down to the boat and get in. He tried to wave at her, nearly lost an oar, and rowed in circles before he remembered how the oars felt when they were right. When he got back to his aunt's dock, Mrs. Garner had gone inside.

Dorrie was cleaning up when she saw Hugo rowing back. He'd been over there an hour, way past the end of his soap opera. She washed her hands and dialed the Garners' number.

"I apologize," she said when Mary answered.

"Dorrie? Apologize for what?"

"My nephew. I assume he hit you for his soap fix."

"He's delightful, Dorrie. We had juice and cookies together. He's the nicest boy. And I didn't even know he existed."

"Well, he does," she said, watching the erratic progress of her rowboat. "I'm his legal guardian now that my dad is dead. I hope he didn't make a nuisance of himself."

"Dorrie, he mowed the lawn. I mean, he was so grateful, it was absurd. And he's a riot about that crazy *Upton's Corner* or whatever it is. Did you know he keeps records on it? He has all these statistics. Oh, Dorrie, he's a sweetheart. And so bright!"

"Don't let him take advantage of you." She pictured Mary and Ross tied to chairs, gagged, their house ransacked, herself hiring lawyers, seeing social workers, bailing Hugo out. She heard Phineas's voice saying, "It was no big deal, and it wasn't even my fault, I don't see why all the fuss."

"We have a little agreement, Hugo and I," Mary said. "He's going to do some odd jobs for us in exchange for television time."

"Well, see that he sticks to it, Mary. And don't let him hang around getting in your way. If you don't want him there just—"

"Dorrie! Don't be so down on the boy. We like children; he won't be a bit of a bother." Reproachful: what had Hugo told her? That his auntie was a disagreeable old bitch who hated kids and wouldn't let him have any fun?

By the time she hung up, Hugo was pulling the boat up on the grass. She watched him turn it over and lean the oars against the tree. Good boy. Maybe not delightful or a sweetheart, but he was trying. It came to her suddenly that she should buy a new television and get the cable company to hook her up. Why not, for heaven's sake? She had the little inheritance from her father; she had put most of it into money markets for her old age and a college fund for Hugo, but surely she could abstract a couple of hundred for his present needs. The thought came and went, like a cramp, and she knew she wouldn't. Not yet, at least. Let him earn it, let him prove himself, she thought fiercely, having no idea what she meant.

Hugo was mooching along the bank. As she watched, he stooped down and unlaced his sneakers, took them off, and tossed them up on the grass with his socks. Then he waded gingerly into the pond, his jeans pushed up to the knee. She imagined the mucky bottom sucking at his bare feet; she hated it, the way some people cringe at a nail scraping a blackboard— the glutinous slime against her skin. She never swam in the pond.

Hugo reached down into the water and came up with a net of weeds. He held it up to untangle it, and the red stripes on his T-shirt gleamed in the sun. His arms, even at this distance, looked white and pudgy, muscleless. He flung the weeds from him, then bent for more and flung them away again, found a stone and tried to skip it. She watched him stand still for a moment, looking out over the water, before he proceeded further along the bank toward the waterfall and the Verranos' property, beyond the trees, out of her sight. She was startled by a mild disappointment; she had thought he would come in. She needed to know what he liked for dinner. Maybe they could drive into town for groceries, have a talk on the way. "I want to get a couple of things straight, Hugo," she said aloud, softly. "I'm not very good company. I work very hard. Don't expect me to—"

She took the rubber band from her hair, brushed it out, and braided it, looking in the mirror at her white, untannable face. The lines cut deeper every day between her nose and the corners of her mouth, giving her a snout like a chimpanzee's. Aunt Dorrie. Hugo's maiden aunt. Perfect.

She used to imagine herself with children. Once, when she was still going with Mark, she had even made up names for them: Eleanor, Daniel, and Jane, two girls and a boy. She wondered if they would look like her or Mark: Mark, she hoped. She had pictures of herself and Phinny as children:

thin and tall for their ages, with skin so white it was nearly blue, dense black hair, light gray eyes. They had looked like no one else, not even their parents, who were both short and brown-haired; it was often assumed that Dorothea and Phineas were adopted. There were snapshots, though, of relatives in Ireland, her father's mother's people. When her father was stationed in England during the war he had visited them in Dublin, and had photographed their narrow pale faces burdened with too much black, lusterless hair—faces and hair and tall thin bodies just like hers and Phinny's. She liked going over the pictures with her father. She liked the narrow gray streets and, in one picture, the mammoth carved doors of a church—in another, a house with window boxes brimming with flowers. All the girls were in limp cotton dresses with falling-down socks, the boys in short pants and caps, the parents unsmiling and dim, keeping back. "They don't look healthy," she said to her father.

"They weren't." He told her how poor those far-off cousins were, how it hurt him to share their scanty food, how he had tucked two pound-notes under the teapot when he left. For years he sent them an international money order at Christmas, but they scattered as they grew up, and he lost touch with them, so that all that was left was the photographs, which no one but Dorrie ever looked at, of the poor unhealthy Irish cousins in the forties.

She still had them, had come across them, in fact, during her search for the clipping about Iris. She stood looking in the mirror, wishing now that she had produced those imaginary children, that they were at this moment fooling around with Hugo down by the pond, fishing out weeds and skipping stones, barefoot. She imagined herself calling them to come in: "Eleanor, Daniel, Jane!" She went downstairs and out on the deck, and called, not very loud, "Hugo!" There was no reply, and she shouted it again. Her voice sounded unfamiliar, and embarrassed her. She waited a few minutes, but Hugo didn't answer or appear. The sun was in the west, and it heated the dock. She shaded her eyes against it. The pond reflected the sky, flat blue. The hell with Hugo, it was too hot. She went back inside and looked at the new issue of *Ceramics Monthly* that had come in the mail.

Hugo returned, eventually, for dinner. He was subdued, though when Dorrie asked him about school he talked a little. His favorite subject was math, music was all right, English wasn't. He had liked his history teacher, Mrs. Selnick, but he didn't like history. He had taken Latin for two years but didn't like it. He had made a bird house in shop and given it to David's mother.

"She likes birds?" Dorrie asked. "So do the Garners. They go out nearly every Sunday. Maybe they'd take you with them."

"I'm not interested in birds," Hugo said.

The conversation seemed inadequate to the occasion. Shouldn't something formal have taken place? An exchange of vows? I, Dorothea Gilbert, hereby swear I will do my best to—what? bring you up? be responsible for you? be a mother to you? And I, Hugo Gilbert, swear to be a good boy, to stay out of the way and not be a nuisance, and most of all to be nothing like my father.

"Birds all look alike to me," Hugo said.

"Was she nice—Mrs. Wylie?" Dorrie asked him.

He looked up at her from his plate of tuna salad, the first time he had met her eyes since she sent him out with his basket of clothes. "I wish I was back at Grandpa's," he said. "I wish he hadn't died."

"Oh, Hugo, so do I," Dorrie said.

They both had tears starting, and this agitated Hugo so much he left the table and went outside. She watched him out the back window, running down to the dock, a shadow among shadows. She washed the dishes and then sat in the living room, trying to think, to take it in. If she looked out the window again, she knew she would see him, a small dimming figure huddled with his grief. The pond would be darker than the sky, and gradually they would merge, the sky going navy blue, then black. Hugo invisible. But there, still there.

❧ 2 ❧

Dorrie's father, Martin Gilbert, had taught Victorian literature at a small, second-rate Connecticut women's college that had shocked and dismayed him when, in the early seventies, it began admitting men: "The Invasion of the Barbarian Hordes," he called it. He never altered his opinion that coeducation leads to mediocrity. He blamed his own disillusion with teaching on the invasion, but the truth was that as he aged he found his job more and more futile and tedious, and he was aware that his students considered him boring and old-fashioned and hard. He even grew tired of his subject. Matthew Arnold and Robert Browning wearied him; their world seemed far removed from his own. He knew by heart the novels of Trollope and George Eliot (from which he had named his children), and he didn't want to read them anymore. After he retired, he hardly read anything at all except magazines and the newspaper, and he discovered television.

But this was years after Dorrie had left home for good. During her childhood, her father had been ambitious and full of schemes. At the college, he served on committees that fought for stiffer entrance requirements, tougher grading policies, more rigorous courses. On vacations, he worked at his cluttered rolltop desk making notes on cards and annotating the margins of his books and filling out grant application forms. He drove all over New England looking in secondhand bookshops for works on his subject, for art books and old prints. He had a true admiration for the sanctimonious paintings of the Victorian age, and he and his wife had dinner table arguments about art, Anna defending modernism, pure form, experimentation, Martin going for realism and moral uplift. The arguments were sincere and informed and a trifle self-conscious: the Gilberts were proud of their ability to carry on a civilized discussion about an interesting subject, and the friction of mind against mind, opinion against opinion, was good for the mental development of the children, even though it was obvious that Dorothea daydreamed through dinner and Phineas bolted his food and then slumped glassy-eyed in his chair until he was excused to go out with his pals.

Martin wrote articles for scholarly journals, and occasionally but not often one of them was published—never in the prestigious publications. His great love was the book he worked on throughout his forties and fifties, a study of the interrelationship of Victorian art and literature. When he finally sent it to a small university press (Anna practically had to pry it out of his hands), it was returned with a letter saying half of it was out of date and the other half had already been done; he hadn't kept up with the scholarship. He burned the manuscript in the fireplace, a few pages at a time, while out in the kitchen Anna pounded her fist on the countertop, cursing the insensitivity of publishers. And then, that evening, they had beef stew for dinner—Martin's favorite—and wine, and apple pie for dessert, and a rousing discussion of Pop Art. Dorrie's parents were as jolly and sanguine as ever. The book was never mentioned again, and the rejection seemed to have left no mark.

Anna Gilbert was a failed artist as surely as Martin was a failed scholar. Failure was her way of life, a source in its own way of pride—proof that she was above the common herd, that her violent, murky oils were a rare and special taste. "I apparently haven't caught the knack of pleasing the masses," she used to say. Her true-grit smile had a wry twist to it, just in case she wasn't a good enough painter for such false modesty. Each time Anna took the train to New York with her portfolio, or sent slides of her work off to a gallery, or submitted pieces to one of the big art exhibitions, Dorrie knew as sure as winter that nothing would come of it—just as she knew that Martin's neatly typed articles would come back speedily, rejected, and that he'd be passed up for promotions and fail to get the grants he applied for. And she knew that his few unimpressive publications, and her mother's occasional group shows in New London or New Haven, were nothing but variations on failure.

They never stopped trying, either of them. There was always hope, always a new scheme: a gallery opening up, a grant available only to World War II veterans, an acquaintance with connections—or, in Phinny's case, a different school psychiatrist, or an innovative program for wayward boys. MAKE THE BEST OF IT, Dorrie thought, should be engraved on their tombstones. And she often wondered how they had produced her and Phineas.

Dorrie's one close friend, Rachel Nye, a fat girl with braces, was even more soured on life than Dorrie. Her witty cruelties made Dorrie feel, by contrast, like a nice person. The two of them used to sit at either end of Dorrie's ruffle-trimmed bed while Rachel ticked off, in alphabetical order, their classmates, first at Chiswick Elementary School, then at Shoreline High, and commented on them one by one. She was impartially nasty. She invented nicknames for the kids they despised most—the popular girls, the goody-goodies, the dumb macho boys they both secretly lusted after. Mary Gonorrhea Harper, No-Tits Farina, Nicholas the Prickless, Gross Gretchen . . . though, even as they sat there laughing until their faces ached, Dorrie wondered if, in another frilly bedroom, No-Tits and Gross Gretchen were cracking up over Horse-Face Gilbert and Fatty Nye. When she said as much to Rachel, Rachel looked at her with what seemed to be loathing and said, "Oh, for Christ's sake, Gilbert, who cares what those jerks think? Are you going to squander your entire precious youth worrying over trivial crap?"

She did, actually. She spent long hours, whole days, enormous chunks of her precious youth worrying: about her looks, her social failures, her unrequited crush on Nicky Moore, and what she would do if she got her period in the middle of English class; about overdue library books whose fines she had to pay out of her allowance; about where she would go to college and what on earth she would study there; about what hanging around with Rachel Nye was doing to her image; about a dream in which she was passionately kissing Lawrence Wynn, the creepiest boy in the class.

And then Phineas. Merely living in the same house with him seemed wrong, a crime against nature, as if a dear little kitten and an evil, no-good polecat were confined in the same cage simply because they belonged to the same family. There were times Dorrie was tempted to make to her parents what seemed like a perfectly reasonable request, that Phineas be sent somewhere else to live, that a foster home be found for him with people of his own kind. What did a person like Phineas have in common with Anna's pressed wildflowers, the threadbare Oriental rug in the hall, Martin's research on the names in Trollope's Barsetshire novels, Dorrie's place on the honor roll, the reproduction of *Guernica* on the dining room wall?

And yet Dorrie had known forever that no matter what outrages he committed or virtues she cultivated, no matter how her mother cried when he slammed out of the house or her father sat at his desk with his head in his hands—no matter what, her parents would always prefer Phinny.

"Oh, you are something," Anna said to him once after one of his dreadful crimes and his ingenious, hypocritical apol-

ogy for it, and she enfolded him in a hug with a look of
such fearful bliss on her face that Dorrie, who had been lurking
in the vicinity, had to back away as if from a painful light.

When Hugo thought of his father, he always remembered
the last time he had seen him. He wished that day didn't
stick in his mind; he would much rather have remembered
the day they had walked on the beach and picked up shells,
or their drive to New Jersey to see his father's friend Connie,
who had a swimming pool, or any of the dozens of nice things
they had done together that were fun or exciting or a little
crazy, but not that last day at Rose's.

His father had drunk too much beer, for one thing. Also,
he and Rose were smoking marijuana. Hugo hated it when
they smoked. He hated the look of glee on his father's face
as he rolled a joint—though he admired the magical deftness
with which he did it, and he liked the texture of the little
paper squares his father gave him to play with; they would
almost melt when he touched them with his tongue. But he
hated the burning smell that was like cloth smoldering, and
he hated the way they laughed at what wasn't funny, and he
hated it that, while they sat and smoked and laughed, his
cousins were allowed to get away with more murder than usual.
It was on one of those marijuana afternoons that Shane and
Monty, tired of his tagging after them and his chatter, had
forced him into the spiderwebbed old chicken house, padlocked
the door, and then forgotten him, and no one heard him yelling
until after it got dark.

But on his father's last visit, Shane and Monty were swimming at the reservoir with the Kushner boys, and Starr was
at her friend Tammie's house, and Rodney, the baby, was
alternately sleeping and crying in his crib, and Hugo was sitting
on the stone step outside the front door playing with Rodney's
Busy Box and listening to his father and Rose talking in the
living room. Their voices were loud, then soft. "On the streets,"
Rose said, and then, "Could be the big one," and his father's

laugh—the shrill, crazy-sounding laugh that meant he was high.

"I'll tell you one thing, Rosita baby," he said, and then Rose must have stood up because the chair and floor creaked so that Hugo didn't catch what that one thing was. But then, clearly, he heard a match rasp and the sound of his father's deep inhaling and then Rose's, and then a pause, and finally his father's voice again. "I can't keep him with me, he just drags me down, Rose, how can I—" The high-pitched laugh came again: *hee hee hee.* "How can I do my fuckin' job with a kid dragging at my heels?" And the two of them exploded with laughter.

"Your fuckin' job," Rose said, squealing. They laughed for a long minute, cackling and gasping, and then they wound down, slowly, saying, "Ooh—oh, my God," their laughter bubbling up and then subsiding and coming again and, finally, with deep sighs, ceasing.

Hugo heard them pass the joint again, heard their breath stop and then start with a whoosh. Rose said, "You be careful at your goddamn job, Phinny. You joke too much. You're too reckless."

"I can take care of myself," his father said. "Just tell me what about the kid."

"He can stay here. Permanently, I mean. What's one more?"

His father let out a sigh. "That's a load off my mind."

They said some more things. Rose said, "As long as you come and see him. You know he's crazy about you."

His father said, "I love the little guy, Rose."

Rose said, "He's a good boy. I wish mine were more like him."

But Hugo didn't listen very hard. He knew all that, what was said and what was left out. He knew Rose liked having him there; he knew she even loved him, probably, better than her own children; he knew his father loved him; he knew too that Rose loved his father, that his visits made her happy—

she hummed and sang for days before his father arrived and cried after he left. He knew too that all this love being passed back and forth amounted, somehow, to emptiness.

His father said, "I'm proud of the kid, Rose." But Hugo knew that too. His father had made a fuss over his last report card—took him out to McDonald's for supper and gave him five dollars, and when Shane forced him to hand over two his father made Shane give it back. Called Shane a little shit. He knew his father was proud of his schoolwork—stupid schoolwork, any dope could do it, except Shane and Monty, who always flunked everything. Hugo knew he was smart, and that his father liked it that he was. Big deal.

What he hadn't known was that his long dream of being with his father—forever, together, permanently—wouldn't come true. He had thought staying with Rose was like (she was sending him to a Catholic school) purgatory, where you waited to get into heaven. A better purgatory than the one waiting up in the sky (or someplace), which was just like hell but not permanent like hell. There was Rose, whom he loved, and Starr, whom he usually loved. And Tiger the dog. And Shane and Monty, who could be nice once in a while, and then they all had fun together. But it was purgatory all the same because heaven wouldn't be until he went to live with his father. And now there would be no heaven. There would only be these visits.

Hugo sat on the step and tried to make it better. Maybe his father would visit more often, at least, and stay longer. Maybe he would even take him on trips, like the one to New Jersey. That had been years ago but maybe now that it was settled, the load off his father's mind, maybe there would be more, the two of them going off in the car together: small heavens because there definitely wasn't going to be a big one. And maybe it wasn't as definite as it sounded. Maybe his father's job that they thought was so funny wouldn't work out. Other jobs hadn't worked out. Maybe then his father would get a job where it didn't matter if you had a kid dragging at your heels, like he could be a carpenter or a bricklayer and Hugo could hand him tools and pack the lunch box.

The voices inside were silent. Rodney stopped crying. The locusts sang *sizizz, sizizz, sizizz.* Tiger the dog came running up the driveway from whatever he'd been doing in the woods, and flopped down on the step beside Hugo. Hugo imagined his father and Rose sitting on the sofa together, dozing, leaning against each other. He would go in, eventually, and sit there with them until they woke up and then he would help Rose get supper. He wondered if his father would leave after supper or stay all night, if they would go for a walk before it got dark, maybe down the road to the old cemetery where his father liked to read the crumbling words on the gravestones, some of them from a hundred years ago or more. He laid his hand on Tiger's rough, sun-warmed fur and concentrated furiously on sending messages through the window to his father's sleeping mind: Stay overnight, stay overnight.

His father didn't stay overnight. In fact, he left before supper. He gave Hugo a snapshot before he left, a color photograph taken in front of his father's old car, the Camaro. His father's arm was around his mother. His mother was smiling a big smile. She was pregnant. Her hands were clasped on her stomach. Somebody's cat was sitting on the hood of the car, washing, one leg in the air. His father wore a black jacket. His mother wore a sundress. She had long blond hair like Rose's. His father wasn't smiling at all.

He gave Hugo the photograph without saying anything about it except "Hang on to this, kiddo." Hugo wasn't even sure it was his mother, but Rose told him later. And that was himself, Hugo, inside his mother's stomach, under her white hands: he pictured a tiny silver fish swimming through green water. He put the photograph away somewhere, and then when weeks and weeks went by, and winter came, and then spring, and his father didn't come back, he hunted frantically for it one day and finally found it in the dust under his bed. It reminded him immediately of that last day, his father saying, "He just drags me down," and "That's a load off my mind," and Rose saying, "Permanently." When his grandparents came to get him, he put the photograph in his jacket pocket and took it along, just because it seemed wrong to leave it behind. But he didn't like looking at it: his mother was a stranger smiling into the sun, and his father looked unhappy, and all it did was remind him of his father and Rose laughing and getting high while he sat outside on the step.

The Gilberts drove up to Rose's place in Massachusetts on a dank day in early spring. Dorrie, bored and carsick in the backseat, listened fitfully to her parents' talk. Anna wondered if Hugo collected stamps. "So many boys at that age are obsessed with collecting—with little finite groups of things they can control. Stamps, baseball cards, that sort of thing . . ."

Her voice trailed off, and Martin took over. "Or chess. It's just the age to learn chess. They enjoy rules, I think—control, as you say."

Dorrie wondered how they knew. Phinny at eight had been interested only in raising hell; control hadn't been one of his interests, nor had rules, not to mention chess and stamp collecting.

They talked about real estate. They were thinking of selling the house by the shore: it was too large, too hard to heat, worth too much to hang on to. They could sell it and buy another and still make a small profit. Martin was just about to retire; many of their friends had retired and moved away; there was no reason to keep the house, and they could use a change. Underneath all their chatter was the promise of Hugo, Phinny's boy, whom they were going to fetch. Every word they said was charged with excitement. This was their second chance. Hugo would be a mini-Phinny, the as-yet-unspoiled son of their son. He would be their atonement.

Phinny's name was no longer being mentioned. Anna had

cried almost constantly for a week after they'd gotten the news of his death. She cried all through the memorial service, cried every time someone spoke to her, cried randomly through the day and in the night. Dorrie, who had been staying with her parents, slept badly, waking in the dark to hear her mother's wild sobbing and her father's murmurs. Then, a few days ago, Anna had taken a loud sip of hot coffee, raised her head, and said, "Well, I suppose life has to go on," and sighed and wiped her eyes. Later that day she telephoned Rose, and then she vacuumed Phinny's old room and put clean sheets on the bed and went out to Child World and bought a Parcheesi game, a jigsaw-puzzle map of the world, an illustrated *Treasure Island,* and a book called *Encyclopedia Brown Saves the Day.*

Dorrie tried to imagine little Hugo moving into her parents' lives. She could think of him as nothing but a small Phinny, trailing trouble wherever he went. As for Phinny himself, she knew she mourned, and that the hard knot in her stomach that was partly carsickness and tension was also partly grief for her brother, for "the waste of human life," as her mother had been calling it all week. But her feelings were complicated. Had she not, all her life, prayed to be delivered from Phinny in some miraculous, unspecific way? And now he was dead in prison. She had been startled, at the memorial service, by the slap of memories she didn't know she retained. Of the time when, age five, he had fallen out of a tree, a fragile apple tree he was forbidden to climb, and had lain there like a doll, limp and white, in a pile of autumn leaves. Dorrie had run to the back door, pursued by loss, screaming that he was dead, that they had to save him. (He'd had a mild concussion and a broken collarbone.) And another time, the first time she had ever seen him high, she'd come home from college for a weekend and he had met her at the train station, his eyes glittering and his walk uneven; his driving down the dark roads from New London she couldn't recall without a lunge of fear. "What have you been doing to yourself, Phinny?" she had asked him—her brother, a junior in high school. He had told

her to fuck off, and after that she'd imagined him in car
crashes—not dying but, after a hospital stay, repenting.

"What about a bicycle?" her mother said. "Do you suppose
he'll have one to bring? I don't know how we'd ever get it
in the car."

"It would be simplest to get him a new one, Anna. I don't
suppose he's got anything better than an old broken-down
thing at Rose's."

"What a lovely idea, Martin! We'll get him a new one.
Something classic—bright red, with a good big basket."

It struck Dorrie that they were like lottery winners spending their new wealth: Oh, yes, we'll have that, and that, and
one of those. . . . Their affection for Hugo, so long unrewarded,
was their winnings, and they were spending it prodigally. Their
reckless high spirits were obvious even from the backs of their
heads—her mother's passé French twist, her father's shiny
bald spot. They gleamed, and their voices rang sharp and metallic in the closed car, always on the edge of pleased laughter.

"I'll get that old sled out of the cellar and spiff it up a
little. . . ."

"Let's call Chuck Thurman about putting the house on
the market. . . ."

"That nice carved chess set must be in the attic. . . ."

Rose lived outside Worcester, on a country road lined with
sagging trailers and junked cars and sparse weeds. Martin
and Anna had met Rose only once, years ago, when she and
Phinny had brought Hugo for a visit, two stilted hours with
Phinny's bad temper and Hugo's whining. Of Rose they recalled gross obesity, a rich and frequent laugh, and what
seemed to be a sincere appreciation of their flower beds: Rose
down on her knees crooning over the pansies. "It was unbeliev-
able how she resembled Iris," Anna said in the car. "It's grotesque. But she seems a good woman, in spite of everything."
The four illegitimate children, she meant. The fat. The bad
grammar.

"We have no reason to believe she hasn't been good to

Hugo," Martin put in, eager to be fair but determined to let no hitch prevent their taking Hugo away. Rose had sounded cooperative on the phone—had seemed, in fact, to welcome their plan. She had, after all, four of her own. Dorrie wondered what a social worker would make of the situation: the orphan son of two junkies poised between an unwed welfare mother and an elderly couple who barely knew the boy.

"Could this really be the right road?" Anna asked, eyeing a yard full of rusting car bodies. Before every house there seemed to be a dog tied up, barking. "This doesn't look quite—"

But there around the next bend was the mailbox by the road: TCHERNOFF in spiky black letters, and a yard full of chilly-looking children, one of whom was unmistakably Hugo.

He was eight, a fat little boy with a runny nose. He came dashing down to meet the car, then stopped in the middle of the dirt driveway and stood with his hands in his pockets, smiling tentatively. When the car stopped, Anna whimpered, "Oh-oh-oh," fumbling with the door handle, and rushed forward to hug him. "There's my boy," said her husband, following more slowly. Dorrie sat in the backseat until she couldn't get away with it any longer (her mother looked back and gestured impatiently, "Come on") and then she got out, stiffly, and followed them all up to Rose's trailer, where Rose stood waiting, the neck of a beer bottle in one ham fist.

No one had foreseen that Hugo wouldn't want to go. Rose hadn't told him yet; that, of course, didn't help. It wasn't that she didn't want them to have him. "I'm reconciled," she said. "That kid deserves better than this." She had said as much on the phone, and she said it again to Dorrie and Anna in the narrow living room, while the kids took Martin out back to see where they'd buried the dog, Tiger, who had been hit by a car. "I love that kid, but I don't mind telling you I'm really strapped most of the time," said Rose. "I haven't been able to work because of my back, and I get food stamps but they don't go all that far when you've got five—and I'll tell you, them boys can eat." She offered them all a beer. Anna and Martin declined, but Dorrie took one and stood there swigging it from the bottle as Rose did. It immediately calmed her stomach. She imagined her mother, on the drive home, saying, If she's so strapped, how can she afford beer, I'd like to know?

The place was in a state of anarchy that was like another world. The living room was bare of furniture except for a sagging sofa that had once been light blue but was now greasy gray and spilling its stuffing, two wobbly upright chairs—one seatless—and a wood-grain Formica coffee table, thick with grime, that supported several empty beer bottles, an overflowing ashtray, a doll's arm, and a pair of cracked eyeglasses fixed with a Band-Aid. On the floor was a piece of tan carpeting, filthy and fraying at the edges. There was an ancient console television, one of its rabbit ears bent at an angle and linked to the window via masking tape and a long piece of wire. Everything in the room was broken in some way: toy trucks without wheels, a mirror with a lightning crack, the latticed mahogany base of the television that looked kicked in, the table propped up with a block of wood where one leg was missing. There was a generalized reek of dirty diapers and a specific, close-up stink that was Rose's bad breath. She said, "I know you can give him all the advantages, Anna, which is something I sure can't," but she seemed unbothered by the state of the room, the lack of clean glasses for the beer, the thin baby-cry from a room down the hall, or the fat sausage of flab like an inflated beach toy that bulged pink from beneath her T-shirt and over the straining band of her jeans.

"He's a good boy," Rose said. "He's my baby. Even though I got two younger than him my heart goes out to that kid, maybe because he's my sister's boy. Iris and I were that close!" She held up two fingers, intertwined like slugs mating. The nails were bitten down. "And now his daddy, poor Phinny—" Her blue eyes filled up. "I just wish that child would have some good luck, for a change."

They called Hugo in, and Rose told him to get his things

together, he was going with his grandparents. Hugo looked
from face to face, at Rose, at Dorrie, as if one of them might
be an escape, the look in his eyes getting wilder and more
desperate. Dorrie had a mad impulse to kneel down by the
boy and hug him and let him bawl on her shoulder. "You're
going to come and stay with us, Hugo," said Anna. "Remember
you used to visit us sometimes, when you were little? You're
going to live with us now. For good. Won't that be fun?"
Hugo let out a howl and leaped at Rose where she leaned in
the doorway.

"Whoa there, boy." She set down her beer and picked
him up with surprising strength and held him against her shoulder, rocking him while he cried. He locked his legs around
her middle. "He'll get over this," she said calmly. "It's just
strange to him."

Hugo did, finally, stop crying, but he wouldn't smile when
Anna asked him to. He stood looking down at his shoes. He
wouldn't kiss Rose good-bye, either; he pulled away, frowning,
but she kissed him loudly on the top of his head and said,
"You come back and see us, you little monkey—hear me?"

When they left, Dorrie's father pressed twenty dollars into
Rose's palm and said, "Buy the kids something," and Rose,
surprised, uncrumpled the bill and held it up. "Twenty dollars?
Oh, you shouldn't, Martin. But thank you. This'll buy a hell
of a lot of diapers."

Three of the cousins gathered at the door to say good-
bye. The baby continued, somewhere, to whine. A little girl
of perhaps five cried and said, "Hugo, Hugo," and a bigger
boy picked his nose and said nothing. A tall boy with pimples
said, "So long, shit-head," and went back into the house. Rose
paid them no attention. She got down on her massive knees
by Hugo and said, "You be a credit to me now," half the
solid edifice of her fat pink back coming into view as she
lifted her arms to force a hug on him.

His Aunt Rose told him that his father had died in a car
crash, and so for a while Hugo was afraid to ride in cars,

especially when his grandmother drove. She tended to slam
on the brakes and point out the window at a bird or scream
at someone she knew. He loved his grandmother; he thought
she was the busiest, smartest person he had ever met. But
he missed his calm, smiling Aunt Rose. His grandparents never
talked about his father; for a long time, Hugo tried not to
think of him, but after a while the idea that he might forget
his father filled him with panic and he began to try to remember. He spent the boring parts of arithmetic and social studies
telling himself stories of Hugo and Phineas—the long drive
to New Jersey, the walks to the cemetery. He always came
back to that last visit, his father leaving early, giving him
the photograph, backing fast down the dirt driveway—still a
little drunk, a little high, even after his nap. Hugo wondered
if his father had been sober when his car crashed, if he had
died instantly or later in the hospital, if he had been conscious,
if he had spoken before he died. No one had told him a thing.
He kept recalling Tiger the dog lying still by the side of the
road, blood coming out of his mouth.

When Hugo was ten, his grandmother died, and his grandfather sold the house, finally. Hugo started fifth grade in a
new school. Everything was always the same: the boring school
day, the kids avoiding him, the teachers nice, the school bus
where he sat alone, and the quiet evenings and weekends with
his grandfather. His grandfather didn't do much, now that
he was retired. Most of his friends had moved to Florida.
There were no more theater tickets and dinner parties, no
more babysitters for Hugo. His grandfather knew hardly anyone but the neighbors: a young housewife on one side with
whom he exchanged courtly remarks about the weather, old
Mr. Murdoch on the other side with whom he played bridge,
the Molinos across the street whose dog ran wild and crapped
on lawns. Hugo sometimes played with the other children on
the street, but they considered him a pest and a sissy and
laughed at him when the Frisbee sailed right through his hands.
He and his grandfather played Scrabble; by the time he was

ten, Hugo was winning regularly, and, when his grandfather bragged to Mrs. Molino or Miss Crake, his teacher, Hugo could tell they suspected the old man of throwing the games. But he wasn't throwing the games. Hugo knew, in fact, that behind the bragging his grandfather—a retired professor of English!—was upset by his losses; if Hugo occasionally let him win his grandfather always knew, and looked sad.

But there was no real sadness, no bad trouble. Life flowed by as smoothly and lazily as the creek down at the end of the street. It was the easiest life in the world, Hugo thought, and the safest. After the daily drudge and humiliation of school, his life at home was neat and simple: TV, food, a few chores, the predictable Scrabble drama, enough money, infrequent intrusions. In sixth grade, he met David, and they became friends. Sometimes he went to the movies with David's family, or stayed overnight. But he didn't mind just being home, talking with his grandfather about *Upton's Grove.* His grandfather never tired of his chatter, and he never tired of his grandfather's old pink face—absorbed, nodding, fond.

Once in a while, his Aunt Dorrie came to dinner. Hugo had no opinion about her. He knew she didn't like him to hang around, and that disappointed him a little. Not that there hadn't always been people who considered him a nuisance, but usually they were kids; adults tended to like him, and to consider his conversation appealingly precocious, though his father used to get impatient and say things like "Drop it, Hugo, for Christ's sake, quit trying to pin me down," or just plain "Shut the fuck up!" His aunt was brisk and unfriendly, with a worried face. She looked like his father, but older and uglier. Her eyes were exactly the same: the light blue irises ringed in black; every time he looked at her, he couldn't believe it. When she wasn't around he never thought about her.

He dreamed several times that his father wasn't really dead, there had been a mistake, and his father called him up and said, "Hugo? It's Dad. I'm coming home." But his chief waking fantasy was that Rodney and Starr and Rose—shorn somehow of Shane and Monty—would come to live with him and his grandfather. Rose would settle her huge self into the chair by the fireplace and drink beer, and she and he and his grandfather would talk, and Starr would play with her Barbie doll, and Rodney wouldn't be crying the way he always did but would be cooing happily on the rug, saying things to himself in baby talk.

It was Dorrie's habit to work all day and to read in the evenings. She liked travel books, biographies of artists, and fiction, and she had a weakness for murder mysteries. During the months before Hugo came to stay she had been reading some of her father's blue-bound Trollopes, but she'd made an excursion to a bookstore in Providence and picked out a stack of mysteries, and Hugo's arrival caught her in the middle of the new Spenser.

"What's that?" he asked her when she settled down with it after dinner on his second evening.

"A mystery."

"Oh—like Agatha Christie?"

"Well—not much, actually."

"Does somebody get murdered?"

"Yes, somebody gets murdered."

"And there's a smart detective? I read an Agatha Christie once for a book report, and there was a really smart detective named Hercule Poirot."

His French accent was impeccable and unselfconscious. Dorrie frowned at him. "Would you like to read this when I'm done, Hugo? It's a lot better than Agatha Christie. It's quite funny, in fact, and the characters are human and real; it's not just a puzzle. . . ."

Hugo was shaking his head, standing with his hands in his pockets looking at her and smiling politely. "Oh, no, thanks. You could tell me the plot when you're done; I'd like to hear what it was about."

"But Hugo—"

They were sitting out on the deck, where the breeze was

almost cool. The light was fading. Soon she would have to go inside, but the house was stuffy and she resisted, even though her book turned gray in her lap and the sun was setting rose and purple over the Garners' roof. Hugo had been exploring the neighborhood; he'd strolled down Little Falls Road as far as the Verranos' and had penetrated the woods—not very far—on the other side of the road. He'd reported to Dorrie a black snake in the woods and what sounded like guitar music coming from the Verrano place.

"A harmless garter snake," she told him. "And it must have been the radio. I don't think either of the Verranos plays guitar."

"Do they have any kids?"

"No—they're a young couple, not married very long. He works for the phone company and she's a nurse, I think." She hated to think of the Verranos. They often walked down the road in the evenings, hand in hand; once they had stopped to kiss right in front of her house; and one evening, walking along the pond picking wildflowers, she had come to the waterfall that marked the property boundary and seen them standing in it as if it were a shower, embracing, the water glancing like diamonds off their naked bodies. Dorrie had dropped her jewelweed and lilies and hurried back home, mortified and near to tears. They hadn't seen her; it was her envy of them, her painful longing, that mortified her. She always thought she was safe, cured, resigned, until someone else's happiness cast its radiance on her meager contentment and bleached it out to nothing.

"But Hugo—" He stood before her, his round stomach straining against his T-shirt and his face cheerful. "Hugo, if you don't read, what do you do? I mean—" She could see he found the question absurd—and it was, in a way. Plenty of people didn't read. What did Phineas use to do while his sister sat in her room with her nose in a book? Get in trouble. "When you lived with Grandpa, how did you spend your evenings?"

"Oh—" He shrugged, paused, smiled again to himself as

if recalling good times. "I guess I did my homework. And we played Scrabble or Monopoly or crazy eights or something, or we watched a little television. And then we talked quite a lot."

It was still unimaginable: her ponderously cultured, quiet, bookish father and' this restless boy. "What did you talk about?"

"Oh—this and that."

"Well." It really was too dark to read outdoors, she could hardly see her book, but Hugo's face loomed pink above her, vivid in the sunset glow. He looked disappointed, his smile gone. He had expected something from her—the magical breaking, with a word, of the spell of his sad boredom. She closed her book. What she wanted, desperately, was to get into her coolest nightgown, pour a cold glass of wine, settle into the comfortable chair by the window fan, and open her book again. The longing to read was sometimes almost a physical sensation, of the same order as the need to drink water or rub her eyes or stretch her arms above her head after a long day at the wheel: reading released tension, it soothed her, it gave her something to think about, it provided company. It did everything *Upton's Grove* did for Hugo; it did what a love affair would have done for her.

She hugged her book to her chest and looked up at Hugo. He said, "Maybe I'll take a walk down to the pond and then turn in early. This country air sure makes me tired."

He would be down on the dock again, crying for those dear dull evenings with his grandfather, and then he'd go off to bed in his alcove to weep himself silently to sleep. She appreciated his good humor, the genuine attempt to conceal his unhappiness from her, even his tries at friendly conversation. He seemed, actually, to like her, and she wondered why. She hadn't begun to be reconciled to his invasion of her life, nor did she have any particular liking for him. She pitied him, tolerated him, would do her duty if it killed her. If they could only get through the summer, school would start and he would occupy himself with schoolwork and friends and the usual adolescent activities. Until then . . . If she thought about it, her heart sank. It wasn't even the end of June.

"The mosquitoes are really something!" Hugo said, slapping his neck.

"I think we'd both better go in." Dorrie stood up and looked out over the water. The trees were spiky and stark against the colored sky; the pond was black. "Would you like to play a game of Scrabble before bed, Hugo?"

His smile was enormous; he hugged himself. "Oh, boy— would I," he said, and she felt bad, even angry with him, that he was so transparently grateful for an offer so grudgingly made.

He beat her. She couldn't believe it. It had been years since she had lost a Scrabble game. She and Teddy used to play, and she had always beaten him—narrowly enough to give him hope, but consistently and without mercy. It had been, she suspected, one of the unacknowledged elements in the breakdown of his love for her. Since Teddy, she had played from time to time with the Garners, whom she beat easily. They didn't mind; a Scrabble evening was a social occasion, and on the nights when they switched to poker Dorrie always ended up a few dollars poorer. Scrabble, though: it was her strong point. "My one talent," she called it apologetically to the Garners. She probably hadn't lost a game since college.

Hugo played silently, swiftly, with a concentration so intense it changed his appearance; he looked almost gaunt, his features sharpened, his eyes narrowed. At first they were close, but Hugo pulled way ahead of her with RAJAH on a triple word score and then a seven-letter word worth eighty-two points: HALCYON, winning finally by nearly a hundred points.

He relaxed when the game was over, clearly pleased with himself but chagrined at her loss. "You really play a good game," he said. He gathered up the letters into a pile. "I mean, that game could have gone either way right up until the end, and then I had some luck."

"Nonsense, Hugo—you're an amazing player." She

watched him as, in careful handfuls, he replaced the letters in the old felt bag her mother had made: SCRABBLE, it said in bold, fraying embroidery. His face was as round and innocent as a doll's. His plump forearms were dotted with mosquito bites. He looked no older than eleven or twelve, and he never read a book unless he had to. "Where did you get your vocabulary?" she asked him, not so much because she expected he could really tell her but to see what he would say.

He closed up the bag, thinking. "Oh—well—I listen pretty hard, I guess. Whenever I hear a weird word or an unusual word it keeps going through my head, sort of. Like music? And then if I learn a word in school or someplace I just sort of keep remembering it." He grinned. "Whether I want to or not."

It puzzled her, that he could have such an affinity for words and not want to use them for anything except to rack up points at Scrabble. "But you don't like to read. Or write? You've never wanted to write poetry or—" She searched her mind. Or what? Do crossword puzzles? Enter spelling bees? And she couldn't imagine Hugo a poet; for all his improbable gifts he seemed the most literal, the most prosaic of boys.

"Reading makes me nervous. It seems so phony or something, but it's really real. Do you know what I mean?"

"I'm afraid I don't."

"Well, like Hercule Poirot. Or even Huckleberry Finn. I've read all that stuff for school; I did a book report on Huck Finn last year. But take somebody like Poirot—"

"Hugo? Where did you get your French accent?"

"Huh?"

"Your accent. Where did you learn to pronounce French like that?"

He looked puzzled. "I've had French in school for the last two years."

"Yes, but—"

"We learned how to talk French. We had a language lab and everything."

"But—" He looked at her politely, waiting, weighing the bag of letters in one hand, and as she looked back at him his face crumpled in a yawn. "Never mind," she said, "I'm sorry. Go ahead with what you were saying."

"Well—I mean guys like Poirot and Huck Finn." He came out of the yawn, grinning, shaking his head. "Excuse me. I mean here we are talking about them as if they're real. Like how Huck Finn escaped from his father by pretending he was dead or how Hercule Poirot solved the crime by asking the gardener what time he was pruning the rosebushes, just like we could talk about Mrs. Garner or my grandpa or somebody, but they're not real, they're just made up."

"But your soap opera people aren't real, either, Hugo."

"But they are. I mean, I know they're just actors and everything, but at least they're real people on TV pretending to be the people on *Upton's Grove.* But in books they're just words." He looked at her helplessly, on the verge of another yawn. "Doesn't that seem really weird? All those little black squiggles on a page and we sit around in English class and talk about how Huck Finn escaped from his father? Doesn't that give you the creeps? That it's so phony and everything?" He let the yawn loose and gave himself up to it; she could see all his molars.

"Not so that I can't read," she said, suddenly impatient with him. What a baby he was, after all, wasting his good brain on petty abstractions and excuses. She stood up. Her hair was hot on her neck, and she gathered it up in her hand. If she were alone she would take a cool shower and go to bed naked. She said, "Speaking of reading, Hugo, I'm going to read a bit more before I go to bed. I'll go in the bedroom so the light won't bother you." She wanted to be rid of him— this bizarre, unwelcome nephew with his useless skills. She wanted her old life back. Empty though it might have been, it had suited her; she was used to it.

"Are you mad that I won?" Hugo asked her.

"Good Lord, of course not!" It was true. She wasn't mad,

she was flabbergasted, but her denial sounded unconvincing, and she made herself say, "We can play again tomorrow night if you like." Even that: it sounded as if she was upset by her loss, wanted another chance. "If I'm not too busy," she added.

"Oh, great," Hugo said. "That would be so great."

She stretched out on her bed with her book, the fan blowing in cool air, and listened to Hugo run water, pee, brush his teeth, spit into the sink (*pyuh, pyuh, tyew*), and then climb heavily into bed. The springs squeaked.

"Good night, Aunt Dorrie."

It touched her: Aunt Dorrie, in his husky boy's voice. "Good night, Hugo." She got up and closed the door gently, then opened it again a crack and sat on her bed, listening. The night before he had lain awake; she'd heard him thrashing around, he'd gotten up twice, restlessly, for drinks of water. Tonight, she could tell, he dropped off immediately. Well, if a Scrabble game a night would send him peacefully to sleep, she'd play him one until he got over his grief. She wondered how long it would take him to settle down—whatever that meant. How could a kid like Hugo settle down into her life? And if he did, what would it do to her existence?

She opened her book and tried to read, but she had lost interest in Spenser and his wisecracks and his perfect though fortyish girlfriend. She thought about the mysteriousness of Hugo, the magnitude of her responsibility, the horrors of parenthood, the unfairness of life. What was she to do with him?

The more she tried to read, the more her mind stuck at Hugo. Finally, she turned out the light and sat in the dark, trying to look on the bright side: it had crossed her mind, when she first contemplated taking him on, that Hugo would save her from a lonely and meaningless old age, the curse of the single person. She had seen herself aged, desperate, foolish, susceptible to causes, an old crone in a kerchief lighting candles in some church, signing away her life's savings to the Moonies, carrying signs on behalf of hamster rights or the banning of fluoride. Hugo would be the antidote to all that. She would be lovable old Aunt Dorrie, who had raised Hugo from a pup, the matriarch of his large and loving family. . . .

She said to herself, What a pathetic hope, and felt tears begin at the corners of her eyes. What a goal in life, to be someone's beloved aunt. She turned off the fan. The light from the rising moon laid whey-colored strips across the sheet. She fell asleep and dreamed, as she often did, that she was locked in a room without doors or windows, that she was hopelessly, horribly late for an urgent appointment, that everything depended upon her escape, and that (as she ran in circles and pounded the walls and screamed for release) she would never get out no matter what she did.

❧ 3 ❧

At the end of June, Hugo moved out of the house and into the garage loft. The room up there was cramped and triangular, rising to a point with the roof, and splinters of light came through between the roof boards where shingles had disappeared. But Hugo considered it far superior to his cubicle off the living room. It had, at least, two small windows.

"One for sunrise, one for sunset," Dorrie said when she climbed the ladder for a look. "I suppose it'll be all right if you clean it up a little." She kicked at a dead mouse with her foot. "A lot," she said. But she didn't question his preference for the garage.

He swept the floor, hitting his head on the low beams where the roof angled down, and then scraped off the bird droppings and scrubbed it. He removed spiders' nests and dried-out cocoons from between the wall joists. He patched a worn-through place in the floor with scrap lumber he found in the garage. He tacked screening to both windows and devised a heavy curtain, from an old canvas awning, for the sunrise side. He had had enough of early rising—his aunt was always up by seven. He packed his clothes into his suitcase and his duffel bag and hauled them up the ladder; eventually, he would put up shelves or something, maybe a system of boxes, to keep things in. It didn't matter. The important thing was to take possession.

He had wanted to do the whole job himself, but he had to let Dorrie help him drag his mattress out there and then twist and wedge it through the trapdoor, a task that left them both sweaty and laughing. "It's like the birth of an elephant," Dorrie said when it was done. They both flopped down on the mattress at opposite ends, each cautiously aware that times like this, when the tension and hostility fizzled away and they liked each other, hadn't been frequent. Most of the last two weeks had been, Hugo thought, like *Annie,* the movie he'd gone to with the Wylies about the kids in the orphanage, except that here nobody sang.

His aunt didn't seem to mind that the mattress had become dented and grimy on its trip over the lawn and up to the loft. Not that it had been that great to begin with. Hugo liked the way his room looked with the mattress in it, like hippie pads he'd seen pictures of. "I've got a cover somewhere that you can zip over that," Dorrie said, and got up to stand by the west window, looking out. "It'll be gorgeous up here with the light from the sunset coming in. I bet it'll turn the whole room pink."

Hugo said, "Actually, I'm going to need a flashlight or something, if you have anything like that—or I could go into town and buy one." He still had the twenty dollars Mr. Garner had paid him for cutting back the shrubs and clearing out the cellar—hard work but good money. He would have liked to earn more, but when he'd finished the shrubs Mr. Garner had said, "Looks like you've just about cleaned us out of chores, Hugo. I bet this place hasn't looked so good since it was first built," so that it was clear the Garners didn't want anything else done—couldn't afford it, maybe. Now it was just lawn mowing for TV time.

"I guess I could get a kerosene lantern," he said.

"My God, Hugo—I didn't realize," Dorrie cried, whirling around from the window. "There's no light!" He was afraid she'd refuse to let him sleep up there after all. She'd see all of a sudden it was too dirty, too dark, too buggy. The problem of winter—snow, dark, no heat—loomed unspoken between them. Hugo couldn't believe he'd still be there by winter; maybe she couldn't, either. He was half convinced that, while he was at the Garners' every afternoon, she was on the phone tracking down orphanages, foster homes, boarding schools. It was the fantasy that put him to sleep on rough nights, the possibility of a nice family somewhere, or a school full of really nice kids, where he would fit in and be cared for and liked.

"Well, you don't read in bed," his aunt said. "So that's no problem. But—" She surveyed him closely, as if trying to figure out just what a nonreader would need light for. "You could probably get along with a good flashlight, don't you think? Or a lantern. No kerosene, please. That's one worry I don't need. But maybe some kind of battery-powered gizmo?"

Why did she always have to be so vague about everything? Mrs. Wylie would have known, Mrs. Garner, Grandpa—they'd know just what to get and where to get it. His aunt merely gazed out the window again in a worried way: did she expect a battery-powered lamp to come whistling through it? She turned to him again and smiled, and he made his face blank, unirritable.

"Make up a list, Hugo," she said. "We'll go into town and get what you need. My treat. We'll make this into a really nice room. Maybe you should have a rug—one of those woven grass things that smell so good? Or a piece of scrap floor covering? What is this place—about fourteen by twenty? And I'll get you a new mattress cover, Lord knows if the old one will turn up. And how about proper windowshades? Or something to keep the rain out—now I wonder what would do it."

He didn't want her horning in, but he liked the sound of all the new things and the idea of shopping. It made him feel good, that she was going to buy him something, even if it was only practical things like rugs and shades, and even if it meant she was glad to get him out of the house. He didn't mind that; it worked both ways.

He was looking forward to going into town again too. They had driven there twice before, both times for groceries. He'd had a bad experience on each occasion. On the first, she had said, at the Stop & Shop, "Why don't you check out the main drag while I get the groceries?" and he left her pushing a cart through the produce department while he walked on down the street. It wasn't much of a town, but Hugo liked the way it looked—dusty and old-fashioned and forgotten in the sun. He passed a drugstore with a display of wheelchairs and crutches in the window, an auto parts store whose windows were so grimy you could hardly see in, a bar in whose gloomy depths he could see a gray game show on TV, a Carvel that looked unchanged since about 1952, a luncheonette, a Laundromat, and at the end of the block a pizza parlor. In front of the pizza parlor were three girls and a boy, maybe a little older than he. The girls were all pastel and white and tanned, in short shorts and sneakers with little white socks, and they had hairdos like Claudette and Tara, those millions of combed-back waves that scalloped over their shoulders like half-moons, like scimitars flashing. The boy they were talking to looked like Crystal's boyfriend, Jamie—Mr. Cool. Hugo had always hated Jamie, with his big biceps and that mumbling way of talking. "In real life, that boy would be in reform school," his grandfather used to say.

"Hi, good lookin'," one of the girls called, tossing back her shining waves. She was speaking to Hugo. Her T-shirt said DURAN DURAN IN CONCERT. Hugo felt his face turn scarlet, and a fever of happiness took him over before he realized it was a joke. Another girl punched her on the arm and squealed, "Kathy!" and they all laughed, except for Mr. Cool, who said, "Jeez," and allowed himself a detached smile. Hugo turned and walked back down the street, hearing their laughter, hearing how quickly they forgot him. "There's Jerry," one of the girls screamed, and another Mr. Cool loped across the street to join them. How did they tell each other apart? Hugo hated them. Twits, he thought. Idiots. Lunchmeat. All the way back to the Stop & Shop he could hear them behind him, their shrill cries, their brainless laughter. He looked sideways at himself in the Carvel window: short and pudgy, a wimp. Nothing had changed, nothing ever would. He would look twelve years old until he died, which he hoped was soon.

He wouldn't have gone along on the second trip into town, but he had been sitting in the boat all morning, rowing back and forth, fishing out weeds and flinging them back, with the sunbleached sky pressing down on him until his eyes and ears and teeth ached. He was hot and bored, so bored it was like being desperately ill, it was like the flu. He hadn't known such boredom was possible. The town wasn't much, but it was better than the boat. He went to the Stop & Shop with his aunt, and it turned out to be sort of fun. She let him pick out his favorite foods—some of them, anyway. Hot dogs and cantaloupe and wheat thins and Breyer's butter almond, but no soda or packaged cookies, and raspberries were too expensive. He had a good time until at the check-out counter he spotted a copy of *Soap Opera Digest.* David used to grab it in the drugstore where they had stopped for candy on the way home from school, and Hugo used to have trouble tearing David away from the thing. Hugo hated soap opera magazines; he had no use for what they had to tell him: lame predictions, rumors that came to nothing, endless summaries of events he already knew by heart. Worst of all were the details of the stars' lives. These were painful to Hugo. He didn't want to know what Tiffany ate for dinner, how many wives Prescott had had, who wore gowns by whom at the cast party after the Emmy awards. He wanted these people to exist for an hour every afternoon—thirty-eight minutes, actually, after the commercials. He allowed them, in addition, that shadowy realm no one was privy to, in which Claudette did actually take dictation from her boss and Crystal had her pregnancy test and Tiffany got up in the morning and put on her makeup and made coffee for Michael—or whatever. But outside *Upton's Grove* he refused to allow them life. And then, in the Stop & Shop, on the cover of that loathsome magazine, while he was helping his aunt stack groceries for the cashier, he saw a photograph of a man and a woman embracing, with the headline UPTON'S GROVE ROMANCE HEATS UP: EXCLUSIVE INTERVIEWS WITH MARCIE AND SCOTT. But it was Paula and Michael, brother and sister on *Upton's Grove*. He stared sickly at the picture. How wrong it was, how disgusting. He wished he hadn't seen it, the two of them pressed up against each other.

"Do you want that?" his aunt asked, beside him, with the isn't-he-cute look on her face. She had two ways of looking at him: isn't-he-cute and what-kind-of-kid-is-this. The way she'd looked when he beat her at Scrabble, four games out of four. They didn't play anymore.

"No," he said, and began piling up toilet paper.

"No, thanks, Hugo," she corrected him. "Please."

"No, thanks," he said. He wished he could tell her about the picture and why it upset him. There was even something in her schoolmarmish correction that he liked, that made him feel almost comforted, but it put him off too—that and the way she had of treating him like a troublesome pet of some kind. Couldn't she see that he was upset? That good manners didn't come into it? But it wasn't a thing he was sure he could explain, anyway. Better just to forget it.

The Stop & Shop, though, like the pizza parlor, became tainted for him. It was like a corner near his old school where a small dead dog no one ever bothered to remove had decomposed slowly, unobtrusively, a white lump by the curb covered and then uncovered by snow and thaw, which could have been a chunk of ice except that Hugo had seen it when it was fairly fresh and still had its whiskers, its teeth bared in a death snarl, its fluffy tail. There was a bakery on that corner where he and David sometimes stopped for doughnuts, but after the dog appeared Hugo couldn't bring himself to go in there anymore.

But he knew it was weird to feel like that. It was like David, worse than David, and he had to overcome it. He knew also that there was more to his new hometown than a bunch of stupid girls and *Soap Opera Digest.* And so when his aunt suggested they drive in and get his supplies he was glad to go.

They went to a big discount store—not as vast and new as the one in East Hartford where he and his grandfather used to buy socks and toothpaste and, once, the new TV, but for East Latimer it wasn't bad. They found a mattress cover and a lightweight blanket (brown, which wouldn't show the dirt, his aunt said) and a battery-powered light bright enough to read by if he'd wanted to. Grass rugs turned out to be too expensive, but Hugo liked a red fake-fur throw rug, so they got that. He couldn't believe how kind, how generous his aunt was being. He wondered if people mistook her for his mother. He hoped they didn't, but aunt—aunt he wouldn't mind.

There was a sale on towels, and while she poked through them Hugo browsed around the store. He thought he might buy her a present—but what? He rejected perfume, cookbooks, jewelry—the things he recalled his grandfather giving his grandmother. They weren't right for Dorrie. He looked at mugs with names on them, but there wasn't a DORRIE. Or DOROTHEA. Not even DOROTHY, which he would have considered risking. But there was a mug with a red heart on it, and inside the heart, FAVORITE AUNT. Hugo pondered. The mug was $3.95; he could afford it. That she wasn't his favorite aunt was a technicality. Rose was his favorite aunt. But he couldn't remember Rose all that well, and she had disappeared from his life—though, standing there with the mug in his hand he remembered what he could of Rose, and imagined giving her the mug, saw her smile and her soft, loose chins and her beautiful eyes, which he knew were just like his mother's. He remembered what it had felt like when she hugged him: she was soft everywhere, and she hugged tight.

He bought the mug for Dorrie, and went back to the towel department. "An impulse item," he grinned, holding up the bag.

"Hang on to your money, Hugo," was all she said.

They got towels and washcloths, in the ugly blue that Dorrie favored, and a plastic wastebasket for Hugo's loft, and she stopped to leaf through a *Time* magazine cover story about some writer she liked while Hugo looked absently at hardware. Then she got Scotch tape and masking tape and a paring knife. When they got to the check-out with their basket, Hugo searched around for a clock, couldn't find one, got a look at the digital watch on the cashier's wrist. It was 3:22. He was missing it. He couldn't believe it. He had assumed he had an inner timesense, as migrating birds do, that kept him in sync with *Upton's Grove*. This had never happened before.

He looked at his aunt. She was counting out bills. "I'm not going to make it," he said. "My program."

She said, "Oh, Hugo," in her irritated voice, paying him no attention. "I thought those towels were on sale," she said to the cashier.

"Not the blue," the woman said. "Just those flowered ones that come in sets."

"Oh, well, never mind, I'll take them," his aunt sighed. He watched her skinny white fingers receive the change and stow it in her wallet. He watched the cashier tuck everything neatly into bags, wrapping the rug in two bags and stapling them shut. Who cared? Was it going to get dirty between here and the car? He watched the minutes dissolve on her watch. It was past 3:30 when they left the store. His aunt stomped ahead, frowning, unconscious of him. Hugo considered tossing the mug into the Dumpster in the parking lot. What a dumb present, anyway, for someone who made mugs all day! He must be losing his mind. But he didn't throw it

away, and when he got back to his loft he tucked it up on
the ledge under the eaves where he kept his secrets (the photograph of his parents by the Camaro, the pottery cat he had
stolen from the basement, the eighth-grade class picture in
which he looked almost handsome). Maybe some day he'd
get the chance to give the mug to Rose—though he doubted
it. Despair filled him.

Later, when his aunt was working in her studio, he rowed
across the pond to see Mrs. Garner. She had not only watched
Upton's Grove for him, she had kept the records on a piece
of her blue stationery. "It looks as though Tara and Prescott
are going to adopt Crystal's baby, after all," she announced.
"What did I tell you? You owe me a dime, Hugo." Betting
on *Upton's Grove* was their latest thing. Hugo hugged her,
remembering Rose again, though Mrs. Garner was short and
thin. "You're a dear boy, Hugo," she said, and his heart light-
ened. That there could be such goodness in the world!

When he got home his aunt was at her table, carving a
blue border of leaves and flowers into the rim of a bowl. He
approached her warily. He suspected her of dawdling at the
store on purpose, so that he'd miss his program, or at least
of being glad it had happened, but she looked up when he
came in and said, "I'm sorry we didn't get home in time,
Hugo."

"You are?"

Her bony smile. "I really am." As always, it seemed, after
she had been working, she looked fagged out but calmed, and
her voice was kind.

He touched a carved bowl on a shelf, a teapot, a plate—
gently, as he had learned. "These are nice," he said.

"But what about your records? This will screw everything
up, won't it?" The hint of laughter was there as usual, but
she looked genuinely concerned—and guilty?

"Mrs. Garner watched it and told me what happened."

"Oh." She bent over her bowl again, with that smile. "Anything good?"

"Yeah, I guess so." He hesitated. "The Palmers are going to adopt Crystal's baby."

She frowned. "Crystal's the teenybopper with the mean parents?"

"Yeah—well, they're not that mean. See, Crystal's boyfriend, Jamie, was trying to back out of marrying her, but then—"

"Hugo?" She put down her knife and looked up at him. "Enough already."

"You asked."

"That'll learn me."

She set the bowl down on a shelf and stood up, stretching. She removed the rubber band from her hair and scratched her head violently with both hands, then bent from the waist so that her dull black hair hung down and nearly touched the floor. "Oh, God, am I stiff," she said, coming up. He watched her. He couldn't believe they were related, though she looked like pictures of his father. His father had been handsome, of course—not so stringy looking. He wanted, suddenly, to ask her a question about his father. Anything: what his hobbies had been, whether he had liked math in school, what he used to do on long summer days.

"What are you looking at?" She pulled her hair back again, smoothed it with both hands.

"How come you never say anything nice to me?" It wasn't what he had meant to say, but he went on. "All you do is make fun of me."

"Oh, Hugo—" He thought for a minute she was going to cry (her eyes closed briefly her forehead furrowed up), but all she did was twist on the rubber band and say, "Please. Give me a break. It's been a long day," and head for the stairs. "Come on. Let's have some dinner."

"He's probably the only child you'll ever have," said Rachel. "Considering."

"You don't have to be so brutal." It was the Fourth of

July. Rachel had driven down from Boston, bringing hot dogs; Dorrie supplied the beer. They were sitting on the dock with their feet in the water while Hugo, up near the house, attempted to start a fire in the hibachi.

"Brutal doesn't come into it," Rachel said. "Let's face it, Dorrie. You and I are pushing forty—not the optimum age for motherhood."

"Or for immaculate conception." Dorrie made herself laugh, not very convincingly. "You're right, of course. It's just that it's not easy to replace a batch of imaginary children with Hugo."

"He's not a bad kid, you said so yourself." Rachel spoke idly, leaning back on her elbows and raising her face to the sun. There was something more urgent than Hugo on her mind. Dorrie had known Rachel for nearly thirty years, and she recognized the symptoms: the secret smile, the bemused staring into space, even the way she was wearing her hair, hanging down from a barrette instead of pinned into a chignon. Definitely: Rachel had met a man. Dorrie braced herself for the ache of envy that would come when the details were revealed, even if he turned out to be a paunchy, golf-mad investment analyst like the last one. "Really, Dorrie. He seems like a nice boy."

"He is, in his own way." Dorrie looked over her shoulder at Hugo, crouching by the hibachi. He wore cutoff jeans. His legs were thick and pink—babyish. He wore a black T-shirt and the Red Sox baseball cap Rachel had brought him. "Oh, hell, Rachel, I wish I liked him better." Dorrie turned back to look at her own legs dangling off the dock. If she were pregnant, she thought, she would look like a stork, puffed up plump above skinny legs and knobby knees. "He can be charming sometimes, and he's very bright, but he's just so empty, Rachel. He gives me the willies. He never does anything on his own but sit down here poking sticks into the water. Or he rows—around and around the pond. And he eats. And that's all—that's absolutely all."

He had been with her not quite three weeks. There had been four shopping trips into town; once he had helped her unload the kiln; they had toasted marshmallows one night over the hibachi while she told him about pottery making, and the next day she had given him a lesson on the wheel and let him glaze a couple of mugs and bowls. He had decorated them sloppily with slashes and arrows and lost interest before he was half done. They had driven into town to see a movie. On the way there, Hugo had chattered about other movies he had seen; on the ride home he'd been silent. They had had several arguments about what he ate: too much junk, not enough vegetables, Dorrie chided him. Hugo claimed she never made anything he really liked and he had to fill up on dessert. And they had argued about the television. He offered to mow the lawn for her, to pay for one; she told him he would have to help mow the lawn anyway, and she certainly couldn't afford to pay him. After conversations like this, he took refuge in the boat, or sat down on the dock looking at the water for hours and hours, and Dorrie sat inside with her lonely anger, unable to concentrate on working or reading, unable to do much of anything but indulge in vain wishes that things were different.

"What about summer camp?" Rachel asked her.

"I don't know anything about camps, Rachel. And they're expensive. And it's undoubtedly too late."

"He can't be as idle as he looks, if he's an intelligent kid. He must think a lot."

"He doesn't have anything to think about. And his conversation, to say the least, is not the conversation of a thinker. Just about all he can talk about is his favorite soap opera. His one passion in life."

"Which one?"

"*Upton's Grove,* for God's sake."

"I used to watch that." Rachel sat up, smiling, and took a long drink of beer. She was a short-story writer, beginning to be known, her first book on the verge of publication. Dorrie still had moments of disbelief in the Rachel who had emerged after their suffering adolescence, when they were in their twenties: attractive to men, sure of herself, almost glamorous. Everything she did had a shine to it, even watching a soap opera. What was dreary or pathetic in other people became magical when it happened to Rachel: desertion, divorce, overweight, rejection. Dorrie had observed her all these years with wonder and curiosity, and with intermittent hope that was always dashed but always lurking somewhere: if good things could come to Rachel, who used to be ugly and cynical, who spent entire summer vacations in tears over her pimples and braces and flab, couldn't they come to Dorrie too? And yet they didn't, so that her fondness for Rachel was tinted, faintly, with bitterness.

"When William left me and I was so depressed I couldn't eat or work or sleep," Rachel said, "I got pretty involved with good old *Upton's Grove.*"

"I vaguely remember this," Dorrie said. She could remember clearly, in fact, Rachel's flamboyant depression; even that had had charm, had caused all sorts of people to rally round.

Rachel laughed. "Don't make such a face, Dorrie. It was entertaining, like eating pastry. Probably bad for you but fun— sort of like William, actually." She sighed. "I still miss that selfish bastard."

"I doubt it." Dorrie knew it wasn't William Rachel had come to talk about, either—that the reference to William was Rachel's way of leading up to her announcement. Dorrie didn't want to hear it, not until she'd had more to drink, but Rachel said, "Well, maybe I don't. Anyway, I've met someone, Dorrie. A man named Leon, a lawyer, forty-two years old, divorced. I've been seeing him every weekend."

"I suspected it," Dorrie said—briefly pleased, after all, that she had read the signs right.

"I met him in my dentist's waiting room. He had an abscess," Rachel went on. "He was pretty doped up. We talked about cheese, and he'd seen one of my stories in *The Atlantic* and liked it. He had to have a root canal, and I waited and drove him home afterward. He was really in bad shape. The next day he sent me flowers, to thank me, and I sent him flowers, because of his tooth, and it just went on from there." It sounded like one of the wacky, improbable courtships in Rachel's stories: in the story they would go to the zoo; she would tell him about her dog Montmorency; he would show her his membership card in the International Telephone Book Collectors' Association; she would give him her straw hat to hold and disappear into the monkey house; she would watch two chimps mating and then look out the window at him, squinting into the sun, patiently dangling the ribbons of her hat in the dust, and she would fall in love with him. Dorrie always had trouble liking Rachel's stories; they didn't seem to be about anything.

Rachel continued: he was nice looking, considerate, good in bed, prosperous . . . Dorrie knew she would meet him eventually, and he would turn out to be a pleasant middle-aged chap with a Williamish taste for silly jokes—Rachel's inevitable choice. "And here's the best part, Dorrie," she said. "He has this absolutely terrific friend. His name is Charles Lind. Divorced, a painter, quite attractive—"

"Sorry, Rachel," Dorrie said immediately. "I'm not interested."

"Why? Have you found a new messiah?"

"I would have told you if I was seeing anyone." As if a prior commitment were the only reason to pass up the divine Charles.

"Then why not just meet him? You don't have to marry him, Dorrie. Just come for dinner, just a nice casual evening, the four of us."

Dorrie closed her eyes. There had been men, since Teddy, whom she had met and liked and who hadn't responded. One she'd met at a craft show and made a fool of herself over, another she'd pursued at a party until his beautiful blond girlfriend had come and taken him away in an instant. Petty humiliations, little failures. And there had been men interested in her too, like the pharmacist in town, newly divorced and pushing sixty, who had invited her for a drink at the Elks' club.

"I'm simply not interested, Rachel. Is that so strange? I'm old and ugly and I don't want to start anything. I don't want to let myself in for it. And I know what you mean by quite attractive. He's a loser just like me. Losers don't like other losers. It's not like matching up tennis players or something. Dog breeders. Losers have their pride, Rachel."

"Dorrie, you're not a loser." There had been many similar discussions over the years. "Christ, you're not beautiful, honey, you're not a glamour girl, but hell—who is?" Rachel was genuinely upset, as always. "You're extremely attractive, Dorrie, you've kept your figure like no one else I know, you're certainly good company—"

"Rachel, stop. Just forget it."

"You make me so angry."

"I can't help it. I don't want to be fixed up. I don't want to be put through it. I just want to—" She paused, looked out over the pond. It didn't sound convincing, that she wanted her solitude, lonely though it might be. It wasn't even entirely true. And wasn't it gone forever, anyway, now that Hugo was here?

Rachel had lost her exuberance. "You're scared," she said. "I guess I don't blame you. You've had a lot of rotten romances." Was that the secret of Rachel's charm? Her ability to switch gears, to shape discord into amity like clay into a pot? And to glaze it over with a bit of undeserved flattery?

"Not a lot," Dorrie corrected her. "If I'd had a lot it wouldn't be so bad. There've only been Mark and Teddy, actually."

"Well."

They were silent, watching the sky begin to hint at the sunset.

"The pond's high," Rachel said.

"It was a wet spring."

Another silence. What if, by some crazy fluke, Charles Lind was attractive and nice and smart and talented? He would hate her. She imagined Rachel's little dinner party: Rachel being charming, Leon slobbering all over her, Charles wishing Rachel were his date—anyone but Dorrie—and herself ugly and tongue-tied, dressed wrong, drinking too much, becoming garrulous and overfamiliar and driving the long road home—alone—to hate herself.

"Listen, Dorrie," Rachel went on in a rush. "Think about it, will you? I promise you, you'd like Charles. He's a watercolorist. On the side, of course. By day he's a librarian or something. By night he paints these incredible pictures. I've seen them. They're really remarkable."

"Rachel?"

"Oh, all right." Rachel sat back on her elbows again. Dorrie looked at her face. She was genuinely cross, and Dorrie was sorry.

"I'm just not up for it," she said.

"All right, all right. I get the idea." Rachel sighed, drank, changed the subject. "I'll have to grill Hugo about *Upton's Grove.* I wonder if Tara and Prescott ever got married. And that awful woman—Colette? Claudette! Enough hair for six people, and this screaming-pink lipstick, and the acting ability of a halibut. She found out about this plot to kill her father—no, I think it was her stepfather, this pompous jerk of a doctor—I'll tell you, I'd rather die than have this guy operate on me—"

"Spare me *Upton's Grove,*" Dorrie said—but amiably. "I get it every night at dinner."

Rachel grinned and kicked her legs in the water; luminous drops flashed in the sun. The pond shone dark as a seal's back. "It really was terrible stuff, but I kind of miss it. I think the reason it's so addictive is that you keep watching it partly to see how bad it can get."

"That's not why Hugo watches it."

"Well, you should watch it with him, Dorrie. Teach him to analyze, teach him to think—since you don't believe he knows how."

"I'll leave Hugo's intellectual development to Sterling High School. It starts two blessed months and one day from now."

"Oh, Dorrie—is it that bad?" Rachel touched her arm in sympathy. "That you count the days?"

"I suppose I'm exaggerating. It's just that whenever I turn around there he is. My brother's wild oat. And it's not as though he came with a dowry. The child is costing me an arm and a leg. Do you know how much a teen-age boy can eat?"

"It really is something, taking on a responsibility like this just when your life is all sort of set." They looked out over the pond, examining Rachel's words. "I mean, I know I've been nagging at you about meeting Charles, I'd love to see you hook up with some nice man, but I have to admit your life here is pleasant. It's so—"

Lonely. Isolated. Set in its tracks. The life of a spinster. The kind of life Rachel, soon, would leave, with one of her lawyers or another. Later, when Hugo was asleep out in the garage, Dorrie knew they would go over it all again—Rachel's relationship with Leon and her advocacy of his unlovable watercolorist friend. It was as inevitable as the sunset.

"He's not much like Phineas, is he?"

"Hugo? Well, he certainly doesn't look like him."

"He looks like your father, I thought."

"He does, I suppose." Dorrie didn't say how much she grudged Hugo that resemblance. "He doesn't take after his mother at all."

"I wonder if he knows what happened to her."

"Oh, God, Rachel, I don't know, I suppose so, in a general way. He never mentions her. Or Phineas, either. He really misses my father. They were pretty close." That too she grudged him.

"He doesn't seem to be a troublesome kid," Rachel said. "I mean—like Phineas."

They were silent, thinking of the troublesomeness of Phineas. At Hugo's age, Phinny had already had a succession of girlfriends. Dorrie had caught him with one on the porch glider, seen the girl's little breasts like snouts and her brother with his pants down, and screamed before she could stop herself. She had been fifteen then, Phinny twelve. The moment (it had been a warm summer night, the sky just losing its color over behind Miss LaPorte's house) was branded into her memory, still hot, still vivid, her horror and embarrassment and comprehension and envy still fresh after twenty-odd years.

"No," Dorrie said. "He doesn't seem to be much like Phinny. Of course, he hasn't had a lot of opportunity. When school starts—" She broke off and smiled at Rachel unhappily. "I have to confess, I don't really care what happens when school starts, Rachel. As long as he's away all day and not wandering around doing nothing and waiting for me to break down and play Scrabble with him or something."

"I suppose you can't blame him. What a life the kid's had."

Hugo's voice came over the grass to them. "Fire's ready!"

Dorrie and Rachel got to their feet. "At least he's always had someone to take him in," Dorrie said.

They walked slowly up to the house. "I envy you in a way," Rachel said. "It must be sort of nice to have a kid around the house."

"You want to borrow him? You want to adopt him?"

"Oh, Dorrie—" Rachel smiled her secret smile again, and paused to finish her beer. She envies me, Dorrie thought. Like hell.

Hugo ran down to meet them. "Fire's ready," he said again. "I think it's just right." The shadow of the baseball cap cut diagonally across his face so that only his big-toothed grin could be seen. His mindless cheeriness, Dorrie thought. The human smile-button. And then the thought jolted her: He's alone in the world, no one loves this boy, and she considered, fleetingly, putting her hand out to touch his pink cheek, but she refrained: he would think she had lost her mind. "I got the hot dogs out of the fridge," he said. "They look sort of strange." He held out the package. "Sort of too brown. Look."

"Those are nitrite-free, organically grown, all-beef hot dogs," said Rachel. "They're delicious, Hugo. Really they are."

"Well—" Hugo fell into step with them. "Dorrie made plenty of macaroni salad. And there's pickles."

"And we can always make peanut-butter sandwiches," Rachel said with a laugh, and punched Hugo lightly on the shoulder, a gesture that startled Dorrie. How did Rachel do a thing like that, so casually? "Don't worry, Hugo, you're going to love these hot dogs." Rachel opened the package and arranged six of them over the coals. "This is a nice little fire."

She was lying, of course; the fire was sparse and chancy. Hugo beamed. "Thanks." He cleared his throat elaborately: a joke was coming. "Uh—maybe there's some hamburger in the freezer."

His silliness, his susceptibility to Rachel irritated Dorrie. "Oh, loosen up a little, Hugo, for heaven's sake. You've got to try things, at least."

Hugo tipped the cap back so the sun fell full on his face. He was grinning widely. "That's just what Claudette said to Charles today."

Rachel looked up from the hibachi. "Did Claudette and Charles ever get married? And Tara and Prescott?"

"You watch *Upton's Grove?*" Hugo took the cap off, as if in tribute, and stared at Rachel. Briefly, with his eyes squinting in the sun and that laughing, eager look on his face, he reminded Dorrie for the first time of Phineas. A memory fluttered at her, of some long-lost picnic, and Phinny's monkey face contorted with the pleasure of tormenting her.

"I used to, at a time in my life when I wasn't responsible for my actions," Rachel said. "I was temporarily insane."

Dorrie spread a cloth on the picnic table and anchored the corners with silverware. She could feel herself giving in to the bad mood that had dogged her all day: a holiday, nothing accomplished, the Boston show only a week away, Hugo under-

foot in the kitchen, and now this—Rachel's happiness and
her own petty resentment. Of course, she was glad for Rachel.
. . . She looked at her friend, tanned and pretty in her sundress,
not plump so much as ample, lovable. No, she wasn't glad
for Rachel: that was the shameful truth. All she felt was self-
pity, and a kind of aversion to Rachel's good fortune, as if
Rachel's being happily in love were a hideous, debilitating
disease.

"So what about Tara and that stick Prescott?" Rachel was
asking Hugo. "And that other couple—Tom? Was there somebody named Tom? And a red-haired woman with a lisp?"

"Sabrina? Sabrina was shot last winter."

Dorrie went inside for the macaroni salad, carrying a beer
with her. Upstairs, she detoured to the bathroom and splashed
water on her face. Bitch, she thought. Unnatural hag. She
inspected her face: pasty, droopy, lifeless. She must get some
exercise, some sun; she must sleep more, work less, get out
and meet people. She ran cold water on her hands and pressed
one palm to the hot back of her neck. She knew she would
do none of those things. She closed her eyes, letting the water
run over her wrists. It was cool and quiet up in the bathroom.
She almost dozed off, standing by the sink. She imagined taking
her razor and slicing neatly into each wrist, following the blue
lines, then watching the blood run pink and diluted down
the sink with the cold water. She opened her eyes and looked
in the mirror again. Hair: all she saw was heavy black hair:
an aging woman oppressed by a mop. She had a sudden impulse
to cut it all off, get rid of the hot tangle on her neck. She
imagined her hair lifting free in tiny waves, so the wind could
blow through it. She hadn't had short hair since eighth grade.

Quickly, before she could change her mind, she got the
nail scissors from the cupboard and sawed off a hank of it,
near her left ear. Hell: it hung there, stiff as crabgrass. Why
had she thought it would do anything else? And it was crooked.
She straightened it out, making it shorter, and then cut the
other side to match and began recklessly on the back without

a mirror, by feel. Her thick hair defeated the nail scissors. She found a better pair in the sewing box—pinking shears, but what did it matter? The point was to get rid of it; she could always go down to Laurelle's House of Beauty in town and have them make it even. She chopped at it urgently, remembering, for some reason—it must have been the beer—that she used to cut Mark's hair, all those years ago: his brown curls that always looked good no matter how she hacked them. She remembered running her fingers through his hair, and bending to kiss him, and what it had been like, kissing Mark. Mark and then Teddy, and that was all—all you could count as romance—in nearly forty years.

When she finished, the sink was full of hair, heavy black clots of it. She was sweating. Snips of hair stuck to her neck and the sides of her face, and she could feel it down her back, scratchy under her shirt. She brushed what was left and looked at the results. Prince Valiant. *Bernice Bobs Her Hair.* "Oh, Jo, your one beauty." She reminded herself of someone: who? Her hair hung down like the ears of a spaniel, but with jagged places. She tried to clean them up, but she only made it worse, so she put down her scissors and frowned at herself, tried smiling, checked out her profile. She thought it didn't look too bad, but she knew she was no judge. She hoped it wasn't ludicrous, at least, but suspected it probably was. But what did it matter? It would be cooler, less trouble. Another slap of memory: once she had gone to a beauty shop in Providence and had her hair done in an elaborate pileup of curls, and had asked Teddy, "How do I look?" He had replied, "You look intelligent."

From the yard she could hear Hugo's voice, Rachel's laugh. *Upton's Grove.* And Rachel had a new beau. And it had become hot in the bathroom, horribly hot. She pulled off her clothes and stepped into the shower, knowing she had done something absurd: she had cut off her hair because Rachel had a lover and she didn't. Then she knew whom she reminded herself of, with her hair cut short: Phinny, she looked the way Phinny would have looked if he had lived into his thirties.

* * *

While the hot dogs were cooking, Hugo's aunt disappeared, and then she came back with all her hair cut off. Rachel had been talking *Upton's Grove* with him, but when she saw Dorrie she let out a little scream. "Dorothea Gilbert! What have you done?"

"If thine hair offend thee, chop it off," his aunt said. "Maybe you could straighten it out for me later, Rachel."

"Straighten it out! God, Dorrie, you should let a professional handle this. It needs thinning desperately, for one thing." Rachel was up, fluffing out Dorrie's hair, standing back and squinting at it as if at a painting in a museum. "Hmm," she said. "Well. You know—it's not bad. What do you think, Hugo?"

Hugo thought it was bad. He hated short hair on women. All pretty women had long cascades of hair. Even Rachel, who was too fat but otherwise pretty. Dorrie hadn't been good-looking even with long hair, especially pulled back with a rubber band the way she wore it, but with her hair short she looked like one of those street kids from someplace in Europe—those French pickpocket kids he'd seen in a magazine at the dentist. Except that she was older. "It looks nice," he said. He meant it to sound inadequate. "Nice and cool," he added with a small, insincere smile.

Dorrie burst out laughing. "And there's always the macaroni salad, and the pickles."

"No! I meant it!" He repented his meanness. "I really like it," he insisted.

Dorrie smiled at him crookedly—her unhappy smile, he knew it well—and got a beer from the cooler. "And there's always beer, thank God."

"Really," he said again. "It's sharp. It's just so different."

"I'll mess with it after dinner, Dorrie," Rachel said. "I could probably shape it some. Do you remember when we started letting our hair grow, back in the ninth grade?"

"Your mother accused us of trying to look like beatniks."

"She was probably right."

"What are beatniks?" Hugo asked politely, making amends, but Dorrie only said, "Ancestors of hippies," laughing, not paying him much attention. What was so funny anyway?

"Those were the days," Rachel said. "Long stringy hair and black stockings."

"White lipstick and men on motorcycles," said his aunt.

Hugo took off his cap and picked at the Red Sox insignia. He hated baseball and especially the Red Sox. He was starving, and the day had suddenly fallen apart. He had been telling Rachel about Claudette and the necklace. It was so great to be really listened to instead of what his aunt usually did, which was to endure patiently and then cut him off short. And now the two of them were off on a nostalgia trip, laughing, guzzling beer. They were on their second six-pack already.

"Men on motorcycles—God, didn't we wish." Rachel took a long drink of beer, tipping her head back so that he could see the three parallel creases across her neck. They disappeared into the shadow of her chin when she lowered her head. "We had the long hair and the black stockings, but that was about it. I was too fat and your Aunt Dorrie was too thin," she said to Hugo. He wondered if he was supposed to say something gallant or if it would sound weird. In any case, he couldn't think what it could be.

"The fifties were medium-size years," Dorrie said.

So are the eighties, Hugo thought. "The hot dogs are done," he said.

They sat at the picnic table. Hugo put mustard and pickles on his hot dog and took a bite. He was about to say, "Speaking of motorcycles, Crystal's boyfriend, Jamie, cracked his up," but Dorrie got going first, asking Rachel about her book, and they dissected some boring problem Rachel was having with her agent, and then she asked Dorrie how business was and Dorrie said business was good. She told Rachel about the big order from the restaurant, and about the local movie star who'd come in and bought a couple of teapots and a dozen mugs and six of the big casseroles.

"He said they make good hostess presents," Hugo broke in, cheered. The movie star's visit had been one of the few bright spots of his stay. "Like when you go and visit somebody for the weekend and you take them something? Some little gift? Like Dorrie says, maybe a piece of cheese or a bottle of wine. But this guy takes these eighty-dollar tea sets!" He still couldn't believe it. And he had sneaked a look at the bank balance when the movie star wrote a check: six thousand plus! In his checking account! He told that to Rachel, "And you should have seen the car he drove up in. It looked like a Rolls-Royce or something."

"A Mercedes, I think," Dorrie said. "And Hugo was trying to convince me not to cash the check because he wanted the autograph. I told him, Hugo, honey, you want his autograph, you can bicycle over to his place and ask for it, for heaven's sake!"

Hugo blushed. He had thought there must be a way you could manage to keep the check and still get the money— talk to the bank or something. And she hadn't called him honey. "I don't want it that badly," he said.

"How was the hot dog?" Rachel asked him. He looked at her in surprise. He'd finished it without noticing. The two women laughed at his expression.

"I guess I could force down one more," he said, getting another laugh. But it only brought back his gloom. He was tired of being laughed at. He wished there were someone his own age around, preferably some pretty, long-haired girl who didn't talk much, who would sit and listen to him without saying a word, and when he was through talking she would say, Hugo, that's fascinating! She would look at him the way Crystal looked at that jerk Jamie.

He ate the hot dog and some more macaroni salad and drank a Coke and a half. Dorrie had bought ice cream, and they ate that down on the dock. Hugo kept going up to the house for more. He felt he could eat ice cream forever. The cold chocolate slipping down his throat was the only thing that could cool him off. God, he was sick of heat. The summer seemed to have gone on for years instead of weeks. But when he started for his fourth helping, his aunt said, "That's enough, Hugo," and he left his dish out on the picnic table and went up to the garage loft, seething, feeling like a baby.

But in the loft, he was immediately soothed. Curiously, it was almost always cool up there, probably because of the two oak trees that flanked it—the branches high enough not to obstruct his view but providing shade for the roof. He looked out of the window: there they were, the two old biddies gossiping down on the dock. He knelt by the window, watching them, watching the sky turn peach and gold, with shreds of mauve. He'd discovered that the sunset was different every night. He wondered if you could keep records on something like that. A painter could, a photographer, even a poet. David would think of a way. But what good would it be to write down "Gold/peach/lavender" one night and "Rose/orange/ light brown" the next?

Bits of conversation reached him:

"He was a dreadful man, a terrible man!"

"Can't imagine him retiring and just—"

"Of course, I'm happy for you! It's so wonderful that you can—"

Their laughter rose to his window, subsided, drifted up the lawn when they walked back to the house for more beer. "Hugo?" his aunt called up to him. He stuck his head out the window. "Hugo, keep that screening up there; you'll be eaten alive with bugs."

"I'll put it up before I go to bed."

"Are you tucked in for the night?"

"I guess so." Jesus: tucked in.

"Well, good night, for heaven's sake."

"Good night."

"Tell Rachel good night and thank her for the baseball cap."

"Good night, Rachel," he said, deeply embarrassed. "And

thanks for the cap, it's really neat." They stood below, squinting up at him. How silly they looked, his aunt with her chopped hair and long neck and beanpole legs, Rachel with her big flowered dress and flabby arms.

"Good night, Hugo," Rachel called. "That looks nice and cozy up there, from here. Is it cool?"

"It's not bad." He wondered if she meant to come up and see it, and he had a terrifying vision of clutching her tight on his mattress. He was glad when they turned and walked back to the house. Their laughter drifted back to his window, and even after he peed out into the dark and got into bed and lay there waiting for sleep he could hear their voices, far into the night—a sound no less sad and lonesome than the whistle of the train that passed, somewhere not far off, every night around ten.

4

Dorrie had dinner with her old friend Gregory Vere on the first night of the Boston Art Center Invitational Crafts Show. Gregory was a successful potter from Michigan who specialized in *raku* and had studied in Japan. He was a large, ugly, good-natured man in his fifties, and he had flirted with Dorrie for years. She told him about Hugo.

"Where did you get a nephew?" he asked her. They were eating at a French restaurant on Newbury Street. They always ate there; Gregory was a creature of habit. They were munching on bread and drinking wine, waiting for their meal; already Gregory had crumbs in his beard.

"He's my brother's boy."

"I didn't know you had a brother."

"He's been dead for years," Dorrie said. "He was a junkie. He died in jail." It sometimes gave her a sick thrill to say this—to spark people's interest with it, as if her wild brother were some buried aspect of herself, some banked-down fire that might still flare in her soul.

"Jesus, Dorrie," Gregory said. It never failed; in some perverse way, she gained status because of Phineas.

"He shot up with some contaminated heroin, and he did it with a dirty needle." She sipped the wine he poured for her. "Not a very pleasant death."

"Your parents—"

"They always expected it. Something." *Phineas,* she thought, with the familiar catch in her stomach.

"What about his wife?"

"They never got married. They lived together for a while and had Hugo. She was killed while Phinny was in jail, by a dealer. She owed him money."

He stared at her. "I almost hate to ask you what your nephew is like, with a background like that."

"He's fourteen now and, surprisingly enough, he seems to be a good kid." She thought for a minute. "In fact, he's a very sweet boy, Gregory. And he drives me right up the wall."

Gregory had a short, yelping laugh, a dog's laugh. "I can't help thinking of the aunts in P. G. Wodehouse. Bertie Wooster's Aunt Agatha, who chews broken bottles and kills rats with her teeth."

"And then there's Hugo's Aunt Dorrie, who refuses to buy a TV."

"Sadistic bitch," said Gregory.

He asked her, after a bottle of wine and two cognacs, to come back to his hotel with him. He asked her every year, and this time she nearly said yes; he was kind and he liked her and he wasn't so ugly in the candlelight. "We could just sit up and giggle all night, if you wanted to," he said. "We could take some wine with us."

"I can't, Gregory," she said—glad, really, that she had an excuse to resort to. If she spent the night with Gregory—then what? In the morning, when the wine had worn off, she would lie in bed beside him and find him pathetic, forget he was a dear friend and a fine potter and a good man and see only that he was overweight and old-maidish and had crumbs on his beard, and he would go, inevitably, out of her life—for the sake of a little dismal cheer, a little ego boost. "I'm staying with Rachel, and I told her I would be back."

"Tomorrow night?"

"She's roped me into a dinner party. I'm sorry, Gregory."

Gregory nodded, understanding; he understood everything, she could see that, and she leaned across the table and kissed him on the cheek.

The show went well. She sold things, she picked up some new markets, and she got two big commissions that would take her through the rest of the year. She was interviewed for *Ceramic Arts Quarterly.* She saw old friends, people she met once or twice a year at shows like this one: her old crony from New Haven, Emma Northrup, newly divorced, wearing a T-shirt that said I'M AN EARTH MOTHER; Emma's ex-husband, Chris, who told Dorrie how when their marriage began to go bad Emma had been making little sculptures of pocketbooks with teeth, inside of which there were tiny women in dresses, wringing their hands and crying; her friend Claudia from California, who had been telling Dorrie for years that she should give up mugs and pots for art.

"I'm no artist," she told Claudia. "I just like to make things out of clay."

"Bosh," Claudia said. "No one could produce such beautiful shapes and designs and not be an artist. You just don't let yourself go, Dorrie."

Dorrie thought of Teddy, who used to say, "You're nothing but a machine—a mug machine. What kind of life is that?"

"It's a living," she had answered. How could she explain how much more it was, that she not only didn't mind turning out the same forms day after day but actually liked it? It sounded so dull, and there was Teddy's square, tanned face, his bright brown eyes and bristly moustache, reproaching her, refusing to love a machine. But the security of it, the absolute mastery—cup after cup, bowl after bowl, identical, complete, beautiful, perfect: that was what she liked. And the fact that a machine could think, could listen to music, could look out her window at the sun slanting off the water.

"You could work on an assembly line someplace and probably make more money," Teddy said. "If that's the kind of thing you want to fritter away your life with. At least you'd have a union."

Claudia said, "You should come and see what we're doing out on the coast. Visit some of the studios out there. You'd learn a lot, Dorrie. You easterners are so timid!" Dorrie looked at Claudia's work: flat brownish porcelain flowers that looked dead and were surprisingly heavy to pick up. She saw that they were backed with metal: paperweights? She chided herself: *objets.* "Maybe you need therapy," Claudia said. "I'm doing group out in L.A.—for potters and woodworkers only. It's really helped me get free from all the old constrictions—the hang-up of functionalism."

"I'll think about it," Dorrie said. "But probably not very hard."

She was glad, at the end of each day, to get back to Rachel's. Rachel lived in a small, clean Back Bay apartment that she used to share with William, a place that had the distinction of being the scene of one of the Boston Strangler's crimes. It was very bare; after William left her, Rachel had cleared out all traces of his presence, including furniture they had bought, books he had liked, even the dishes they had eaten off together. There were still empty spots that Rachel hadn't refilled, and the small rooms echoed. "I really should get married again," Rachel had said once to Dorrie. "My life is like this apartment; I can't seem to fill it up by myself." Dorrie thought of her own house: crammed to the rafters. Did that mean her life was full? Despite appearances?

On the second night, when Dorrie arrived, Rachel was rushing around her tiny kitchen, simultaneously lining a large glass bowl with lettuce leaves, chopping nuts in the food processor, and drinking gin. She was wearing a low-cut black dress and a calico apron.

"How was the show?" Rachel shouted at her over the noise of the Cuisinart.

"Great," Dorrie shouted back. "Profitable! But an alarming number of my colleagues seem to have gone off the deep end."

"What?" yelled Rachel. She turned off the machine.

"I said, why did I let you talk me into this damned dinner party?"

"Cheer up, it'll be fun." Rachel raised her glass, clanking ice cubes. "Remember fun?"

"No," Dorrie said.

"Well, have a drink, then. Take a bath. Put on your dancing shoes. You know, your hair really looks nice, Dorrie."

"Thanks."

She went into the bathroom, ran water in the tub, and looked in the mirror. She'd had her hair trimmed at Laurelle's House of Beauty. Feathered, Laurelle called it. The ugly duckling, Dorrie thought. She pulled at the wispy ends. Her mother used to say, "Cleopatra wasn't beautiful, she just had a good personality." Why do I remember these things? Dorrie lay back in the tub, perfectly still so that the water was a flat sheen, marbled with Rachel's bath oil. "When you're grown up and married, Dorrie, with children of your own—" Her mother must have started a million sentences that way. Grown up wasn't enough; there had to be marriage too, and children. As if they'd provide some kind of answer. She looked at her long toes sticking up under the spout. This little piggy went to market, she thought. Et cetera. Children. Well, maybe they did provide an answer. She and Phineas: had they constituted an answer for their parents? The thought was unimaginable. They'd been nothing but wrong answers, the two of them— like something gone bad early in an equation, so that the solution came out absurd, contrary to logic. And yet her parents had seemed to be people with answers. She wondered, not for the first time, how much of it had been feigned—that confidence and optimism. How much of it had been cultivated, like an ornamental hedge. And she thought—again not for the first time—that she had probably been an even greater disappointment to her parents than Phineas. At least Phineas had had a child. She doubted, though—sitting up, scattering oily drops, reaching for the soap—that Phinny had ever found any answers. Had Phineas even known there were questions?

Rachel called from the kitchen, "Dorrie? Are you almost ready? Come out here and have a drink with me. People will start coming any minute."

She soaped energetically. She would stop thinking about Phinny, stop brooding, stop asking herself what she was doing here, anyway, sitting in this tub scrubbing her elbows in preparation for an evening she would no doubt remember all her life with humiliation. "How do I look?" "You look intelligent." She thought, If you could end your existence, this minute, in this tub, by saying a magic word—just extinguish yourself with a shazam—would you do it? Not quite, she thought. But if it would whisk her away, out of Rachel's bathroom and back to her house, her deck, where she could be sitting, this minute, fighting off mosquitoes and watching Hugo row down the pond, and back, and down again . . . yes, that. Anything but this (drying off with Rachel's plush new towel), anything but this evening, these people, this misplaced effort (zipping up her dress, applying the Moonglow eye shadow and Peachflower blusher Laurelle had talked her into, fastening gold rings in her ears), this strange man who was destined, whoever he was, to make her unhappy. *Shazam*, she thought. *Shazam!*

Hugo was spending the weekend at the Garners'.

"It's not that I don't trust him alone," his aunt had said to them. "It's just that he's still new to the place and I think he'd feel strange by himself over there." She had looked at Hugo and smiled. The truth was that he had begged her not to leave him there alone—not because he would feel strange but because he saw a golden opportunity to sleep in the Garners' sun room.

"We'd love to have him," Mrs. Garner said emphatically. Her husband, less emphatically, nodded and said, "Sure—why not?"

It was good enough for Hugo, but Dorrie kept saying,

"You're positive? You didn't have any special plans this week-end? If he's going to be in the way just say so"—until Hugo would have felt like an ape being delivered to the wrong zoo if Mrs. Garner hadn't put her arm around his shoulders, squeezed, and said, "We're always glad to see Hugo, Dorrie. It'll be a treat to have him for the weekend."

After Dorrie left, and after *Upton's Grove,* he was shy and awkward. He wandered around aimlessly outside, waiting for dinner. In the house, he felt in the way—presumptuous, somehow. He sensed the Garners' awareness of him, their special smiles. A fourteen-year-old kid, he could hear them think-ing, too nervous, too much of a baby to stay alone. "Let's be extra nice to Hugo," he muttered aloud to himself, balancing on the end of their dock. "Poor old Hugo, let's make him feel at home." Across the pond, his aunt's place looked de-serted, shadowed by trees—abandoned. For a split second he was homesick for his loft. He had it fixed up now the way he liked. He loved the cool nights up there, the dimness, the strangeness even of the way it sounded: "sleeping in the ga-rage." He dreamed of bringing girls up there, impressing them with his ingenious window shutters, the shelves he'd made, his *Upton's Grove* statistics.

Dinner was formal, served in the dining room on the good china. The Garners poured themselves red wine, in thin glasses shaped like tulips, and after a minute Mr. Garner poured some for Hugo.

"Oh, Ross, I don't know," said his wife.

"A little wine won't hurt. If they learn to take a little alcohol at home they won't go out and drink in bars."

"That's what we learned last year in our Drugs and Alcohol unit at school," Hugo said. This was a lie, and as soon as he uttered it he had the wild, scary feeling that he would tell more lies as the weekend went on. Immediately, a second one came to mind. "Besides, I always have a little at my aunt's."

"Well, then," Mr. Garner said, and another half inch of red wine went into his glass. "Now," he said, unfolding his napkin. "It's time we really got to know you, Hugo. Aside from your lawn-mowing abilities."

"And your taste in soap operas," Mrs. Garner said, smiling her dear-boy smile. He smiled back. He loved Mrs. Garner, he wished she was his grandmother, but his smile was apprehensive. What did they mean, get to know him? He thought back to fairy tales, of old people who win the confidence of children and then wham! into the oven!

"Tell us what you want to be when you grow up, Hugo," Mrs. Garner said.

Hugo drew a blank. He couldn't remember how he usually answered that question. It was weird enough to contemplate being grown up, much less what he would be when it happened. He frowned down at his food, pretending to think. He wished they would forget about getting to know him, talk about *Upton's Grove* or tell funny stories about their grandchildren. But they waited. I want to head up to Alaska and work on the pipeline, he said to himself. I want to make big bucks and screw lots of women. That was what Shane used to say. Hugo smiled, imagining Shane and Monty sitting here at the Garners' elegant table, and what would happen to the silver knives, the crystal glasses, the bottle of wine.

"I guess I'll probably be a professor like my grandfather," he said at last. "Only I wouldn't teach English. I guess I'd teach math."

"Math is your best subject?" Mr. Garner wanted to know. Everything was different with the Garners in the dining room. He wished he could be sprawled out on the sun room couch with Mrs. Garner or out in the yard with Mr. Garner. This was like being on television, being interviewed on some teen talk show. He sighed. "Well, I'm good at some others too, but math is the one I like best."

"What did your father do, Hugo?" It was Mrs. Garner's turn.

"He worked in a garage, I think. He liked cars. He didn't go to college or anything. I think he was pretty smart, though."

Hugo helped himself to more beef stew. He liked this substantial food, not the little salads and things his aunt made. Once they'd had crackers and cheese for dinner. "He died in a car crash. It was irony, my grandfather said."

He saw the Garners look at each other: the poor child. He'd seen the look before. Mrs. Wylie used to have it, his teachers, the people at his grandfather's funeral. It always made him feel sorry for himself, the poor little orphan boy whom Fate had bereaved again and again.

"My mother died when I was a baby," he said. "She was in a car crash too."

"Oh, no!" Mrs. Garner put down her fork.

"Yeah," Hugo said. He was feeling the wine; at least, he supposed it was the wine that tingled the top of his head and made him want to wring sympathy from the Garners. "I never knew her, really. I used to live with my Aunt Rose, but then when my father died I went to live with my grandparents."

"And were there cousins there to play with? At your aunt's?"

"Yeah, but they used to just tease me, mostly. They were—" He thought. He wanted to say something like "juvenile delinquents," but he wasn't sure it was a strong enough description of Shane and Monty. He contemplated telling his third lie: They're in jail now. Wow! Maybe it was true; he wouldn't be surprised. A memory flashed by him, of Shane holding his hands a foot apart and saying, "I just crapped the biggest turd!"

"They were a pain in the neck," he said, and amplified: "They used to lock me in the chicken coop. Then when my father came and gave me money, they used to steal it."

"My goodness," Mrs. Garner said.

Mr. Garner cleared his throat in a troubled way. "Have some more of this stew."

"Could I have just about a quarter inch of wine to wash it down?" He realized as he spoke that the Garners' glasses were still nearly full. "Or maybe some water would be better. I'm just so thirsty!"

"Tell you what," Mr. Garner said. He put a little wine into Hugo's glass and then poured in some ice water from a pitcher. "How's that?"

"Great." He took some more stew and washed it down.

After dinner, he helped load the dishwasher and then he went outside. He had a mission. In the evenings, when he went for his long, bored walks around the pond, he had been hearing the guitar music from the Verranos' place again— loud, mournful, sometimes discordant music. Lately he'd thought he'd heard a voice too.

He had a method for going around the pond. You could do it two ways. One he called the chicken way: you went down past his aunt's property until you came to a road, a little causeway over the stream that fed the pond, then over to the Garners' and down the shore on their side, then there was a swamp you skirted via another road that crossed the stream (wider here, though not quite a river: Marsden Creek, it was called) and passed the Verranos' driveway, and then the waterfall, and beyond it a sort of track back to his aunt's. The gutsy way was to go right through the swamp, getting your sneakers wet, and detour past the waterfall, stepping on boulders in the frothing water and getting everything else wet.

It was a hot night, the water would have felt good, but he didn't think he ought to return to the Garners' sopping wet. He thought Mrs. Garner might not like it, though his aunt never seemed to mind. He took the long, chicken way, starting from the Garners' and heading for the Verranos'. The pond lay dark and motionless; it could have been an oil slick. Hugo stumbled a little: the wine. He remembered his father drunk, and Rose, and the fear of death clutched him suddenly when he came to the road. He looked both ways, and then looked again, before he crossed. The poor child, everyone would say, if he was run over and killed. And no more Hugo. He wondered if he would see his mother and his father, if stuff like that was true. The things they'd told him at St. Michael's when he'd gone there, back in first and second grades. He stopped at the bridge over the creek to take a deep breath.

He had eaten too much stew, too much blueberry pie. He wondered, if the Garners adopted him, if they would eat in the dining room every night. He hoped not. And he knew the Garners wouldn't adopt him; they were too old. But it was one of his going-to-sleep fantasies.

The music began, suddenly, as he stood there looking down at the water. He turned his head toward it. The Verranos' house sat on a little hill. The front room was lit up; as he listened the music grew louder and he heard the voice. It was eerie, loud and thin, a ghost's voice. The top of his head tingled again. It was a girl, singing and playing the guitar.

It was nearly dark. If whoever it was looked out she probably couldn't see him, but, just in case, he approached the house roundabout, from the back. He crept up on the lighted window. The Verranos' place was old, and most of the windows were too tall for him to see into, but the lighted one was in a little addition that had been put on the back—probably to take advantage of the waterfall view on the other side of the driveway. He stayed back in the shadows, stood on tiptoe, and looked in.

There was a red-haired girl in overalls. She was standing in the middle of the room playing a guitar, and if her head hadn't been thrown back in song she could have looked right at Hugo. He moved further away, staring at her. She was short, skinny, frizzy-haired, intent. He listened to the words:

"Well, can't you see I'm just a kid?
And I don't care what you did.
A kid like me can't understand it all—
Well, don't you know I'm only fifteen?
Absorbed in my teen-age dreams,
I don't hear the sound of your fightin' down the hall—
damn!"

She broke off, and the guitar stopped. She stood in silence for a minute, then nodded and said aloud, "All right—take it." The music began again, and then her voice:

"Well, don't you know I'm only fifteen?
I just don't know what you mean,
When I hear the sound of your fightin' down the hall."

Her voice was high and piercing and right on key. She stopped, then sang:

"The sound of your fightin' . . ."

and stopped again. The guitar dwindled away to chords, then to two notes picked fast, over and over, then silence. "Well," she said after a while. "The hell with that, Listerine. Right?" Then she was still. Hugo was sure she could see him, but she just gazed straight ahead, frowning. She had very thick eyebrows; her frown was impressive. She stood like that for a while, and then turned suddenly and left the room, and he couldn't see her anymore. A huge black cat jumped to the windowsill and stared out at the night.

"You look gorgeous," Rachel said when Dorrie emerged from the bedroom.

"Gorgeous may be going too far," Dorrie said.

"You're right. You actually don't look one bit better than suicidally beautiful." Rachel poured her a drink, and Dorrie began to cut up vegetables for crudités. "You must always wear blue, dollink," Rachel said in her Russian accent. "And you must get your hair cut every six weeks without fail. And promise not to forget your old friends when you and Charles walk off into the sunset together to the sound of the throbbing balalaika."

"You're so silly you must be nervous, Rachel."

"Of course I'm nervous. The damn bean dip is too runny, and this dress makes me look fat, and it's hot in here." Rachel's mood changed suddenly. She pushed back her hair with both hands, sighed, took a gulp of her drink. "And Leon and I aren't getting along all that well."

This was news to Dorrie. She had met Leon the night

before; he had been there when she arrived home at midnight, tired out from the show. He was the jovial, paunchy man Dorrie had expected—stretched out on the sofa with his shoes off and his head in Rachel's lap. They were watching *The Thing* on television. Leon leaped to his feet, hugged Dorrie, told her he'd looked forward to meeting her, asked her how the show had gone, told her he loved her work, loved the teapot and mugs Rachel had given him for his birthday. "Leon is interested in everything," Rachel had told Dorrie, describing him. "And he likes everyone. A bitchy old complainer like me doesn't deserve him. He's so *good,* Dorrie." This was obviously true: goodness shone out of his small brown eyes; it seemed to reside even in his bushy hair, his beaked nose, his quick smile. Rachel could do a lot worse than marry him.

"You don't look fat, Rachel," Dorrie said. "You honestly do look gorgeous."

Rachel looked up from the bean dip. She had tears in her eyes. "I really wanted to fall in love with him. I really tried."

"I thought you *were* in love with him."

"It's just not working. I like him very much; he's wonderful and all that. It's not his fault—it's mine." Rachel lifted the dish towel to her eyes and dabbed gently, preserving her eye makeup. "I still miss William, of course."

"Oh, God, Rachel. William." For a moment life seemed silly and futile. Not much more than a year ago, she and Rachel had spent hours together, analyzing the shortcomings of William: his selfishness, his lack of understanding, his childish temper tantrums. His mother had spoiled him rotten, Rachel said. He wasn't fit to be married. He filled her with a blank, black rage. She was glad to be rid of him. If he hadn't left her she would have left him. Et cetera. Hours and hours of anger and scorn. And the relief Rachel said she found talking it over with Dorrie, getting it straight. Had all that been for nothing?

Rachel blew her nose. "I don't suppose it's William, really. It's just cheap nostalgia."

"For what?"

"For marriage, I guess. I want so much to get married again. And I thought Leon was the one. But when I begin thinking about that rat William I can tell I've just been fooling myself. Again. I never learn." Rachel laughed mournfully, almost proudly; she opened the refrigerator and bent down to look in. The kitchen was a mess, as if it reflected this new disorder in Rachel's life. "I've met a lot of men, Dorrie. Why can't I fall in love with one of them?"

Dorrie couldn't think of a reply; it was a problem she had never encountered. She was always falling in love; it was the men who didn't. The doorbell rang.

"Oh, hell—" Rachel took a container of sour cream from the refrigerator. "If I add this to the dip will it make it more runny or less?"

"Less, I should think. Try it."

"Will you let in whoever that is, Dorrie? I'm sorry, I'll be right there."

Dorrie left her stirring in the sour cream—it didn't seem to help, after all—and went to the door. It was Leon, with Charles Lind, both of them carrying bottles of wine. Leon hugged Dorrie again and introduced Charles. He was not as Rachel had described him: he was not "quite attractive." He was tall, dark-haired, beautifully dressed, and horrifyingly handsome. Dorrie took one look at him and steeled herself.

He smiled at her, a smooth, manufactured smile, meant to devastate everything in its path. Shaking his hand, she perceived dismay behind the smile, and thought, The hell with him, wondering where her indifference came from. Rachel's discontent? Fatigue? The approach of middle age? Her feeling that no one should have fingernails as flawlessly manicured as Charles Lind's?

Rachel came out, lamenting the bean dip, and she and Leon disappeared into the kitchen with the wine. Charles

poured himself a drink and sat down beside Dorrie. His smile
became dutiful. He cut a slab of brie and placed it squarely
on a cracker. Dorrie imagined him having his nails done, prac-
ticing his smile on a fawning manicurist. "Cheese?" he asked
her, and she took one of his precise constructions. His after-
shave was overpowering, and smelled somehow kitcheny: cin-
namon?

He wasn't, it turned out, a mere librarian; he was a high-
level archivist at the new Kennedy Library, and he launched
into a detailed recital of his duties there, and his gripes—a
dull tale, full of the injustices done to Charles by his boss.
Dorrie tried to remember he was a gifted painter; she could
conceive of him doing self-portraits, not much else. Nudes,
maybe: his gaze kept falling to her cleavage. She said to herself—trying to be fair—that a more aggressive, more self-confi-
dent, more interested woman could have stopped the flow of
egotism, maybe even brought out his better side. Everyone
had a better side. She knew he was rattling away at her because
that's what you did when you were stuck with a plain woman
who didn't talk much. She sat quietly nibbling crackers, noting
with fascination the small regularity of his teeth, his clear,
tanned skin, the deep blue of his eyes, the thick black lashes.
One was not often this close to perfection. She was reminded
of Iris, so beautiful she had seemed unreal. There was something disquieting in such inhuman beauty, or so it seemed to
her—something out of joint. Flawlessness was not a human
attribute.

He sat with her for the space of one drink and four slabs
of cheese, and then he wound up his monologue, looked at
her brightly, and said, "I'll just see if I can help out," and
headed for the kitchen. Dorrie heard him and Leon talking
computers. She thought, I should be humiliated—dumped after
fifteen minutes. But she felt serene, proud of herself. There
had been plenty of occasions on which simple dislike of a
man hadn't insulated her against being hurt by his coolness.
Progress, she thought, and sat sipping gin and turning the

pages of a magazine containing one of Rachel's stories. The story began: "Vanessa met Christopher in the supermarket. He had just knocked over a display of Puppy Chow, and Vanessa helped him put it back together. Maybe that was why, for as long as she knew him, he reminded her of a puppy: cute, impetuous, untrainable, devoted but inclined to bite."

Rachel poked her head out of the kitchen. She looked flushed and distracted, the calico apron discarded, her hair beginning to descend from its careful arrangement. Too much gin in the kitchen. There was a painting in one of Dorrie's father's art books—*Mother's Ruin:* a harassed, aproned, disheveled woman, leaning against a big black late-Victorian stove, swigging from a bottle.

Rachel asked, "You okay, Dor?" with a trace of reproach in her voice. For what? Dorrie wondered. For failing to ensnare the divine Charles? For not even trying? For screwing up the symmetry of the party?

Dorrie said she was fine; Rachel gave her a look and returned to the kitchen. Dorrie heard her say, "I'd be terrified to write on a computer. What if it just swallowed something and lost it forever in its dungeons?"

"There goes the Nobel Prize, honey," Leon said, and Rachel's rich laugh floated out to the living room, a banner announcing Dorrie's failure. It was like being back in high school—on the outside, watching the popular girls. So that was how you did it: you loaded on the eye makeup and pretended to be afraid of computers. But back in high school Rachel and Dorrie would have been outsiders together, making nasty cracks. And Dorrie would have been, beneath the cynicism, despairing. She looked absently out the window and saw the sun setting over the Boston rooftops: a golden, tranquil scene. She felt no despair. Maybe she had outgrown despair. The closest she could come to it, listening to the men's voices out in the kitchen, was a kind of listless nostalgia, as if she mourned a lost world.

Another couple was due for dinner, and when the doorbell

rang Dorrie abandoned Rachel's story and let them in: a writer-
friend of Rachel's named Margo Cornell whom Dorrie had
met before, and a tall man with a drooping moustache. "Alex
Willick—Dorrie Gilbert," Margo said. "It's nice to see you
again, Dorrie."

"Good to see you, Margo."

Alex Willick shook her hand and said, "You don't write
for a living, do you?"

"No."

"Thank God," he said fervently. "Margo is having contract
problems."

Margo turned on him. She was a small, vivid woman, a
writer of a series of novels about women in the American
West. She wore braids and a flower-sprigged dress with puffy
sleeves—as if she were a character in one of her own books,
the doughty pioneer wife. "Up yours, Alex," she said, destroy-
ing the illusion. "We all know why my contract problems
bug you so much."

"Because of my low boredom threshold?"

"Guess again," said Margo. Alex looked at Dorrie and
raised his eyebrows in mockery—an expression so intimate
that she wondered for one mad moment if she knew him from
somewhere, if they were old friends.

Rachel came in from the kitchen followed by Leon and
Charles, and the party reassembled over hors d'oeuvres and
drinks. The conversation turned to Margo's option-clause problem and Rachel's eternal troubles with her agent, Leon coming
in with the legal point of view, Charles contributing an irrele-
vant anecdote about the gallery that handled his paintings.
Alex Willick stayed silent, drinking whiskey, and Dorrie, sitting a little apart in a rocking chair, listened for a while to
the dull talk of contracts and commissions and then—antisocial
and not caring—she picked up the magazine containing Rachel's story and began to read. The evening, she felt, had already gone subtly and irreparably wrong: she and Charles
disliked each other, Rachel was unhappy with herself and dis-

appointed in Dorrie, Margo and Alex were on the outs. Dorrie was tired out from the weekend, from worrying about Hugo at the Garners', from her anxieties over this pointless party. She considered doing something outrageous and dreadful: sneaking down the fire escape to go to a movie, getting royally drunk and tap-dancing in the nude, stabbing Charles with the cheese knife. But she knew she lacked the genes for outrageousness; they had all gone to Phinny.

She finished the story. This one ended sadly, with Christopher the puppy slinking off with his tail between his legs and Vanessa alone in Quincy Market, sitting on a bench eating croissants from a bag. Dorrie didn't believe anyone would sit on a bench eating a bag of croissants. It didn't sound right: a bag of candy, maybe, or a bag of cookies. Peanuts. Grapes. Croissants were too much. And think of the crumbs! the grease! Earlier in the story, Vanessa had bitten her knuckle until the blood ran down her hand and dripped on her dress. Dorrie didn't believe that, either.

Alex came over and sat on the floor beside her chair. "Okay, you don't write," he said. He spoke with an ironical air of doing the proper thing. "What do you do?"

Dorrie put down the magazine, folded her hands in her lap, and produced a cooperative smile. "I'm a potter."

"Did you make that?" He gestured to a footed bowl on the shelf behind her: a post-William gift to Rachel.

"Yes. I went through a period when I put feet on everything."

"What period are you going through now?"

"I carve flowers and leaves on everything."

"Where do you live?"

"Out in the country. In Connecticut, about an hour from here."

"In a house?"

"Yes. A little white house on a pond." She was conscious as she said it of how idyllic it always sounded, how romantic. She thought of the sunset on the pond, missing it.

"You live alone?"

"At the moment I'm looking after my teen-age nephew." Into the picture of the pond came Hugo, rowing back and forth in the boat. "But usually alone, yes."

They looked at each other curiously. She liked the questions, the way his face sharpened with interest. He wasn't a handsome man, but he looked intelligent and—what was the right word? rakish? It was the long gunslinger moustache. He sat cross-legged on the floor, and she could see that his legs were bony, his knees compact squares under his khakis. He wore a striped shirt. His tie hung loose, unknotted, a frayed label visible. Everything he wore looked old, from the sixties, maybe. She wondered if he shopped at campy secondhand-clothing stores or if he simply never threw anything away. And his hair: it was blond and graying, thin in front, long in back like the hair of a tortured musician. Why did he wear it like that?

"I know you don't write," she said to him. "What do you do?" She expected something weird and unique: a broom designer, a hamster raiser, a tuba cleaner.

"But I do write," he said. "At least, I used to. I've come down with a terminal case of writer's block."

"Alex is just plain lazy," Margo called from across the room. It was a surprise, that she had been listening to their conversation. "He's only looking for sympathy."

"True," Alex said. "It's a long time since I had any." Dorrie wondered about their relationship and stole glances over at Margo, trying to decide if she was attractive. Her small, red-cheeked face looked pleased with itself. Dorrie deduced from the bits of conversation she heard that Margo was on the verge of some large commercial success. She was sitting beside Charles, quite close. As Dorrie watched, he handed her a cracker and cheese, and Margo smiled at him, conspicuously coquettish. Alex sat with his back to them, stroking his moustache. She asked him, "What do you write when you don't have writer's block?"

Alex told her he was working on a novel. He had published his first novel two years ago to some acclaim, had made a little money, had signed a contract for a second book—the one that was giving him trouble. "My contract's been renewed three times, but people are losing faith in me," he said. "I am rapidly on my way to becoming a flash in the pan." His voice was doleful, and his hands sketched a hopeless, palms-up gesture, but the look in his eyes remained amused, as if he had trouble taking it all seriously. Dorrie had read his book; she recalled a sardonic tale of a young man on the make and the beautiful woman who ruined him. She remembered that the heroine was idealized, that the hero refused to feel sorry for himself, that his bravado had made her uncomfortable.

His new novel, he said, was called *An Infinite Number of Monkeys,* and it was about a writer who tried to get away from it all to write a great book but who kept getting involved with people. "It's lousy," he said. He looked cheerful enough; she wondered if it was genuine. "But I keep plugging away." He refilled Dorrie's glass and began to ask her questions again: where had she learned her craft? Did she support herself at it? Had she ever studied in Japan? in England? He seemed to know a lot about it. He said he had a potter friend in Denver—Doug Levine, a man Dorrie had met once or twice. Alex leaned back on his elbows, looking up at her, asking her about clays, about kilns, about her house and her pond, absorbing the answers with a thoughtful look, pulling at his long moustache, steadily drinking whiskey. She wondered if he was interviewing her, if he had suddenly decided to put a potter in his book.

By the time dinner was ready, the party's skewed grouping began to seem quite natural. Margo and Charles were obviously hitting it off; they sat talking with Leon while Rachel hustled to the kitchen and back, stopping now and then by Dorrie and Alex to say a few words. Once she asked Dorrie's help in the kitchen, and Dorrie followed her there, leaving Alex on the floor staring down at his ice cubes.

"I guess you and Charles aren't exactly a match made in heaven," Rachel said. She ripped up lettuce and tossed it into a bowl while Dorrie chopped mushrooms. "He's really very sweet, you know, if you'd give him a chance."

"Rachel, I can't cope with a man who looks like that. How could you do this to me? Not to mention to poor Charles. He looked at me like I was somebody's old spinster auntie." She laughed. "Which I am, actually. That reminds me, I ought to call the Garners and see how Hugo's doing."

"Forget Hugo, Dorrie. He's undoubtedly doing fine. Better than you are."

"I'm perfectly happy," Dorrie said. "I'm having a lovely time."

Rachel looked up from the salad bowl and said, "I should tell you—Alex Willick and his wife were divorced last year and he and Margo have been going together ever since. They fight a lot but I think they're pretty serious."

"Rachel, can't I sit and talk to a man without your trying to marry me off? This is life, not a Jane Austen novel, damn it!" Dorrie dumped the mushrooms into the bowl and wiped her hands on Rachel's towel. She was angry; she felt like throwing something, or like slamming out of the kitchen and into her room to fling herself on the bed and pound the pillow in rage. "First you fix me up with that pompous mannequin in there and then you warn me off the first attractive, decent, intelligent man I've talked to in years."

Rachel laid a hand on Dorrie's arm. "Calm down," she said. "At the risk of sounding like *Upton's Grove,* I just don't want you to get hurt."

"At this point, it would take a lot more than a conversation with a man at a party to do that."

"You think you're a pretty tough old bird, don't you?"

"Damn right," Dorrie said, but when she returned to the living room something was changed. Rachel's caution had bro-

ken the spell of her indifference, and when Alex looked up
at her, smiling, her heart turned over.

"Do a good deed and tell me dinner is ready," he said.
She had the impression that he hadn't moved since she left,
had brooded in silence over his drink thinking bitter thoughts.
"We ex-writer types get pretty hungry."

"Dinner is ready," she said obligingly. He held out a hand,
and she helped him up. She liked the way his hand felt, lean
and dry, and his lightness as he leaped to his feet, his thin-
lipped smile, the rough quality of his voice and the trace of
an accent she couldn't place.

"The less I write, the more I eat," Alex said. "And the
thinner I get. If I didn't have writer's block I'd write a book
about it. *The Writer's Block Diet.*"

"Maybe when you waste away to nothing you can ghost-
write it," Leon said. He slapped his stomach. "I'll be first
in line to buy a copy. Lord knows I need something." Rachel
emerged from the kitchen bearing a platter of chicken. Leon
took it from her and set it on the table. "Looks good, darn
it," he said, with a tentative smile. Rachel looked distracted,
unhappier than ever. Did Leon sense her dissatisfaction? Did
he blame it on his paunch?

They gathered around Rachel's new butcher-block table,
Charles and Margo approaching slowly, still talking computers—Charles, it seemed, was explaining the computer system
at the library, and Margo was listening round-eyed. Leon
poured wine for everyone, and Alex clanked Dorrie's glass.
"To food," he said. "Among other things."

While salad and bread and bottles of wine were passed
up and down, Dorrie thought about Alex, conscious of his
rolled-up striped sleeve next to her, his bony forearm covered
with blond hairs, his long legs not far from hers under the
table. Objectively speaking, she didn't much like his looks;
she never would have picked him out in a crowd. He was
skinny, lazy looking; everything about him seemed indolent,
his thin light hair, his mocking greenish eyes, his shabby

clothes. She imagined him sitting at a desk all day—a horribly cluttered desk, worse than her father's, worse than her own— staring at a blank page, doodling, looking up bizarre words in a dictionary, drinking coffee with a shot of something in it, dozing off, checking on the weather outside his window, watching a bird skim across the sky. And he frightened her: she had a feeling he knew everything about her, that if he imagined her life as she was doing his, he would be accurate, would know the most secret facts about her: that on long car trips she sang sentimental songs in a squeaky soprano; that now and then she looked in the mirror and saw not an ugly crone but a magical creature of staggering beauty; that holding his hand and then releasing it had made her desire him.

The food was good and plentiful. Dorrie picked at it, her stomach in knots. She was silent, listening to the others talk about traveling—a subject to which Dorrie, who never went anywhere, had nothing to contribute. She looked for an opening in which she could say, "I don't know why, but I never go anywhere; I just read about other's people's travels," but she never found it, and decided, finally, that the remark made her sound even duller than she was.

"There's this *auberge* in the Laurentians," Rachel said. "I was there a couple of years ago. It was run by a very chic expatriate Frenchwoman—gracefully aging—and this handsome young Canadian who was obviously her lover. It was right out of Colette. I'd love to go back and see if they're still together or if he's left her for some young thing." Dorrie knew Rachel had been to the inn with William—their last vacation together before he left her for a twenty-three-year-old schoolteacher named Janet whom Rachel always called The Slug.

"It was a wonderful place," Rachel went on, looking sad. A bad sign, this Williamish reminiscing, this talk of deserted women. "She did the cooking, good wholesome food and lots of it, and this killer dessert called *trempette*. And there was a beautiful garden, vegetables growing alongside the flowers. I wonder if it still exists."

It was at that moment, at that image of broccoli and squash flanked by roses, that Dorrie became conscious of Alex's knee, under the table, pressing hers. She looked at him, felt the blood rush to her face and neck. He smiled at her.

Charles began talking about a trip he had made out west. "Did you get to the Grand Canyon?" Alex asked him. His voice was even, his face calm and humorous; maybe he thought it was the table leg he was caressing. "I asked because I was thinking of sending my hero out there. In my book," Alex explained when Charles looked blank. Under the table, his leg twined around Dorrie's. "I've wanted to see the Grand Canyon since I was a kid and I'll probably never get there, so I figured the next best thing would be to send him. But I don't know. He's terrified of heights. I wondered how badly it would affect an agoraphobe, to look over the edge of that chasm. I hate to put the guy through a bad time, but—" He paused, smiling to himself at the prospect of rocky immensities and sunset colors. "I've got my heart set on it," he said. Under the table, he put his hand on Dorrie's thigh, and squeezed.

"I really couldn't help you," Charles said with a short laugh. "I don't have those hang-ups."

"Alex's hero is based rather heavily on Alex, needless to say," Margo put in. "His only friend is a dog named Woofy— isn't that cute?"

"I've changed his name," Alex said. "It's not Woofy anymore."

"What is it?"

"It's Margo. And I've decided to make the dog a bitch."

Margo pretended to smile. "You're such a scream, Alex."

"That was uncalled for," said Charles.

"No, it wasn't, actually," said Alex. "But what'll it be? Pistols at sunrise? Or do you want to step outside right now?"

Charles looked at Alex with disdain. "Come off it, Willick."

"Do I have to? It's such fun."

Rachel looked close to tears. "All of you come off it," Leon said. "Quit quarreling and eat, for Christ's sake."

Alex leaned across the table and said to Rachel, "I'm sorry. I'm being a shit. This is an incredibly good meal. I'm going to quit making an ass of myself and start making a pig of myself."

Rachel summoned up an unhappy smile. Margo sat with her teeth clenched. Charles tore into the French bread as if it were Alex. Leon began talking again, about his travels in Europe as a young man. Dorrie closed her eyes for a second and had a vivid, startling vision of herself and Alex, hand in hand, looking over the edge of a Grand Canyon–like abyss. Where had that come from? A previous incarnation? Alex glanced at Dorrie regretfully and removed his hand from her thigh so he could help himself to more chicken. She had an insane desire to laugh. Their legs, still entwined, began to sweat cozily together.

The girl with the guitar was named Nina. Hugo met her on Saturday afternoon by the waterfall: a girl even smaller than he had thought, and skinny as a water bug, though Hugo sensed she was his age, maybe even older. She was still in her overalls, and her bare feet stuck out pink below the frayed pantlegs. She sat cross-legged on the rough grass, her guitar in her lap. "I live in town, actually, but I'm cat-sitting," she said. "For Susan and Paul. The Verranos? They're in Europe. Susan is my sister. I come over twice a day to feed Listerine and play my guitar." She took a stack of rubber-band-wrapped cards from her back pocket and peeled one off. Hugo took it. It said:

NINA SLAUGHTER

"RHYMES WITH LAUGHTER"

Songs to go

"I'll bet you've never heard the name Slaughter pronounced like that," she said. "It was my own idea. Otherwise, it sounds so violent, and I deplore violence in any form. Don't you?"

"Yes," Hugo said. He sat down beside her on the grass. Up close, in daylight, her hair was dark red and wild; no attempt had been made to tame it down—though Hugo couldn't imagine what would do it. No mere elastic or ribbon: metal bands, maybe. "I live with my aunt in the white house," he said, and smiled at what it sounded like. "I don't mean the White House, like in Washington. I mean over there." He pointed through the trees.

"Well, obviously," Nina said, and he blushed. His dumb jokes.

The guitar slung across her chest hid most of her. She strummed a chord. "Do you like music?"

"Sure. Everyone likes music."

"Not true. My mother doesn't. Which is why I have to sing my songs over at my sister's."

"You mean she doesn't like any music? Or just—you know—" He nodded at her guitar.

"Rock and roll, she calls it. Or country and western. She doesn't know which is which. She only likes the classics." Nina pursed up her mouth and lifted her eyebrows and waggled a little finger—a parody of a lady at a tea party. "Mozart," she said in an English accent. "And Beethoven, dahling. And all that jolly old craperoo." Hugo laughed. She held her pose for a minute, then smiled at him. "Who do you like? What's your favorite group?"

Hugo thought hard. He knew very little about pop music. "Oh—Duran Duran, I guess."

She stared at him, strummed a chord. "Really? I thought only girls were hot over Duran Duran."

"Oh—well—I'm not really hot over them, I wouldn't say."

"I don't like rock much. I loathe New Wave, especially, and that little creep Michael Jackson. I have to admit I really prefer country and western. I adore Dolly Parton, don't you?"

"Sure. Kind of." He remembered a big-breasted blond woman in a movie he'd seen with the Wylies. He remembered her breasts better than he did her singing.

"But the kind of music I really want to write is unclassifiable," Nina said. "I want to write songs about what no one has ever written about before. You know the kind of things I mean? Like I heard of this chauffeur once that was named Parker. Isn't that a fantastic name for a chauffeur? Wouldn't that make a song?" She raised her face to the clouds, lifting her chin. Around her neck she wore a choker made of knotted and braided string. On the back of one hand was what looked like a tattoo—or maybe it was just a ballpoint pen drawing—of a large, heavy-lidded eye, realistically rendered. Looking at her, Hugo had the same feeling he had had when David Wylie sat down next to him in the lunchroom one day and took out of his lunchbox a dog-eared notebook filled with poems: that he was in the presence of a weird and special person, someone to be listened to. "And there's this tribe in Africa, or somewhere," Nina went on, "that has this ritual where boys have to prove their manhood by cutting off one of their fingers and roasting it and eating it. Can you imagine what a song about that would be like? Or about water striders." She pointed out toward the glittering bugs on the water. The eye on the back of her hand looked straight at Hugo. "What do you think? Or about cats. Could there be a good song about cats? Or does it have to be love love love all the time? I think about that a lot. Why do songs have to be about love and practically nothing else?"

"I don't know." He decided to be honest. "Actually, I don't know that much about music. I'm not really into it."

She seemed to forget him as he spoke. She began to strum another chord, built it into a tune, and sang:

"Well, I don't know much about music,
No, I don't know much at all;
I just wanna be with my baby,
Hangin' out at the shoppin' mall."

Her voice was eerie, sharp and high—a witch's voice, Hugo thought. Her lips were pink, with high peaks. She slapped her palm against the strings, abruptly, and the music stopped. She looked down at her feet over the top of the guitar and said, "Well."

"Is that one of your songs?" Hugo asked her. He reached out one finger and plucked a string: a deep-voiced twang. "You wrote that?"

"What? What I just played? Are you kidding? I just made it up now. That's crap."

"It didn't sound so bad to me."

"You were right, then. You don't know much about music if that didn't sound bad to you."

Hugo wrapped his hands around his knees and stared out over the pond, casually, as if he was about to change the subject, about to yawn or get up and leave. He was sick of the way she kept insulting him. She didn't even know him. "Not that it was great or anything," he said.

Again she ignored him and began to play. He turned his eyes to watch her fingers creeping over the strings like lithe, white little animals—retreating, advancing, pouncing, retreating again, picking the same notes over and over fast, then slower, stopping. The eye—it was drawn on with a pen, he was sure of it—watched him. The waterfall made its endless sound, which, if you closed your eyes, was strangely like the sound of fire. Nina rested her chin on the guitar, looking glum, and said, "All I want is to be a famous songwriter."

"Ah," he said, hoping to wound her. "The what-do-you-want-to-be-when-you-grow-up game."

"I don't mean when I grow up," she said. The gloom in her voice was replaced with disdainful amusement. "I mean now. I'm sixteen; I could leave school any time if I could support myself—if I had a career."

Hugo blushed. What was he doing here talking to this girl who would always one-up him, who knew things, who was sixteen years old and ready to quit school for a career? "Hmm," he said, implying boredom, sophistication, skepticism, aware that it was all undercut by his red face. He had imagined being in his loft with a girl. What a load of crap. How could he have forgotten what it was really like, being with girls? How they terrified him. How he always said the wrong thing. How he turned into a hopeless nerd.

There was a pause, while he stared across the pond and Nina, so far as he could tell, stared at him. He refused to turn and meet her eyes. He would sit looking over at the swampy pine woods and the high scatty clouds forever before he'd acknowledge her existence.

She stood up suddenly and held out her hand. He saw it—white, freckled, tiny—stuck in front of him. The thumbnail extended thick and yellow; the rest were bitten short. The eye, close up, was not so well drawn. "Come on," she said. "Come and meet Listerine the Purring Machine."

He looked across the pond one last time, as if he loved it, and then put his hand in hers. She pulled him to his feet and stood grinning. "Listerine is expecting kittens any day— we think. She's huge, but of course we have no way of knowing when she's actually due." She kept hold of his hand, and they began walking up to the Verranos' house. "We can't exactly ask her when she went out and did it."

He laughed. His laugh sounded strained and stagy. Nina scared him: how could he live up to her? And, small and flat and frizz-haired though she was, she seemed to him very sexy. The day in general was very sexy—the hot, sun-filled July afternoon, the impassioned guitar music, the pregnant cat, the rhythmic chirp of insects. There were times when all of life seemed sodden with sex. Even pronouns—it struck him again, as it often had, how sexy pronouns were: how every time you said "he" or "she" you were acknowledging the mysteries of sex. And how he wouldn't exist, and Nina wouldn't, and no one would, if it weren't for sex. Even Listerine wasn't merely a cat, she was a female cat; her sex was an essential fact that it was impossible to forget. Nina said "she," "her," "she," "her," and Hugo could see in his mind not only the huge pregnant cat but the photograph of his pregnant mother leaning against the Camaro, and Rose vast and sleepy with Rodney in her belly. He remembered the day—he had been at the reservoir swimming with his cousins—when he'd realized that the parts of people that were always covered up were the parts where men and women differed from each other. It was without doubt the most embarrassing day of his life, until this one.

"I'm glad I met you, Hugo," Nina said, surprising him. She squeezed his hand and then let it go. "I hate school when it's going on, but when summer comes it's so boring around here."

"Do you have brothers or sisters?" he asked, thrilled. That meant she didn't find him boring. "Or friends. You probably have a lot of friends."

"I told you," she said in an elaborately patient voice. "My sister is married. This is her house. I'm cat-sitting for her."

"You don't have to condescend to me," he said, astonished at himself for using the word. He didn't think he had ever uttered such a word before.

Nina took it in stride. "You're right. I'm sorry. Of course, I could have other sisters, or brothers. But I don't." She grinned at him. "Thank God. I like my privacy. I love my sister, but her wedding was the happiest day of my life, and not only because I got to wear a gorgeous dress and a picture hat." Hugo tried to imagine her pixie face under a big hat; he wouldn't have expected her to care for such things. "As for friends," she went on, "forget it. This town is full of idiots and creeps."

"I think I've seen some of them," Hugo said. "In town— like at the pizza parlor on Main Street."

"Exactly. The teen queens and the macho heroes. Oh, God, how it all makes me want to throw up. I mean, most people's value systems. Don't you agree?" Hugo nodded. He tried to think of something smart to say, something to convey to her his feelings about that afternoon on Main Street, but Nina spoke first, changing the subject. "Why do you live with your aunt?"

"My parents are dead," Hugo said. He thought with guilt of the little lies he had told the Garners. With Nina, he would stick to the truth. "I lived with my grandfather but he died in April, so I had to come here. There was no place else for me to live. She's my only relative." He had resolved to be honest, but already this sounded misleading—too pathetic. He didn't feel pathetic, but he didn't know how to modify his statement.

Nina was gazing at him sorrowfully—a Mrs. Garner expression. "You poor kid! What's your aunt like?"

He hesitated. He didn't want sympathy from Nina; it put him at a disadvantage. And he wasn't sure he liked the way she called him a kid. And he didn't know how to answer. His aunt. He had been glad when she left him with the Garners, glad to see her go. Then, unexpectedly, he had awakened that morning feeling funny and out of place at the Garners', wishing he were home. Home? At his Aunt Dorrie's. Missing her, sort of. Not much, but enough to confuse him.

"She's all right. She's nice," he said. "She makes pots and things. You know? Like teapots and bowls and stuff."

"You mean she's a professional potter—right? That much I knew from my sister. But what's she like? Do you mind living with her?" Nina was watching him intently as they climbed the hill. He felt she would probe into his soul if the fancy took her; she would fish down in the depths of his being and come up with everything he feared and was ashamed of. "Where would you rather be if you didn't live with your aunt?"

"I don't know," Hugo said, beginning to be miserable. How could he answer such a question? Honesty was one thing, but having his bedtime fantasies dragged out of him by a girl he didn't even know was something else.

But by then they were at the house, and Nina seemed to forget about him again. She threw open the porch door, pulling her guitar strap over her head. Pregnant or not, Listerine jumped down from the porch windowsill to greet them as they entered—the black cat who had looked out at him in the dark. "There's my big baby," Nina said. She set her guitar down carefully and fell to her knees. Hugo knelt beside her, conscious of his babyish fat legs. He wished he had worn jeans instead of elastic-waist shorts. The cat climbed onto Nina's thighs and kneaded there, her paws seeming too small and delicate to support her body, which was distended on each side and strangely lumpy looking, as if she had swallowed baseballs. Her fur was as black and shiny as the pond at night, and when Nina petted her she purred with such fervor that at first Hugo thought some appliance had begun to hum, maybe the refrigerator. "Come here," Nina said to Hugo. "Pet her." He obeyed, fascinated by the cat. Her fur was softer than any human hair, and she arched her back under his hand. "Isn't that a fabulous purr?" asked Nina, talking not to Hugo but to the cat. "Isn't she a sweetums? Hmm? Isn't she?" Hugo could feel something moving inside the cat as he petted her, a soft batting against his hand that filled him with an odd kind of rapturous panic, and he quickly pulled his hand away and began to scratch Listerine's head, watching Nina. He thought about cutting off his little finger, roasting it over a fire, crunching into it as if it were a piece of chicken. He felt no revulsion, only reverent curiosity: he would do that for Nina if she asked him, he thought—half knowing he was being absurd. He would have liked to tell her how some people seemed like another species entirely, aliens from another planet—the kids at the pizza parlor, for instance—and how he knew deep in his heart that he and Nina were of the same outcast stock. But he couldn't find the words, and he sensed that any such statement would be premature. His deepest concern at that moment was not to screw up.

"Do you want a Coke?" Nina asked him.

"Sure."

They went into the kitchen—a big, bare, clean room. Hugo liked seeing the inside of other people's houses—how different they were from each other. He thought of his aunt's tiny, cluttered, messy kitchen, and the Wylies', full of electric gadgets and stainless steel, and Mrs. Garner's, all cozy and old-fashioned. He smiled, picked up a spoon rest in the shape of a pair of kittens with a ball of yarn. "You sure your sister won't mind if we drink her soda?"

"She said to make myself at home," Nina said. She took two cans from the refrigerator. "Let's go sit on the porch. Unless you have to get somewhere. I'll sing you some of my songs if you like."

"I'd love it!" He wished he hadn't sounded so enthusiastic, but Nina smiled at him in delight and he changed his mind. He would rather make her happy than be cool.

She said, "You mean it? I can hardly ever get anyone to listen."

"Well, you can get me, anytime. I like your voice."

"You do? That's wonderful. My mother says I sing like a cat in heat."

She sang the song he had heard the night before when he lurked in the dark outside the porch. She had changed it slightly, worked out the bad rhymes, and at the end of each verse added a little humming bit that Hugo loved. She nodded as she hummed it, raising one eyebrow and making the hum sound somehow angry, almost threatening. When she was done, he said, "Wow," and Nina laughed.

"I hope that means you like it."

"It's great. I really think it's great." He wished he could think of a supplementary word that didn't sound phony. Instead he asked her, "Is that a true song? I mean, did all that really happen to you? Are your parents really divorced?"

"Oh, no—they're utterly devoted to each other. In fact, they're quite disgusting about it, when you consider they're fairly old." She reached across her guitar for her can of Coke and drank. "Singing is like walking through a desert. I get so dry!" He watched her throat pulse, and looked at the little hollows of her collarbones on each side, and then she coughed and said, "I love making things up. Every one of my songs tells a story. I think that's important."

"I had an idea for a song once—actually a poem. I have this friend who writes poetry."

"Yeah? What kind of an idea?" Did he imagine belligerence? He would have to remember, always, to tread carefully.

"Just a dumb idea. About how life is missing people. I mean—you meet someone and then you move away or something and so you miss them."

"Oh, great. Terrific. Brilliant."

"No, but then when people die, not just leave you but actually die, then they become—this was sort of the point of the song, which I warned you was dumb—then they become missing people, like missing persons, only if you say 'missing people' it's more of a pun. Not a very good pun but sort of a dumb pun. It helps—well, it doesn't help much, but it helps if you put the emphasis on 'missing' first and then on 'people,' so that you can really see what you're talking about."

"I get it, Hugo. You have this fatal tendency to overexplain."

"Yeah. Sorry. I probably talk too much. Anyway, it's not much of an idea."

"No. It's okay. It might make a song. It's kind of interesting." Her voice was neutral; he couldn't tell what she really thought. He thought, suddenly, that nothing could make him happier than to have her turn to him and say, Oh, Hugo, that's fantastic! He closed his eyes for just a second, to imagine it, not daring to go further and imagine her falling into his arms. . . . He would save that for before bed: it would be his treat.

He said, "Why don't you sing me another song?"

She sang several, most of them either sad or angry sounding. There was one called "Midnight Roads." The chorus went:

"I'd like to travel those roads,
Those long dark midnight roads—

Those roads where nobody knows my name,
Where I can play the driftin' game,
Where the miles can swallow up all my pain—
I'd like to travel those roads with you."

Something about it made Hugo want to cry. It wasn't only
the song itself, though it was sad, and Nina's voice dipped
down at the end into what he recognized as a minor key,
but the combination of the music plus Nina's face as she sang—
ruminative and alert, as if she listened to herself and heard
something surprising—and, outside the porch screens, the sun
low in the sky making a golden path across the water, and
most of all the way he felt. This day, he said to himself—
clenching his fists tight to keep back tears—was one of the
biggest of his life, a turning point. He was on this porch,
not three feet away from a girl—a strange, exotic girl who
became more beautiful to him every second. He longed to
reach over and touch her wild hair, and when he realized
that perhaps one day soon he would have the freedom and
familiarity and ease with her to do that, then again the tears
nearly spilled over.

Nina broke off suddenly in the middle of a verse and said,
"What was that?"

Hugo composed his face. He had heard nothing but Nina's
voice. Then it came again: a low yowling sound from inside
the house.

"Listerine?"

They hurried into the kitchen where, in one corner, Nina
had set up a bed for Listerine to have her kittens on, an old
sofa cushion covered with a tattered beach towel. Listerine
was lying there, and when she looked up and saw them she
made the long, yowling sound again. Her eyes were large and
round, the same gold color as the sun on the pond. Nina
went over to her and knelt down. "What's the matter, my
baby? Oh, Hugo!" She clasped her hands before her chest.
He knelt next to her. "Hugo, look—the kittens are here."

On the towel with Listerine, nearly lost in a fold, were two moving creatures, wet black rats. Hugo could see their small snouts, their tiny paws, their closed-up eyes. They resembled a mole he had seen once behind Rose's trailer, little rooting things. He put out a finger. "Don't touch them," Nina said, and laid her fingers across the back of his hand. "She might not like it yet; they're too new."

He leaned down closer and said, "I think there's something wrong with Listerine."

"What do you mean?"

"Is there a light we could put on?" Nina got up and turned on the overhead light. Listerine stared up at them, and her golden eyes narrowed in the glare. She yowled again, a noise rich with desperation. "You see?"

"It's a kitten coming out," Nina said.

"It looks like it won't come." He bent closer. He could see the tiniest possible paws and a stringy tail hanging limply from Listerine's behind. He wondered why there was no blood, no struggle, just this bit of a kitten dangling there and Listerine's pained eyes.

She made her noise again. Nina sobbed. "Hugo, what can we do? I think it hurts her."

"Call the vet?"

"I don't know who the vet is! And vets don't come to your house and deliver kittens. Oh, Listerine!" She reached out a hand to the cat, and Listerine leaned toward it and yowled, and then she opened her mouth and began to pant. Hugo had never heard a cat pant; it was a harsh little sound that scared them both. "Hugo, do you think we should do something?"

"I think we should pull it out."

Nina clasped her hands before her chest again. They knelt close beside one another, their faces close enough to kiss. He thought, I will remember this moment all my life. Then he leaned down to Listerine and grasped the dangling kitten and pulled. He was too gentle, afraid Listerine would bite him

or scratch, but she only panted. With his fingers around the
kitten he sensed that it was dead—shouldn't it squirm? Maybe
that was the trouble, maybe dead kittens didn't come out so
easily. "I've got to pull hard, Nina," he said, and looked at
her. Her eyes were small and brown; right now they brimmed
with tears.

She said, "Can you do it?"

Tears came to his own eyes; he couldn't help it, and he
knew somehow that it was all right to cry a little. He touched
the kitten again, felt the slimy fur, cool under his fingers.
He got a good grip, felt the little paws, the taut stomach,
and he pulled. The kitten came out, and behind it a knotty,
muscled cord, and blood. Hugo suppressed a cry and set the
kitten on the towel. "That's it," he said. He looked at Nina
again. Tears were rolling down her cheeks. He put an arm
around her shoulders.

"That's it, Nina. She should be okay now."

Listerine reached her head over to the kitten, nosed it,
began to lick it. It didn't move, no matter how ferociously it
was licked. "It's dead," Nina whispered. "The poor thing."

He tightened his grip on her shoulder. They watched while
Listerine chewed at the cord, and bit it off. Then she expelled
a bloody mass that they thought at first was another kitten
until she licked at it and chewed it until it was gone. Neither
of them spoke. Hugo wondered if what was happening was
what was supposed to happen. He wondered if Nina knew,
but he didn't like to ask and break the silence between them—
an absence of talk in which it was possible for his hand to
remain across her shoulders. He felt awed and reverent, the
way he imagined people felt in church, the way he figured
he was supposed to have felt at his grandfather's funeral when
all he had been able to feel was panic, and the knowledge
that he was wearing sneakers with a suit. But he felt it now,
watching the cat: the sense that he was in the presence of
something miraculous, beyond his comprehension, perfect and
ancient and real.

He had no idea how long they knelt there. He had lost track of the time while Nina was singing, and that seemed hours ago. Now he remembered that the sun had been low across the pond, and he wondered, without caring, if the Garners were waiting dinner for him. He knew he wouldn't leave until Nina did. Eventually, Listerine ignored the dead kitten and began to pay attention to the other two, licking them until they squeaked. They nuzzled at her and finally found the part of her they wanted, and began blindly to nurse, pushing at her with their paws opened out like stars. Listerine lay back, purring. Hugo heard Nina take a deep, shuddery breath, and then she said, "Oh, Hugo," and turned to him, and he held her close against his chest.

After a while, he took the dead kitten outside and buried it down by the pond. It didn't need much of a hole: he dug it with a wooden spoon Nina gave him from the kitchen, and he set the kitten inside on some green leaves. The fur had dried to a glossy black, the front paws were white, the tiny claws sharp and perfect. "Mittens," he whispered, and covered the little body with leaves before he filled in the hole. On top he placed a bunch of jewelweed.

When he returned, the atmosphere had changed. It was no longer religious, or quiet. Nina was singing to the kittens, a version of Brahms's "Lullaby." She fetched some more Cokes, and they toasted Listerine, clanking cans. They petted the kittens, gently, though Nina said they'd better not pick them up yet. She had heard of a mother cat who rejected her babies when humans showed too great an interest in them. Nina crouched over the cats, crooning to Listerine. "Was she my little pumpkin? Was she? My little pumpkin mama? And does she have the bestest little kittens?" Hugo scratched Listerine's head, wondering how anyone could talk like that in public to an animal without sounding foolish. It seemed to him that Nina would never sound foolish, or look it, even in a large blue picture hat, and he wondered why that was. He believed it was true that they were of the same species, but she was a superior form of it, that was for sure. He watched her, down on her knees, with her red hair a frizzy cloud around her head and her teeth bared in a doting grin, crooning silly things to a cat named Listerine the Purring Machine, and he was aware, at that moment, of yet another great truth, on a day that seemed full of great truths: that what he wanted was to become her friend, if that was possible, and to win her esteem, if he could. To learn from her, if she would let him. Sitting on the floor there with Nina, he felt his hand almost tremble on the cat's head, the idea was so daring, so preposterous, so necessary.

When Dorrie arrived home from Boston on Sunday afternoon, Hugo and Nina were sitting on the deck drinking orange juice and eating fried egg sandwiches and cookies. Dorrie was hot, tired, and scared: she and Alex Willick had parted with plans for the next weekend, and she had been worrying about it all the way home. Singing "Danny Boy" hadn't helped; the Red Sox game on the radio hadn't helped; all she could think was that she was crazy to be setting herself up for another failure, an unknown quantity of pain, and a store of bitter memories. In three months, a year, even five years, when the inevitable happened, she would look back on this hot July afternoon, and the long dull drive down Route 90 and Route 86, and she would wonder why she had allowed herself to hope. For that was what she was doing, at some level below the worries: like termites at their work of undermining, mini-hopes were flourishing, dooming her to collapse.

The sight of her house, and the green water behind it streaked with light, never failed to steady her. The pink swamp roses all in bloom along the fence. The island in the water where she had once seen a snowy egret. The shabby outbuildings, the ancient beech tree, the mountain laurel fading by the garage. Here was home, where she was in control, had her routine, could think straight. She was even glad to return to all her familiar concerns about Hugo, whom she had not exactly forgotten but evaded: the weekend in Boston had been a vacation from the necessity of thinking about him, but now she welcomed the thought of her nephew, the sight of him out on the deck.

He stood up when she pulled in, and waved at her. The wave seemed friendly enough, and he called, "Welcome home," as if he meant it, but she had the impression that he hadn't expected her so soon, that she was an interruption. Then she saw that there was a girl with him—a skinny, wild-haired little person in overalls. Dorrie's first reaction was simple confusion; seeing Hugo with someone his age was as unexpected and inexplicable as seeing him out there on the deck with a penguin.

"Why aren't you at the Garners'?" was the first thing she said. She supposed she could have been more cordial, but he hadn't offered to help her lug her suitcase across the grass, and the friend sat there looking her over, cool as a queen, as if it were her house and Dorrie an unwelcome guest.

"I wasn't sure how many meals I was supposed to sponge off them," Hugo said. "And I kind of felt like coming home for a while. This is Nina. Mrs. Verrano is her sister, and they're away in Europe, and Nina is cat-sitting."

"Hello, Nina," Dorrie said.

Nina didn't get up; she squinted into the sun and said, "Hi."

"The cat had kittens, Dorrie," Hugo said. He used her name awkwardly, putting too much emphasis on it. She had told him before she left that he could leave off "Aunt"; this was the first time he had managed to do it. Impressing the girl.

"Great."

"Yesterday. We saw them being born. Two live and one dead—all black, with white paws."

"Terrific."

Dorrie stood there with her suitcase. Hugo looked at Nina, and then back at Dorrie, smiling uncertainly. "Can I have one?"

"One what?"

"Kitten. Nina's sister said she could have one and to find a home for the other if she could. They're really cute, and I'd take care of it. It could live with me up in the loft. It could catch mice."

"It could sleep on your bed and keep you warm," Nina said. The innocent remark seemed suggestive, as if it contained a double entendre, and though her voice was childish—clear and brittle and high-pitched—Dorrie could see she was probably older than Hugo, and a million times more worldly-wise. How in hell had Hugo picked her up?

"I'll have to think about that," she said. "But not right now. I need a shower and a cold drink. Excuse me, please."

She carried her things into the house, thinking, God forbid either of them should open the door for me. As the screen door closed behind her she heard Nina say, "I see what you mean." Dorrie stopped. There was silence on the deck behind her. She imagined Hugo frowning at Nina with his finger to his lips, and Nina suppressing a giggle. "I see what you mean." Had a war been declared over the weekend, then? And this rude girl was Hugo's ally?

She went upstairs and took a shower. She remembered Alex again, and shivered under the warm water. He had said, "Can we get together next weekend?" and she had replied, "Yes," and he had said, "I'll call you midweek so we can work out the logistics of it," and she gave him her phone number, and that was all, except that before he left he managed to waylay her in the kitchen and say again that he would call. She didn't know what she dreaded more: his calling or his failure to call.

She changed into clean clothes and poured herself a beer. The kitchen was a mess—an eggy pan in the sink, eggshells and spilled orange juice on the counter, a nearly empty bag of cookies left open, a knife on the table thick with mustard. It was Hugo, she knew, who ate mustard on egg sandwiches, but it must have been Nina who had spit plum pits into the sink. Hugo never ate plums.

She looked out the back window; he was alone. "Hugo, come up here and get rid of this mess in the kitchen."

He lifted his head. "I'll be right there." His back was to her, turned toward the pond. Dorrie looked, and there was Nina, walking along the water toward the Verranos' place. Hugo watched until she was out of sight. Oh, God, Dorrie thought: young love. She couldn't imagine his small, indifferent, ferretlike Nina not hurting him, and she pitied him profoundly.

"Who is that girl?" she asked when he came up. He was carrying plates and glasses.

"I told you—Mrs. Verrano's sister. She's sixteen. She'll be a junior this year. She's an honor student—she's never had less than an A in anything."

"Sounds like you."

"I guess so. And she plays the guitar and writes songs. Her father's an eye doctor. Her mother is a real estate salesman in Providence."

"Saleswoman, maybe? Salesperson?"

"You know what I mean. She sold a million dollars' worth last year and won this huge gold trophy. They keep it on the mantel. And Nina grows mushrooms in her bedroom."

"She grows what?"

"Mushrooms. I'm serious. And they're really good. You grow them in dirt, in a cardboard box. Nina sent away for it—it's a kit."

"You ate a mushroom?"

"Sure. Lots of them. These aren't like regular mushrooms, they're these huge brown things. They're delicious. Anyway, Nina's really nice."

"I'm sure. What did she mean by 'I see what you mean,' Hugo?"

He set the dishes down on the table and asked, "What did she mean by what?" There was a wide-open eye drawn with blue ink on the back of his left hand.

"What did your friend Nina mean when she said, 'I see

what you mean'? And what in hell is that on your hand?"

"This?" He made a fist and studied the back of his hand, smiling. "Nina drew it on."

"For what?" She imagined a demonic cult, complete with hallucinatory mushrooms.

"For nothing. Just for fun."

"And what about her little remark?"

"Oh, that." He pursed up his lips, grimaced, looked up at the ceiling and down again at his hand before he looked at Dorrie. "Well, I guess I told her you were kind of—I don't know."

"Yes, you do, Hugo. Kind of what?"

"Well. Hard to get to know. Kind of stiff or something."

"I see." She suppressed a desire to laugh. What had she expected? Something sinister masked by a sullen refusal to confess. Something Phinnian. She had forgotten what Hugo was like. Whatever else the child was, he was honest, and innocent. In spite of the awful Nina, and even in spite of his unfortunate genes.

"What's so funny?"

"Oh, Hugo, I don't know." She couldn't tell him that what made her smile was simple relief at the harmless normality of him and Nina sitting around and bitching about their elders—a picture so unlike that of the lonely, solitary Hugo she had left behind. She said, "I'm sorry if I've seemed stiff and hard to get to know. I guess I'm not used to people your age."

"Well, sometimes you're okay. Like right now, you're not even mad that I said that to Nina. It's just I never know how you're going to react to things."

He sat down at the table across from her, and she studied him. He was pudgy and grimy and sweaty. His blue eyes were round and earnest, his eyebrows drawn down in a little frown, his hair falling in his face. He needed a haircut and probably a bath. His black T-shirt, too tight across his chest, was ripped at the neck. He looked the way he always did, but there was a subtle difference, and she tried to figure out what it was. Did he seem older? More assured? Less lost? Happier? She said, "I'm glad you've found a friend, Hugo."

He blushed violently, as if a light bulb had been turned on behind his face. "Yeah," he said. "I really like her"—casually, pushing with a fork at a bit of egg on one of the plates. Dorrie made sure not to smile. "She seems to be an interesting girl," she said.

"Yeah, she is."

"Does she live nearby?"

"In town. She rides her bike over to cat-sit. She plays the guitar there too, at her sister's. Her mother doesn't approve of her music."

"What's wrong with it?"

"Nothing. It's great music. It's—" He struggled for a word. "It's really beautiful sometimes. She writes songs that are sort of unclassifiable. They're not just songs, they're really—" He paused again, considered, and said, "Great," again, smiling at his inability to articulate. She could see that he was wound up, and wanting to talk about her. She remembered that stage of infatuation: was she not, in fact, about to tumble into it herself? In spite of her dread. "Her songs are about everyday life," Hugo said. "What people feel and everything. You're going to think this is really stupid, but they remind me of *Upton's Grove.*" That was it, of course: the change in him that she was trying to pin down. Talking about Nina, he was as happy and interested as he always was when he talked about *Upton's Grove.*

"Since I've never seen *Upton's Grove,* I can't tell if that's stupid or not."

"Maybe you should watch it," he said, teasing her—their old conflict, made funny by his new happiness.

"Not me, kid," she said. Maybe Nina would wean him away from it—though when she considered Nina she wondered if there would come a day when she would think *Upton's Grove* wholesome and uplifting by comparison. "I'd like to hear some of Nina's songs, though. Do you think she'd come over and play some for me sometime?"

"Sure," he said, and then, "Maybe." He took a cookie from the bag and bit into it, considering. "I'm not sure she really trusts grown-ups. She says nobody likes her songs."

Dorrie was ashamed of herself. She had no doubt that she wouldn't like Nina's songs, either. Nor did she especially want to hear them. What she wanted was to check out Nina. "Well," she said. "Maybe sometime."

"Yeah."

He sat absently eating cookies, his eyes distant, his mind on Nina. And what would Alex think of Hugo? And how was she to work a love affair around this child? And would there be a love affair?

She tried to recall Alex's face but could remember only his absurd moustache, and the tense atmosphere of Rachel's dinner party, and her strange vision of the two of them at the Grand Canyon. Her voice had been shaky when she gave him her phone number. She wondered if he'd understood her nervousness, if it had put him off, if he could be patient with her until it departed. It worried her that now, the party over, she felt nothing but this uncomfortable, cold fear. She remembered that, a week or so ago, she had stuck a pin straight through the webbing between her third and fourth fingers and there had been no blood, she had felt nothing, and she had said to herself, This is what I have come to, a bloodless creature without feelings. She had an urgent desire to go and look at herself in a mirror. What could it be that he liked about her? She was nearly forty years old, she wasn't pretty, she was awkward with men, she was too tall and too skinny, she had wrinkles. What did he want with her? Did he want anything? And if he did, who would be the lover, who the lovee? Who would call and who wait for the call? She knew perfectly well. Oh, God, was it worth it?

Hugo said, "I guess I'd better do the dishes." He stood and gathered up the plates, humming to himself.

"Is that one of Nina's songs?"

"Oh—I guess it is," he said, blushing again. "I didn't even know I was humming it."

Like hell, she thought. "Hugo?" He turned, and his resemblance to her father caught Dorrie's heart. "You can have the kitten if you really want it."

His face lit up. "Oh, that's great! That is so great."

"You promise to take care of it? Keep it fed, and don't let it wander?"

"I promise." He stood up and began to pace around the kitchen, too elated to sit still. "I've always wanted a cat or a dog. We used to have this dog at Rose's, named Tiger. I loved him so much, and then he got run over and I really missed him. We had a funeral and everything. For years and years whenever I thought of him I'd cry." He smiled slightly and sniffed. "I'm starting to cry now, even. I can't believe it."

"I used to have a cat," Dorrie said. "When I first got out of college. He was a really sweet cat, named Hodge."

"Why Hodge?"

"My boyfriend was writing a dissertation on Samuel Johnson. Eighteenth-century English writer. Johnson had a cat named Hodge." She could see it surprised him: the boyfriend.

"What happened to Hodge?"

"Feline leukemia." She had nearly forgotten Hodge, who used to try to crawl into the refrigerator whenever she opened it, and who slept on her bed, a warm, soft mass behind her knees. Mark used to bring him catnip. "I really missed Hodge too," she said.

"Why didn't you ever get another one?"

"The old story, I guess. I didn't want to go through that another time. Losing it." He nodded solemnly, surprised again—that she not only had boyfriends but felt pain at the death of a cat. "It'll be nice to have a cat," she said.

"It'll be a good cat. I'll try not to let it sleep all over the furniture and stuff."

She laughed at his scrupulousness. "Hugo, does this look

like the kind of place where anyone cares about cat hair on the furniture?"

He looked around the kitchen and snickered. "I guess not." Then he sobered and said, as if it had just occurred to him, "Oh—I was wondering if I could go over tonight and visit my cat. Nina gets there about seven to feed Listerine."

"That's the mother cat?"

"Listerine the Purring Machine."

"I guess you can go." She wished she could caution him not to, to avoid his sullen popsy for his own good, to stick with the unattainable babes on *Upton's Grove*. He stood there smiling at her, perfectly, purely happy, with bits of cookie between his teeth. Hugo. She hadn't yet absorbed it, the fact that he had a friend, much less a girlfriend. And maybe it wasn't even true. Maybe she was imagining his devotion, projecting onto Hugo what she was unable to feel herself. She faked a smile back at him and asked, "Was it okay at the Garners'?"

"They were really nice to me." He carried the plates to the sink and said, with his back to her, "They let me have some wine at dinner."

She sensed that this was a confession, and that he made it because he was grateful to her about the cat. "That's all right, Hugo. I assume they didn't let you get soused."

"I only had a little."

"And did they treat you well?"

"I really love the Garners," he said, and the pang of jealousy she felt startled her.

"They're awfully nice people." She drained her beer. "I think I'll take a walk down to the pond while you do the dishes."

"Do you want to play a game of Scrabble after that?"

"I don't think so, Hugo. It's too damned hot."

She walked over the burned grass to the water, took off her shoes, and sat on the end of the dock. The sun beat down on her head. This is going to give me a headache, she thought, and immediately it did. She wished it was tomorrow, that she was up early, and it was cool, and she was at her wheel. She had come away from the show with a dozen ideas. She lay back on the warm wood and closed her eyes, giving in to the headache, listening to the absolute silence. No: not absolute. There was a cardinal's tireless whistle, and from the Verranos' the faint whoosh of the waterfall, and behind her on the grass an insect buzzing. And then, from the house, the sound of the phone and Hugo's voice calling her. Don't let it be Alex Willick, she thought.

But it was. "You're home," he said. "Good. Suppose I drive down there tomorrow afternoon and take you on a picnic."

"You said the weekend."

"Your enthusiasm is infectious."

"I'm sorry, I don't mean to sound—I mean, I usually work on weekdays."

"So do I, but I decided I'd rather see you."

She felt, for a moment, disoriented. What was he saying? Was she imagining this? She remembered his hand on her leg. Her head pounded, her chest felt tight, her breath came short, as if she were about to be sucked into the mucky bottom of the pond. "Okay," she said. "The hell with work." She took a deep breath. "I'd rather see you too."

Part Two

❧ 5 ❧

Hugo and Nina were sitting on a blanket down by the pond. It was a hot Sunday in August. They had spent the morning with the kittens—Daisy and Dolly they were called, still too young to leave their mother—and then eaten a lunch of root beer and potato chips down by the waterfall. Dorrie was out of town—"in Boston with her weird paramour" was how Nina put it—and after lunch Hugo and Nina walked along the pond to the white house and took over the deck. They idled through the days, now, like this—together, aimless, in the sun, sometimes in Nina's backyard in East Latimer, more often at the Verranos' or at Dorrie's when she was away, so they could take the boat out on the pond.

Hugo had had a series of fierce sunburns; his skin was blotched and peeling. He had taken to wearing jeans all the time, for protection, and to slopping suntan lotion on his vulnerable arms and the back of his neck. He had his bottle of Coppertone beside him on the blanket, and he waited for the day Nina would offer to apply it to his back.

The afternoon was hot and quiet, the pond wavy blue glass, shimmering in the heat. Nina was singing her "missing people" song, the one she had written for Hugo. "You gave me the idea," she said, "and you'll get half the profits when I'm famous and it's published." It was a prospect that saddened him— Nina's fame—implying as it did their separation. What use would a rich and successful Nina have for him? Imagine Dolly Parton still hanging out with the fat neighborhood kid she used to know when she was sixteen.

Nina sang, in the strange shrill voice he had grown used to and begun to love:

"They're not missing, they're gone to Jesus,
To that Missing Persons Bureau in the sky;
You don't need no passports, you don't need no visas,
'Cause we'll all be missing persons by and by."

It saddened him also that he didn't like Nina's song. "Missing Persons Bureau" wasn't, to say the least, what he had had in mind when he devised his "missing people" pun. He had thought the song would be, somehow, about his father and his mother and his grandparents, something that would cheer him up when he was down because it said what he felt, and it had been his idea. But Nina's song seemed to him just another country-and-western tune, the sort of thing that most of her stuff was better than. He hummed along with her at the end, though, and when she said, strumming chords on her guitar, "This is the song that's going to put you through college and send you to Europe and buy you a Rolls-Royce," he nodded and agreed. "No doubt about it." She beamed at him, and he felt his love for her like a hunger pang deep in his stomach. He would never confess to her, ever, that her song didn't please him.

"Tell me some more about your parents, Hugo," Nina said. She sat as she always did, cross-legged, with her guitar slung across her middle. He wondered if it was there to keep him away. He wondered if she was his girlfriend—if, in the unlikely event that he ever again had to introduce her to someone, he could say, "This is my girl, Nina." He wondered if you could call someone you had never even kissed your girl-friend. Most of all, he wondered if the idea was absurd: if he introduced her as "my girl, Nina," would she laugh, or throw up, or scream in horror?

She said she had never had a boyfriend—had hardly ever had a friend, even, except for a girl named Mary Lou who had been her best friend from seventh grade to ninth grade but who had moved to New York to do television commercials. "She was in a Skippy peanut butter commercial a couple of years ago," Nina told him. "The one where the kids are gathered around the table for lunch and the mother can't find the peanut butter and they refuse to eat anything she hauls out and then one of the kids pulls a jar of Skippy out of her backpack—did you ever see it? That was Mary Lou, the one with the backpack."

Hugo vaguely recalled the commercial, though not the girl with the backpack. "Was she your only friend?" he asked.

"Except for my cousin Courtney, in Michigan. She tried to commit suicide once, or so she said. Over some boy. She took ten aspirin. I don't know if that counts as a suicide attempt, but I guess her parents were really scared. I don't consider her a true friend, though. She's too strange—but she's strange in a sort of ordinary way. Do you know what I mean?"

She was always wanting to hear about his parents, or about his years with Rose or his grandfather, or about the Catholic school Rose used to send him to. She liked people to tell her things. She sat happily listening for long stretches of time, her face raised to the sun and a slight smile on it. "My life is so dull," she would moan. "I love to hear about yours. Yours is so full of characters. What material! If I'd had your life I would be the greatest songwriter in the world—instead of about the fourth greatest." He loved her grin; he loved the jokes she made about her talent that he knew weren't really meant to be jokes. "I have had the most depressingly regular childhood," she would go on. "I have the world's most normal parents, the world's dullest sister; all my schools have been just regular old schools—I mean, it's all so *nice*. Mary Lou might be in New York playing people in TV commercials, but I've *lived* like someone in a TV commercial. All those super-normal people with nice neat kitchens and concerned moms and no troubles in the world except what kind of peanut butter to buy. Miss Average American—that's me."

Hugo doubted this. He had met her family—her eye-doctor father, and her million-dollar salesperson mother, and her sister, Susan, and Susan's husband, Peter, even her grandmother, old Mrs. Slaughter, who went to Florida every winter and whose only distinction was that she wore a red wig—and their nice ordinariness made him ache with longing. But Nina herself was another story: he couldn't imagine what a commercial with her in it could be selling.

He was flattered by the way she glamorized his sad past. "What were they like?" she asked him. "That's what I want to know. I don't want facts, I want feelings, Hugo."

"How do I know what they were like? My mother died when I was a baby. All I know is what Rose told me. Nobody else ever talked about her. And my father died when I was eight. I've told you everything I remember about him." He had told her how the inability to remember tortured him, and how often he had tried to gather together what fragments of his childhood he could—of his father and Rose and Tiger the dog and his grandparents—making lists to hold in his mind like a book on a shelf he could browse through whenever he wanted. He didn't tell her, though, how he worried that at some future time these afternoons they were spending together, this blanket beneath his elbows, this film of gnats flitting around their heads, the flat green water and Nina's wild hair and the peeling skin on her nose and the sun polishing her guitar to the color of maple syrup—all this would be nothing but memories, or, worse, might be gone, unrecallable, nonexistent. He frowned with the intensity of the effort to seal it into his brain, to forget nothing, to keep it alive: that was his mission, his purpose in life.

Nina said, "I wonder why no one ever talked about your mother."

Hugo shifted uneasily on the blanket. "Because it was so tragic, what happened to her. I suppose." But he had wondered that too. She had hardly ever been spoken of, even by Rose, her sister. He had scarcely anything of her to put into his mental collection.

"You'd think they'd give you pictures of her, at least. I would expect you to have a framed photograph of her next to your bed. Or letters from her to your father. Or stuff like her old report cards and her graduation picture. That sort of thing."

"Well, I don't have anything," Hugo said irritably. Nina seemed to be reproaching him for his lack, as if he hadn't cared enough about his mother to seek out a memento. He took the cap off the Coppertone, poured some into his palm, and rubbed it on his forearms. "Just the picture of her and my father. I showed you that."

"Big deal," Nina said. "There must be more, somewhere. People just don't disappear without a trace. I'll bet your aunt has stuff. I'll bet she just doesn't show it to you. She probably thinks it's morbid. Or it could be sheer meanness on her part. I wouldn't put it past her."

Hugo began to feel uncomfortable. Was it his fault that Nina disliked Dorrie so? He was always trying to remember what he had told Nina when they first met to make her so down on his aunt. He couldn't think of anything, but he must have implied by his tone of voice or the expression on his face that she was an ogre. Dorrie was all right, really, he liked her fine a lot of the time, and Nina's attitude disturbed him—but it was also exciting: Nina and Hugo against the adults. Nina was working on a song about Dorrie, she said. He couldn't wait to hear it, even though he knew it would make him feel awful.

"I don't think she'd do that," he said. "And I doubt if she'd have anything, anyway. I don't think she even knew my mother very well."

"I'll bet you a million dollars she's got at least some photographs or something. Your parents would have had them, and when your grandfather died your aunt would have taken them."

Hugo thought it over and decided that it was probably true. Of course—somewhere there had to be photographs of his mother, probably right there in the house. His mother's things. Cold sweat broke out on his back, chilling him, and the sun was all of a sudden painfully bright. The smell of the Coppertone was sickening. Nina stared at him. "Are you all right?"

"She said she'd be home for dinner," he said. "I'll ask her then." His voice sounded strange and hoarse, scaring him. He cleared his throat. He hadn't known how much he wanted what Nina had said—a picture in a frame by his bed, old report cards and letters. My mother, he thought, and wanted to cry.

"Why wait?" Nina asked him. She got to her feet and looked down at him, hands on hips. She was a goddess, her hair all aflame. "Come on. Let's have a look."

"You mean just go through her stuff? I can't do that, Nina. It's her house."

"It's your house too, Hugo. And besides, the stuff belongs to you, not to her. They were your parents."

"But I can just ask her. She'll give me whatever she's got. Not that I think she's got anything." Arguing, at least, removed the urge to cry and made Nina look less like a goddess of war and more like a human being. "We can't just go sneaking through everything."

"She'll never know. Oh, Hugo—" She squatted down beside him again, her guitar bumping her knees, and put her hand on his shoulder. "Don't you see that she'll never give you anything like that? You know what she's like. She'd do anything to avoid a scene. She probably figures you couldn't handle it, you'd go to pieces and she'd be stuck with a basket case."

"I'm not going to go to pieces. I just don't see why I

shouldn't have a picture of my own mother."

"Well, of course!" She squeezed his shoulder. He wondered
if she knew what happened to him whenever she touched him.
He wondered if she knew he was trying to get up enough
nerve to kiss her. The idea of kissing her had begun to consume
him, and he worried constantly about bad breath. The night
before, there had been a full moon: lumpy, yellow, and swollen,
looking ready to burst. He had been with Nina at the Verranos',
and they had sat outside watching fireflies and listening to
the night sounds. The train whistle had sounded from over
beyond East Latimer. He had thought that the time was right
for kissing her, and just as he was about to she had said,
"Doesn't the moonlight look exactly like frost on the grass?"
and then, quickly, "Let's go tuck the kittens in for the night,"
and the spell was broken. What he had wondered all day was
if she had done it on purpose, because she had sensed his
decision and couldn't bear to be kissed by him.

"Come on," she said. "Let's go check it out."

"Let me ask her first, and if she says no we'll go and
look." As he spoke, he knew she had won.

"All right," Nina said. "But let's just have a small hunt
for ourselves first. I don't mean go poking through her personal
junk. But maybe there's something you've never noticed, like
an old photo album. She wouldn't mind if you looked in something you found right out in the open, or on a closet shelf
or someplace like that. I mean, you live there, Hugo. Suppose
you were looking for a tennis racket, or your old sneakers?"

He sighed, and she took her hand from his shoulder, and
they both stood up. "You're right," he said.

"Right as usual," she said, and he had to laugh at her.
They walked hand in hand up to the house.

His aunt's studio looked as if it had been abandoned suddenly by a person under attack; things were piled any which
way, a pot of glaze had been left open on the worktable, there
were uncleaned paintbrushes stuck in a can, dirty rags in a
heap on the floor. "What a mess," Nina said.

"She's been away a lot lately."

"The weird paramour up in Boston must really turn her on."

"I wish you wouldn't call him that." It seemed irreverent, there in Dorrie's house, for Nina to make fun of her. With Dorrie gone and Nina there, the house was different—foreign and almost threatening, as if it could hear Nina's mockery and retaliate somehow.

"Well, what should I call him? The gigolo? Or just the WP?"

"You could call him Alex."

"I hate the name Alex. What about him? Do you like him?"

"He's all right. I have no opinion. I've only met him a couple of times."

"He hasn't tried to win you over yet? Get on your good side to win your auntie's heart?"

Hugo laughed nervously. "I haven't seen any signs of it. Mostly he just ignores me."

"Well, watch out. He'll be wanting to take you to the circus and make you play catch with him out in the yard."

Nina parked her guitar inside the door and they climbed the stairs to the living room. It was hot up there, and stuffy, and only slightly less chaotic than the studio. Hugo had no idea where to look for such a thing as a photo album: in the bookcases, where the books were lined up two deep? in the piles of magazines that filled every odd corner? under the stacks of old letters and bills and God knows what on the desk and beside the easy chair and stuffed into baskets and falling off shelves?

Nina stood in the middle of the room and closed her eyes. He watched her, thinking again about kissing her, about kissing in general. It seemed to him an unbelievably gutsy, horribly intimate thing to do. It was like an invasion of someone else's territory. The kissing on *Upton's Grove* always bothered him, those big, wet, close-up kisses they performed with their mouths wide open, as if devouring each other. Nina was watching *Upton's Grove* with him now—they watched it at the Verranos'—and she always groaned during the kissing and said something like "Give us a break." And yet he knew that even if it looked a little weird it was something good to do, and certainly something he wanted to do with Nina.

"What are you doing?" Hugo asked her.

"I'm divining. I'm calling to the spirit of your mother and asking her where her pictures and things have been hidden."

"Come off it, Nina." Nina began scanning the room with narrowed eyes, her head thrust forward and her jaw clenched. Hugo laughed. "Now you look like a red fox stalking its prey."

"I doubt it," Nina said. She had a way of dismissing what he said by raising one eyebrow and tossing her head; she did it less often than she used to, but enough to make him, sometimes, afraid to speak. He turned away from her and began going through a pile of papers. He had wanted to say for a long time that she reminded him of a fox: the fox, specifically, that he had seen out behind Rose's once, a sleek, quick-eyed apparition, ruddy and beautiful. That was Nina, with her red hair and her pointed face and her air of wildness.

He felt her hand on his arm; she had come up behind him. "Unless you're my prey," she said. He put out a hand to draw her closer to him. He was always remembering how, on the day the kittens were born, she had come into his arms. He had imagined a hundred times how his hands would feel on her bony shoulders, her back. But she smiled at him and pulled away. "Just kidding," she said. "Let's start with the closets."

He hadn't meant it to be much of a search, but once they started he couldn't stop. "Just be careful, Nina," he kept saying. The excitement of being in the empty house with Nina was overwhelming, but his nervousness didn't go away. He couldn't believe he was doing what he was doing. He kept listening for his aunt's car to pull in, and looking around trying to see things with her homecoming eyes. "I don't want this place to look ransacked."

Nina waggled her fingers at him. "Have no fear, darling. Another successful job by the Little Falls Pond cat burglars. High-class ransacking at reasonable rates."

She was, in fact, more painstaking than he, and not nervous at all. Her attitude appalled and fascinated him. She would have gone through his aunt's underwear if he hadn't stopped her, and she found a slinky black dress in the closet and held it up against herself, looking in the mirror. "Nina, please!" he cried in horror and tried to take it from her.

She wrenched it away from him. "Calm down, Hugo, you'll have a heart attack. Now admit it—" She went back to the mirror. "Wouldn't this look better on me than on her?" She lifted her chin and let her eyelids droop. He stood beside her, looking down at her smooth freckled skin, the long dark eyelashes against her white cheek, her electric hair.

"It would look beautiful on you," he said. His heart pounded so hard he could hear it inside his head: was this a heart attack? But he knew it wasn't. He knew just what it was. He wanted, suddenly, to leave, wished he could, knew he couldn't.

Nina grinned at him. "You are cute," she said, and hung the dress back in the closet.

They found an old picture of Dorrie and Phineas as children, and an album full of snapshots of people Hugo didn't know—some were soldiers, and the settings looked European. "These must be from the war," he said. Some of them he thought were of his grandfather as a young man. He liked them, and he liked the old pictures of his father and his aunt; as children, they had looked almost exactly alike. "Look," he said to Nina. "They could have been twins."

"He's better looking," Nina said. "She hasn't changed a bit, has she?"

There were no pictures of them as adults. His aunt's high-school graduation picture was the most recent. And there were none of his mother.

Until they looked under the bed and found a dress box full of junk. Inside, right on top, was the clipping—old and brittle, and so yellow it was brown. They stared at it together: TEEN MOTHER SLAIN IN DRUG DISPUTE. BABY SLEEPS THROUGH IT.

Having a love affair was simpler than Dorrie had expected. Lying in Alex's bed on August afternoons, walking with him down the Boston streets, sitting across the table from him in her kitchen drinking beer while the hot sun beat down outside, she was ashamed of the trepidations of July.

Within a week after they met, Dorrie and Alex had been lovers; by the first of August they had decided they were in love. "There's something wrong with the terminology," Alex said when they discussed this. "How can two people be lovers before they fall in love with each other?"

"For a writer, you have an awfully literal mind," Dorrie told him, though she too was bemused—not by the terminology but by the fact, and the readiness with which she had, after all, accepted it into her life.

"It's so modern of us," Alex said. "Sex before love. It makes me feel young. I used to think I was such a proper gent. Used to spend weeks hoping and praying and sending flowers and little mash notes."

"Bilge."

"It's true! Then I met you and we were in the sack inside of a week, without so much as a bunch of daisies. You've corrupted me." It made her happy to be the kind of woman of whom such things could be said, even in jest.

Her friend Rachel asked, "Didn't I tell you you could get any man you wanted if you put your mind to it?"

"I don't think you ever said that, exactly," Dorrie replied. "Besides, I didn't put my mind to it. If I had, I would have run as fast as I could in the opposite direction. What I had to do was keep my mind out of it."

"Well, good luck," Rachel said. She and Leon were still planning marriage, maybe a little wedding in the fall. She had stopped talking about it to Dorrie, but her voice on the phone had an undertone of pessimism that Dorrie couldn't miss but didn't know how to respond to. "Alex has quite a history, you know."

"Oh, well, everyone does, Rachel," she said. "Except maybe me."

Alex was forty-seven. The veins on the backs of his hands stood out in ridges, and his hair and moustache were mostly gray, and there were hollows under his eyes that merged with parentheses of wrinkles on either side; otherwise he seemed no older than her previous lovers had been. But he talked, sometimes, like an old man, and he tended to lose energy in a way that seemed to Dorrie not physical, nothing to do with age, but mental, as if the will to be young had left him. He was a self-confessed failure, prone to nightmares, perpetually short of cash. He drank too much, and he was possessed by his desire to see the Grand Canyon.

He had been born in England, moved to the States as a child, and retained a trace of accent, a tendency to let his voice fall instead of rise when he asked a question. He had spent several years hitchhiking around Europe, a time he referred to as his crazy days. His eyes were gray and sad, washed-out looking, experienced. The inner depths of his mind she imagined to be as cluttered and full of riches as the rooms of her house.

The apartment he lived in, by contrast, was insanely bare. He had two rooms, and owned practically nothing, all of it shabby: a trunk left over from college, full of manuscripts; a card table; two ancient Windsor chairs in bad shape; an oak press-back rocker with a broken rung; a maple desk with a portable manual typewriter; a travel poster of the Grand Canyon tacked up on one wall; the sagging daybed on which he slept. All his books were paperbacks, and tattered.

"I can't stand to have possessions," he said. "A roomful of nice furniture would make me feel ill. Literally. I couldn't live there—I'd be weak in the knees all the time. And clothes—

buying new clothes makes me feel like I'm suffocating. It's not because I'm cheap. I love to spend money. I spend a bundle on whiskey. Ephemeral things, that's what I like."

Dorrie wondered if that included her. He seemed impermanent to her, tentative, like someone she imagined. He was all gaps and loose ends. Nor did he, at first, tell her much of importance about himself. She knew that he and his wife, whose name was Beth, had been divorced for thirteen months. Beth and their two teen-age sons had moved to California. The divorce had been painful for Alex, in ways he seemed unable to explain. His relationship with Margo, however— because it didn't matter—he described in detail.

"It was my little fling with masochism," he said. "That woman is a barracuda. I guess I hoped her self-confidence would be catching, that I could latch on to some of it by some kind of literary osmosis. And then of course she was so goddamn sexy." This surprised Dorrie, who considered Margo dumpy and dowdy, though she remembered how easily she had captivated the divine Charles. "Sex makes strange bedfellows," Alex said.

Another time he told her, "I can't stand gorgeous women." It was an opinion he expressed often, but the first time he said it they were in bed together, and Dorrie gathered the covers around herself and said, "Thanks a lot."

"Oh, hell, Dorrie," he said, and pulled the covers away to kiss her neck. "You know what I mean. I'm not saying you're not a good-looking woman. I like the way you look. If I didn't, would you be here in my bed?"

"I don't know. People are weird." She turned her back to him and inspected the room: the digital clock radio on the floor by the daybed, a plastic laundry basket in the corner full of folded underwear, a six-pack containing four empty bottles and two full ones. Nothing superfluous, except the sun coming in through uncurtained windows to reveal the fact that there was no dust, anywhere: his neatness, she knew, was fanatical. "Maybe you're having another fling with masochism," she said. She watched the square red numerals on the clock flashing the seconds by. Dorrie hated it, considered it a useless electronic miracle, all that technology just to let you know that you were older by one second, two, another, another . . . Alex was surprised at her attitude; he said precision was a positive thing, it was always good to have things exact, to know where you were. The clock beamed at her, 5:14:07, 5:14:08. She said, "Maybe ugly women turn you on."

"Well, they don't. Neither do gorgeous women. But you do." He ran a fingernail down her back. "You should know that by now."

She relaxed, sighed, turned around to him and smiled. It was absurd to be hurt by his words. At least she had a man she liked, was beginning to love, enjoyed spending all those lost seconds with. She shouldn't expect flattery as well. "I'm sorry," she said. "I have a thing about my looks."

"Your looks?" He leaned over her and retrieved his wire reading glasses from under the bed, put them on, and stared at her. "What's wrong with your looks? God, the things our society does to women. Dorrie! You're a fine figure of a woman. You're damned attractive. Look, neither of us is going to be offered a modeling contract. I'm no beauty, God knows. But we're nice-looking people, Dorrie. And you look awfully good to me. I think we make a handsome couple." He took off his glasses again and pulled her close to him, and with her head against his chest she listened to the marching sound of his heartbeats, and believed that he meant what he said. "You have a thing about your looks," he went on. "Well, quit having it, will you? It's ridiculous." He let her go and pulled the tops off the two remaining beers.

But it was something she thought about. He wouldn't tell her she was beautiful; he would only tell her the truth. Teddy used to murmur to her sometimes, always in bed, that she was beautiful, and his insincerity made her uneasy, but so did Alex's tepid adjectives: attractive, nice looking—handsome, for heaven's sake! Whenever she looked in the mirror,

all that hot summer when she and Alex were falling in love,
she thought of those adjectives and mourned: she was nearly
forty years old, and she would never get a crack at it, would
never know what it was to be beautiful. It seemed an enormous
deprivation.

And yet she was happy. How could she have forgotten,
and undervalued, and pretended not to want, the joy and comfort and excitement of having a lover? It was as if she had
emerged from a dark place into not only light but bright color
and brilliant music and lush tropical warmth. He asked her
why she had never married, and instead of acting on her first
impulse, which was to tell him that she'd never been asked,
she said, "I'm not the type. I don't know why, but I've always
known I wouldn't get married. Even when my mother used
to talk about it as a given, I think I knew that it wasn't going
to happen to me." This was true: the sense that the peculiar
and vivid apartness that had been with her all her life encom-
passed a kind of absolute solitude unrelievable by husband
or children—though she had never articulated this belief before, and had barely been aware that she held it. She was no
longer sure she did, but she didn't say that, either.

"I think children do have intuitions," Alex said. "Not about
the details, but in general I believe they can imagine their
lives at a very early age and be right about them." He looked
reflective, perhaps recalling some early intuition of failure.

She said, "Maybe I just had the wrong attitude. Maybe
I made it come true."

"But you've been in love?"

"I suppose so. Yes."

"You seem doubtful."

"It's just that it always ended badly."

He put his hand over hers. "Don't think about endings."

There must be no one on earth easier to be with than
Alex Willick. In spite of the vast tangled life that she sensed
sticking close behind him like his shadow—wife, children, divorce, knotty relationships, capricious muse, foreign childhood,

footloose travels—he seemed to her a restful presence. After the first excitement, in fact—those first passionate weeks spent mostly in bed—what she found in him, and treasured, was comfort and repose. She was as peaceful and at ease in his presence as she was snug in her house at night with a storm ranting outside. His insubstantiality made no demands on her.

And he loved her. She had never been so sure of love before—not from Mark, certainly not from Teddy, maybe not even from her parents. It wasn't true at all that she was the pursuer, he the pursued. He couldn't seem to get enough of her, and her great delight was to wake beside him in the morning, after the nights they spent together, and find him gazing at her with a besotted smile on his face. He loved her in odd, original ways. He liked to move his lips delicately over her wrists and the soft insides of her arms, and press his tongue against her skin. He liked to stop in the middle of lovemaking and lie with her, joined together, talking, drinking beer; sometimes half the afternoon slipped by before they resumed. He called her "love," sounding English. He gave her presents: a woolly stuffed sheep standing on spindly black legs, a jar of honey from Scotland, a silver frame containing a picture of his sneakers. He told her she had saved him from despair, had cured his writer's block, had restored his youth. His devotion astounded her; it buoyed her up and kept her from her own melancholy, which had been, before, such a part of her life she had scarcely taken notice of it—like a long allergy for which a cure had just been found. When she wasn't with him, the thought of him sometimes rose in her mind, hot and clear and overwhelming, bringing tears to her eyes. If loving her saved Alex, his love for her turned Dorrie's life around and gave it meaning beyond the safety of her potter's wheel.

Her work suffered. As the affair progressed it became a favorite thing of Alex's to drive down to her place in the afternoons and go for a swim in the pond, and then sit out on the deck in the shade writing in a large spiral notebook while Dorrie worked at the wheel. Sometimes he came in and read aloud to her what he wrote—long, rambling, disconnected portions of a novel that seemed to her full of rare insights and studded with his special gift for the brilliant image, the *mot juste.* She saw traces in the manuscript of parts of his life and personality that were known to her, and hints of the things he kept secret—though these might have been fictional. She didn't know. "If only it went somewhere," he said when she praised him. "If only it added up to something. But at least I'm writing," he always ended up. His relief at the breaking of his writer's block was enormous. "I feel like someone in a fairy tale—one of those paralyzed princesses who has to be awakened with a kiss."

"You don't kiss like a paralyzed princess," she said to him.

His presence there distracted her. She would work a while, but then they would begin to talk, and she would turn from her table or her wheel, get cold beer from the refrigerator, sit with Alex in the shade. They talked about their childhoods, people they knew, Alex's writing, her attitudes toward her work. It seemed years since she had had anyone to talk to, except Rachel—years since she had been that close to a man. "I think you're the first man I've ever been able to be honest with," she told him.

"That's a great compliment," he said. "It's true too. You can tell me anything, and I'll keep adoring you, no matter what it is. Try me."

She didn't mean to, but one day she told him she used to plan the killing of her brother, a fact she had forgotten. She remembered it one afternoon in the Boston Museum of Fine Arts. They were standing in front of a Cézanne, a painting of a row of cottages down a wooded lane—red roofs and blue, and the road winding out of sight, out of the picture. As she looked at it, her head began to ache, a pinpoint of pain that tapped behind her temples until she remembered. *Phinny,* she thought, and the tiny needle of pain became a hammer.

"We used to have a reproduction of this." She needed to talk, and to hear Alex's voice in reply. "My mother was a great one for art reproductions. We had *Guernica* in the dining room. Can you imagine trying to eat in front of all that suffering?" She was trying to speak lightly, as if the story she was about to tell were a funny one, but she knew from the way he looked at her—suddenly giving her his full attention, not looking at the painting at all—that she must be failing. She went on. "This one hung in the upstairs hall. The light from the window used to shine on the glass, so you had to stand very close to see it."

"I'm glad to know your parents liked it," Alex said. His voice was even and soothing. "It's one of my favorites."

"This is so odd," she said. It was as clear as anything, as if it had appeared out of her headache, as if the pounding in her head were a slide projector: that sunny hall at the top of the stairs, the foreign-looking roofs and trees smaller, and under glass. "To see it here." She stared at the painting, and it went out of focus, doubled itself; the crescent-shaped road became two, the little woods a major forest.

She hung tight to Alex's arm. He looked down at her steadily. "Are you all right?"

"I'm having a Proustian experience," she said, trying to laugh. "But not a very nice one."

"What, love?"

"I remember—I just remember this now, I haven't thought about it in years, twenty-five years, thirty—" She stopped. It wasn't something she wanted to tell, and yet she knew, instinctively, that by telling it to Alex she would exorcise it. There was Alex, the beautiful painting, the silent gallery, a bright afternoon outside: nothing to fear. "I stood in front of this painting one day, I must have been ten or eleven, and planned how I would kill my brother."

"Ah, Dorrie." He moved as if to put an arm around her. "It's normal to think things like that. Kids are naturally bloodthirsty little devils."

"I don't think this was natural, Alex," she said, standing

stiffly, clutching his arm. "I don't remember exactly what he had done to make me hate him so much; there was always something. He wrecked my tenth birthday party, I remember that—terrorizing all the little girls I invited, squirting them with his squirt gun, running through the house yelling dirty words—God, even at seven, he knew all of them. Maybe it was around that time, I don't know. Anyway, I stood in front of that painting, and I thought about how I would get the weed killer out of the garage, the stuff my father used on the lawn, and I would put it into a glass of root beer because I figured you could never see it or taste it in root beer, and I would get Phinny playing ball or chasing me or something, get him all tired out and hot and thirsty, and then I'd go in and get him this glass of root beer, and take it to him down by the creek where we sometimes played. Phinny used to catch tadpoles there and watch them flop on the dirt until they died."

"Dorrie."

"They used to get dried out, and turn from black to brown, these little brown husks like seeds, and after a couple of weeks in the sun they would crumble like powder in your hands."

"Dorrie."

"He did worse things than that, Alex. He was a very curious child. He always wanted to see what would happen. Usually something horrible happened. Oh, God, Alex, there were a million things, a million horror stories. He never quit, he never just let things be. I was full of fantasies of deliverance—car crashes and fires and kidnappings. Anything, just so he would be gone. I suppose the weed killer in the root beer was the worst."

Alex frowned. When he drew his brows together he looked worn out and old, older than he was. They sat down on a wooden bench. She would have liked to stroke his face, smooth out the lines between her fingers, make him smile. She was sorry she had brought up this unpleasant subject.

"Okay," Alex said. "So you thought about murdering him."

"Do you want to hear the details?"

"I want to hear whatever you want to tell me."

"All right." She took a deep breath. "So I would bring him the root beer and he would drink it and—I didn't know what would happen, except that he would die, somehow. I didn't think about the actual process; I just imagined him not moving, sort of going to sleep, and then I would drag him to the water and put him in it face down so it would look like he had drowned."

"Dorrie."

She looked up at him: his grave, gray gentle face, his knowing eyes. "And that's all. Except that once I worked it out I thought about it all the time. I'd go up in the hall and look at this painting and think how life would be peaceful with him gone. It would be like that little town in the painting, with the neat white houses, the road turning off. Green and peaceful. No Phinny."

"Dorrie—what kid with someone like your brother to put up with wouldn't have fantasies of doing away with him? You know you wouldn't actually have done it. I hope you're not blaming yourself for it."

She shook her head. It wasn't that; it was the suddenness and vividness of the memory that had jolted her. "I'm just overcome with remembering it," she told him. "I really don't think about Phinny much anymore. I forget how much I used to hate him."

They left the museum, and walked to a place near the Fenway for dinner. In the dark bar, two young men played a noisy video game, laughing, baiting each other. Their language was violent, profane, casually filthy. Instantly, they reminded her of Phinny. "He was trash, Alex," she said. "He made no one happy, ever. He ruined my childhood; he ruined my parents' lives." She thought about it: no, that wasn't quite it. He should have ruined her parents' lives. He somehow didn't. She remembered their incomprehensible ability to bounce back, to keep forgiving him. That must be what it was to be a parent. She wondered if she would have been capable of it, if Daniel, Eleanor, Jane had been realities instead of dreams. If they did become realities, ever. The thought of Hugo glanced through her mind but didn't stay.

"He was a human being, Dorrie," Alex said. "He must have had some redeeming qualities."

"No," she said. "None. Nothing. He was trash."

The boys playing the video game shouted and called each other names: "ass-hole," "shit," "fucker." She remembered Phinny calling his own parents those things; she remembered seeing him dragged by two policemen into a patrol car; she remembered the time he had pushed her father into the kitchen wall, the sound of her father's head hitting it, how her father had moaned: "Oh, Phinny, Phinny, my boy, my boy." Tears came to her eyes. Alex said, "Dorrie," and she picked up her glass and drank.

"Let's forget it," she said.

"It must have torn you up when he died."

"It would have if I had let it," she said. "I do my best not to think about my brother."

"I can understand that."

"I know the unexamined life is not worth living and all that, but there are some things that if you examined them too closely would make life—I don't know." She pressed her fingers, cold from the glass, to her aching head. How unfair it was that those hard-forgotten things could be brought back so easily. " 'Unbearable' is probably too strong a word, but you know what I mean."

She dried her eyes, sipped her drink, nibbled peanuts. She was beginning to feel irritable now, more than anything, as if she were getting better after an illness. Crabby. Needing to be pampered. She wanted to forget Phinny. She would have liked to think instead about the possibility of Daniel, Eleanor, Jane. She looked at Alex, trying to imagine a baby with his face. It wasn't too late. The seconds were ticking by, but it wasn't too late if they hustled. Let's go back to your apartment, she wanted to say. Let's make love without my diaphragm.

The waiter came and took their order. "I don't care," she said. "I'm not hungry. Anything. Chicken. Fish." She let Alex order for her.

"Dorrie," he said when the waiter had gone. He took her hand again and held it tight. "Talk to me about him some more if you want to—your brother. Everyone has something in their lives like that, some unresolved bit of hostility, some long grudge. It helps sometimes to talk it over and get it straight, even if it's unbearable. It's easier to bear with someone else."

She closed her eyes, and opened them again to see Alex sitting across from her, looking concerned. "Oh, God, I'm so glad I met you," she said. He smiled his sad-eyed smile. "I just want to forget Phinny, Alex. At least for now. I promise that if I ever need to talk about him I'll let you know, I'll talk to you."

Afterward, she thought it might have been his own secret grudges he wanted to talk over and get straight—all the simmering parts of his life he hadn't told her about. When dinner was over and they returned to his apartment she was unable to say what she wanted to say—about time running out, about her mythical children. She didn't know why she couldn't speak; she had resolved to lay it all before him. It was Phinny, she half thought, coming between them. Or Alex's own unexamined life. Something. Whatever it was, they made love, as usual, with the diaphragm in place, while the red seconds flashed by on Alex's digital clock.

Once they had settled down into their affair—a remarkably quick process—Dorrie began to worry about Hugo. She knew she was neglecting him. Even when Alex was at her place (and he was there more and more; his apartment was so hot, and he claimed he couldn't work well without the sight of her), she didn't see much of Hugo. He was spending most of his time with Nina, down at the Verranos' house. Nina's sister and her husband were back from Europe, but both of them worked all day, and Hugo and Nina seemed to have made the place their headquarters. What they did there Dorrie hated to think, but she had met, formally, Susan and Peter Verrano as well as Nina's parents, the Slaughters. "We're so delighted that Nina has a nice friend like Hugo," Mrs. Slaughter said. She was a chain smoker, and her voice was fast and nervous with a lot of laughter in it. Her husband hovered behind her, frowning, short and frizzy-haired like Nina.

"It's good for her to be outside too," he said. "Out at your place in the country. Sunshine, fresh air . . ." He gestured vaguely, looking unconvinced. The two of them made Dorrie think that the reason Nina hung around with Hugo so much, and spent all her time at her sister's, was a simple desire to get away from her parents. And she wondered what Nina's other friends were like, that her parents should be so glad about Hugo. But they were good reliable people, Dorrie thought. A nice family. Behind this perception was the hopeful idea that whatever the kids were up to it probably wasn't drugs or crime or anything more degenerate than excessive television watching—though in her worst moments, she imagined Nina getting pregnant and Hugo being hit with a paternity suit.

"Hugo?" Alex chuckled when she told him her fear. "Be realistic, Dorrie. Babies can't make babies."

"He's fourteen."

"He's the most immature fourteen-year-old on earth."

"He's in love with that girl."

"Puppy love. And puppies can't make babies, either."

If Hugo and Nina worried her, Hugo and Alex worried her more. Alex treated the boy like a troublesome pest—like, in fact, a puppy no one wanted. He told her that Hugo was the wimpiest kid he had ever seen. "If you don't do something about him, he's going to grow up to be the kind of guy who goes around with a plastic pen holder in his shirt pocket. The kind of guy whose idea of heaven is going to his company's annual convention in Chicago. The kind who puts an 'America Number One' license plate on the front of his car."

"He's not like that at all, Alex," she told him. It was the only time he angered her, when he made fun of Hugo. The worst was when he contrasted Hugo with his own sons— two California teen-agers who played soccer and basketball and had just taken up windsurfing. He kept their photographs squirreled away in a drawer but he took them out once to show her: Jeffrey and Jeremy, dark-haired boys with similar smart, handsome faces. They resembled his wife, Alex said, keeping his voice expressionless; Dorrie thought they looked arrogant, but didn't say so. She wondered if his wife had winged, smugly lifted eyebrows like Jeffrey's, the same ironic curl to her lips that Jeremy had. Alex told her Hugo should go out to California and spend a couple of weeks with them; they were normal, noisy, exuberant kids who didn't sit around and brood all the time: they would straighten Hugo out. It made her furious, not only that he criticized Hugo but that he stuck up for his sons' way of life only, it seemed, as a reproach to Hugo's. Alex was not normally a man who thought much of things like ball games and windsurfing. If Hugo had been a jock, Alex would have laughed at him and called him a meathead.

She wondered too what would happen if she took Alex up on his idea to send Hugo out to Santa Barbara to be re-formed by Jeffrey and Jeremy. She suspected that the terms Alex was on with Beth didn't include much contact with the boys; the photographs were slightly out of date, and he didn't seem to know as many details of their lives as a doting father should. And they were spending their summer vacation at soccer camp instead of in Boston with Alex. She could be cruel: she could say, "What a marvelous idea, I'm sure Hugo would love a trip to California, let's call up and arrange it." She didn't, of course, and she asked nothing about his sons; the untold details, she knew, were painful. She merely requested him to lay off Hugo.

"If you got better acquainted with him you'd have a higher opinion of him," she said. "I admit he needs to grow up a little, but he has a lot to offer. Play Scrabble with him some time," she suggested with a wicked smile.

"And have the little bastard gloat over his victory? No thanks."

"He doesn't gloat, Alex. He's really a very good kid." She remembered the day he'd cleaned the garage, how hard he had worked. She thought of all his silly *Upton's Grove* jokes.

"I didn't say he isn't a good kid. I just like him better when he's off with his girlfriend than when he's hanging around here."

"When he's off with his girlfriend I worry about him."

Alex sighed with exasperation. "You told me you used to worry that he didn't have any friends his own age. Now he's got one and you're still worrying. Leave the kid alone, Dorrie."

"She's not his age. And he doesn't seem like himself since he's met her."

"Maybe it was before that he wasn't acting like himself. How do you know? You barely knew him before he moved in with you."

"He was never this distant," she said. It was a Sunday evening. She and Alex were sitting on the deck having dinner. She had hoped Hugo would be home in time to eat with them, and she had grilled hamburgers outside just for him, because he used to complain that they never had real food like hamburgers and pork chops. "We just have snacks," he said in the good-natured way she never took seriously. Maybe Nina supplied him with hamburgers and potato chips and unlimited cans of Coke; maybe that was the attraction. While the hamburgers cooked, she found herself hoping that the smell of meat would waft over to the Verranos' and draw him home. "I think that girl is turning him against me."

Alex was thumbing through the phone book while he ate, searching for a name for a new character in his novel, but when she spoke he closed the book and stared over at her. "I'm not imagining it, Alex," she said. "Hugo and I were getting along fine until he met this Nina person."

"Don't you see what you're doing, Dorrie?" he said. He spoke hesitantly, reluctant to continue with a subject that made them bicker. If Hugo would only go away: she could imagine that idea always behind Alex's pained eyes.

"No. What am I doing, Alex?"

He set the phone book gently on the floor and leaned forward across the table. In the failing light, his delicate, angular face was full of purple shadows. His thin, light hair hung lank; his moustache drooped. He lay awake at night, he said, thinking of her, of his book, of his sons, of the threat of nuclear war, of his nightmares; only when she was there could he sleep properly. He said, "You've condensed the entire parent-child relationship into one summer. You go through postpartum depression when he arrives, and then you find that he's really a dear little fellow and you have lots of jolly fun together, and then he begins to leave the nest and you go into a panic and become all clingy and pathetic like someone who writes to Ann Landers because her baby is being stolen from her by a girlfriend who's not worthy of him."

"I am not all clingy and pathetic!" She put down her hamburger; she wasn't hungry. "I'm trying to look out for his interests, and it happens to be true that he's become withdrawn and sullen and he's never home. I really don't think that's healthy behavior for a fourteen-year-old kid who never before showed any particular signs of alienation." Or had he? Was rowing around the pond for hours an alienated activity? Or not finding any friends? Or refusing to read books? It seemed to her that she hadn't seen Hugo smile in weeks—that babyish grin that used to irritate her with its readiness. And hadn't she read somewhere that a sudden change in behavior was one of the danger signs for parents of adolescents to look out for: was he on drugs?

Alex put down the phone book and leaned over to take her hand. "If this seriously worries you, tell him, Dorrie. Have a talk with the little bastard. Even if he doesn't tell you a damn thing, you should be able to judge from his behavior if anything is wrong. At least, it'll set your mind at rest if you tell him what's bothering you."

"I do feel responsible for him, Alex." She was grateful for his about-face, and for his warm handclasp. She was grateful for everything, for his very presence on her backyard deck, at her table, and she believed that eventually he and Hugo would become friends. If she was very careful and did everything right, her life, and Hugo's, and Alex's, would stretch out luminous and winding and calm, like the road in the Cézanne painting—their lives would take on the kind of beauty and clarity she hadn't allowed herself to dream about in years—had never really, perhaps, thought possible. Alex had never thought it possible, either. Or Hugo. But she would achieve it for them. If she didn't allow Hugo to get away. She took a deep breath and let go Alex's hand to pick up her hamburger again. It was getting dark. The light on the pond made a path between the dark reflections of the trees. "He should be home any minute. I'll talk to him tonight."

"I should probably be on my way."

They looked at each other ruefully. "I guess I would like to get this straightened out with him. And it would be better if you weren't around."

"Did you ever think that that's what may be alienating him? You and me? Or can't you be Oedipal over an auntie?"

"I suppose I've been neglecting him. Maybe that's it. But you're right, Alex. I don't know him well enough to judge."

She walked him out to his car. He had washed and waxed it that afternoon in her driveway—a newish little hatchback, absurdly small for him. She leaned in the window for a kiss. "I wish you could stay."

"I'll see you in Boston on Tuesday. Right?"

"Yes, I have to deliver those pots."

"And you'll stay over?"

She straightened up and made a face. "I guess that depends on my talk with Hugo."

"Well, call me." He took hold of her wrist and pulled her down to him again. "Don't forget that we postadolescents need coddling too."

Hugo didn't get home until after dark. He knew, as he came across the lawn from the Verranos', that Dorrie was waiting for him. It wasn't only that she had turned on the backyard floodlight. He could feel her presence—her aura, Nina would call it—up there in the living room window, watching for him. He had taken to going directly to the garage loft when he came in at night, not even stopping in the house to brush his teeth before bed. Tonight as he stepped into the path of the light she called to him, and he gave a deep sigh that he hoped she heard and turned toward the house.

When he went upstairs she was there, in a nightgown and an old sweatshirt, curled up in the rocking chair. He leaned in the doorway of the living room with his hands stuck in his pockets and said, "Hi."

"Hi."

"I guess I'll just say good night and get to bed," he said. "I'm really tired."

"I wondered if we could talk for a couple of minutes, Hugo."

He had known it was coming. You couldn't live in the same house—or nearly in the same house—with someone for a week without talking. Or she couldn't, anyway. He wasn't having any trouble. It seemed an okay arrangement. "About what?" he said.

"Come in and sit down, for heaven's sake. I can't talk to you while you're slouching in the doorway like James Dean or someone."

He didn't know who James Dean was. He came in and sat on the edge of the wing chair. "About what?"

"About your behavior," she said. "Your rotten attitude lately. I'm sorry, I don't mean to be harsh, but I don't know what else to call it, Hugo."

He could tell she was trying hard not to get mad at him, she was trying to be sympathetic and understanding. He didn't care. He felt his rotten attitude bubble up inside him like Coke shaken up in a bottle. One more shake and it would spill over. If he had an aura, it would be a dark, purplish black. "I don't know what you mean," he said.

"Hugo, you never smile! you never talk to me! It's not only that you spend all your waking hours with Nina, but that's part of it too. And you never bring her over here. And you haven't been to see the Garners lately. They've been asking about you. And—" She paused, and sighed. "Well, everything. You know what I mean. There's obviously something the matter, Hugo. Aren't you happy here? I thought we were getting along pretty well until lately."

He waited patiently through her speech, looking first at her, then down at his hands, then at a vase full of some kind of huge red flower. Probably a present from the weird paramour, flowers so big and bright and spiky they made his eyes hurt to look at them. When she was through talking, he said, "I think we get along fine. There's nothing wrong. Really."

There was a silence. He inspected the flowers again, then a pile of old newspapers on the floor. The headlines he could read said JOB SEEKERS GET SUPPORT OF SENATOR and WARM WEEKEND AHEAD FOR AREA. Teen mother, he thought. Slain in drug dispute. Baby sleeps.

"Will you bring Nina over for a cookout one of these nights?"

"Sure," he said. "Sounds good."

"When? Tomorrow?"

"I don't know. I'll have to ask Nina. She said something about going somewhere with her family, I think."

"So you'll be home for supper."

"I guess so. Sure."

He thought if he had to sit across from her and eat dinner he would choke, or faint, or explode. He knew why he couldn't ask her, What happened to my mother? Is it true what I saw

in that newspaper? Was that my mother? Not only because
he had snooped and would have to admit it but because he
knew the answers. And because he would have to blame them
all—all his missing people: Rose and his father and his grandparents. It wasn't just Dorrie who lied, it was the whole bunch
of them, almost everyone he had ever known. His teachers,
even. They'd probably known. The Garners. When he thought
about it all, it was like a wall crumbling. Had he seen it in
some movie once? A vast wall made of stone that buckled at
one end and then, bit by bit, slowly, methodically, collapsed
into a heap of rubble. Teen mother. What did it mean? He
had asked Nina. "My God, Hugo, it means your mother was
a junkie." What else? he had asked. "It looks like she was
murdered. She was murdered by some dope dealer. Oh, Jesus
fucking Christ, Hugo." He had never heard Nina swear so
much before.

"Shall we cook hamburgers? Or what? What would you
like?"

He looked away from the flowers and at his aunt. He would
bubble over and explode any minute. "What would I like?"

"For dinner tomorrow night." She was being so patient
and nice, even though he was acting like James Dean and
had a rotten attitude. Nice hamburgers. That would be nice.
Mommy died in a nice car crash, Hugo. So sad, poor Mom.

"Oh," he said. "Anything. That would be great."

"Hugo?" He had to look at her again. "If something's
bothering you, you can tell me. Really you can. I'm on your
side, you know." He didn't speak. She said, "Let me tell you
something, Hugo. When you first came, I wasn't all that pleased
about it. I felt I was being intruded on. I'd been alone for
so many years, it was strange to have someone here. I know
I wasn't always pleasant about it. I'm quite sure I was short
with you plenty of times. And stiff, as you said. But I want
to tell you something, Hugo. I like having you live here. And
I'm sorry if I spent a couple of months being a bitch."

"Oh, that's all right," he said, and forced a smile. He doubted that it fooled her, but he didn't care. "I think I'll go out to bed now, if that's okay."

"Just one more thing."

"Sure." He sat back down on the edge of the chair. Didn't she know he was going to explode? One more thing. Oh, yes, your mother was murdered, she was shot three times in the head, she was a junkie. "What is it?"

"I hope you and Alex will get to be friends, Hugo. He really likes you a lot, and we both hoped you'd be here this afternoon, so he could sort of get to know you a little. I— he and I are very fond of each other, Hugo, and I think it's important that you get to be friends. You know?"

"Sure," he said, and stood up. "I think that would be great."

She sighed, and frowned at him. "Well," she said. "All right, Hugo, go to bed. You do look tired. I just—you'd tell me if anything was seriously wrong, wouldn't you?"

"Sure."

"Remember what you said that first day?" She was smiling at him, being pals. "That I was your surrogate mother? Well, I am, you know. Legally. You can think of me that way if you want to."

"Sure," he said, "right," and escaped down the stairs and out to the dock, where he sat looking into the water and letting the mosquitoes bite him until finally she turned off the flood-light and he didn't have any tears left and he didn't feel like exploding anymore.

🌿 6 🌿

It was an autumn full of sunny days. The bright leaves reflected in the pond made a selvage of color around the blue, and when they fell the water became thick with them, red and orange and then a dull faded brown that washed up to the shore. Every day, from her window, Dorrie could see more of the Garners' house and barn, more of the wooded hills at the horizon.

She was making new things. She had devised an elongated, nearly angular shape for a pitcher, and she made a dozen or more of them, working obsessively until the proportions pleased her. She was firing the kiln almost weekly, beginning to feel secure again with the rows of ghostly pots, unglazed and ready, lined up on the shelves of her studio. She devised a gray-green glaze with a spill of dark blue for the pitchers; the movie star came in again, bought one of the pitchers, and ordered a tea set to match. She was sorry Hugo missed him. He drove up this time in a silver sports car that could have been a Maserati, and with him was a young woman who looked about Hugo's age; her hair was crew cut and pale blue, and she wore a row of jeweled earrings in one ear and a long black feather dangling from the other.

While Hugo was in school, Daisy the kitten made herself
at home in Dorrie's studio, pouncing with her tiny paws on
the bits of crumpled paper Dorrie threw for her, curling up
to sleep in a patch of sun on the table, meowing now and
then to be let out the back door. Outside, she never went
far. Dorrie would see her black shape stalking down the lawn,
head down and tail low like a cat in the jungle, and then a
few minutes later she would be asleep on the deck rail or
meowing at the door again to come in. "I'm so glad you brought
her home," she said to Hugo. "She's awfully good company.
I should have gotten a cat years ago."

"Great," Hugo said with a wan smile. "That's great."

Hugo wasn't communicating any better—worse, maybe.
Dorrie was trying to be home more, to be there especially
when he arrived from school, and it was putting the strain
she had expected on her relationship with Alex.

"I'm the one who needs you," he complained. "He's a
kid, with his whole life ahead of him. I'm an old geezer, this
is my last chance."

He was only half kidding, but she laughed at him anyway.
"Teaching will keep you busy. All those adoring students."
He had been offered a one-night-a-week fiction-writing course
at BU, an emergency opening created when a writer in residence committed suicide.

"The thought of teaching that poor bastard's course makes
me sick," Alex said. "One writer profiting from the troubles
of another. I feel like a strikebreaker. I feel like dirt."

"Don't make it complicated, Alex," she begged him. She
was beginning to see that always, at the borders of his perennial
good humor, was a small besieging army of depression. "His
suicide may have had nothing to do with his being a writer."

"He hadn't published anything but book reviews in eight
years. He was fifty-six years old, a former Guggenheim, trying
to put two kids through college on his teaching pay. Do you
know how little they pay someone without a Ph.D.? A Ph.D.,
for Christ's sake, to teach a bunch of teen-agers that writing
is a lot harder than they think it is and that there are other

kinds of books in the world than science fiction."

He complained, but he was also honored—pleased that his book still had a reputation good enough to get him hired. He had taught before but not in years, and he took the course seriously.

"You won't miss me at all," Dorrie told him. "We'll spend every weekend together but during the week you write your novel and read student papers and I'll tend to Hugo and make pots and try to keep the wolf from the door."

All summer, she had been hopelessly behind in her work. She went through the Guilford show in a dream, understocked, and she was late with a commission, something that had never happened before. "That's how dull and regular my life was before I met you," she told Alex. "I used to deliver everything early." Now she needed time alone, and she remained firm: weekends only. But her firmness scared her; it made her wake up sweating in the night. Was it true, then, what Teddy had said, that deep in her soul, for whatever reason, she cared for nothing but working? That she was willing to risk Alex for the sake of a few casseroles and soup bowls? For she believed that it was a risk to hand him over to his students. She joked about them but she had no trouble picturing them, all female, all twenty-one and beautiful and brilliant, lined up outside his office door ready to be seduced over their short-story outlines.

"I'd be scared to death of creatures like that," he said when she told him this fantasy. "Not only because they'd make me feel like somebody's grandpa but because they write. God, deliver me from writers. Give me a sexy sensible woman who makes pots."

She tried to believe him, and tried not to be haunted by the fear that he would one day, in Teddy's scolding voice, call her a mug machine, a maker of empty vessels.

In only three months, in the passage of time from high summer to Indian summer, she had come to rely on her relationship with Alex, to accept it as something permanent and necessary in her life. The details of that permanence and necessity she didn't examine closely. When Rachel asked her about the possibility of marriage, she said, "We're both probably too old and set in our ways to get married," realizing after she spoke that "probably" was her safety word, her tentative reach toward marriage to Alex. Immediately she put the thought from her. If she allowed herself to consider it, even lightly, even as a daring nibble at the edges of her mind, she had to whirl away from it as if from a glimpse of some alien paradise too bright and startling in its perfection for her to confront. She found herself looking at babies in supermarkets and on the street, and made herself concentrate not on their lovableness but on their snotty noses and stinking diapers and piercing whines. When she looked into Alex's face and tried to imagine a baby, she saw a wizened little thing with deep wrinkles and a long, unruly moustache. Out of a long habit of self-denial and low expectations, she told herself to forget it.

Rachel still didn't approve. She and Dorrie met for lunch at a restaurant halfway between Boston and East Latimer so that Rachel could repeat her various warnings. "Of course, he's a very charming man," she said to Dorrie, her tone of voice implying some qualification of his charm that she was too polite to specify.

"We really get along very well, Rachel," Dorrie said, smiling to herself at the understatement. Their ecstatic times in bed, their long conversations and companionable silences, their jokes and shared tastes, their delight in the mere act of looking at each other across a table: all this was summed up, correctly but inadequately, in "getting along very well."

"He's had an awfully messy marriage and divorce," Rachel went on. Whenever Rachel made one of her negative remarks about Alex and his past, Dorrie was tempted to ask her for details: what exactly had the mess consisted of? But she didn't want Rachel to know that Alex didn't discuss it with her. His failure to do so hurt her. She thought, When he tells me what went wrong with his marriage—but it was a thought she never finished.

"I think he's recovered nicely," she said to Rachel. She dug happily into her quiche in a manner that she recognized as smug.

"It's just hard to imagine Alex Willick settling down again."

"I told you—nobody's talking about settling down." Dorrie heard her voice—snappish, dismissive, scared—and changed the subject to Rachel's wedding.

Rachel and Leon were getting married at the end of October. Rachel had revealed no more doubts, and Dorrie didn't like to ask, but over coffee, in case Rachel's pessimism about Alex was a signal that she had troubles of her own she wished to spill, she asked, "I assume you've worked everything out?"

Rachel's reply was ambiguous: "It's worked itself out," but she smiled as she said it and, in fact, she had been smiling often, and seemed perfectly content, so that Dorrie had to conclude that either Rachel was, after all, marrying for love, or she didn't want Dorrie to suspect otherwise. Either way, Dorrie kept the conversation at the practical level of wedding, honeymoon, and housekeeping arrangements. The wedding would be simple, the reception lavish; they were traveling to the south of France afterward; Rachel was giving up her apartment and moving into Leon's condominium. "I can't believe I'm finally getting out of that Strangler apartment," she said. "Now I'll really be erasing William from my life, at last. God, second marriages are wonderful. Everyone should have a second marriage. Too bad you have to go through a first marriage to get there."

"All this blithe talk of marriages," Dorrie said. She felt, suddenly, full of resentment. Here was Rachel, on her way to a second husband, cautioning Dorrie away from her first. "What about me, Rachel? Why shouldn't I have a chance at it—to make my own mistakes, if nothing else?"

Rachel looked at her woefully and said, "Oh, Dorrie, you

do want to marry him, I was afraid you did. I've said all
the wrong things. God knows, I'm not to be listened to. Look
at the swamps I've gotten myself into over the years." She
put down her coffee cup and touched Dorrie's sleeve. "Go
for it, Dor. If that's what you want. Good Christ, you deserve
whatever happiness you can snitch."

Dorrie burst out laughing. "You sound like you're recom-
mending that I start robbing banks. And I meant it when I
said I don't think Alex and I will ever go so far as to get
married. Believe it or not, I'm managing to snitch quite a
bit of happiness just having an affair with him." She leaned
forward and lowered her voice. "I mean, if nothing else, we
do have a terrific time in bed, Rachel."

Rachel looked shocked, then—what? envious? before she
laughed and said, "Really, Dorrie!"

Rachel's book came out not long before the wedding. The
reviews were ecstatic. Alex sat in Dorrie's kitchen one Sunday
morning, with the kitten on his lap, gloomily reading aloud
the *Times* review. "Listen to this," he said. " 'Rachel Nye
may have a surer ear for the rhythms of American speech
than any other writer since Hemingway. In her own very different way, in her own milieu, that of the sophisticated young
urban eccentric, she is every bit as pungent as Hemingway,
every bit as true, every bit as valuable a contributor to the
excellence of the American short-story tradition.' Holy Jesus
Christ and all his saints." Alex put the paper down. "I'm
very glad that your friend Rachel is having some success,"
he said. "She works hard; she's an intelligent, sensitive person.
But to compare her trivial, cold, precious little stories with
Hemingway's is like comparing rabbit turds with the Taj Ma-
hal. And I don't even like Hemingway."

"I know how you feel," Dorrie said. "It's hard enough
for me. I never know what to say to her about her stories.
I'm usually reduced to telling her I love the way she describes
what her characters eat, or asking her where she ever got
the idea for somebody's weird name. Or sometimes I can tell

her I recognize a bit of someone I know, somebody from our adolescent past—or William, of course. She's always putting William in. It's difficult. But for you it must be torture." She reached across the table to touch him. "I mean, you're a real writer, Alex."

He took her hand and stroked it thoughtfully, nodding. One of the things about him that made her happy was the renewal of his belief in his talent. "I suppose I am," he said. "I just wish I knew whether what I feel is a real writer's regret for the bad influence she's having on literature or plain old sour grapes."

"No, you don't. That's the last thing you wish."

He grinned at her. "You're right. Let's wait and see what I say when my new book comes out and they compare me to Henry James."

"You'll say, 'Aw shucks, I owe it all to my muse.' "

"Damn right," he said, and pressed his lips to the palm of her hand. "So how about my staying over tonight?"

She wished he wouldn't ask. She knew that without her he suffered from insomnia and his old plague of nightmares, but when he stayed with her on Sunday nights Monday was usually lost, and his version of coming for the weekend was to show up for lunch on Friday. A three-day week, she kept trying to explain to him, was not enough for a full-time potter who needed to support herself, not to mention a ravenous, rapidly growing teen-age nephew. If she gave in, she felt guilty and desperate about the bills coming in; if she didn't give in, she worried about Alex. "It would make life so much easier if we just stuck to our agreement—if you didn't keep putting temptation in my path."

"I'll leave first thing in the morning. Before dawn," he promised extravagantly. "I'll slip away like a shadow while you're still lying there dreaming about making soup bowls."

"It's just too complicated, with Hugo getting up for school and everything."

"Everything—what's everything? So he gets up, pees out

the garage window even though you've told him a hundred times not to, puts on the same filthy shirt and jeans he wore all last week, wolfs down a bowl of Cocoa Puffs, and trots up the road to get the bus. Where's the problem? Or do you have your auntie-nephew chats at seven A.M. on Monday mornings?"

"We're still not having auntie-nephew chats at all. Alex, I don't know what to do. Things aren't improving. And I keep remembering how Phinny never talked to anyone, just slammed out of the house and disappeared for hours and hours, getting into trouble." She thought again of the Cézanne painting, her murder plot, all the petty hates she had revealed to Alex. Would she, perhaps, at age eleven, have murdered Phinny for real if she had known he was destined to reproduce himself and put her through it all again? "I'm trying hard to love him and to be understanding. My God, Alex, I don't want him to turn out like Phinny."

"Tell him to try out for the soccer team. It would do him good to get outside and run around and quit brooding about whatever he broods about and, incidentally, lose some of the baby fat."

She stayed silent and angry for a minute. Why was she sitting here, lingering over coffee with a man who didn't understand a thing about her? She had a kiln to unload, pots to glaze, the movie star's tea set to pack up in a box. She had a nephew to worry about—where was he now, for instance? Out in the garage loft or rowing up and down the cold October pond. She looked out the window: no Hugo, just the autumn morning mist on the water. She imagined him alone in the dim loft, doing nothing, lying on his mattress. "Don't make fun of him, Alex," she said.

"I'm not, damn it." He slapped his palm down on the table, on top of Rachel's review. The kitten jumped down and began to wash herself. "Every time I make a constructive criticism of that kid you accuse me of being hard on him or making jokes. I mean it, Dorrie. He needs to get out and do something, for God's sake. It's not natural for boys that age to sit around all the time."

Don't mention your wretched sons, she thought. Don't tell me again about those hard-faced all-American boys. "He rows," she said.

"He rows. Oh, great. Send him to Oxford."

She stood up and began to clear the table. Daisy trotted ahead of her, hoping for scraps, and Dorrie crumbled up a piece of cold bacon for her. "I've got work to do," she said to Alex.

"Dorrie." He came over to where she stood by the sink and, with any encouragement, would have taken her in his arms. She stood scraping toast crusts into the wastebasket. "Don't think I don't sympathize," he said. "I'm sorry I get so impatient with the kid. It's because he gets in the way of us, our being together."

Of course she turned to him, leaned her head on his shoulder, hugged him hard, though she didn't feel comforted so much as appeased and stalled. "It's all too much for me."

"It'll work out," said Alex. His dismissive optimism only made her grouchier, but when Hugo came in soon after, silently got himself a glass of orange juice, and took it, the kitten, and his algebra book back out to the garage, Dorrie felt so lonely, so defeated by his hostility that she told Alex he could stay the night, after all.

Dorrie hadn't understood, until school had been in session several weeks, that Hugo was no longer seeing Nina. She suspected school wasn't going well, though Hugo was getting A's in everything. Dutifully, without comment, he showed her the tests and reports he got back, his biology lab book, his French *dictées:* A, A+, "Excellent work," "*Magnifique.*" But it was obvious that his grades weren't making him happy. He was spending his evenings at home but when he finished his homework what he did was sit with Daisy on his lap, out on the deck, or, when it got too cold, up in his loft. Finally, by the chilly nights of early October, he occupied Dorrie's living room, doing nothing. Answering when he was spoken to. Petting the cat, who purred furiously and dug her little white claws into his leg. Dorrie assumed at first, optimistically, that these evenings with her and Daisy, instead of with Nina over at the Verranos', were meant to reestablish their old friendly relationship, but it eventually became obvious that this was not the case. He wouldn't talk, couldn't even be lured into a Scrabble game. She had the impression—from what source she couldn't have said—that he was waiting for something from her. She tried asking him questions—about everything, anything, hoping to hit on the problem, hoping to say the right thing.

"What happened to *Upton's Grove?*" she asked him one day.

He shrugged. "By the time I get home from school it's too late to go over to the Garners'."

She sat down beside him on the sofa where he was sprawled with Daisy. The kitten's green eyes opened; she looked up at Dorrie with interest, closed her eyes again. Her purr intensified. Hugo kept his gaze on the cat, on his own hand stroking her black fur.

"Hugo? I have an idea. I thought I might get a television, and call the cable people. What do you think? For your birthday." Any mindless TV show, she thought, would be better than this glassy-eyed idleness, but she tried to keep that idea out of her voice. "I have a feeling we're both missing some pretty good stuff on television. I'm always reading about things in the paper and wishing I'd seen them. And I hate to admit this, but it seems a shame for such a loyal *Upton's Grove* fan to have to miss it after all this time."

He gave a weak half-smile, being polite. "Oh, thanks, but— well, I mean, not for me. If you want one for yourself don't let me stop you, but—you know—"

"No, I don't, actually, Hugo." She clasped her hands and looked earnestly into his face, forcing him to meet her gaze.

He did, but only for a moment. She saw that his eyes were wary, adult, infinitely sad; then he lowered them back to the cat. "I *don't* know," she persisted. "Why won't you tell me? Whatever it is that's the matter. This may be hard to believe, but I might actually be able to help." He was silent. "You don't see Nina anymore, do you?"

Another silence, then he said, heavily sarcastic, "We go to the same school, you know. We ride the same bus."

"Yes, but—after school, you don't seem to—"

He changed his tone, polite again. "It's different when school starts. They really load on the homework."

"Have you met any other kids you like? If you ever want to bring anyone home, you know, it's okay."

"Oh. Sure."

What did that mean? Sure, he'd met other kids, or sure, he knew it was okay to bring them home? She wasn't handling this right. She thought back to herself at that age, her gawky, dissatisfied adolescence. She too had been uncommunicative, different, in a state of perpetual resentment, bad at making friends. But it was an unfair comparison: she had had parents, a stable home, books to escape into. The complication of Phinny, but there had been Rachel to make up for it. And hadn't life been easier in the fifties? So it seemed now, though she knew the gloom she recalled from those days was a true memory. Damn it, at least Hugo knew what it was to be doted on. And wasn't she knocking herself out for him? Surely, whatever his miseries, she deserved better from him than this sullen cat petting.

"Another thing, Hugo," she said. She would get it all over with now, once and for all. She was hating the conversation as much as he was. "It's going to be too cold before long for you to sleep out in the garage." He did look up at her then, stricken. She laughed. "Well, it happens every year, doesn't it? Winter. Right on schedule." Her laughter was a fake; she was angry with him, her sympathy on hold for the moment. Was it that bad, moving back into her house? "Snow and frost and sleet and white bloody Christmas." Christmas, she thought, and her heart sank—trying to imagine Hugo trimming a tree, opening presents. She put it out of her mind. Surely, by Christmas, this would have been resolved. "It was below zero around here for most of last January," she said.

Hugo wore his death-sentence face—the appalled, desperate look that she recalled from the day, years ago, when she and her parents had gone to take him away from Rose. "How about a sleeping bag?" he said in a voice severely under control. "I could manage with a sleeping bag, one of those down-filled things. I think I have enough money left to get myself one."

"Hugo." She put her hand on his arm, and removed it quickly, so that it was almost like a slap, though she hadn't meant it that way. Or had she? She felt her anger turning to hysteria. This wasn't going to work. Why even try? Call the Department of Youth Services, find him a foster home. "No," she said, and took a deep breath. This was an absurd conversation. What kind of kid wanted to sleep in an unheated garage during a New England winter? "You're not sleeping in the garage anymore. It's back to the alcove, like it or not. There's an old door somewhere that goes on the opening. I'll put it up so you'll have some privacy."

She thought with despair of her weekends with Alex. Would they have to go to a motel to make love? Or stay at his place in Boston, leaving Hugo to God knows what? Or sneak out to a down-filled sleeping bag in the garage? It was like one of the wacky situations in a Rachel Nye story, only Rachel would probably have the three of them end up in one bed eating take-out Chinese.

"I know it's hardly an ideal solution, Hugo, but for six months of the year it certainly won't kill you."

He hesitated. He was obviously reluctant to talk to her, and yet this was a subject on which things needed to be said. He couldn't just say sure and shrug his shoulders. "It's awfully small," he said finally. "It makes me feel sort of closed in, sort of—"

" 'Claustrophobic' is the word."

"Yeah. But I mean—what else is there? Right?"

She sighed. "This is a tiny house, Hugo, with the shop and studio taking up so much of it. It really only holds one person with any comfort. Or—" A couple, she didn't say. Alex and me. "I was thinking maybe next summer we could build an addition. On the side, off my studio. A nice big space, all yours."

"Yeah, that'd be great." He spoke without enthusiasm, and again she felt her anger rise. What more did he want? What else could she do? And did he have any idea what it cost to add on a room? Daisy put her head back and yawned, and Hugo smiled down at the kitten and stroked her under the chin. Then his smile faded, and he heaved a sigh. "So I guess it's the alcove or nothing."

"I'm afraid so, for the moment." She stood up. His bent head, his false humility and resignation irritated her. Alex was right: he was a spoiled brat. "Damn it, Hugo, it could be worse. You could be out on the street, you could be in an orphanage," she said, and she went out into the kitchen to start dinner, cursing herself. How could she say such a thing? How did matters get to this point?

It occurred to her as she fried potatoes and snipped the ends off the beans that this was a crisis in her life and she didn't know how to deal with it. There would come a time, years from now, when she would look back on her taking over of Hugo and see how what she did was either just fine or all wrong, depending on what happened in the next few months. She needed advice. She wished for that tearful moment that she could ask her father. Or that Alex would be more help. It frightened her that, beyond getting a meal on the table, she had no idea what she should be doing.

When dinner was ready, she called Hugo. He was still sitting on the sofa with the cat. His eyes were pink around the edges. Full of remorse, she let him have seconds on everything.

Two days later, in the midst of the bills and the junk mail and the new *Ceramics Monthly,* there was a letter in her mailbox from Mrs. Wylie. How odd, she thought, walking up to the house with it, sitting out on the porch with it in her lap. She sat there a while contemplating it, until it occurred to her that she was afraid to open it. She acknowledged to herself that she had, at some secret level, wished this: an appeal from the Wylies for the return of Hugo. And now what? There was Hugo's laundry on the line; there was Daisy the kitten stalking something in the grass; there were the sunflower stalks, their flower heads picked clean by the birds, outside Hugo's loft window. She looked at her watch: in two hours she would hear the school bus roar into the turnaround up the road, soon after that Hugo's shuffling steps on the porch, then his retreat to the alcove to do his homework. She would make him take down his laundry and put it away. She would ask him about his social studies test. She would wait in vain for something more, something unasked, and it wouldn't come, and eventually they would eat their supper, with a news program on the radio to keep the silence from embarrassing them both.

And here was this letter she feared to open. The envelope was pink and lineny, the handwriting the tortured backslant she recalled from last spring when Hugo's school records had arrived in a manila envelope, like a school application. She hadn't felt very kindly toward the Wylies when they had dropped Hugo off in such a hurry, en route to the Cape—or was that only because of her own panic, her desire that they keep Hugo just a little longer, just for the summer? It seemed years ago, that innocent panic. She thought back to Barbara Wylie, a smarmily oversincere woman who spoke psychotherapists' jargon, and her husband Maxwell, who spoke hardly at all. And little David, of course—skinny, bespectacled, suffering, tongue-tied, a parody of the oversensitive nerd. He wrote poetry, Hugo had told her. The Wylies had three televisions, and an electric garage-door opener, and a computer. Mrs. Wylie had the birdhouse Hugo made in shop. He's never given me anything, she thought. She looked down at the letter she owed it to Hugo to open. It's probably something else entirely, she thought, and ripped into the pink linen paper.

Why I'm writing you a letter about this I don't know. I suppose I'm afraid to call you about it, it's such a terrible thing to ask. What will you think of us? To put it as simply as possible, we would love to have Hugo come back to us, at least temporarily. David has been such a problem since Hugo left. Except for Hugo, he has never made friends easily, and now he really has no one, and is alone too much. Maxwell and I are dreadfully worried about him. He's not bright like Hugo, he seems to have no interests besides writing his very strange poetry that no one can make head or tail of, his schoolwork is suffering, Hugo would make such a difference. Of course, it's bound to be awkward at this time of year, school having just begun, but on the other hand it might be best to do this now before Hugo gets too settled in his new environment. God knows what you must think of me for asking, but we're pretty much at our wits' end with this and I only hope you—

Dorrie let the letter fall. It wasn't right for prayers to be answered so promptly and efficiently. There was too much good luck in her life lately: her affair with Alex was enough to make her suspicious of fate, and now this. Why was she to be spared pain with such ease? She read the letter again, looking for the catch. Barbara Wylie didn't sound smarmy, she sounded unhappy and desperate and well meaning. Presumptuous, maybe. As if Hugo were an aspirin or something the Wylies wanted to borrow. No mention of what it would cost Dorrie to give up Hugo. Well, what would it cost her? Hugo's laundry flapped in the breeze. After school, when she asked him to bring it in, his obedience would be immediate, not because he was so obliging but because it saved conversation with his aunt. He had, for some reason, begun to hate her. All it would cost her, if he left, was the chance to retrieve him.

Daisy followed her into the house, and Dorrie watched while she ate some Kitten Chow, crunching intently at the dish that was kept in a corner of the studio. Dorrie sat in her rocking chair with a cup of tea. The kitten ate, washed, and jumped to Dorrie's lap, where she purred a while, then slept. Dorrie had asked Hugo once why he named her Daisy, and he had said, "I should have thought it would be obvious." She had given up trying to figure that out.

Dorrie sat a long time, not thinking, dozing a little. The fall sunshine was warm through the window; the room smelled pleasantly of clay and the bunch of chrysanthemums on her worktable. All around her were the hard-baked bowls and mugs and dishes waiting to be glazed, the new pitchers with their gracefully bulging bellies and their beveled handles. The studio, now, was full of Alex. His old jeans hung from a doorknob along with the binoculars he'd used to watch the Canada geese on the pond. The wicker chair he always sat in was pulled up to a window, some books piled on the floor next to it. An old *New York Review* was spread out under the bowl of cat food. Slowly, in his gentle, inexorable way, he was infiltrating her life. If she was free of Hugo, she and Alex could get married. She could have her own child. Was it as simple as that? Yes, she thought it was—that easy. She sat there with the cat on her lap, gripping the pink letter, until she heard Hugo's school bus up the road, and then she ripped the letter quickly in two, and then in four, and stuffed the pieces deep into the pocket of her smock.

Hugo was sitting in algebra class when the idea came to him. It was a Tuesday, the worst day of the week. On Tuesdays he had gym (that was bad enough; he hated gym) but the way the class periods were arranged around those humiliating, endless forty minutes meant that he arrived at the science lab just as Nina was leaving it. Invariably, no matter how he dawdled in the hall, he passed her in the doorway. Invariably, she smiled at him and said, "Hi, Hugo"—the old intimate smile, the old Nina-voice, but different now, moved to a level of artifice, as if their summer friendship had been a rehearsal for a play that would be put on in the fall. A very bad play, badly acted. Hugo hated it, and didn't understand it. He wanted her back. He thought he had never needed anything so much; nothing, in his whole needy lifetime, compared to the way he needed Nina to be his friend.

After bio lab was algebra, his favorite class. At least it kept him alert, even though it was at the end of the day. He was always tired, got up late, went to bed early, yawned all day, and in his other classes he was in constant danger of falling asleep. But in algebra, as soon as Mrs. Feinberg started writing the quadratic equation on the blackboard, he woke up, and his pencil got going. This was what he liked: finding out what a was, performing his lightning calculations and watching them work out—groping through a dark forest toward the light. He couldn't think of anyone but Nina to whom he could say that the rest of school was boring and simpleminded and too easy to bother with.

The day he got his idea was an October Tuesday. There was a substitute in algebra class, a cool little man named Mr. McGee, who didn't actually teach but assigned them a mimeographed page of easy equations to solve while he sat up at the desk marking papers. Hugo got bored, looked up from his work, and watched Mr. McGee biting his cuticles, digging wax out of his ears, playing with his moustache, surreptitiously picking his nose. He raised his head and met Hugo's gaze. "Anyone who doesn't finish those problems by the end of this period will have to tangle with me personally."

Hugo bent his head over his paper and thought about Nina. He had been absorbed for several days in the problem of how to get back at Dorrie and get Nina back: that was the way he put it to himself, liking the way the two objectives echoed each other. Sometimes he thought getting back at Dorrie wasn't quite what he meant: to challenge her, maybe, was more like it. To make her tell him the truth. He wanted desperately to know the truth, every bit of it, all the little crannies of truth that made up his life, his mother's life, his father's. He thought, This way, I don't exist, I'm no one, there is no Hugo.

But having Nina back was part of it too. He had never been so happy, never so complete—so true—as when he was hanging around with Nina. It seemed, when he thought about it, like something he had made up, some going-to-sleep fantasy. Had he really spent the entire summer with her? Had there really been those long, lazy days by the pond, over at the Verranos', out in the boat? Had Nina really sung him her songs and told him her dreams and assured him he was her best friend ever, that the two of them were indeed a breed apart, special people who belonged together? Had he really, all summer, been close enough to kiss her?

He should have, that was the trouble. Or was it? He didn't know, but he had come to the opinion that, if he had been more romantic, more aggressive, more mature about things, maybe he wouldn't have lost her. All that time he had been hovering timorously over her, wondering if he should kiss her, if she would like it or hate it—hell, he should have been all over her, that was probably what she wanted, someone masterful, and he had blown his chance by being a cowardly wimp. That was it, it had to be. He should go out and get drunk sometime and do it—just grab her. He remembered how the wine at the Garners' had made him feel, and was imagining for the hundredth time what it might be like to kiss Nina when it came to him: *Do it.* Get drunk at the Garners' with Nina. Break into their house while they were away. Take Nina with him; she would do it, she'd like that kind of adventure, look at the way she'd gone through Dorrie's stuff. Get a bottle of wine out of that cupboard. They could drink it in the sun room, sprawl out on the floor, watch a little TV, Nina in his arms.

He felt a chilly excitement deep inside his bones. In a daze, he finished the algebra and waited for the class to be over. He kneaded his hands together on the desk, trying to calm down, rehearsing what he would say. In the crowded corridor he walked the familiar route to his locker without knowing what he did. Say it on the bus. No: get off at her stop and say it. Nina, I wondered if you'd like to . . .

He always tried to board the bus first so he could sit right in front, behind the driver. The nerd seat, he was aware. The Jamie-types and their girls sat in back. As the bus emptied, the kids who were left moved toward the back, so that he became more and more isolated up in front with Mr. Wicker, the driver, who never spoke but who whistled old songs, a sad, burbling sound that Hugo rather enjoyed. He didn't know where Nina sat, or whom she sat with. He didn't want to know. From his front seat, with his face turned antisocially toward the window, he could sometimes hear her voice, joining in the general fooling around, but often she seemed on the ride home to be as silent as he.

The bus ride that day was unbearable. Wasn't there some book, *The Agony and the Ecstasy?* That was the ride home. He would force her to speak to him. He would get her back. She would scorn him. She would laugh at him. She would fall into his arms. She would get off the bus at her stop and there would be some boy in a car to pick her up. She would cry and say she was sorry she'd been so mean to him. She would cry and say her mother was terminally ill, her father, her grandmother; and she hadn't been herself. She would say, Oh, Hugo, my darling. She would refuse to speak to him. He leaned his head against the cold window, enduring the bumps as the bus leaped along the roads. It went too fast; it went too slow. Agony, ecstasy, agony.

The bus was half empty when they got to her stop. Several kids got off there—it was the town stop, on Main Street, by the drugstore—and Hugo joined them. Mr. Wicker didn't notice or didn't care that Hugo got off three stops early; his whistle didn't cease. Hugo went down the steps last and walked behind Nina. There was no boy in a car. Nina walked alone down Main toward her street, and Hugo walked faster to catch her up. She had on her old summer overalls, and a dirty tan windbreaker. Her hair billowed out behind her like autumn leaves. "Nina," he said in a voice not his own.

She turned. "Hugo! What on earth?"

His heart turned over. She was smiling, even looking pleased. Her beauty nearly blinded him, her little brown eyes, her pointed lips. Under her windbreaker she wore a blue sweater. There were tiny gold hoops in her ears: something new.

"I want to ask you," he said.

"Well, what?"

She stood facing him, still smiling, her books propped on her hip, but he could see that her friendliness was phony and polite; she would just as soon be gone. But he went on, forcing it out: what else could he do? "I wanted you to go somewhere with me."

"Oh. Well. I don't really know, Hugo."

"I wanted you to break into the Garners' with me and get drunk." It was the only way to do it, blurt it out wildly before she turned and walked away. "Some Saturday night when they're out of town or something."

Her eyes widened, and then her smile spread out and became genuine. He felt blessed, glorified, rewarded. She said, "What?"—spilling the word out slowly in the intimate, confiding way she had, that he remembered so well, as if they had just been lured together into some magical place, some chamber of wonders.

"I just want to get drunk for once in my life," he said. It came easily now, the kind of thing to say and the nonchalant way of saying it. "I'm sick of everything. School, home, the whole bit. I just want to—" He shrugged. "Let's just get drunk and say the hell with it, Nina." He couldn't believe he was uttering these words. In the midst of his triumph he felt intense shame. He almost despised her, just for a moment, for responding so easily. It was like a bad day on *Upton's Grove,* one of those episodes when the scriptwriters seemed to have fallen asleep. She shouldn't be standing there smiling—impressed. She should tell him he was a fool and walk away from him. She should say, I am perfectly aware that all this is just a ploy so you can kiss me, poor Hugo. "They're going away some weekend soon, I know that. I heard Mrs. Garner tell my aunt. I can't remember when, exactly." He wished he had listened better, even joined in that boring conversation: Mrs. Garner at the door collecting money for some disease. He tried to remember. Where were they going? A wedding? No, it was Dorrie who was going to a wedding. "Their place would be simple to break into. I've been all over it. I could get their cellar door open in about five seconds."

She stood looking at him, her eyes bright. "Are you sure you're not drunk right now, Hugo?"

"Do you want to do it?"

"Need you ask? Of course I do."

"I'll find out when."

"Let me know. I'm available."

What did that mean? Did it mean anything? Now was the time to do something masterful. Grab her right here on Main Street? No. Don't screw up. He remembered when she had drawn the eye on the back of his hand with a pen, how when she had leaned over her hair had brushed his arm. He had wanted to pick up a bit of it and press it to his lips, but he hadn't. He remembered how he had held her tight when the kittens were born. He searched for what to say. "Bring your guitar."

It seemed the right thing. She touched his arm, his jacket, with one finger, and said, "I'll play my song for you. The one about your aunt. I wrote it, finally."

"Oh. Yeah. I'd really like to hear it."

"It's called 'Heart of Clay.' Isn't that a great title?"

"Yeah, it sounds really good."

She looked seriously into his face, and there was a moment of silence. "I'm sorry, Hugo," she said at last. "I've been preoccupied since school started."

"That's okay, Nina." Everything was okay. She would come to the Garners'. She was apologizing. God, he hoped it wasn't her mother, her father, dying hooked up to tubes. He imagined comforting her at the funeral. She would turn to him in her grief as her truest friend.

"I've been in love," she said.

"Oh." He clutched his books to his chest.

"But it isn't working out."

"Oh."

"I'll tell you about it," she said, and her smile returned. "Over drinks."

His aunt said to him, "Would you like to go and see the Wylies?"

It startled him. He hesitated, then decided the only safe response was "Why?"

"I had a letter from Mrs. Wylie. They would like to see you, Hugo." He made himself look interested. "I thought you might like to visit them. Maybe over Christmas vacation."

They were at breakfast. Alex, the weird paramour, was asleep in the bedroom. Hugo looked down at his eggs. *Nina Nina Nina* was all he could think. "It's hard to say. I mean—"

"Your friend David seems to miss you a lot. What's he like, really?" Her voice was false and bright. What did she care?

"You met him that time."

"Yes, but he didn't say much. I guess he just stays quiet and observes people, and then writes about them. I suppose there are some writers who work that way." She smiled, thinking no doubt of Alex in the bedroom, who was certainly anything but quiet and David-like. "What kind of poems does he write?"

"Oh—just poems. Not the kind that rhyme or anything."

"His mother says he seems to be having some trouble making new friends."

"He's kind of shy."

"He seemed nice, though."

"He's nice, yeah. Dave's a good kid." He thought: why all this pumping? What did it matter? David and the Wylies seemed far away, long gone. He remembered David sitting on the floor with his notebook on his knees, writing poems. When he finished one he would look up and say, "Da *da!*" and read it to Hugo. "I kind of miss him sometimes. Yeah, I guess I'd like to see him one of these days. Sure." His aunt's face was expressionless behind a bland smile. Was she going to send him back to the Wylies? "I don't know about a whole vacation."

"Well, you don't have to decide now."

There was a pause while he looked at his eggs; like everything else in his life, they said, *Nina Nina Nina.* He and Nina had cooked eggs in this very kitchen, eaten them off these very plates. Heavy blue plates, made by his aunt, with carved borders of lilylike flowers. "These aren't bad, actually, considering," Nina had said, running her fingers over the carving. He looked up at his aunt and said, uncontrollably, "Nina and I are sort of friends again."

She understood that this was not a non sequitur, and said, "Hugo, that's wonderful," overdoing it. "I thought you seemed more cheerful the last week or so. Even this—I mean, getting up at a decent hour and having breakfast with me."

He shrugged. "I woke up hungry." That wasn't all the truth. He had woken up, in the alcove room he hated, hungry for human companionship—specifically, for someone to whom he could say her name.

"Well, I'm glad you're here. Have some more bacon. I don't want to pry and intrude and all that, but I think you've been needing a friend like Nina lately, someone you could talk to."

We have a date to get drunk, he thought.

"I knew you were missing her."

He looked at her cautiously. How had she known that? "She just got busy," he said. "School and everything."

"And now she's not so busy."

"Right." She had been in love, it hadn't worked out, she would tell him about it, cry in his arms. He pushed the eggs around on his plate, imagining, then suddenly wolfed them down in three bites and reached for another piece of toast.

"That's wonderful, Hugo, I'm so glad," his aunt said again. Why was it so wonderful? he thought. She didn't use to like Nina much. He studied her suspiciously. Her intelligent eyes were exactly like his father's, that funny pale blue. He remembered, suddenly, his father, with a clarity of detail that hadn't come to him in years, and with the same incredulity with which he remembered his summer with Nina. His father's eyes, his square white hands, his thick black eyebrows. His father's monstrous belches when he drank beer. His father's crazy laugh. Had he really been with him, sat at tables with him and ridden in cars? His father used to swing him up and carry him on his shoulders. Once he had taken him for a motorcycle ride, Hugo propped in front of him on the narrow part of the seat, held there only by the force of his father's right arm clasped tight around his stomach and his father's strong, lean body behind him. He remembered terror and absolute confidence, both at once. He had been—what? five? six? What had happened to the motorcycle? What had happened to anything? He thought, suddenly, that what he would like to do when he was drunk was to demand the truth from his aunt. Otherwise he'd never have the nerve. The Garners' wine would be a medicine to make him brave and carefree. Drink a little wine and you could do anything. Kiss Nina. Demand the facts. Tell people off. The very thought of it made him daring. "How long is *he* staying?" he asked, gesturing across the kitchen and living room to the bedroom door. Behind it, he heard the bed squeak.

"He has to get back to Boston early," Dorrie said. "He'll

probably leave after breakfast." It annoyed him, the infatuated way she said "he," as if she were talking about a king.

"Maybe we should go over and see the Garners later." She stared at him, and he realized what a bizarre suggestion it was, after these solitary and hostile months. He thought about how he would do better, now that he had Nina, now that he had resolved to get his aunt to tell him things. He made himself smile. "Just to kind of pay a call," he said, spreading jam carefully on his toast. He took a bite. "I feel bad I haven't seen them lately," he said with his mouth full. "They've been so nice to me." He swallowed his toast, feeling like a rat. The truth was that he wanted to go over there and check out the place once more, and also find out when they were going to be away. But as he spoke he knew that he did miss them, that they *had* been nice to him, nicer than nearly anyone. They had even sent him a birthday card—a funny Snoopy one signed "Love, Mary and Ross Garner." How could he even consider sneaking into their house to drink their wine? *For love,* he answered. There was no other way. Dorrie never kept more than a couple of bottles of beer in the refrigerator. Everything else *he* drank up. It would have to be the Garners. But just take maybe one bottle, he said to himself. Forget the sun room and the TV. They could bring the wine back to his abandoned loft, with a blanket. Two bottles? Three? How much wine would it take to get drunk? How much could he remove without the Garners' noticing? Eating his toast, feeling his aunt's eyes on him—his father's eyes—he kept himself by an act of will from blushing red. What would his father think of him? He was a rat: a rat in love.

The bedsprings squeaked some more, and Alex emerged from the bedroom, old and rumpled in jockey shorts and a denim workshirt that, like Alex, had seen better days. Hugo thought he looked disgusting, with his hairy bare legs. He couldn't believe his aunt slept in the same bed with this man; it was an idea he didn't care to dwell on. Alex muttered,

"Good morning," and headed for the bathroom. Dorrie jumped up and began scrambling more eggs. From the bathroom, Hugo heard unabashed farting.

When Alex came in and sat down he said to Hugo, "To what do we owe this honor?"

"I was just going."

"Hell, don't go," Alex said at the same moment that Dorrie rushed in with, "Stay and have some more eggs, Hugo." Hugo shrugged, and sat on the edge of his chair.

Alex drank some orange juice. Hugo watched his Adam's apple go up and down. When he finished, there was juice on his moustache, which he wiped away with his napkin. "Give us a report on the younger generation," he said, starting on his eggs. "How's life in the world of Michael Jackson and cocaine and algebra?"

"Do you want any of these?" Dorrie held out the pan of eggs to Hugo.

"No. And I don't want to be made fun of, either."

"Hugo, no one's making fun of you," Dorrie said. He saw her pull some kind of face at Alex, some unfathomable smirk.

He said, "Well, I've got to go, anyway."

He escaped down the stairs and outside. Behind him, he heard Alex say, "I tried," and then a clatter of dishes. Raisin bread and eggs and bacon. Such extravagances were only for weekends, when *he* was there. Hugo would have liked another helping, but he couldn't stand the way Alex talked to him, as if he were something from another planet and Alex a scientist trying to make contact. The comparison amused him and he slowed down and changed his course. He had been running toward the garage, but instead went down to the water and got the boat out of the shed. The pond was paved with the blue of the sky, but it was harder and colder than the blue of summer, in spite of the sun. He rowed across the water, imagining it turned to ice. Winter wasn't far off. Where would he be then? He shivered, and rowed fast.

The Garners were at breakfast, reading the newspaper.

Mrs. Garner wore a pink bathrobe buttoned up to the neck;
Mr. Garner was all dressed, in neat brown pants and a V-
neck sweater. They welcomed him with happy surprise, made
him sit down and eat a corn muffin with apple butter on it,
asked him about school and his kitten. Without his even having
to worm it out of them, they told him they were going to
Albany to see the grandchildren next weekend. There was a
new one—had Dorrie told him? A little girl named Alison.
They were so nice that he almost felt they wouldn't mind if
he took away a bottle or two for a good cause. He could see
the cupboard where he knew the wine rack was, crammed
with bottles lying like corpses in a vault. He wouldn't take
anything good, nothing French or old; he knew that much.
Mrs. Garner offered him another muffin, and refilled his milk
glass. In English class they discussed the stories in their book,
and Mrs. Dean was always asking things like "Where in the
story did Nick go over the edge? Where is the point of no
return?" That was where Hugo was, poised on the cliff, ready
to go over. He was a rat, he was no better than Shane or
Monty, he wished he wasn't going to do it, but he knew he
was, he was.

7

At the wedding reception, Rachel insisted on throwing her bouquet. She tossed it straight at Dorrie: an autumnal arrangement of chrysanthemums, purple and white, that would have hit her in the face had she not, reflexively (in the act of remarking to Alex on the absurdity of Rachel's enslavement to tradition), caught it. There was laughter and applause. Margo Cornell, there with the divine Charles, clapped harder than anyone. Dorrie blushed and thrust the bouquet at Alex, who hugged her and whispered, "I guess that settles it. We'd better do the proper thing and get married."

Rachel whisked Dorrie away with her—upstairs, for the ancient ritual in which the maid of honor helps the bride change out of her finery and into her traveling clothes. The wedding had taken place at city hall, with Dorrie and Alex, and Leon's brother and his wife, acting as witnesses. It had been done in a minute, an emotionless ceremony they had had to wait in line for. When it was over, there were kisses all around, and handshakes, and smiles, and then they stood there in the brightly lit corridor looking at one another. Outside, it was raining, and they dashed under umbrellas to their cars. Rachel's white shoes got muddy. They arrived at the reception far too early and had to sit at the bar drinking until people began to arrive.

"I knew what a city hall ceremony would be like. That's why I didn't want to be done out of all the rest of it," Rachel explained to Dorrie, apologizing for the bouquet, the white woolen dress and impractical shoes, the hat with its little veil, the lavish reception at a country inn outside Boston, with champagne and a tiered cake. They were sitting in one of the inn bedrooms, finishing a bottle of champagne—Rachel in her slip, Dorrie still bemused by what Alex had said. She had left him holding the bouquet, smiling at her over the blossoms, the purples garish against his shabby, inappropriate tweed jacket. Another answered prayer. After all these years of futile yearning, what did it mean? What crucial conjunction of planets had taken place that the man she loved could say, with the trace of an English accent that she loved so much, "We'd better get married"? Or had it been a joke—an extension of her comment about Rachel's silliness? What was she to say when she emerged with Rachel and faced him again?

"I had to make it real, Dorrie," Rachel said. "And of course I missed out on all this traditional crap with William."

Dorrie remembered Rachel's first wedding with affection: a mid-seventies affair, with fruit and cheese and homemade carrot cake set out on trestle tables in someone's rural backyard. Dorrie had met a nice man there—Philip something? A friend of William's, tall, fair, and (it turned out after a disastrous night) sexually confused.

"That wedding was such fun," Dorrie said. "We danced on the lawn, and there were roses in bloom, and people playing guitars. And you had that gorgeous Mexican wedding dress."

"You were necking with Philip Lerman," Rachel said, and sighed. "Poor Philip."

Dorrie didn't ask for details: AIDS, drugs, death, disaster—she didn't want to hear about it. "And you and William actually wore vine leaves in your hair," she said.

"Were we really that young and silly?" asked Rachel. She smiled, remembering, and in the next moment her face distorted and became a mask of sorrow, the face of an old woman. She lowered her head into her hands and began to cry. "Oh, God," she said. "I want to be back there, I don't want to be here, I don't know why I'm doing this."

Dorrie thought instantly of Leon, downstairs, jubilantly pouring champagne for his friends and relatives—Leon, whose adoration of Rachel was already legendary. "He's so happy, he's like a teen-ager," his brother had said. "Only Leon was never like this as a teen-ager. I honestly think this is the first time that son of a gun has taken the time to fall in love!"

"I don't love Leon," Rachel said. "I just don't want to be alone. I can't be alone anymore, Dorrie. I'm thirty-nine years old." She raised her head, gave a harsh sob, and covered her mouth with one hand—the left one, where Leon's mammoth diamond and the new wedding band gleamed. "I need to be with someone," she said. The words came muffled through her fingers, and the tears ran fast from her eyes. Black makeup streaked down from the corners. "But I shouldn't be doing this. I don't love him, Dorrie, I just don't."

"Rachel, Rachel," Dorrie said. She got up and found tissues in her purse, and gave one to Rachel. Rachel stopped crying and blew her nose, then started again. Dorrie was horrified. She felt Rachel's outburst was somehow her fault: she never should have mentioned the vine leaves. "It's postwedding jitters," she said desperately. "Everyone has them. So they say." Who said? It didn't matter. "It's perfectly natural, it happens all the time."

"They're not just postwedding, they're prewedding and during wedding." Dorrie handed her another tissue; she wiped at her nose violently and took a deep, shaky breath. "He's a dear, sweet man, but it's just not the same. I know what it's like to be in love. It's not like this. Oh, I don't know—maybe I can't do it anymore, the ecstatic bit. Maybe I'm too old."

"Of course you're not," Dorrie said, thinking of herself

and Alex. But Rachel's face, streaked with tears and makeup, did look old—worn out and battered. Her crying spell had done away with the blooming bride.

"Well, maybe I should have hung on longer," Rachel said. "What I'm doing is settling, I know I am. I'm doing it with my eyes wide open because I need to be married to someone and Leon is all there was."

"Oh, Rachel," Dorrie said. She didn't know what else to say. It seemed a tragedy to marry for anything but love— the ecstatic bit. And yet the deed was done, and Leon was a nice man, he loved Rachel, surely they would have a good life. She leaned over and took Rachel's hands away from her face, and looked her in the eye, feeling like someone in a movie: Katharine Hepburn, the sensible one, giving advice to Olivia de Havilland, who was weak and flighty. "Rachel, listen to me." Rachel's face stayed crumpled, the tears flowing again. Dorrie said, "Rachel, you are going to be happy with Leon. Yes, you are. I know you are. You are very lucky to have found him. You think you don't love him, but you do. You do, Rachel." She felt like a hypnotist, she felt ridiculous and stagy, but Rachel's tears stopped, and she slumped in her chair quietly, holding Dorrie's hands.

"It's not going to be like with William," Dorrie went on. "It's different, it's another way of being in love. And don't forget what a bastard William turned out to be. Leon will never make you unhappy, Rachel. You live with him for a year, and then try and tell me you don't love him. You'll be the happiest couple on earth. You'll lick his shoes, you'll love him so much." Rachel snickered, and freed one hand to wipe her eyes. "I mean it," Dorrie said. "It's not like fiction—life isn't. It's much messier and more confusing, and it's not like it is in your stories. Not often, anyway," she added quickly. "I mean—well, you write about these young things having wacky romances, and here's Leon, a nice, solid middle-aged man, and you're in a situation without much plot or conflict, I admit, but—hell, Rachel, isn't that better? Maybe not in fiction, but in life. You had plenty of plot with William. Now you'll have character, with Leon."

She smiled at her metaphor, and Rachel, through fresh tears, giggled. The tears, Dorrie knew, were no longer despairing. Rachel reached awkwardly across the space between their chairs to hug her. "Dorrie, you are wonderful," she said. "What would I do without you? You're right, you're always right, you've always been able to set me straight." She blew her nose one last time—a resolute honk—then stood up and went over to the mirror. "Oh, God, what a hag I look like," she said cheerfully. "Never cry after thirty—doesn't that sound like a book title? Something by Jean Rhys? I guess I'd better go wash my face and start over."

She went into the bathroom and ran water. Dorrie poured herself the rest of the champagne. She wondered if Rachel had engineered the tearful scene as part of the wedding drama—a variation on the tradition of the blushing bride going reluctantly to the altar. Dorrie listened to the merry, purposeful sound of water splashing in the sink. Rachel was as ebullient as one of her own jolly heroines—all her charm risen to the surface like cream. Any minute she would emerge, looking radiant again, and get into her knit dress and tweed jacket and beautiful new boots, and drive with Leon to Logan Airport for a night flight to Paris. What a life. And Dorrie and Alex would go back to East Latimer. . . . The ride there was unimaginable to Dorrie. Rachel's bouquet would lie wilting on the seat between them. What would they talk about? Their own wedding? What if Alex didn't mention it again? Could she actually bring herself to ask him if he had really meant it, or if it had been one of his ironic jokes? And if it had been a joke, was she supposed to laugh? Ha ha, very funny, Alex, you're such a card.

She drained her glass. She had undoubtedly had too much champagne. Something about the scene was beginning to make her feel middle-aged and depressed: the empty champagne bottle, the little pile of crumpled tissues on the floor, Rachel's carefree mangling, from the bathroom, of "Some Enchanted Evening."

"Once you have found him, never let him go," Rachel sang. Right. Good advice. An omen? The second of the day, maybe. Just that morning, before she left the house, she had received in the mail the proofs for the *Ceramic Arts Quarterly* interview. She had liked it, had thought that, for someone who really had very little to say about her work, she had spoken pretty well—except for one exchange. The interviewer, a preppy young man named Hal, had asked her, "This may be none of my business, but why do you live alone? Do you find that necessary for your work?" She had answered, "No. It just happened that way. It has nothing to do with my work. I'm certainly not temperamental. I could work whether I lived with someone or not; it really doesn't matter." She would pencil through the question and answer when she got home, and scrawl, "Delete this," in the margin. Bad luck, to say it didn't matter. Or would it be bad luck, to anticipate?

"Ne—ver—let—him—go-o," Rachel warbled from the bathroom, going up, off key, at the last words.

"Rachel, come on," Dorrie called. She couldn't sit forever in this stuffy hotel room, sifting through good omens and bad while she waited for her fate to be revealed.

Hugo had arranged to meet Nina after dark, down on the dock. He saw her flashlight wobbling along the track by the water, and then the light disappeared, and a moment later her voice in his ear said, "Gotcha!" and she clutched his arm.

"I knew it was you," he said, and clutched her back, but she pulled away to turn her flashlight back on and shine it in his face. Her guitar, in a canvas zip-up case, was slung over her shoulder.

"I'm staying overnight at my sister's," she said. "Isn't that brilliant? Where's your auntie?"

Hugo shielded his eyes. "At a wedding, in Boston. She won't be home until late."

"A wedding. Not her own, I assume."

She turned the light away from him, and he saw her smile. "No—her friend Rachel."

"The writer."

"Right." He was pleased that she remembered this trivial, peripheral detail of his life.

"Well," Nina said. "Let's get going. Christ, it's cold. I sure could use a drink, ha ha. Is it going to rain again?"

"Maybe it won't," he said. He felt apologetic about the weather. It was a chilly night, and a drizzly rain had fallen, off and on, all day. He had on his best sweatshirt and a windbreaker and his new black jeans that made him look thinner. Nina was wearing a thick white sweater and jeans; she had tied a plaid scarf around her hair. She looked tinier than ever lugging the guitar. He considered offering to carry it, but knew she would refuse. "Maybe it's let up for good," he said. "We'll be inside, anyway. All we've got to do is get over there."

"Are we going to take the boat?"

When he first devised the plan, he had meant to. He'd had a longing, all summer, to row the pond in the dark, but he had imagined a starry, moonlit night. This night was so dark he could see nothing; even with the flashlights he imagined the boat getting stuck in the marshy weeds, or going over the falls. He had concluded it was a bad plan. And now that Nina had asked him—humbly too, deferring to him as the expedition leader—he felt obliged to veto the idea. "Too dark," he said. "Too wet. Too damn much trouble. Let's walk around by the road."

They took the chicken way, shining their lights ahead of them—two circles on the wet grass, then the shiny black causeway, then the Garners' grass and the concrete steps up to the house. Nina took his arm the whole way, chattering to him in a half whisper. "I hope you're positive that they're gone for the weekend, Hugo. They would kill us, everyone would kill us if we got caught. My sister would kill me, and then she'd tell my parents, and they'd kill me, and then I'd have to kill myself I'd be in such trouble." The guitar bumped between them; Nina stumbled and tightened her grip on his arm. "I hope you don't think I'm joking. Don't forget what super-conventional people my parents are—not like your wacky auntie who lets you do whatever you want. And don't forget what a loss to the world it's going to be if I have to commit suicide."

He knew she was joking, of course—and yet from her nervous chatter he could tell she was having second thoughts. Panic and dismay choked him. What if she decided to fink out? What if she said, Let's just forget this, Hugo, I'm going back to my sister's to watch TV? He didn't think he could bear it. It wasn't just to be with her. Even if he spent the evening in her company, watching television at the Verranos', it wouldn't be the same as this—this daring act that would bind them together, plus the wine that would give him the courage to kiss her.

He tried to make his voice sound off-hand and reassuring. "The Garners aren't coming back until Monday afternoon," he said. "They're all the way in Albany, New York. They have this new grandchild they haven't even seen before. They're not exactly going to leave the minute they get there, Nina."

It was the first time he had spoken her name. In the dark—they were hurrying over the causeway—it sounded intimate and thrilling. He wondered if it did to her. She said, "Well, if we get caught I'm counting on you to get me out of it. Say you kidnapped me and forced me into it at gunpoint."

"Believe me, I would, Nina. It's all my idea. I'll take full responsibility."

She squeezed his arm, and he tensed it, making a muscle.

It was raining again, lightly, as they approached the Garners' house. "Around back," Hugo said. They were still talking in whispers—absurd, but he couldn't stop himself. What if—it had never occurred to him—what if they had some kind of house-sitter staying there? Somebody to water the plants and look after the place? "Let's check things out first," he

said, and they circled the house, making far too much noise,
he thought. Nina's guitar bumped against the porch post and
she cursed, and when he kicked a metal trash-can cover that
had blown into the path it sounded like a whole orchestra
tuning up. But the house seemed deserted. There were no lights,
no movement, no strange cars. He and Nina stood by the
cellar door, her arm still through his. He could hear his heart
beating, Nina's soft breathing, the rain pattering down through
the leaves: no other sound.

Nina said, "Well?"

"Looks okay to me."

"So let's get in, Hugo, I'm sopping."

"Right," he said.

The cellar door was closed with a padlock. He had spent
two days in that cellar clearing out old lumber and boxes
of junk and the dirt of ages, and he knew that the padlock
no longer had a key, it didn't need one, all you had to do
was press down on it hard with your palm, wiggle it, and
pull up.

"You shine the light," he said, and bent to the lock. He
could see his hands in the circle of light, and the old wooden
cellar door, and the latch across the middle, padlocked. What
if they'd changed it? he thought, and the familiar panic rose
up again. But it was the same, an ancient brass lock that
gave instantly when he pushed and pulled. He crouched there
looking at it. This was it, then. He felt sick—were they really
going to do this? Nina hit him lightly on the back with her
fist and said, "Come on, Hugo. Let's go," and he pulled the
padlock through and lifted the latch and the doors. The cellar
loomed like a dungeon, pitch dark. He felt, for a moment,
dizzy, looking down into it. He thought of rats, burglar alarms,
traps.

"Shine the light in."

It revealed nothing but the Garners' cellar, still tidy from
his cleaning. He turned around to Nina and grinned nervously.
"Okay, then, this is it!"

"Well, it would be if you'd just get in, Hugo. This guitar case may not be one hundred percent waterproof."

"Sorry," he said, and held out a hand. "Follow me. Watch out, these steps are slippery."

They weren't, but she put her hand, trustingly, into his, and negotiated the steps down with exaggerated care, two feet on each step. "We're in," she said. "What's down here?" She pointed her flashlight randomly into a corner, revealing metal shelves full of canned goods. "What's this? Peaches, tomatoes—what else?"

"Nina, forget it. Let's just go up." He had begun to worry about the upstairs door. What if it was locked? What could he do? Break it down? Bang his head against it and weep? Sit down here in the cellar with Nina getting drunk on canned fruit? Go home, he murmured in some silent corner of his mind. Go home, get out of here, forget all about this.

"If you're going, go," Nina said.

They proceeded slowly, using flashlights. Up the stairs to the kitchen, and the door: it opened silently when he turned the knob. He nearly wept with relief, or fear, he didn't know what was what at this point, and when the tears stung at his eyes he realized that he was horribly on edge, horribly frightened, horribly sure deep in his soul that this was the dumbest thing he had ever done.

He steadied himself and shined his light into the kitchen. Nothing. No one. And there was the wine cupboard, right in the beam of light. "Here we go," he said to Nina.

Her guitar bumped against him from behind, and she giggled. "Would monsieur prefer a red? Or perhaps monsieur fancies a white this evening."

His hands were sweaty, and sweat ran down from his armpits. He stopped, looking at the cupboard and thinking about fingerprints. Should he pull his sleeve down over his hand before he opened it? Or would Nina laugh at him?

"Don't you think we could turn on a light now, Hugo? I mean, this house isn't even visible from anywhere but your auntie's."

He wished she'd quit saying "auntie." "No lights," he said. He set his flashlight on the counter, and it illuminated the room—everything unnaturally neat, everything put away. The Garners' kitchen as he had never seen it. It gave him a funny feeling, as if the Garners had died.

"We're going to stay here all night in the dark? Nothing but these flashlights? They're not going to last all that long, Hugo."

He was startled: all night? "I thought we could take a couple of bottles and carry them over to my loft to drink."

"Your loft? In this weather?" She pulled her guitar strap over her head and set it down, and shined her flashlight in his face again. "Spare me, Hugo. I don't get drunk in garages in the cold and rain, thank you. I stay right here and watch television where it's warm and cozy. I'll go along with no lights, but I'm damned if I'll go along with rain down my neck and my feet freezing off."

"But we can't just stay out all night!"

"Look, Hugo, as far as your auntie knows you're tucked up in your little bed already. Right? I mean, she's not exactly going to be getting home early, is she? And doesn't she still bring her weirdo loverboy with her? They'll probably just fall into bed in a fit of passion, and won't know whether you're around or not. Won't care."

Her fierce face scared him. "What about your sister?"

"She's used to my late hours. I've got a key."

He said, "Who do you keep these late hours with? The guy you're in love with?"

She looked at him angrily, then her face changed and she astonished him by stepping two paces toward him and laying her head on his chest. His arms went around her, automatically. "I want to tell you about that, Hugo. I need to talk to someone."

"You can talk to me, Nina," he said. He laid his cheek against the scarf that bound her hair, and they stood like that for a moment. Then she pushed him away—gently, though, giving him hope for later—and said, "Open the cupboard.

Let's see what they've got." It was understood that they would stay at the Garners'.

The cupboard wasn't quite as full of wine as Hugo remembered. There were seven bottles lying in a rack on their bellies, and a squat upright bottle of brandy.

Nina took out a bottle. "Château dum-de-dum," she said. "What's this? Ah. Red table wine, it says. Sounds cheap."

"Are you sure? That's French, isn't it?"

"Hugo, just because wine is French doesn't mean it's expensive."

Her patient, condescending voice. How was he supposed to know these things? How did she? And how did he know it was true? But he didn't want to argue with her; he was tense enough.

"All right, then. Let's take that one. I just don't want to mess around with anything good."

"Monsieur prefers ze cheap red? Très bon. And perhaps some caviar to go weez it? A beet of truffle?" She giggled again, and then said, "Shit!"

"What's the matter?"

"You need a corkscrew for this thing, Hugo."

He had another of his small panics, and then he said, "Well, obviously. Right here." He opened the drawer where he knew things like spatulas and mixing spoons were kept. It had to be there. He thought hard. Had he seen where Mr. Garner got a corkscrew from? Here? No. Next drawer. Cocktail napkins, little toothpicks, an ashtray. Wait. He moved the flashlight. "Here," he said, "I knew it was here somewhere," and pulled out the corkscrew.

"Monsieur is very clevair," Nina said. "I see monsieur has—how you say—cased ze joint."

It took him a minute to figure out how to get the cork out. He managed to work the corkscrew in—a little crooked, but all right—and then tried to pull the cork out with it, until he realized that all he had to do was push down on two little wings that had come up, and the cork came out by itself. "Hey! Neat!" he said. "Look at this, Nina."

But Nina had opened the refrigerator and was rummaging inside. "Peanuts," she said. "Here's a big can—already opened, don't worry. Let's just liberate a handful. I'm starved."

"I don't think we should," he said.

She grinned at him over her shoulder. "Stealing wine is okay, but you draw the line at peanuts?"

"I don't want to just—" He couldn't tell her that the wine had a purpose, that the theft of the wine was a noble act, in a way. The wine will bring us together, he couldn't say. He shrugged, and smiled foolishly. "You're right, of course. Let's eat peanuts."

"And salami," she said. "There's a lot of salami here, Hugo. Pounds of it. They'll never miss a couple of slices." She took a bite and held out the rest of the slice. "Here. Mmm. Delicious." He took it and ate it, pressing his tongue against the side where her teethmarks were. "What about glasses?" she asked.

"Here." He got two wineglasses down from over the sink. He had once unloaded the dishwasher and put them away up there. He thought of all the things he would do for the Garners, to pay them back for a crime they would never know about. He would shovel their snow all winter. He would give them for Christmas the wrought-iron book rack he was making in shop. He would remember to ask questions about the new grandchild.

Nina put the salami and peanuts on a plate. "Don't worry, I'll wash it. And we'll wash the glasses. Don't get all paranoid, Hugo, and spoil everything." She picked up the plate in one hand and her guitar in another. "Now let's get comfortable. Let's watch some TV or something."

He led the way into the sun room, carrying the wine and glasses. "You said you wanted to talk."

"I do. After I have some wine."

"Did you mean it, or were you joking?"

Alex looked at her quickly, then back at the road. They were driving down the Massachusetts Turnpike, back to Dorrie's, in the rain. It was the wrong time. Dorrie immediately wished she could take back the words, and his answer made things no easier: "Did I mean what?" Nothing. Forget it. "Hmm? Speak."

She steeled herself, gritted her teeth. She nearly hated him, for dragging it out of her. "What you said. About our getting married."

"Oh, that." She stole a look at him and saw he was smiling. "Of course I meant it. I don't joke about important things."

"Yes, you do," she said, smiling too. The relief that filled her was like the cessation of an ache. The pure happiness of being chosen, accepted, loved, wanted, she assumed was waiting in the wings: for now, all she felt was the release of the tension that had been building since she had caught the bouquet, and seen Rachel through her last-minute despair, and picked up the fragments of that despair when Rachel cast it aside.

"But you don't really think I was joking about that."

"No, I guess not."

"Well, then. Marry me."

She studied his profile in the rainy light. He drove with concentration, with the ironic seriousness he brought to everything. She liked to imagine him teaching, talking about Poe's poetic theory and Hawthorne's use of the grotesque, making erudite, poker-faced jokes that his students wouldn't know whether to laugh at or not. His response to "Have a nice day" was "God forbid!"

She said what she had had, all this time, prepared to say on this occasion. "I don't think we should talk marriage until you tell me about your first wife."

He turned his head full in her direction and looked at her in surprise. "I haven't told you before?"

"Alex, you know you haven't. I know it's painful, but I have no idea why. I think I ought to hear about it. Something, anyway."

"Like a Le Carré novel," he said. "The defector has to

spill everything before the other side will take him in. What's
it called—debriefing?"

She wished, as she sometimes did, that he didn't always
joke. "I don't mean to be grilling you. If you're going to look
on me as the KGB, forget I asked."

He sighed, and there was a silence. His face against the
rain-streaked window lost its smile and looked grim, but she
recognized the look as the one he wore when he was writing.
He was finding the right words for it—this story he had so
long avoided telling her. She knew that now, having committed
himself to her, he would tell her what she wanted to know:
in a sense, she had him in her power. The car slowed and
pulled into a rest stop. "Let's get a cup of coffee," he said.
"And food. If I'm going to talk, comrade, I've got to eat."

They ran hand in hand through the rain to the nearly
deserted Howard Johnson's. They sat in a booth and drank
coffee. Alex ordered a hamburger, Dorrie a grilled cheese sandwich, and when the waitress had gone away he said, "All
right. My first wife. Beth. You really want to hear this?"

"Only if you really want to tell me."

"All right," he said. "Yes. What the hell." She thought
he looked tired. She thought she should probably spare him,
say, "Some other time," but she didn't. She waited silently,
and he said, "I've never spoken about it because it's very sordid.
I don't like to think about it." He sighed. "All right, the first
thing you need to know about Beth is that she was a bitch."

At first that was all he said, with variations: a total bitch,
a bitch with no redeeming qualities, a bitch who had put him
through hell, who had spent years doing her best to blight
his life, who had damn near succeeded. A world-class bitch.

The waitress brought their food, and Alex paused and tore
into his hamburger as if saying even that much had worn
him out. He ate steadily while Dorrie nibbled at her cheese
sandwich, watching him. "Bitch": that meaningless word men
use to describe women who have done them wrongs. She
waited. Alex would do better than that.

He wolfed down half his hamburger and put it back on the plate. "The second thing you need to know is that she was the most beautiful woman I've ever seen," he said. "The kind of woman people turn around and stare at. Gawk at. She should have been a movie star, or a model, someone whose face goes up on billboards to stun people with the possibilities of the species."

"What was she? I mean, what did she do?"

"Beth?" He snorted. "Nothing. She stayed home and worshiped herself. Actually—let me be fair—she was a secretary when I met her. In one of the offices at that little college in New Hampshire where I taught for a semester. A lousy secretary too, her boss told me—jokingly, when I took her away to marry her. They kept her on for her looks. She was spectacular. I'm sure she increased the enrollment at that hellhole. I've never seen anyone so beautiful, and I hope I never do again. She couldn't keep her mind for two seconds on anything but herself, and she was as cold as a clock. And of course, paradoxically, she slept with anyone. Everyone. Any creepy guy who gawked at her on the street, anyone who came to the apartment to fix the phone or wash the windows." He no longer seemed tired; he seemed to relish his tale. "She had an affair with her dentist, her gynecologist, the super of our building, one of the kids' teachers. Anyone who wanted her—and everyone wanted her, of course. As far as I know, she never said no. Or probably it's more accurate to say no one ever said no to her, since I have no doubt that she's the one who did the asking." He took another bite of his hamburger, and looked over at her accusingly, chewing. "I told you I can't stand beautiful women and you got mad at me."

"You should have told me then. Why."

"But you were so cute when you were mad."

She laughed obligingly, thinking: how funny it was, how perfectly like an example of Alex's ironic humor, that it was her own safe lack of beauty that had drawn him to her. She didn't resent this; she felt almost proud of it. Here was her small victory against one of those golden girls who had always aroused her envy and misery and dislike: Beth had blighted Alex's life—she had renewed it.

"She told you all this? About her—affairs?"

"Oh, yes. In detail. We had a very sick relationship." His voice was flat and detached, amused, as if he were recounting the plot of one of Rachel's stories. "Giving me the dirt about all her tedious conquests was her revenge on me because I was the one man she couldn't captivate. I found out about the first one by accident—her carelessness was insulting. And I forgave her. I made a scene, called her names, made her cry, the whole bit, but in the end I forgave her. Big-hearted guy, right? Then it happened again. That was the super. I caught them. And realized that if she'd screw the goddamn super, this overweight slob who stank of years and years of accumulated sweat and stupidity and general grossness, then she must be going down for everyone, with the possible exception of the poodle in the next apartment."

She almost wished she hadn't asked. Perhaps it was wrong to force him to dredge all this up. She hated his detached amusement; it must be put on, for her benefit, and she wished he wouldn't do it. She wanted to tell him to stop, that was enough, and at the same time, she wanted to know more: what had taken place when Alex had come in on Beth and the super, what he had said, what everyone had done. She had a quick vision of a fat man fleeing down the fire escape, pulling on his overalls.

Dorrie said gently, "May I ask why you didn't leave her?"

He shrugged. "We had two little babies. And no money. I drank instead—it was easier and cheaper. But I never slept with her again after I found the super stinking up my bed. This seemed perfectly logical to me, although she called it priggish and perverse, among other things that were less flattering. It wasn't even that I hated her. I mean, I don't hate the garbage in my trash can. I just don't want to have anything more to do with it. I don't want to touch it."

"You are a very fastidious person," she said, thinking of the obsessive, stripped-down orderliness of his apartment, the way he moved around the room while he talked, tidying up.

She hadn't meant to be funny, but he grinned. "Yes," he said. "I am." He wiped his mouth, ostentatiously, on his napkin before leaning across the table to kiss her on the forehead. "One of the reasons I love you is that you're so neat. No messy intrigues in your life. No garbage. No layers of deceit. What you see is what you get."

"I'm not sure anyone is that simple, Alex."

"I don't mean simple. I mean honest."

The waitress refilled their coffee cups. Dorrie said, "So why did you finally break up?"

"It wasn't because I hated her. I didn't. I didn't even hate the goddamn super. I didn't even insist that we move. I'm not a hater—too lazy, or something. But she hated me—quite a bit, I think. I can be a sarcastic bastard. And I was so obviously indifferent to her and the poor slobs she lured into her net. Genuinely indifferent, I promise you." He put his hand on his heart. "I was never a jealous husband, never pissed off at being a cuckold. I honestly didn't give a damn. I wish now that I did care a little. I hate to think that I lived without feeling much of anything for eight years, but that's what I did."

Could that have been true? Warm-hearted Alex? She took his hand from his chest, and held it. He looked down at their hands, clasped on the Formica, and went on, smiling slightly. "Anyway, all that sort of built up. We gave each other a hard time, to put it mildly. And the boys got older, and took her side every time. She was an incredibly devoted mother. Of course, they were sons. Daughters I think she might have liked a little less. But the boys were her slaves. Still are." He paused, thinking of his faraway sons. Dorrie wondered if she would meet them, if they would come to the wedding: dressed up in suits, chatting with Hugo about sports. They would scare Hugo to death. They'd scare me to death, she

thought. "They're lost to me," Alex said. "They're her kids—
I'm not sure I'll ever see them again. I accept that." He gave
her a hard, defiant look. "Let me be honest, Dorrie. I don't
even like them. My own children. I haven't liked them for
years."

"Oh, Alex."

"What the hell. You wanted to kill your brother; I can't
stand my own kids. Now we know the worst about each other."

She squeezed his hand. "From their pictures," she said,
"they don't seem anything like you."

He shook his head, dismissing the subject. "They're just
lost," he said. "Not something I want to dwell on." He looked
beyond her into the back of the restaurant as if into the complex
parts of his life that were, despite his outpouring, closed to
her.

She said, "I'm sorry, Alex," and he focused on her again
almost with annoyance.

"Forget it," he said, so harshly that she was unable to
go on and say, I'll make it up to you, you'll have other children,
you'll get another chance.

There was an awkward pause, and then he sighed, and
continued, "So finally I made a little money. And divorce
became possible, and once it became possible it became a necessity, like some drug I'd heard about but could never afford
before. I had to have it." He shrugged. "And so we split.
Just in time, probably. One of us would have gone mad if
we'd hung on together much longer. Me, probably. I'm sure
Beth is as impervious to madness as she is to most things."

He seemed to be done. He finished up his hamburger, drank
his coffee. She was sure he had told her the whole story, and
yet she felt she knew nothing. How could such a marriage
have endured for so long? What had it been like, day to day?
Had they ever talked? Had they gone out? Gone to movies?
Had they looked at the paintings in the Boston Museum? All
those Millets Alex said used to be there, a roomful—had he
looked at them with Beth? And the little boys: had there been

picnics, parties, the Freedom Trail, Sturbridge Village? Or had
Alex sat alone in his room, drinking? Warm-hearted Alex:
how had he endured it? Perversely, against her will, she wondered if Beth had a sad story too—if Alex had blighted her
life while she was blighting his. She wondered what it was
like to be someone people turned around to look at. Beth
walking down Boylston Street with her pretty little sons, stopping traffic. She wished, suddenly, passionately, that Alex was
a bachelor, that he was bringing to her a past as neat and
uncomplicated (dull, flat, empty, she thought) as her own.
She didn't want beautiful, bitchy Beth trailing behind him—
Beth and the lost boys. She believed him, that he had been
glad to be rid of his wife, that she meant nothing to him,
and yet she knew he must have loved her once. And the boys.
He must have cuddled them as babies, kissed them, lifted them
high in the air to make them squeal with delight. She thought
of her parents and Phinny. You might not like your children,
but surely you kept loving them.

"Any more questions?"

"Only one," she said.

"Grill on, comrade." He smiled at her. "But I know what
your question is. The answer is yes, I did. But not with anyone
I cared about. I couldn't find anyone to care about. I thought
everything was over for me."

It hadn't been what she was going to ask, but she looked
at his weary, shadowed eyes, the wisps of graying hair around
his ears, the stitching of wrinkles around his mouth, and said
to herself, Drop it, Dorrie. Lately, in the parts of his new
novel that she had been reading, his hero, Henry—the writer
with the dog—had been thinking a lot about the passing of
time, about growing older, about the unlikeliness of his ever
seeing the Grand Canyon before he died. Alex had told her
that Henry would reach it in the end. He and Woofy would
stand before the immensity of it, red rock and vast vistas,
and Henry would be happy. For the first time in his life, Alex
had said. He had also said that it was because of Dorrie that

his book would have a happy ending. She said, "When you say everything was over, I assume you mean what Rachel calls the ecstatic bit."

"Hey, don't writers have a gift for it? Yeah, that's what I mean. No more ecstasy. And then I met you."

It hadn't been her question, but his answer was exactly what she wanted to hear—was what, for years and years, she had assumed no man would say to her. Everything over, until now. "And it's been unbridled ecstasy ever since," she said lightly, tears behind her eyes.

"Damn right."

They sat looking at each other, holding hands across the table. His hand was long, thin, veined, yellowish with the remnants of his summer tan; hers, held in it, looked pure white, and young. She liked it, she realized, that he was so much older than she: nine years. He would keep her young; she would always be his young wife.

"How could we not get married?" he asked. He was smiling at her as he had over Rachel's bouquet. "It's been inevitable since the night we met." It was true, she thought: love had pounced on them quickly and dragged them down. There had been no games, no fooling around, none of the fears she was so used to in her relations with men. She had never had to doubt him. But something was tugging at the calm surface of her mind—some hitch? Something besides Beth and the boys and Alex's past. It came to her: *Hugo.* She shoved it away again; it would work out. How? The question kept bobbing back, like an ice cube in a drink. How, precisely?

"I do love you, Alex," she said, as if apologizing.

He said, "Isn't this where we go into a clinch? And the orchestra starts and we sing a duet, and the customers and the waitress and the guy out back thawing stuff in the microwave all get together and do a reprise while we tap-dance a little and then we sing it again and go into another clinch and curtain?"

"End of Act One."

"Right. Now what about Act Two? You've heard my story, comrade. When are you going to marry me?"

"Whenever you like. Now. Soon."

He stood up. "In that case, we'd better get going so I can take you home and do some of that ecstatic bit to celebrate."

They left money on the counter, and ran back to the car. The rain was wild. Alex, at the wheel, had to lean forward and peer through the windshield. Conversation was difficult, carried on in shouts over the noise of the defogger, the tires swishing, the rain beating down. They did resolve to get married soon—before winter, Alex said, so they'd have each other to snuggle with under the covers every night. And they'd take a trip to Arizona, to the Grand Canyon. Tax-deductible research, Alex said, because Henry was going there. But how would they pay for it? That they'd have to work out.

"That and ten million other things," Dorrie said.

"Not ten million."

"Nine, then."

"Nonsense," Alex said, squinting into the rain. "All the important things have been settled. The rest will fall into place."

Hugo, she thought. How would he fall into place? But neither of them spoke his name.

Nina told Hugo all about her tragic love affair while they watched a movie about a mad bomber. She was in love with a boy named Carl McGrath. Hugo knew him by sight—a senior, a football player, always in a crowd of noisy boys just like him—indistinguishable. Carl McGrath? Was he even good looking? He was big and beefy and always looked like he needed a shave. What else? Nothing. God, Carl McGrath. If Hugo had an opinion about him, it was that he was one of those Jamie-ish jerks—someone so outside his own experience that he seemed not even human. Someone who ran around a football field bashing into people. He couldn't believe Nina cared about him, and said so.

"It's all sex." Nina spoke in a reasonable, explanatory tone that nearly broke his heart. He wanted to take her in his arms and tell her to forget that hulking brute Carl McGrath, that big-nosed hunk of lunchmeat. She had had a date with him; they had gone to a movie and then necked in his car for hours and hours. "It was fantastic, Hugo," she said. "I fell in love with him when he kissed me. I can't explain it. It was some chemical thing, I'm sure." They had made out until the wee hours, and he had taken her home, and he had never called her again. "He says hi to me at school," she said. "He's in my trigonometry class. He treats me exactly the way he did before we went out. It's as if he's forgotten all about it, that we spent hours in the backseat of a car kissing each other."

He took a sip of wine, thinking of Carl McGrath's gross red hands, his five o'clock shadow against Nina's soft cheek, his big flabby mouth on hers. That jerk hadn't had to get up the nerve to kiss her, he'd just done it. He would hate Carl McGrath as long as he lived.

The wine gave him the courage to ask her, "That was all? Just kissing?"

"Hugo, I'm not a loose woman!"

"Well, but you're in love with this jerk."

She began to cry. "Oh, Hugo, I thought if I didn't let him get away with anything else he'd call me again. Isn't that what you're supposed to do? Not be cheap?"

"How would I know?" he said, but too low for her to hear.

"I can't believe he hasn't called me, it's been five weeks, he treats me like I'm his sister, not even like his sister, all he says is 'Hi there, Nina.' " She sniffed loudly, and wiped her nose on her sleeve. Hugo got up and went into the kitchen to get her a tissue, putting on lights. When he returned, she was composed; she blew her nose quietly. "He's going with Marilyn Hayes now," she said. "Everyone knows what Marilyn Hayes is good for." Hugo didn't; he wasn't sure who Marilyn Hayes was. "So I guess I played it all wrong." She drew a long breath of resignation. "Anyway, that's over. I'm fighting

it. I'm not even going to those stupid football games. I try
like hell to avoid him."

Hugo thought of how he had avoided her. Was the world
one long chain of people in love with people who weren't in
love with them? "He's not good enough for you, Nina," he
said.

"Oh, I know." She smiled at him almost absently. She
had calmed down; the movie caught her attention. The mad
bomber was on a bridge, looking over his shoulder. He began
to run frantically, pursued by men in suits and hats. There
was an explosion, and a commercial. She turned to Hugo again.
"Frankly, I found it kind of appalling that I fell for such a
conventional guy. I mean, a football player! Total triteness!
Just because he's got muscles and—whatever." She smiled in
Hugo's direction, unexpectedly, sweetly. "As far as company
goes, Hugo, I vastly prefer you, you know."

He didn't know what to say. Here, he realized, was where
he should kiss her. Thank her, at least, for the compliment.
Reciprocate. Something. But he waited too long, and suddenly
she jumped up and said, "My guitar! What did I do with it?
I've got to play you my song."

She found the guitar in the doorway, and settled down
on the sofa with it, tuning. He realized, watching her, how
much he had missed her more even than he missed *Upton's
Grove*—her songs, her strange high voice, the look of her with
the guitar across her lap, her eyes lowered and her eyelashes
a thick dark line. He thought about how he had told Dorrie
that Nina's songs reminded him of *Upton's Grove*—that same
friendly, involving feeling. O God: *Nina, Nina.* She hummed,
adjusted a string, played it, hummed again. Her wineglass,
on the table before her, was still half full.

He picked up the bottle; it was nearly empty. "I guess
I've drunk most of this," he said with a grin, and emptied
the bottle into his glass.

"That must mean you like it."

"Sure—it's good." He didn't, actually, like it very much.

He thought maybe it went better with food than by itself—
the salami and peanuts weren't enough. He didn't feel like
rummaging through the refrigerator for more. He wished he
had brought potato chips, but Nina wasn't complaining. Now
that she had told him her sad story, she seemed to need nothing
else. He wondered, though, if the evening was going to be a
bust. He hadn't kissed her yet; he was a long way from kissing
her, he wasn't half drunk enough. He took a long drink; the
wine was sour on his tongue.

She looked up. "Okay. Ready? This is the one about your
auntie." She played an introduction, a loud, jazzy-sounding
tune in a minor key, and then she began to sing:

"Oh, Heart of Clay,
Let me tell you how I feel;
I'm gonna crush that Heart of Clay
Underneath my heel."

He felt an impulse to move across the room, to recoil
from its loud violence. This was a song about his aunt? It
went on:

"Oh, you Heart of Clay,
You think you're so tough,
But I wanna tell you, Heart of Clay,
That I've had about enough."

It was a terrible song, repetitious and just plain noisy, in
a way Nina's songs, whatever their failings, had never been.
He wondered if she had been listening to rock music. Something
was different. Had her night of passion with Carl McGrath
ruined her talent? And then—the violent music pounded
around the walls of the little room, drowning out the explosions
of the mad bomber—how could Nina hate his aunt so much,
to write this song? Nina had seen her only a couple of times.
If she hated her, it must be his fault; she had prepared this

poison song for him, she had thought he would like it. At
the end of each verse she looked up at him with a wolfish
smile.

"Your Heart of Clay,
It's an easy one to break;
A heart that is only made of clay,
That's a heart that's just a fake."

Oh, God, what a lame song. What was he going to say when
she was done? But it went on interminably, with long, harsh
instrumentals between the verses that pushed him away as
rock music always did. Hugo drank some more wine, and
felt himself getting drunker. The wine worked in stages, it
was like waves on a beach: calm and then a surge. The top
of his head was numb and tingly. He realized, as he sat there,
that he didn't feel well at all. He thought: did he hate his
aunt? The answer came instantly: no, not hate. But righteous
indignation, along with passionate curiosity—that was what
filled him up as he sat there listening to Nina's music. Heart
of clay. He wished he could have it out with her, right that
minute, with the wine working in him. Tell me, he would
say. Tell me. Tell me everything. I'm not a little kid, I can
take it, tell me, tell me.

Nina said, "Here's the last verse," and sang:

"Oh that Heart of Clay,
I can smash it on the floor,
And after I break your Heart of Clay
I'll be goin' out the door.

"Yeah, Heart of Clay,
Let me tell you how I feel;
I'm gonna crush that Heart of Clay
Underneath my heel."

She ended with a flourish of loud chords, and looked at him triumphantly. "Well? Isn't it great? Isn't it the absolute pinnacle of my songwriting career?"

"I don't know what to say." He knew she would take it as a compliment.

"Of course, it's a very personal song, Hugo. I wrote it just for you. I know how you feel about your aunt, about what happened. I thought you needed a song." She took the guitar from around her neck and looked at him earnestly, seriously. "Hugo, I have missed you. I have. I've wondered about you, and felt so sorry for you. Did she ever say anything? About—you know. That newspaper. Did you ever ask her?"

"I never had the guts," he said.

"Well, of course, she probably wouldn't tell you anything, the old bitch."

"No," Hugo said. "I think—" He couldn't defend her too much, or Nina would know that her song had given him not comfort but a headache. "I think I could probably make her tell me. I guess I'm afraid of hearing it."

Nina took a sip of her wine. "You mean the truth about—all that, what we read."

"About my mother being a dope addict who got murdered," Hugo said. His voice came out loud and belligerent, as if it had been Nina's fault. "And what about my father? That newspaper never even mentioned him." It was this that had stayed in the front of his mind all summer and fall.

"Oh, Hugo, Hugo, poor Hugo," Nina said. She set down her wineglass and, with a long sigh, moved closer to him on the sofa. She put her arms around him, he felt her soft electric hair against his face. "My poor Hugo," she said, and kissed him gently on the mouth.

Kissing her was better than he had dreamed. It was impossible to imagine what kissing was like: you had to do it. They lay together on the sofa, lips together, one of her hands behind his head, on his neck, in his hair. She smelled of peanuts and shampoo. The mad-bomber movie ended in a series of explosions, then music, and was followed by something with penguins in it. Hugo heard, "The emperor penguin of the Antarctic has evolved a remarkable temperature-control system. Arteries carrying warm blood to the feet run alongside veins carrying cold blood back to the—"

Nina's little body was pressed against his. He felt her warm blood running. She was impossibly small, delicate, vulnerable. He would protect her always. He kissed her neck. "Nina, Nina," he whispered, and she took his hot face between her hands and opened her lips to him again.

Dorrie's house was warm—besides books, heat was her one extravagance—and upstairs in the living room they pulled off their wet coats and sank down exhausted on the sofa before they noticed that all the lights were on, Hugo's alcove was empty, the place was deserted.

"Hugo?" The kitten leaped from the kitchen table to stretch and rub against their legs. "Hugo?" Dorrie called. "Damn it, he's probably out in the loft. In this weather!"

"I'll go out and drag him back in," Alex said.

Dorrie imagined a scene. "No, let me."

Alex shrugged and went to the refrigerator, looking for a beer, and Dorrie put her raincoat on again and went down the back stairs. She turned on the outside light; rain fell straight down like nails. She ran to the garage and called up to the loft. "Hugo?" She could tell he wasn't there—and why would he have gone out to the loft, anyway, in the rain, when all his things had been brought inside weeks ago? Nothing up there now but spiders. But she climbed the stairs and called again. The loft was pitch black, empty, and somewhere water was dripping in, striking the wood floor with loud ticks.

She stood in the empty garage, trying to think. She could think only of disaster. "Hugo?" she called, and her voice in the dark, against the muffled, gray sound of the rain, scared her.

Back in the house, she said, "Something's wrong, Alex.

He's not here. I can't imagine where he would go on a night like this."

"Out with his girlfriend," Alex said. He was sitting on the sofa drinking beer, the cat on his lap. His hair hung in wet stripes over his bald spot. "Relax. The little darling is growing up. Probably losing his virginity this very minute."

She shook her head. "He wouldn't just go, not without leaving a note or something. Besides, she's not his girlfriend. Although—oh, I don't know. He did say they're friends again. Maybe he's with her over at the Verranos'."

"No doubt. Watching the telly with one hand and losing his virginity with the other."

"Alex, can't you stop joking? I'm worried about him. I'm responsible for that child." She felt sick with the certainty that something was wrong, and Alex sat there grinning with his can of beer, petting the cat, ridiculing Hugo as usual. "I can't just assume he's somewhere and go to sleep and forget about him."

"Then call the Verranos," Alex said. "Obviously."

"Oh, God—it's one o'clock in the morning, how can I call them and say, 'Is Hugo there?' "

"You just do it. Just pick up the fucking phone and call, for Christ's sake, and quit talking about it. It's not as if you're calling in the middle of the night to chat, Dorrie. The kid is missing, isn't he? Or so you seem to think."

She did her best not to get impatient with him. "I'll drive by and see if there are any lights on."

"Good," Alex said. "I'll sit here with Daisy and stay warm and dry like a sensible person."

"You do that."

She took his keys and went out into the wet again, slamming the door. The rain seemed fiercer. She gunned the motor and backed fast out the driveway, hoping he was watching her from the window. The road was unlit and dimmed by a thin fog, but she could see that there were no lights at the Verranos'—not in front, at least. She got out of the car and went down their driveway to the back of the house. Pitch dark: no lights in house or yard.

"Hugo?" she called softly. She felt foolish, but he had to be somewhere. Why not out behind the Verranos' house, sitting in the rain? What if she found him there, sitting on the grass, staring out at nothing as he used to, all those evenings down on the dock? "Hugo?" But the only sound was water beating down, and flowing out of the Verranos' gutters, drowning the sound of the waterfall.

She drove back to her house, then decided, on an impulse, to pass it and circle the pond, slowly. Maybe Hugo was on his way home from somewhere. She would meet him on the road. Maybe he was at the Garners', watching television. She took heart. That was certainly a possibility. She would kill him for not leaving a note. And she hoped he hadn't rowed across—remembering in that moment that the Garners were out of town. Damn. Then their house became visible from the causeway, lights in all the windows.

She stopped the car down the road from their place, watching. The lights didn't make sense. Even if they had decided not to go to Albany, they never—come to think of it—stayed up this late. Hugo wouldn't be there watching television until one o'clock. Maybe he was staying all night. But Mary would have made him let Dorrie know. If he'd forgotten to leave a note, Mary would have made him come back and write one. Dorrie leaned her head on the steering wheel. It wasn't right: the absence of Hugo, the presence of lights. She gripped the wheel hard, trying to think. All that came into her mind were guns and knives and child molesters and perverts and thieves.

She put the car in reverse and backed across the causeway until she could turn around, and then she drove home fast and burst in on Alex. He hadn't moved. He and the kitten looked up at her sleepily.

"Alex, please believe me, there's something wrong. Please don't joke. Just come with me over to the Garners'. The lights are on and I know they're out of town. I don't understand any of this. There's no reason for him to be missing."

"Why don't you just call the Garners?" He held up a hand before she could protest. "No. Don't tell me. It's one o'clock in the morning. You can't call people at one o'clock in the morning."

"No, I can't. What if—oh, never mind. Maybe I should call the police." She stood wringing her hands, realized she was doing it, and folded them tightly together at her waist. "I don't know, I don't understand this."

Alex sighed deeply, picked up the kitten and deposited her on the floor. He stood up and finished his beer in one long drink. "All right. Let's go." He reached for his trench coat and said, "Not because I think there's anything wrong, Dorrie. Only because I don't want you getting hysterical. The kid is obviously over there watching television."

"Alex, they're away for the weekend. They went to Albany to visit their daughter and her new baby."

"So they decided not to go. They came home early and invited the kid over. There's obviously an explanation. Ockham's razor—the simplest explanation is the most likely. Of course, I admit that Ockham never met Hugo."

The kitten followed them as far as the door, then withdrew when the rain blew in, and began washing herself on the rug. "Smart cat," Alex said. He ran ahead, shoulders hunched, toward the car. "He has to do this in the rain, of course," he called over his shoulder. "He can't decide to visit his surrogate grandparents on a nice summer night." He wiped his face with one hand and slicked back his wet hair. "Damn the little bastard."

But his gallantry was uncompromising: even in the rain, he opened her door, waited until she was in, and slammed it before going around to his side. "That was crazy," she said as he got in.

"Too old to change, love."

She touched his arm. She sensed that he was fed up, that the fact of Hugo, which he had been ignoring while they made plans, was becoming real to him. Here was a teen-age brat, a troublesome presence you had to go out in the rain for.

Here was the woman he wanted, saddled with the brat. Here he was pushing fifty, trying to write, teach, support himself, in search of peace and a quiet life and a last grab at the ecstatic bit, dripping wet at one o'clock in the morning because of the brat. Himself and the brat like weights on either side of a balance. She said, "Thanks for doing this, Alex."

"My pleasure," he said, grimacing at her. "Anything for that gallant little nephew of yours."

They started down the road. If Hugo was sitting there with Ross watching a late football game, she would never hear the end of it. It would become one of Alex's jokes: the night Dorrie and I went out in a flood to rescue dear little Hugo from the New York Giants. Why was it that Hugo always turned Alex's ironic humor caustic? She supposed the answer had something to do with his own sons—so beautiful, so superior to poor Hugo, so lost. She looked out into the dark night and prayed vaguely, to no one: *Please.*

"Don't park right in front," she said as they approached the Garners' house. "I know I'm being absurd, but all I can think about are people breaking in, people doing things to him." She had a lurid, horror-movie vision, suddenly, of Hugo and Mary and Ross lying on the kitchen floor with their throats slit.

Alex made a grunting sound, suppressing a laugh. "I'd like to do a couple of things to Hugo." He opened the car door and got out. "All right, Watson. Let's go peek in the windows."

All the way up the house, he cursed. Dorrie, in her wedding shoes—little heels, with straps—felt her feet sinking into mud and puddles. Her teeth began to chatter. She took Alex's arm.

"Have you still got those shoes on? Christ, Dorrie."

"Never mind, it doesn't matter." The shoes were disintegrating—her only decent pair. She smiled grimly in the dark; for her own wedding she would have to get new ones. "Just please don't make noise, Alex."

"I'm not making any fucking noise, damn it."

They came to the Garners' garage, and she looked in. By

the lights from the house, she could see that there was no car. She said, softly, "Alex, it isn't right, that there's no car."

"Quit worrying," he said. "Think of Ockham's razor."

She stopped and faced him, the rain streaming down her face. "Alex, the Garners are obviously not home, someone is in their house, and Hugo is missing. What am I supposed to think?" Her voice had become shrill, too loud.

"Try this," he said. "The little bastard broke in to steal the silver."

She turned away, toward the house. He caught her up and said, "Dorrie, wait," holding her arm to stop her. "All right. I'm sorry. I know you're upset, I didn't mean to be flippant. I'm just so sure there's nothing wrong." He put his arms around her, in spite of the rain. "I don't know what it is, the cat or what, all those piles of newspapers in your living room—something. The place didn't feel as if some evil act had taken place there. I'm sorry—I just think the kid is up to something. He and Nina. They're out making mischief somewhere. I mean, it's what kids do, isn't it?"

Her hair dripped water into her eyes. His moustache hung down wet. She felt tired all of a sudden, soaked and chilled through, angry with Hugo for putting her through this, and with Alex for not caring what had happened to him. The kid, the little bastard, the gallant little nephew, Alex called him, always with derision. She couldn't tell him her greatest fear, that he would someday throw himself into the pond. How many times had she pictured him floating there, fat and buoyant and dead, with seaweed in his hair? Alex would say, Hugo? he wouldn't have the guts to drown himself. He would say, Hugo can't be in both places, Dorrie, drowned in the pond and bleeding on the Garners' kitchen floor.

"Dorrie?"

The surprising certainty came to her, as she stood there with him, that one way or another she would lose something. As soon as the thought entered her mind, it was as if it had been there always. How could she not have known this—during their ride home, and all these last happy months, and when she used to imagine little wrinkled babies mustachioed like Alex? How could she have kept herself from knowing that there were things that would wash away, into an abyss more massive than the Grand Canyon? Alex's face, dimmed by the rain, was peevish in the hazy light. She remembered her surprise when, at Rachel's wedding, he had turned out to be a graceful dancer, light on his feet, leading her expertly, slightly drunk, humming along with the old tunes. And then he had smiled at her over Rachel's flowers. And then they had drunk coffee together and talked about marriage and a trip out west. And a week ago Emma Northrup had called her and asked, "How are you, Dorrie?" and Dorrie had begun babbling at her that she was fine, she was wonderfully well, she had never been so well and happy in her life—astonishing Emma, who had known her since the days of Mark.

We could just go back, she thought. Go home and get into bed and hold each other, and forget the rain.

Alex said, "Dorrie? Believe me, the kid is all right. He deserves to have his ass kicked, but he hasn't met some terrible fate at the Garners'. Come on. Buck up."

What he loved about her was the neatness of her life. He had said that. She kept her voice even and cheerful. "I'm sure you're right, Alex. I'm sure there's some cute boys-will-be-boys explanation."

"But you still want to look in the windows."

"Yes."

"Let me."

She shook her head and moved away from him toward the house.

As far as she could tell, the lights were on in the kitchen, the living room, the sun room. The windows were too high to see in. Alex, behind her, put his lips to her ear and hissed, "Okay, baby, this is it. You grab onto the sill, and I'll give you a leg up to the porch. Watch out for cops."

She took hold of the slippery sill, then stepped out of her muddy shoe and put her foot into his cupped hands. The certainty of some loss to come had calmed her down: things couldn't get much worse, and if they did she could deal with it—which didn't keep her, as she hoisted herself to the level of the window, from dread. Of a twisted face peering back at her. A maniac pointing a gun. A gory head. Mary Garner gone mad, with a carving knife. She braced herself and looked in.

From the end window, she had a clear view of the room. The first thing she saw was the television, and once she saw it she found she could hear it too, over the noise of the rain. There was no other sound. And no one there, she thought at first, until just below her, on the sofa, she saw Hugo—asleep, it appeared, lying on his stomach. Those awful black jeans against the flowered slipcovers. Thank God: Hugo. She slipped in Alex's hands and jumped to the ground just as she saw that it wasn't Hugo alone, that he was lying there with someone. Clouds of wild hair and a skinny little arm around Hugo's back.

She leaned against Alex, her bare foot in mud. He was in there safe—the little bastard. Wild laughter rose up in her. "Ah, God."

"Well?"

"All right. You win. He's in there with Nina."

"Is that the telly I hear?"

"Yes. And they seem to be necking on the sofa."

"Hugo?" Alex snickered, no longer bothering to keep his voice down. "No kidding. Well, good for him, maybe there's hope for the kid after all."

"I don't think the Garners are here, Alex."

"Then how did Romeo and Juliet get in?"

"Who knows? Maybe they gave him the key. He never tells me anything. Let's go around to the door."

The front door was closed and locked. So was the side screen. In back, they saw the open cellar door, with the rain driving in, made clear by the light from the kitchen window.

"Like father, like son, I see," Alex said.

They stood looking at each other in the rain, and then Dorrie pushed past him down the cellar stairs.

🏵 8 🏵

Hugo was sick in bed with the flu compounded by a hangover. He awoke in the night with his skin burning and an urgent desire to throw up. He had a temperature of 102, his bones ached, his throat felt scraped raw. All that night, and all day Sunday, in between trips to the bathroom, he slept, or lay on his bed dazed, looking at the picture on the opposite wall— purple flowers painted in watercolor by his grandmother. Whatever he did, even in his sleep, while his head pounded and his stomach churned, the thought stayed with him: I don't deserve this.

He knew, though, that when he recovered there was worse punishment in store. Dorrie had told him he would have to go over to the Garners' with a bottle of expensive wine (picked out by Dorrie, paid for by Hugo), admit his crimes, and apologize. He thought of this obsessively as he lay there. It would be awful, it would be the worst moment of his life—not counting lying there with Nina and having Dorrie and Alex burst in on them like maniacs—but he was willing to do it; he considered it a suitable punishment. The remorse he felt was bound up with the Garners: it had nothing to do with Dorrie, or

with her repulsive lover. The weird paramour. His aunt had
no right to abuse him, or pass judgment, or punish. Alex
had no right to say those things Hugo had overheard in the
middle of the night.

It was Dorrie's fault, anyway. If she had been honest in
the first place—told him about his mother long ago, last summer, when he first came to live here, instead of hiding the
facts in a box under her bed—none of this would have happened. As soon as he wasn't sick anymore, he would have it
out with her. As soon as his head cleared, as soon as his
stomach settled, as soon as he could summon up the strength
to do anything but stare at those depressing purple flowers
and think about the futility of just about everything that came
into his mind.

Sunday was a long, sick blur. On Monday, he was a little
better. He lay listening to the sounds of Dorrie moving around
the house. From time to time, she looked in on him, bringing
ginger ale and feeling his forehead with her cool hand—not
saying much. He heard her downstairs working at her wheel,
then someone coming into the shop, then someone else. Daisy
jumped to his bed and blinked at him from the valley between
his knees. He slept, dreamed, and woke to the distant whir
of the wheel again, and the phone screaming into his headache.
He wondered if Nina would call, then found he couldn't think
about that without despair. There were calls from what seemed
to be the furnace man, and one of his aunt's Boston galleries.
He heard her talking to the doctor: "Yes—all right—a hundred
and one—yes—no, I don't think so—yes—thank you—I will."
Later, she went to the grocery store (he could tell by the
clank of bottles to be returned) and while she was gone he
dreamed of an endless algebra problem, a formula that twisted
and looped and snaked around corners, teasing him by length-
ening no matter how fast he followed it with his pencil.

When he awoke it was dark out and his cheeks burned.
He kicked off the sheet. Dorrie was doing something in the
kitchen. She heard him stir, and came to the doorway. She

was still mad as hell at him, that was obvious. Maybe not as mad as she had been Saturday night, when she had looked like she wanted to hit him. He knew she'd fought with Alex about him too; he'd awakened in the night to hear her and Alex yelling and then Alex slamming the door and driving away. The fight in the night, was the way he thought of it. The words wove through his head, into his dreams: the fight in the night, the fight in the white night, the night fight.

She said, "Let's take your temperature again." He lay there sucking on the thermometer, gazing at the ugly purple flowers in the painting. He closed his eyes, opened them again, closed them. His head felt like a knife was in it, probing. Life had never been so bad. Everyone hated him; he hated everyone. And he had been having such crazy dreams. He tried to grab at the last one, the algebra dream, but the details were gone, leaving only the sense of angry frustration.

"It's down another point," Dorrie said.

She shook the thermometer and sat by his bed in silence, studying him, leaning over absently to pet Daisy, who woke up and yawned and went back to sleep. The house was still except for the faint sound of rain, gentler now, dripping on the porch roof outside his window. The rain had been coming down for almost two days. He imagined it swelling the pond, points of wet hitting the rough, gray water.

After a while, Dorrie said, "Do you want to tell me why you did it, Hugo?"

"No," he said. He turned his head to look at her. She wore a bright red sweater that hurt his eyes. If he didn't tell her, his getting drunk and breaking into the Garners' was pointless, childish. Fleetingly, he thought of Nina, her tiny soft lips. He made up his mind. It would be a relief to talk, even though every word was like a nail in his head. "All right, yes," he said. "I did it because everything was so rotten."

"Everything was rotten," she said. "I see."

He knew exactly how much she saw: nothing. "I couldn't take it anymore," he said. "I had to do something." He pushed himself up to a sitting position, and she lifted the pillow into place behind him. When he moved, the knife stabbed. He considered, for a moment, his illness: what if it wasn't flu? What if it was something worse, and fatal? He couldn't remember ever feeling like this. He'd had the flu last winter, but there had been no weird dreams, no knives and nails. He hadn't had this feeling of detachment from life, as if he were a boat cut loose and heading for the waterfall. He realized that he didn't care how sick he was, any more than he cared about anything else. There was no point to anything, least of all his life. The idea scared him: if that was true, what was left but to die?

"Your life doesn't seem so rotten, Hugo," she said. "Unless I'm missing something." It seemed to him that she was choosing her words carefully, speaking with exaggerated calm—the way you talk to a crazy person. Is that how it had looked to her, his breaking into the Garners'? Like the act of a nut case? He wondered if she would send him to a psychiatrist. He tried to imagine himself lying on a couch like they did in movies, telling some old guy with an accent about how rotten his life was. The idea was ridiculous. It wasn't some doctor he had to tell, it was Dorrie. Out with it, Hugo. Now's your chance.

"You're missing something, all right," he said.

"Well, why don't you just give me a little hint?" Before he could speak, she went on. "Tell me one thing first, Hugo. Why the Garners' place? When they've always been so nice to you."

"That's why," he said.

"What do you mean, that's why?"

"I couldn't just break into some stranger's house."

"Hugo." For a minute he thought she was going to laugh, but it was just her voice; her face was as stern as ever. "Hugo, I guess what I really want to know is, why break in anywhere at all? Why didn't you and Nina come here if you wanted to spend the evening together?" She said that with heavy sarcasm, as if spending the evening together was a filthy thing to do. Heart of clay, he thought. "There was no one home. You would have been alone, if that was the idea."

"It wasn't just that," he said. "I needed to get drunk." Hadn't he already said that? Maybe in the dream where he had it out with her and cried. "I knew the Garners had some wine."

She took a deep, annoyed-sounding breath and let it out. "All right. Let me keep asking questions. Why was it so important to get drunk? Just because everything was so rotten? Whatever that means. I don't like this, Hugo. It's against the law to break into someone's house, it's against the law to steal, and it's certainly against the law to drink at fifteen. I assume you're aware of all that?"

He turned his head away. "Obviously," he said.

"Why this insane desire to get drunk, at your age?" she asked.

He stared at his grandmother's painting and his entire body was flooded with what, in his illness, he had been trying to avoid: the remembrance of kissing Nina. He had felt it picking at the edges of his consciousness, bringing with it only regret for what might have been. Now it possessed him like a fever, 102 degrees of *Nina, Nina.* At last, after all those months of ignoring him and falling in love with Carl McGrath, after he had thought over and over again that he'd lost her, there was the miracle of her turning to him on the Garners' sofa and kissing him. What did it mean? Her tiny body pressed to his, her firm little breasts against his chest. He had buried his hands in her hair and kissed her, one long kiss that had lasted—how long? Hours. And then she hadn't spoken to him in the car, had sat there with her arms wrapped around her guitar, hadn't even looked at him as she got out. She had said a sullen good night to no one in particular, and had run in the dark and the rain up to the Verranos' door without looking back. It hadn't meant anything, her kissing him. It was part of the long series of letdowns that was life. This one thanks to Dorrie and Alex barging in on them at the

Garners'. "Oh, Christ," Nina had said, and pushed him off the sofa.

"Hugo?"

Nina faded away. Dorrie held out the ginger ale to him, and he took a drink through the bent straw. It was mercifully cold. He looked at her and lost his nerve. How did people say such things to each other: You lied to me, everyone lied to me, my mother was murdered, my mother was a junkie. It all seemed unreal. Maybe he'd dreamed that too—the newspaper under the bed. He wanted to turn his head away and go to sleep.

"Hugo?"

"I told you," he said. "Everything was rotten."

"All right. Then tell me something else."

"What?" he asked, in dread. It had been in the back of his mind all day that he had done something more, something worse, something he'd forgotten, something that did give her the right to hate him.

But all she said was "Do you realize that what you did was wrong?" Her voice was no longer calm, no longer so considerate of his sickness. He moved his head painfully to look at her again. There were lines in her face, worse than usual, half-moons under her eyes, angry roads mapping her forehead. Her eyes were burning and intense, as if everything that had happened was her hell, for some reason, as much as it was his. She said, "I need to know—are you sorry about it? Do you regret it? At all?"

He sighed. His stomach cramped, let go, cramped again. What did it matter? He closed his eyes, and when he opened them she was still looking at him, waiting. Heart of clay. "All right," he said. "I'm sorry about the Garners. I'm sorry I did it to them. That was stupid. But I don't see that it's got anything to do with anything else." With you, he meant, but her face was clenched with anger, and he couldn't say it. The long speech tired him; he swallowed some ginger ale and finished, "I don't see that it's such a big deal."

She brought her fist down furiously on the side of the

bed—once, twice, shaking the mattress beneath him. The ginger ale in his stomach was like seawater, like sludge. He was going to throw up; he was going to die. She said, "Don't you dare say that, you little bastard."

He gathered his strength. She had no right to talk to him like that. He said, "If I did something wrong it's my business, not yours."

His voice was barely audible, but she heard it. She put her face close to his. "It is my business, damn you, Hugo. I won't have this kind of thing, I won't live with it, I've been through it all before." She spoke through gritted teeth, her voice low, but it rose at the end with something approaching hysteria, and the knife in his head plunged in deep. He had no idea what she was talking about, and he didn't care.

"You made me look like a jerk with Nina." The seawater churned and soured in his throat. "I'm going to throw up," he said, and stumbled out of bed, dislodging the cat, catching his foot in the sheet, pushing past Dorrie. He just made it to the bathroom, and leaned over the toilet, puking. He seemed to throw up forever. It was horrible, but he felt instinctively that this was the last time, he was better. Somewhere at the back of his mind it occurred to him that he was probably losing weight.

When he was done, he sat back on his heels, the cold rim of the toilet bowl against his forehead. The toilet smelled of vomit. He reached up and fumbled for the handle to flush it. His aunt was there, and flushed it for him. Shit, she had been watching him. He stayed where he was. He felt better, but weak. He would have to get up, walk by her, get back in bed.

She was crouched beside him with the washcloth. She wiped his face, put her hand under his arm to help him up. "Do you feel better?"

"Yes." He shook off her arm. "I'm fine," he said. "Just don't fuss at me."

"Suit yourself," she said, and threw the washcloth into

the sink. He sighed, and lowered his head to the toilet bowl
again. All right: he had hurt her feelings when she was trying
to be nice. He should be sorry. He was sorry. He just didn't
care.

He got back into bed, and as he fell asleep he heard her,
in the kitchen, slamming things around and swearing.

She sat at the wheel while Hugo slept. She was making
more soup bowls for the restaurant on the shore: that tricky,
low-slung shape, not too shallow. She discarded more than
she kept; it didn't matter, she was ahead of schedule, for once.

She thought obsessively of Alex. She was waiting for him
to call her. The phone had rung constantly: never him. Surely
he would call—wouldn't let a curse and a slammed door be
his last words. How, she wondered, had the farcical elements
of this night—Hugo's teen-age libido, the prowling around
in the rain, her crazy fears—how had they escalated to the
point of madness?

"I don't understand you," he had said. "Your brother you
wanted to murder. You wanted to put rat poison in his root
beer, for Christ's sake. His kid you defend to the death. He
needs discipline, Dorrie—not defense. That's how your parents
ruined your brother. They never made him pay."

She said, "You know he's nothing like Phinny"—hoping
it was true. She thought of Hugo's stricken face when they
walked in on him, of how he had cried in front of Nina, embarrassed, unable to stop.

Alex said, "How did such a charmless little bugger turn
you into a mother hen?"

Anger took her over. He was like some vast powerful dicta-
torship making war on a harmless little state, Russia invading
Afghanistan. "You go to hell, Alex," she said, hating him.
And yet it all seemed false; she kept waiting for him to laugh,
make a joke of it, put his arms around her and offer comfort.
The look in his eyes, it seemed to her, was more anguished
than cruel.

She imagined him driving home in the rain, tired and angry, the tiredness eventually taking over, the anger dissipating by the time he reached his apartment. She had thought he would call her then, remorseful. She waited, still awake, her own anger dwindling down. All right, he had been wrong; he had been hasty; he had been, she supposed, upset by their discussion of his own children. Had taken out his own pain on Hugo. She understood that, it was a pattern, it would pass in time. And Hugo was no saint. Why had she felt she had to defend him so violently?

She had been sleepless all that Saturday night. Hugo got up twice to go into the bathroom and vomit. Around 4 A.M., she took his temperature. "Leave me alone," he said. His pillow was wet with sweat.

The rain dripped down. At dawn, she could see nothing out the window but mist: no pond, no road, no trees, as if her little house had been cut loose from the rest of the earth. When she turned on the light and tried to read, there, all over her bedroom, were Alex's leavings: a sweatshirt, a pair of gray wool socks, a worn-out belt. A copy of *The Great Gatsby* that he was taking notes on for his class. On the wall, the absurd photograph of his sneakers: grungy black basketball sneakers—no Nikes for Alex. What would she do with these things? They constituted a little museum of Alex Willick— all sides of his personality represented: literary, poor, old-fashioned, humorous, lovable. Cruel? There was no room for cruelty, for shouts and insults, in her picture of him. Nothing made sense. Was she dreaming this cold, wet, wretched night?

She shivered in her bed, and got out of it to turn the heat up, but it didn't do any good. The icy rain and the slamming door had chilled her to the bone. Winter was coming; already, on these cold mornings, there was a delicate skin of ice at the edges of the pond. Winter would come, and it would go on forever, every night as cold and comfortless as this one.

Alex didn't call: he must have dropped exhausted into bed. He would call her when he woke up. But Sunday passed, and half of Monday. The rain was over, and she sat at her wheel hoping for solace from the cold clay and the pale sun out her window—some comfort for the silent phone. Was this it, then? The course of her life changed so radically, blown apart as if by a bomb, only because of an accident of fate— because Hugo had had a mad whim to get drunk and impress his beloved? No bomb, just the juices of puberty. Or some genetic madness, a spark from that sick flame that had made Phinny what he was.

The bowl she was making was wrong—lopsided and heavy-bottomed. She mashed it into a ball and dropped it into her pail of slurry, took another hunk of clay and began to center it. She wished she could talk to Rachel; Rachel was in Paris, sleeping off her jet lag by the side of her new husband. Was it only two days ago—less—Dorrie and Alex had plotted to get married? It seemed like weeks—long weeks of sorrow and sleeplessness and the sound of Hugo being sick in the bathroom. "We'll fly out to Arizona," Alex had said. "We'll hike down into the canyon from the North Rim—that's where nobody goes. We'll climb down to the river, and then we'll look up, and we'll see the canyon rising all around us, and—that's it, Dorrie. That's what I need to do. I feel almost religious about it, as if it's a pilgrimage—don't ask me why. I need to see it, and I want to see it with you."

Maybe that was the ridiculous thing, the idea of herself and Alex on that pilgrimage, on any pilgrimage. Maybe what she had foreseen all those years ago was true, after all: she was destined to be alone, to be husbandless and childless, to live by herself in a little house with immensity and grandeur denied to her. She looked out the window. Instead, she had Little Falls Pond. It was choppy and dull, swollen looking after the rain, nudging the top of the dock. She felt a fierce love for it, for her house, for what she possessed—the sure things in her life. Her own personal pilgrimage stopped here. This would have to be enough.

She worked at the wheel longer than she needed to, and

she quit only when she was exhausted, her shoulders and back tight and sore. She stood up, bent from the waist, and dangled, shaking her wrists, moving her neck to unkink it. One thing about having a husband, there was always someone there to rub your back.

Upstairs, Hugo coughed, but when she looked in on him he was still asleep, the kitten curled up in the bend of his knees. His breathing was even; his cheek felt cooler. His hair had dried in slick points across his forehead. What to do— how to make the rest of the day pass? She sat in the wing chair and tried to read. She was in the middle of a book about a train journey through Italy. When this is all over, she thought, I'll have to go traveling. The thought brought her up short: when what was over? Her grieving for Alex? Her responsibility for Hugo? Her anger and disappointment and worry? She threw the book aside; it was impossible to concentrate on olive groves and piazzas.

She felt the need, all of a sudden, to get outside, away from the silent house. She combed her hair. Her face, in the mirror, looked aged and pale—eyes sunken, cheeks thin: her pre-Alex face. He had transformed her, over these few months, into a "handsome woman," a woman whose face, if nothing else, reflected the certainty of being loved. Now, like the evil queen, she had reverted to a hag. She rubbed in some Jolie Jeunesse and put on blusher, wondering why she bothered. She peeked at Hugo again, left a note saying BACK SOON on his bedside table, and took the phone off the hook.

Outside, the late-afternoon sun was struggling to shine. The leaves that were left on the trees gleamed from the rain, and the air smelled clean. She walked over the wet grass down to the water. She remembered the magical day she had looked out of the window and seen a deer make its slow, dignified way along the shore to the pond—just here, by the lightning-struck oak—where it had bent its beautiful head and drunk, the spring sun on its brown back. She had gone out and seen the prints of its hooves, felt them in the grass with her fingers as if they were messages left for her to interpret. And the day the snowy egret had stood for long minutes on the tiny, bushy island at the north end of the pond. She had watched it through binoculars the whole time—it did nothing, except to turn its head around, inspecting things with its wicked black eye and darting its black bill into the water—and then, seemingly for no reason, it lifted its wings so that she saw its bright yellow feet, and then it slowly, slowly rose into the air, away.

Now there were a pair of Canada geese near the shore, gliding on their own reflections, browsing in the weeds. Alex said they looked like accident victims, their necks bandaged in white, their heads held stiffly. They mated, she knew, for life.

She turned away from the pond. She was tired, she had nowhere to go, she should stay upstairs with Hugo, but she didn't want to be up there with the uncooperative phone, the book she couldn't concentrate on, the Alex Willick museum. She got in the car and sat there pondering. There wasn't much to do on a Monday evening in East Latimer. She could go to McDonald's and get a Big Mac. She could go bowling. She could go to Ernie's, the town's one bar, and drink a beer. She could walk along the darkening streets, skirting puddles, and look at the shabby old houses and stripped trees.

She started the motor. For want of anything better to do she could drive to the discount store and buy some Tampax. Get Hugo some more ginger ale, some ice cream. See normal people doing their normal shopping. Smile at the clerks, chat a little. She would treat herself to something nice—a plant, a nightgown, maybe a magazine. Go home and eat a bacon sandwich. Listen to the Monday night concert on public radio. Go to bed early.

A thought struck her as she eased the car out of the driveway: what if Alex showed up instead of calling? What if he arrived while she was gone, to find only Hugo and Daisy? She pondered this idea, driving steadily toward town. Well, he would have come for her—that was the point. He would have shown he wanted her. Even if he didn't wait, even if he turned right around and drove back to Boston—the gesture would have been made, the reprieve given. She imagined Hugo saying, in a tone of disapproval, *He* was here. She would call him, and he would say, Damn it, Dorrie, I drive all the way down there to see you and all I find is the kid coughing at me. And everything would be well. She would be summoned back to Saturday, back to the edge of the Grand Canyon. She would be a handsome woman again.

Fat chance, Dorrie. He's not going to show up. But the hope persisted, even as she drove into town, parked the car, pushed a shopping cart around the discount store: you never know—an irrational hope that came from the same source that had prompted her to put on blusher, to contemplate a new nightgown, to think about the deer and the snowy egret with simple happiness, to defend Hugo to Alex. You never know: even when you do.

"Dorrie?"

She turned around in the appliance department (she was considering a new hairdryer) to see Monica Scully, a woman who had taken pottery lessons from her a few years ago. Monica raised an electric kettle in the air, gesturing hello.

"How are you doing, Dorrie? I haven't seen you since Lord knows when."

She was a stout, pretty woman, still in her late twenties, who wore her hair in two blond braids, thick as skeins of yarn. She and her husband struggled to keep a small dairy farm going. The Scullys had been dirt poor, barely making it, and Monica'd had to give up pottery and devote her time and money to the farm.

"Roseanne's helping me pick out a new teakettle," Monica said. "Aren't you, honey?" She beamed down at her daughter, a timid little girl in a sweatshirt that said THE DEVIL MADE ME DO IT. "Ours burned out this morning just in time for breakfast, wouldn't you know." Dorrie remembered Monica's jokey self-deprecation: "wouldn't you know" and "just my luck," and the rueful grin.

"How are things going, Monica?"

Monica's grin widened. "Just terrific, thanks to the goats.

I saw a thing on television about making goat cheese, and we added a couple of goats to our herd, and now I'm the goat cheese queen of northeastern Connecticut." She burst into laughter. "I'll tell you, Dorrie, they're bad-tempered, smelly little devils, but they've turned our lives around. I don't mean we're rich or anything, but we sure are doing a lot better. Hey—maybe I'll come out and do some pottery with you again."

"That would be great, Monica," Dorrie said, and realized that she meant it. She had sworn not to teach anymore, now that she didn't have to, but she had enjoyed having Monica around—a large, relaxed figure, always in a tent dress. That had been back in the Teddy days. Seeing Monica, she was reminded of Teddy: for some reason, she thought of a shirt he'd had, one she'd always disliked, a dark purplish plaid. "I'm glad to hear things are going so well. You were having a tough time for a while there."

"How are things with you? I'm sorry we lost touch, Dorrie. I've been so busy. Did you ever do any more with your salt kiln?"

Dorrie said she'd neglected it, she'd love to get back to it, maybe Monica could come out and they could work together. She heard herself saying these unaccustomed things and realized how solitary she had become. Before Alex, she'd seen hardly anyone—occasionally the Garners, sometimes Rachel. Then there was only Alex—and now, nothing, no one. She barely knew her neighbors. Her customers were strangers—even the steady ones like the movie star, and the galleries she sold to. When her one good friend was in Paris, she had no one to talk to.

On impulse, she said, "I've got my nephew living with me now. My brother's boy—Hugo. An orphan, just turned fifteen."

"Oh, my God, I feel sorry for you, Dorrie." Monica raised her eyes to the heavens. "That has got to be the worst age. My sister Linda's fifteen."

"She's my aunt," Roseanne piped up.

"That's right, baby, she is. Dorrie, she's putting my mother through hell. Tantrums? Hostility? Let me tell you. I can imagine what you're going through, taking him on. That's wonderful of you, to do that."

"I didn't have much choice," Dorrie said.

"Still, he must be company for you."

"Oh—" She thought of Hugo telling her to mind her own business, to quit fussing. "I suppose he is, when we're speaking."

They laughed, and parted. It was agreed that Monica would call her to arrange a time for lessons. She would bring Dorrie some cheese. She wished her good luck with her nephew. "It'll pass," she said. She took Roseanne's hand and steered her toward the exit. "Before you know it, he'll be away at college and you'll miss him like crazy."

The hell I will, Dorrie thought, but then—passing bemused through the appliance department, thinking of Hugo going away to college, of the pristine little pots Monica used to make, of Teddy's plaid shirt—she saw a display of television sets on sale. Small ones, color, really very cheap. Why not? He could keep it in his room; she wouldn't even have to know it was there. The idea entered her mind without her permission. She turned guiltily, as if she expected Alex to leap out from behind the refrigerators shouting, This is discipline?

She needed advice, but Monica was nowhere in sight. And how absurd, to ask if she should buy a television set. You don't have a TV? Monica would say. Well, Dorrie, no wonder that child doesn't speak to you!

One set was tuned to *Monday Night Football*—men crashing into each other, pulling each other down, slipping in the mud. Football meant nothing to her; it looked like insanity. She stood watching, figuring out her finances, and then, feeling insane herself, she removed the Tampax and the philodendron from her shopping cart and hefted in a boxed television set. Put back the Tampax and the plant. Wheeled it all to the check-out counter, thinking, What the hell, why not, and damn Alex.

On Tuesday Hugo's temperature was normal, his flu gone. The doctor had diagnosed, over the phone, "this forty-eight-hour thing that's going around," and prescribed bed rest, no food but ginger ale, and, once his stomach calmed down, aspirin for his headache. Dorrie drove him, wrapped in a shawl, to the Garners', where he presented the wine and made his apologies. He felt her stern eye on him the whole time, but the Garners were nice about it. Mrs. Garner fussed over his flu, and wanted to make him some hot tea with lemon. Mr. Garner had ready a little speech about learning from his mistakes; he twanged his watchband as he talked, and his voice sounded embarrassed and dutiful. Hugo cried a little. Mrs. Garner hugged him, saying, "Who cares about germs?" And then Dorrie hustled him home, where he fell into an exhausted sleep.

He awoke bored and starving, and, though the knives and nails were gone, his cough was worse and his head was stuffy. Dorrie came in when she heard him sneeze, and looked at him with exasperation. "Don't tell me you're getting a cold," she said, as if it were his fault.

"I'm hungry."

She sighed. "You can have soup."

He hated soup, but he ate two bowls of it and then, grudgingly, she let him have some ice cream.

He watched television all day. He couldn't believe it when she brought the set home and put it up on his dresser. "It's yours," she said, plugged it in, and left the room as if she was afraid she might become contaminated. What did it mean, her getting him the television? She still seemed pissed off—barely spoke to him, just set down the food and ginger ale and went away, looking preoccupied. He wondered if Alex had walked out on her for good, and hoped so, then felt like a rat for hoping so. She could do better, he thought vaguely.

Wouldn't anyone be better than Alex? He couldn't help it, he'd be glad to see the last of him—his silly-looking cowboy moustache and his crummy old clothes. He hated the way Alex made fun of everything, and the way he had just taken over, leaving his stuff around as if he owned the place. When Hugo lived in the loft, it hadn't been so bad—they'd hardly ever run into each other. If Alex and Dorrie got married, he'd move back to the garage, he didn't care what anybody said. If they didn't let him, he'd walk up to the highway and hitch to the Wylies' place in West Hartford.

He was waiting for Nina to call. When he thought of Nina, his nose clogged and his throat hurt more, as if invisible tears were choking him. All day he thought about calling her. He said her number over and over to himself, like an incantation: it was full of 5's, his lucky number, the number he most liked working with in math. If he said it enough, he would get up the nerve to actually dial it. But he didn't.

Thinking about it—his need to talk to her versus his cowardice—made him restless. That and his determination to have it out with Dorrie, another thing he didn't yet have the guts to do. Her unhappy obliviousness put him off as much as her hostility. He had no idea how to break through it.

He was glad of the television—it was company, and distraction—but after half a day of it, he was having trouble concentrating. *Family Feud* came and went and he hadn't even noticed it. He would call Nina after school—no, after *Upton's Grove*. I wondered if you were mad at me, I called to apologize, I'm sorry, Nina, I'm sorry . . . And then he would confront Dorrie. I know how my mother died, why did you lie to me, tell me the truth.

He sat propped against pillows, muttering to himself through *Ryan's Hope* and *One Life to Live*. He tossed and turned on the bed, dislodging the cat, who looked at him with reproach, then found a new spot and went back to sleep. Daisy fascinated him: all she did was sleep and purr. Was that all she wanted out of life? Plus a little Kitten Chow, a little affec-

tion? He envied her. He thought of all the things he wanted.
First, to have Nina call him. Second, to get out of bed; his
rear end was sore from sitting. Third, to have Alex disappear
from the universe. Fourth, to have his old *Upton's Grove* notebook from the shelf in the garage where he'd left it. Fifth,
to have some more ice cream. Sixth—

"So this is the famous *Upton's Grove,*" his aunt said from
the doorway.

Hugo was startled. It couldn't be three o'clock already.
But there was the frieze of white houses and church steeples
and trees and winding streets, the familiar music starting, the
words UPTON'S GROVE carved in chunky wooden letters. Then
the commercials, all those concerned mommies, all those sexy
girls going crazy over diet pills and deodorant soap. Then a
woman sitting on a narrow bed in a small room, crying.

"Oh, my God," he said. "That's Claudette! She's in jail.
They must have found out about the necklace."

"That jail seems to have a good hairdresser," said Dorrie.

He ignored her. The scene changed to a posh business
office. Big desk, Oriental rugs, a man on the phone. "I can't
wait that long, Prescott," he said. "I'm warning you. Three
more days. After that, Jason is mine."

"Who is this guy? That's Crystal's baby he's talking about!
How can he get Jason from Prescott and Tara?" Hugo looked
up at his aunt; she was gone.

But Claudette was there, and Charles, and Tiffany and
Michael and Harley, and Crystal and that stupid Jamie. Even
Jamie seemed somehow lovable, it had been so long since he'd
seen him. He hadn't watched the *Grove*—that was what Nina
always called it—in two months. He didn't seem to have missed
a whole lot, thank God. No one had been killed off, as far
as he could tell. He sat sucking on cough drops, smiling at
his favorite characters, even those in trouble, like Claudette.
Don't worry, Claudette, he wanted to say to her. You'll get
out of it, you'll be all right. He remembered his grandfather
saying that Claudette looked like a cocker spaniel, and he

grinned—well, she did, a little, but prettier. And how his grand-father had hated Harley. At his age, Grandpa had said, the old geezer should have more sense. Hugo blew his nose. Watch-ing the *Grove* after all this time was a little like being home with his grandfather again. He tried to pretend those comfort-able, predictable days were back again—that the whir of Dorrie's wheel from downstairs was—what? His grandfather's electric shaver? Some kitchen noise? That his grandfather would come in and sit with him and ask, "What's that old goat up to now?"

When it was over, he turned the set off and sat there think-ing about his notebook, out in the garage. He would like to have it so he could start updating. There were new characters, a huge batch of new statistics. And Dorrie had acquired a supercalculator, one that did everything. If she let him use it, he could figure things out faster, do more complicated charts. He heard her out in the kitchen, boiling water for her tea break. He gave a couple of fake coughs, hoping to sound pa-thetic and draw her in, and then he got into a real coughing fit, and she came in with water and cough medicine.

"Looks like you'll be out of school a while," she said, as if she didn't relish the prospect. "Well. Do you need anything else?" What a joke, did he need anything else. He said, "I need my notebook. I left it in the garage. Can I go out and get it?"

She stared at him. "Did I hear you right, Hugo? Did you just ask me if you could go out to the garage? With a cough like that? Have you lost your mind?"

The coughing had brought back his headache. Her red sweater hurt his eyes, and he closed them. "I might get pneu-monia and die. Who cares?"

"Come off it, Hugo," she said. "Quit dramatizing."

"I just want my *Upton's Grove* notebook."

She sighed massively. "I'll go get it. Where is it?"

"Up in my loft. My ex-loft," he said. "On the ledge over the west-side window."

"I'll get it after I have my tea."

He lay back bored to death, breathing through his mouth. He wondered how many days off his cold was good for. The whole week, he hoped—boring though it might be. He realized that not only could he not telephone Nina, he was afraid even to see her in the halls. She must despise him. What a baby he was. He couldn't believe he had cried in front of her, had let Alex push him around. Even now, tears threatened under his closed lids. I don't deserve this, he thought defiantly, and if anyone had asked him what he meant, he would have said, Everything: his stuffed nose, and Nina's rejection, and having to wait for his notebook, and those ugly purple flowers framed on the wall of his room.

Dorrie sat in the kitchen drinking her tea. Thank God the television was off. She had made Hugo turn it down twice, but there was no real escape. Even downstairs in her studio, the noise came through as incoherent jabbering punctuated by music; it was like having a loud, brutish neighbor. As soon as school started, she would make rules: no television but *Upton's Grove* after school and, if his homework was done, one additional program at night. She had seen the headlines on magazine covers: TAME THE TV MONSTER, TURN YOUR KIDS ON TO READING, DON'T LET THE BOOB TUBE RULE YOUR LIFE. She supposed she'd have to start reading them—all those dreary articles for parents. YOUR SON'S PUBERTY PROBLEMS. TEEN SEX: EPIDEMIC OR EXAGGERATION? RAISING HEALTHY KIDS IN TROUBLED TIMES. She sipped her tea, thinking, How did this happen to me? What good had been all her birth-control precautions over the years? Here she was, in the same situation as an unwed mother, saddled not with a cute little baby who snuggled in her arms and called her Mama but a surrogate son with puberty problems.

Alex wasn't going to call. Nor was he going to drive out to see her. Nearly three days had gone by. She imagined him in Boston, living his life without her: going out into the rain in his ancient London Fog, talking to his students about *The Great Gatsby* and the American dream, making Spartan suppers in his tiny kitchen. Drinking, probably, more than he should. Lying awake, a prey to the old nightmares he always said she abolished with her presence. Missing her? Suffering his own agonies over the teapot and mug she'd made for him, the books she'd lent him, the Grand Canyon poster on the wall?

She was still sleeping badly. She had been trying, during the long nights, to think of a solution so she would be ready if Alex did call. Not that he would. But he might. She would present him with Plan A, backup Plan B, compromise Plan C. So far, she had come up with nothing—except that Alex ought to be a little nicer about the situation, a little understanding. No help there. What did people do in this kind of crisis? People with children got married all the time; the world was full of second marriages and step-families and unorthodox households, some of them containing not just immature, mixed-up kids like Hugo but black sheep like Phinny. People survived. Give and take, she thought. Accommodation. Compassion. Love conquering all . . .

It occurred to her that it might, in fact, be simpler if Hugo were her son: her stake in him would be greater; Alex would have no choice but acceptance. This thought made her feel oddly tender toward Hugo. She heard him yawn, then give his metallic cough, and sigh—fagged out after a day of television. She imagined Alex accusing her of choosing Hugo over their relationship, of loving Hugo more than she loved him. Well, she supposed the first accusation was true; the second was nonsense. She didn't love Hugo at all. She didn't even like him most of the time. And she would love Alex, she told herself, until she died. But she would stick by Hugo; she would keep him from turning into a Phinny. The appalling firmness of this resolution surprised her. Monica had said it was wonderful of her. She wished she could feel heroic. All she felt was sad, and not quite resigned.

She finished her tea and went out to the garage. Hugo and his damned obsessions. It was getting dark, and the wind hit her as she went down the path, whirling leaves around her head. What if those headlights coming down the road were Alex's, what if he pulled into the driveway and bounded toward her, took her in his arms, murmured her name? She would bury her face in his old plaid jacket, breathing in the woolly smell, and they would forgive each other, they would come up with Plan A, Plan B. Send Hugo to boarding school, wish him on the Wylies, arrange a marriage between him and Nina, ship him off to his Tchernoff relatives. Anything, anything. Hugo was a good boy, but she didn't want Hugo; she wanted Alex. Damn.

She had forgotten the flashlight, but there was enough light to see by, dimly. She climbed the stairs to Hugo's loft. It hadn't taken long for the spiders and the mice to reclaim it. She heard rustlings and scurryings as she stood there getting oriented in the dusk. The west window was a square of lighter gray; a large and intricate spider web stretched across the bottom half. She felt around in the dust above the window, cringing from what might be there. The notebook, dusty and swollen with damp, and something else beside it on the shelf: a mug? She took it down and in the window light she made out FAVORITE AUNT.

She leaned her head against the frame and stared out a. the darkening view. Oh, Christ. Oh, damn. That dear pathetic boy. All right. All right. She would try to love the child, try to be some sort of parent for him. She would read the articles, shut out the sound of his television, put up with his taste in girlfriends, forget Plan A and Plan B, settle down with her work and her house and her nephew. All right.

When she got back inside, Hugo seized the notebook and bent over his crabbed writing with a small smile on his face.

She said, "Hugo?" He looked up, and she held out the mug. "I found this out there too."

He stared at it, and said, "Oh," then snickered in an embar-

rassed way. "Oh, yeah, I forgot. That was supposed to be a
Christmas present."

"Here. Take it. I'll pretend I didn't see it."

"No—no." He waved it away, not looking at her. "Keep
it. It can be a Halloween present or something. I'm sorry it
got so dusty." He snickered again, and coughed. She was surprised by the impulse to reach out and ruffle his hair or stroke
his cheek. He said, "I guess it's sort of a dumb present. I
mean you make those things all day."

"To tell you the truth, it's nice to have one made by someone else," she said, smiling at him.

"Oh—yeah, well, maybe."

"Anyway—thanks, Hugo."

She reached out one hand and touched it briefly to his,
where it lay, crumpling a tissue, on the filthy cover of the
notebook.

Hugo found, stuck inside his *Grove* notebook, the two old
pictures he had hidden up on the ledge: one of him, in sixth
grade, with his class; the other of his parents standing by
the Camaro. He looked at his small face, hemmed in by Matthew Purvis and Jason Cantrell, and tried to find a resemblance
to his mother or his father. His mother's face was young and
pretty above her swollen-up body; she looked more like Jason
Cantrell than like Hugo. His father, in this picture, looked
exactly like Dorrie—could have been Dorrie, if her hair were
a little shorter and she didn't have breasts and she wore his
father's old jeans and T-shirt and that western belt with the
big buckle. Well, he didn't resemble them, but they were his
parents all the same. The thought, suddenly, overwhelmed
him. His parents. How he missed them, how different his life
would be if they hadn't died. He almost took the familiar
comfort in tears, until he remembered that all that crappy
daydreaming was over. His parents hadn't been so wonderful.
His mother had been a junkie, murdered by a dope dealer.
And who knew what his father had been?

He stuck the photographs under his pillow and toiled over

his notebook until dinnertime, working variations on last summer's statistics. He was comparing Tiffany's time with Claudette's when the doorbell rang. His aunt bustled out from the kitchen, went downstairs, opened the door, and there was the miraculously beautiful sound of Nina's voice. *Nina,* oh God, *Nina.* He heard her clattering up the stairs, and then she stood before him in the doorway. She was dressed like a witch, and she was holding Daisy on her shoulder.

"Trick or treat," Nina said. She wore a black mask; when she pulled it off her hair flew out around her head. The kitten jumped down. "She sure got big. You should see Dolly, she's gigantic." She grinned at him; her front teeth were blacked out. "Like it? I used Black Jack gum."

He couldn't speak; he smiled weakly at her and pulled his blanket up higher. He was in his oldest pajamas, and his plaid bathrobe looked as if he'd had it on all week, which he had.

"You look terrible," Nina said.

He coughed, drank some ginger ale, and said, "I've had the flu. I've still got this cold."

"Your aunt told me. I had it too. I puked my guts out for two days, and I slept all day yesterday, but today I was better, damn it. Back to school. But I was a mess."

She didn't look like a mess; she looked beautiful. He drank her in as if she were some magic medicine: her pointed nose, her electric hair, her freckled wrists against the black costume. He had dreamed about her, one of the turbulent dreams at the height of his illness. She had been naked, yelling at him; he remembered nothing of the dream but her nakedness, how small and pale she had been, her little breasts like muffins.

"I'm not really out trick-or-treating," she said. "I just came to see you. I thought the costume would be good for a laugh."

Hugo sipped his ginger ale and looked at her. He couldn't believe it: here she was. He said, "Nina?" She was scraping the gum off her teeth with a fingernail. "Nina, you're not mad at me?"

"Of course not." She sat down on the bed and bared her teeth. "Did I get it all off?"

"Most of it."

"Why would I be mad?" She took his hand. "Did you get in much trouble?"

"I had to go over to the Garners' and apologize and pay them back with a twenty-dollar bottle of champagne."

"She made you do that?"

"I didn't mind."

She nodded. "Actually, I think you got off easy. I'll pay you for half the wine."

How good she was, he thought. How generous and beautiful and perfectly, utterly good. "You don't have to," he said.

"I want to. Tell me what they said—the Garners."

"He was kind of mad at first, but she wasn't. They wanted me to stay, but Dorrie said I had to get back to bed. Mrs. Garner showed me pictures of the new baby."

"Boy or girl?"

"Girl. Named Alison."

"What a drippy name. Let's name ours Lurette and Drake."

He stared at her. "You mean our kids?" His voice creaked, and he coughed again.

"Hugo, we're going together, aren't we?"

"Nina—"

"Aren't we?" She tried to take her hand away. "Shit—don't tell me you're going to pull a Carl McGrath on me."

"Nina, believe me—" He squeezed her hand to his chest, pressed it to his lips. "Nina, I love you so much I can't even think about anything else."

She smiled and leaned on his shoulder. "I've missed you, Hugo. All that time when I was sick I kept thinking of you in school without me, and I kept wondering why you didn't even call. And here you were sick in bed. We probably had the same germ. Romantic—right?"

He was overcome with admiration; she had doubted him,

but she had come to see him. He hadn't even been able to dial her number. He thought, I'll never live up to her; I'll never deserve her.

She turned her face up to him. "You could probably kiss me without infecting me." There was her warm breath against his mouth, her lips that tasted of chewing gum. She had always reminded him of a fox—elusive and quick, on the verge of darting away from him—but now she seemed softer, less jittery. She bloomed in his arms like a wildflower.

But, kissing her, he couldn't breathe, and he had to break away, embarrassed, to blow his nose. She stroked his chest, his old bathrobe, murmuring, "Poor baby." He stuffed the tissue down behind the bed and lay back on his pillows. She sat propped against the wall, her legs slung over his, leafing through his *Grove* notebook. He studied her, loving the absent-minded way she got distracted by things—the way she took everything in, not wanting to miss a trick. She sat there frowning, chewing on her nails. The witch costume sagged around her in waves of black. Hugo thought: I love her more than I'll ever love anyone, ever again.

She looked up from the notebook and said, "I should have brought my guitar. I wrote a song about the *Grove* while I had the flu, and I'd like you to hear it. I could serenade you back to health."

"I'm not really all that sick." He added hastily, "Not that I don't want you to sing to me."

"Well, obviously," Nina said. She paused, thinking. "I really value your opinion, Hugo. I want you to always be honest with me about my stuff." He thought guiltily of her "Heart of Clay" song. Was he really supposed to tell her he hadn't liked it? Probably not.

"You can judge better than I can," he said.

"But I need constructive criticism, Hugo!" She looked at him with wide eyes and leaned over to touch his cheek. "I mean, if you're going to be my manager you've got to tell me when I'm good and when I'm lousy."

"I'm going to be your manager?"

"Unless you've got something else in mind. I mean, don't you think about what you're going to do with your life?" Her hand slid down his cheek, across his neck to his shoulder.

"Well, yeah, but I've never been able to decide." Her hand on his shoulder pulled him closer; he drew her to him and buried his face in her hair. He thought, Someday I'll actually make love to her. "I always thought I'd be a math professor," he said. His voice trembled, and he cleared his throat. "At some college."

"Forget it, Hugo. You can do better than that. You be my manager, and we can travel all over and make a lot of money. We'll take Lurette and Drake and a nanny and a governess with us wherever we go. People in airports will turn around to look at us. We'll have luggage on wheels that says 'Nina Slaughter—Rhymes with Laughter' in silver lettering." She spoke fast into his ear. These must be her daydreams, he thought, the things that went through her mind when she was sick in bed, when she sat in silence on the school bus, when she was bored. She had thought all this up, and he was part of it. He saw himself thinner, taller, in a white suit, striding through airports followed by servants, children, people trying to reach out a hand to touch his sleeve.

"I don't ever want a gold guitar, though, or one with jewels all over it," Nina said. "I don't think I'm the flashy type. A plain guitar is good enough for me—like the one I got my start on, only better. We'll go to Spain and have one custom-made."

Spain, he thought. His life seemed to be opening out like a fan, full of surfaces he had never suspected. "It sounds great," he whispered. Nina's arms went around his neck, she lifted her face, and, breathlessly, he kissed her again.

She jumped up. "I've got to get going. My sister's waiting to drive me home. Wait—" She hiked up her witch dress. She had jeans on underneath. "I brought you some Halloween candy—here." She held out some candy corn and pumpkins and a little sugar witch, linty and soft from being in her pocket. "A bit mangled, but still edible."

"Do you have to go?"

"I'll be back tomorrow. Maybe I can come after school and watch at least part of the *Grove* with you."

"Like last summer."

"But different," she said, smiling, leaning over to kiss him again. Then her face became serious. She jerked her head toward the stairs, where they could hear Dorrie running water in the studio sink, and said, "Have you asked her yet? About your mother—you know "

"Nina, I've been sick." He looked at her helplessly, and she gazed back at him with infinite understanding and wisdom and love. She whispered, "Don't be afraid." She took his hand and put it to her cheek, his palm against her soft skin, his fingers touching the silky-frizzy hair of her temples. The gesture affected him in a way nothing else ever had, not even those long kisses on the Garners' sofa. He moved his hand over her face, the bony hollow below her eye, the hard plane of her cheekbone, the curved softness of her lips. She closed her eyes, and he touched the spiky little lashes. *Nina.* Whatever happened, that word would be magic, this moment would be with him forever: Nina's face, the yellow lamplight, the tangled bedcovers and the cat curled in a ball.

"I'll talk to her tonight," he said.

Nina opened her eyes and smiled at him. "You owe it to Lurette and Drake."

When she was gone, he sat looking at the candy she had left him, and then he picked up the linty witch and ate it, slowly, as if it was a sacrament.

Dorrie came upstairs, and he heard her in the kitchen getting dinner. He worked on his notebook some more, his vow to Nina spinning in his head. He practiced, Tell me the truth, damn it, damn it, damn it. He would draw strength from Nina. Every time she kissed him he would become less of a jerk. He would be transformed, gradually, into the tall man in the white suit carrying a custom-made Spanish guitar through airports. He took the photographs from under his pillow and looked at the one of his parents. He thought of Lurette and Drake, frizzy-headed little babies sleeping in his arms.

Dorrie appeared with his dinner on a tray. "I decided to let you eat," she said, and set it down next to the bed. "Hot dogs and french fries and frozen peas. Your favorite junk."

He said, "Why didn't you ever tell me about my mother?"

"What?" She looked down at the photograph in his hand, took it from him and held it up to the light to peer at it. "What was I supposed to tell you?"

"How she really died."

When he said it, out of the blue like that, without even thinking first, his aunt just gaped at him. Then she tensed up, as if braced against her red sweater. Her mouth was open, but she didn't say anything.

"I know she was murdered. I snooped. I saw the newspaper clipping. I know everything."

She closed her mouth, handed him back the photograph, and sat down on the edge of his bed. "What do you mean, you snooped?" she said, as he had known she would. As if he was a little kid.

"Go ahead. Call me names." He slumped down in the bed and put his hand over his eyes. What was the use? "Go ahead. I broke into the Garners', I stole their wine, I told lies, I snooped in your room and found the clipping about my mother. Who cares? Call me anything. Who gives a damn?"

Dorrie was silent. He lay there with his eyes squeezed shut. He wasn't going to say another word. He would remain without speaking until morning if he had to. He would concentrate on Nina. What else mattered? The silence stretched out, and he began to wonder what she was doing, how she was reacting. She shifted on the bed, and he opened his eyes a crack. She said, "Hugo?" and he took his hand away.

"What?"

"You didn't know about your mother?"

"That she was murdered? That she was a dope addict?" Saying the words made the damned tears come: damned, dammed tears. The stupid pun rolled uncontrollably into his mind. "Did I know that somebody killed her for drugs and it was all over the front page of the newspaper? They said she died in a car crash, like my dad," he said. "Nobody told me anything. If I had known it I would have—" Would have what? Killed himself? Died of grief? He shook his head and said, "Shit," willing the tears to dry up.

Dorrie put her hand on his arm, and he pulled away. "Hugo, I assumed you knew. I had no idea no one told you the truth. I figured Rose or someone—my father—"

It had never occurred to him that she thought he knew. His resentment seemed, all of a sudden, stupid. Typical, he thought. Hugo, the eternal jerk. "I'm sorry I snooped," he said.

"Why did you?"

He wouldn't tell her it had been Nina's idea. "I wanted a picture of her."

"Did you find one?"

"Yeah, the one in the newspaper." TEEN MOTHER. God.

"I have some other photographs up in the attic," she said. "Do you want me to go up and get them?"

He wiped his eyes on his bathrobe sleeve. "Yeah, I guess so." She sat there watching him, frowning and looking thoughtful, with her chin resting on her fist. He had a terrible, mad impulse to fling himself against her and weep like a baby.

"I'll be right back," she said, getting up.

When she was gone, he cleared his nose and breathed deeply until the crying stopped. He had turned fifteen at the end of last month. When would he stop crying at things like this? Making an idiot of himself. He wished that he were twenty-five, thirty, old and settled, with his crumpled life smoothed out and himself firmly in control of it. Nina by his side.

He heard Dorrie climb the attic stairs, then footsteps over

his head. Something dragging across the floor. He waited. Nina had said he ought to keep a picture of his mother in a frame by his bed. He wondered if he should do that. Would he ever be able to look at it and think, That's my mother, without adding, the junkie, who was murdered?

Dorrie returned with a cigar box, smiling, anxious. "I forgot all these were up there," she said, then gave him a shy look. FAVORITE AUNT, he thought, and felt guilty about the mug, meant for Rose. "Shall we go through them? Would you like to?"

He shrugged, and she settled herself at the foot of his bed and handed him a photograph. "Look at this," she said. "Guess who that is."

He knew immediately that it was Dorrie and his father. Two skinny little kids hand in hand, their black hair hanging wet in their faces. "It's you and my dad," he said.

She seemed pleased. "You could really tell? Lord, but we looked alike. Except that Phinny was always better looking." That was true, though he supposed he should have argued. But she was holding out another photo. "Here. Did you ever see this? Phinny in his cowboy suit."

Hugo studied it. His father must have been no more than five, and he was sitting on a horse, pretending to fire a revolver in the air. Hugo could imagine him shouting, "Yippee!" or "Hi-yo Silver!"

"Whose horse?"

"A man used to come around with a horse and camera, sort of an itinerant photographer, and he'd take your picture up on his horse—preferably in a cowboy suit. Can you believe that everyone had a cowboy suit? Girls too, with little white skirts. And cap guns."

Hugo set the picture aside; that one he might keep framed by his bed, if she'd let him. His father looking happy.

There were browning snapshots of his grandparents, old-fashioned prints with rippled edges, the two of them looking so young he hardly recognized them. His grandfather like a

gangster in a hat pulled down low. His grandmother in a suit
with big shoulders. Another one of her in a bathing suit looking—God! sexy! And a bunch of Dorrie: in a sunsuit, in the
snow, in front of a Christmas tree. Not many of his father—
a few blurred photographs he looked like he'd been forced
into. And down at the bottom of the pile, a couple of his
mother: the one with the pearls that had been in the newspaper,
a picture of her holding a puppy, and a variation on the Camaro
shot—same car, same big belly, no cat washing this time, and
his father's arm around her. His father was frowning.

Dorrie chattered at him, turning up photo after photo,
telling him old stories. The time Phinny had fallen out of
the apple tree. That old swing in their backyard. Here she
was with Rachel—can you believe that's Rachel? And that
puppy must have belonged to—

Hugo sat staring at the picture of his parents. His mother
looking so beautiful and joyful. Was she high on something?
Himself in her stomach, waiting to be born. Was that why
he was always so weird and out of it, because his mother
had been on drugs?

He pushed the pictures away from him, and they slithered
to the floor. Dorrie stopped talking. No one spoke. The smell
of the untouched hot dogs filled the room. "Just tell me,"
he said finally.

She told him about Iris, about her beauty and sweetness,
as well as her tragic end. About that Thanksgiving dinner,
the teddy bear named Pooh, the Christmas when she had sent
Iris a hand-knit sweater and a wooden duck on wheels—though
she left out the fact that Phinny had been in jail at the time,
and that her mother had ordered her to send gifts to Iris
and her baby, who were living in New London on welfare.
She told him about a note she'd had from Iris, reporting that
baby Hugo was cutting a tooth. . . . Here she improvised
madly, remembering that Iris had once sent her a note about
something, she had no recollection of what—though the large,

childish handwriting had stuck in her memory. She was reduced to telling him where Iris had gone to high school and
that she had once planned to be a secretary but had Hugo
instead.

Hugo interrupted. "I assume they weren't married."

"You assume right."

"Did they ever catch the guy?"

"The one who killed your mother? Yes. He went to prison.
I suppose he's still there."

Hugo sat in silence for so long that she thought the conversation was over, and she was about to slip away to the kitchen,
when he said, "You're leaving a lot out, aren't you?"

She sighed. "I can't remember all that much, Hugo. Listen—I'll tell you one thing. Your mother loved you, I know
she did." Well, it was true. She remembered Iris holding Hugo,
her rapturous face. Should she tell him he was breast-fed?
Only loving mothers breast-fed their babies. It would probably
embarrass him. "She was a good mother. But she was very
young, and misguided."

Hugo gave her a belligerent look and said, "Spare me."

All of a sudden she had had it. It wasn't enough, the
mug in the garage, the flashes of goodness, the differences
from Phinny. Damn it, she was doing her best. And she had
her own tragedies, her own sad past. She said, "Don't talk
to me like that, Hugo. I know this isn't a very nice story,
I'm sure you're upset about all this, but—"

"My father," Hugo said abruptly. "What about him?"

Phinny. It was as if Hugo had pulled a switchblade on
her. She felt sick to her stomach. She could never wish Phinny
on Hugo, no matter how angry he made her. Iris was one
thing—angelic Iris, with her yellow hair and sweet smile.
Phinny was something else. Let him remain a myth. Poor
Phinny, who died young in a car crash.

"I know there's something funny about him," Hugo said.

Something funny about Phinny: no, there was nothing
funny about him, not one thing. Just for a moment, the present

fell away, and she was a child—pig-tailed, gawky, resentful, and Phinny was kicking her, pinching her, calling her Horse-Face, performing the star turns from his vast fraternal repertoire of minor tortures.

"What makes you think there's something funny about him?"

"No one ever talks about him. Grandma and Grandpa never did. You don't. Why not?" he persisted. "What is it about him? Or are you going to keep lying to me?"

She looked at Hugo's angry face—his lips pursed tight, his eyes hard. Behind the anger, she could tell, was tremendous courage, to ask her these things. She thought to herself, Here's the truth: your father was a junkie and a dope dealer, he died in prison of an overdose, he was a creep who ruined your mother's life. Other lives. Who knows how many lives he ruined? Forget about him.

She said, "Hugo, I'm sorry you were lied to about your mother. I suppose they thought you were too young to handle something like that."

"I'm not so young anymore," he said.

"I'm aware of that." Fifteen—a terrible age, as Monica had said. She imagined him up here with the witchy Nina, the two of them necking, and thought of her own aging face in the mirror.

"I'm old enough to have people tell me the truth."

"All right. You've been told," she said, speaking more sharply than she meant to. "What else do you want from me?"

"What about my father?"

She drew a deep breath and said, "No one lied to you about your father. There was nothing funny about him. He— I suppose you'd have to say he wasn't ever very successful, he kept losing jobs, he didn't help much to support you and your mother. But he wasn't a bad man." God forgive me, she thought, and searched her brain for what to say. "He was sort of the family black sheep, I guess. A little weak,

maybe. A little selfish and immature. He wasn't much like
Grandma or Grandpa. He wasn't even much like me. I was
always the good girl—you know? The older sister who did
everything right. I must have made him suffer."

Hugo nodded slowly; she could see him believing what
she said. Lies worthy of Phinny, the champion liar. What
irony.

They sat in silence. Daisy yawned and stretched, and
jumped from the bed to the windowsill. It was pitch dark
outside, but the kitten stared out as if there were something
to see, and then began to wash herself. The two of them
watched her. It was Halloween night—a good night for honor-
ing the dead, whether they deserved it or not.

"Don't think badly of your parents, Hugo," Dorrie said
after a while. "They were—honestly, they were good people.
I'm telling you the truth." She almost held her breath, waiting
to be struck dead.

Hugo looked up at her with tears in his eyes and said,
"Thanks." Lord, how easily the kid could cry. Well, good
for him. Phinny, so far as she could recall, had never shed a
tear.

She stood and picked up the tray—cold hot dogs, limp
fries. "Want me to reheat this?"

He was studying the photograph of Phinny on the horse.
"Oh—yeah—thanks," he said, and smiled at her: the first genuine smile she'd had out of him in a long time. Well, that
was something. Worth all the lies? Maybe. They were stuck
with each other: might as well smile.

In the kitchen, she looked out the window at the night.
Her own reflection looked back at her, hazy on the dirty pane:
Phinny's face. The old photographs had brought back what
she would rather have forgotten. Unfair, the way the remains
of childhood persisted, whether you wanted them or not. Her
mother in a paint-daubed smock made from an old shirt of
her father's. Her father emerging from his study, rubbing his
forehead with the heel of one hand. The Cézanne print in
the upstairs hall. The bowl of papier-mâché fruit on the hall

table, the Mexican rug on the floor there, her father's shabby leather briefcase, the parchment lampshade in the study, her mother's voice reading *A Girl of the Limberlost,* Phinny with his cap gun. "You're dead, Dorrie, fall down." None of those memories, or the crowd of others waiting to rush in, made her happy. None of them made life any easier to endure. And yet there they were, as inescapable as the face of her brother looking back at her from the window.

You can't help whom you love, she thought, and realized it was Phinny she meant. Well, of course she had loved him. Against her will, and hating his guts, she had loved him because he was her brother. She looked into his eyes, and thought, I'll keep your son safe from you or die in the attempt.

Two days later, she had a postcard. The Grand Canyon at sunset, rose and orange and copper, the sun a hot mass outlining the North Rim in gold. The message read, "Took off after class—here with Henry and Woofy en route to California to see kids—forgive me for running—forgive me for everything—thinking hard—love you forever."

She sat with it down in her studio, in Alex's wicker chair, reading it over and over, as if his handwriting—so precise it could have been typescript—were an obscure hieroglyphic that only close scrutiny could interpret. He had gone to see his kids: that was good. And to the Grand Canyon. He would climb down the trail, take his notes, have his epiphany, think hard. Good. "Forgive me for running": that was the part that hurt, the words that, however often she read them, rang like bells of doom. Why run? And was he running from her and Hugo, or to his family out there in California? He hadn't waited for a vacation—just took off in the middle of the semester. The urgency of his act was unfathomable. She had the feeling she had never known him at all. She had known his sad-eyed face, his lean and vulnerable body, the crosshatch of scars on his thigh from a bicycle accident, his dry knobby elbows. But the real, complete, interior Alex: was it possible he was still a stranger to her? and she to him? How had he not known that, if it came to this absurd choice, she would stick by Hugo? Or that this casual postcard, laid out nakedly to be read by the postman or Hugo and Lord knows who else, would cut her to the heart?

"Love you forever." However many times she read it, it sounded like "Good-bye forever."

She went upstairs and made herself a cup of tea in the FAVORITE AUNT mug with its garish flowered border. Ugly though it was, she treasured it; the ugly and unlovable things of this world should be loved and treasured nonetheless. She remembered how Rachel had said, "I can't be alone," and how she had agreed without thinking twice: of course, of course, there's nothing worse than being alone, no love, the lonely bed, the sameness of the days, the dread of the years ahead. But she had been alone—plenty. She had become adept at solitude, and at finding company in inanimate objects, in nature, in work. Now she would have Hugo. Good old Aunt Dorrie. There were worse things.

She was finishing her tea when Hugo came in, breathless and coughing, with Nina—his first day back at school.

"How did it go?"

"School? Lousy as usual."

"I suppose what I mean is, how do you feel?"

"Oh—fine, fine."

"He coughed all the way home on the bus," Nina said. Nina was still shy with her, apologetic under the brassiness. "I think he needs some cough medicine or something."

"All I need is the *Grove,*" Hugo said. "It's one minute to three."

They went into Hugo's alcove. The usual commercials, the theme music, the buzz of inane yakety-yak, Hugo flipping through his notebook, coughing, the two of them arguing: "They're not going to let her die."

"Hugo, she's got a brain tumor, for heaven's sake. That happens to be serious."

"She's survived worse."

"Oh, give me a break. Even Dr. Wendell says she hasn't got a chance."

"When has he ever been right about anything?"

Dorrie smiled. It was Paula, she knew, who had the tumor. Dr. Wendell was her former lover. Paula's brother, Michael, was married to Tiffany, who had also had an affair with Dr. Wendell. Did all that have anything to do with Dr. Wendell's pessimism about Paula's brain tumor? Or with Paula's daughter's illegitimate son, Jason, who had been adopted by Prescott and Tara but was now about to be kidnapped by something called the People's Syndicate? Lord! Was she becoming hooked on *Upton's Grove*? Never—she wouldn't give Hugo the satisfaction.

She would have to add on a room next summer, a place for Hugo to watch television, entertain his friends—lose his virginity, Alex would say. And she'd have to call the cable people; the TV reception, she knew, wasn't good. What else? Pottery classes again, maybe. Some work with the salt kiln. Italy in the spring. Or Greece. Somewhere. Something.

She drank the last of her tea and took her mug into the kitchen. A weepy voice from the television said, "All we can do now is hope."

"Fat lot of good that's going to do anybody," said Nina. "Why don't they get in that specialist from New York?"

Dorrie washed the mug in the sink, dried it carefully, set it on the shelf. She took the postcard from her pocket and read it again. "Forgive me for running . . . love you forever." Well, maybe he would, but she had a fast, desolate premonition that she would never see him again. He would end up in California. His tan would never fade. He would become a handsome old man, growing old in the sunshine with some other young wife, with his boys nearby. They would never let him go: how could they resist such a father, such charm? How could he resist his own children? He would finish his book sitting under a lemon tree. She would go into a bookstore sometime next year and see it:

An Infinite Number of Monkeys

by Alexander Willick

In the last chapter, Henry and Woofy would climb down the North Rim to the Colorado River, and Henry's moment of truth would be authentic, researched, the real thing. The dedication she knew he had planned would stand: "For Dorothea Gilbert." People would read the book and wonder who Dorothea Gilbert was—might notice that their two names set up the same rhythm. Then there would be the next book, dedicated to someone else. She would read reviews of it; she would go to a bookstore and buy it. It would be full of things that were strange to her, told in Alex's familiar voice.

She looked out at the pond, clear and still in the cold autumn light. This was it, then: the end of something. Here was the abyss she had seen that night in the rain. She stood there thinking that: The end, the end; and without warning she began to cry, the old familiar tears, while the old familiar banners waved through her consciousness: UNFAIR and LIFE IS CRUEL and WHY ME? She looked again through her tears at Alex's postcard, his crabbed writing. She turned it over and stared for a long time at the hot gold sun setting over the Grand Canyon, and one thought came vividly, from nowhere: I can't let him go.

In the phone book, she found the area code for Santa Monica, and dialed information. No, there was no Beth Willick, but there was a number for Elizabeth Willick. Breathless, the blood beating hard in her temples, Dorrie scrawled it down. She imagined Rachel telling this as one of her wacky stories: So of course the logical thing was to call his ex-wife in California—right? And get him on the phone and say, "Listen Buster, if you think you can get away with this you're out of your mind. You think I don't see through you? It's not some mixed-up teen-ager you're afraid of, it's *me,* the Big C—Commitment, sweetie, that's the name of the game."

Dorrie hesitated, frowning. Was that true? She didn't know, had no idea; she didn't even care. Fear of commitment, the unresolved relationship with his own children, the specter of Phinny hovering over Hugo—whatever it was that had driven Alex away in the rain, it wasn't lack of love. Of that she was sure. She must have been crazy to let him go without a struggle.

She dialed the number, watching dreamily as her finger moved the dial around. All those digits. Dust on the phone. Her finger with its ragged nail. All we can do now is hope. All we can do now is grope, mope, cope. . . .

"Hello?" A pretty, musical voice, just the voice she had expected.

She said, "Is this Beth Willick?"

"Yes?" the voice said, sounding rushed and impatient. Dorrie pictured a man climbing half dressed down a fire escape.

"I wonder—I was wondering—is Alex there, by any chance? Alex Willick."

"No, he's not, I'm afraid. Is this Dorrie?"

"What?" Dorrie leaned her head against the wall. Her cheeks burned; her mouth was dry. "I mean—yes, this is Dorrie. How did you know?"

"Well, my Lord, he did tell us about you, you know."

The voice sounded amused, beautiful, condescending. Dorrie said, "Told you what?"

"Well, I mean, that you exist! That you two are engaged. All I can say is good luck." She laughed. "I don't mean that the way it sounds. I just mean, sincerely, good luck, best wishes to you both. The boys are thrilled; they're dying to meet you."

Alex. "Is he—can I reach him somewhere?"

"He's en route back east. Jeremy and I just took him to the airport. I let Jeremy cut school. Jeff had a physics test, so I wouldn't let him." She laughed again. "I know I'll never hear the end of that one." Dorrie tried to imagine the woman behind the voice: blond, petite, curvy, with a wonderful smile. In Beth's voice, Dorrie heard Alex's history as he had told it to her; it was a my-last-duchess voice, one that wanted to be liked and loved and admired. "On the other hand," Beth said, "Alex went to Jeff's soccer game last night, so that evens things out, in my opinion."

Dorrie relaxed. I couldn't help it, she heard herself telling Rachel. I did like her. She said, "They all had a pretty good time, then."

"Are you serious? Listen, this was the event of the year—Daddy coming for a visit. I'm glad Alex is getting his act together. Those kids are at an age when they need a father, if you know what I mean. I assume I can thank you for some of this."

"Oh—well." She still held the postcard in her hand; she pressed it to her cheek.

"I get the impression from Alex that you've had a pretty good effect on him."

"I don't know, I suppose he—I have this nephew," she said impulsively. "He complicates things."

"We heard about the nephew. A real eccentric, I take it. I wouldn't worry about it; these step-family things work themselves out." Again the musical laugh. "Look at who's talking. I haven't exactly hustled off to the altar again myself. But the quality of available men these days is not terrific, as I'm sure you've noticed."

"Ah—"

"Don't get me wrong, I don't mean Alex."

"Oh, I—"

"Listen, Dorrie, I'm late, I've got to run. It was wonderful to talk to you. I'm sure we'll meet one of these days. Alex's flight gets into Logan around eight fifteen, your time, if you're thinking of meeting him. Something like that—eight fifteen, eight thirty-five, I forget. TWA, anyway. You can check it."

"Thanks, I—"

"And next time Alex comes out here, you come with him. Okay? Promise?"

Dorrie promised, and hung up in a daze. Alex. He was

on his way back—in the air now, slumped over a book, drinking beer, irritable because there wasn't enough room for his long legs, scared—flying frightened him, she knew, as heights did. He would look out the window, think of his boys, replay Jeff's soccer game, worry about whether the pilot was on amphetamines, plan his lecture for Monday night. Think of her, maybe. Resolve to call when he got in. And there she would be at the airport: waiting, like his suitcase, to be claimed. She should bring a big sign and stand under it: FIANCÉE CLAIM. She imagined his smile, his generous laugh. Alex.

She went over to the sink. Her cheeks felt tight where the tears had dried on them, and her eyes burned. I won't let him, she thought. That's what she would say: I won't let you get rid of me so easily. Okay, my life is messy. All life is messy. And then she would kiss him. Kissing, she would say. Kissing is messy. So is sex. So is literature. So is pottery making. So is the Grand Canyon, for heaven's sake. So is love. Only death is neat, Alex. She would say that, and then they would drive to his apartment and make love.

She splashed cold water on her face. Then she stuck Alex's view of the Grand Canyon to the refrigerator with a magnet and wandered into the living room, to the door of Hugo's alcove.

"She's just being wheeled into surgery," Hugo said to her. She asked, "Who's doing the operation? Dr. Wendell?" "Yeah, but he's been drinking."

The eyes of the nurses, above their masks, were heavy with makeup. They exchanged worried looks. Cut to the doctor; his eyes were narrowed and red-rimmed, his hands trembled as he reached for the scalpel. Cut to the waiting room, where a woman with glycerin tears seeping from her mascara said, "Everything will be all right, Gus. I know it, I feel it."

"Ha," said Nina.

Dorrie watched it with them to the end: Dr. Wendell collapsing in the operating room, another surgeon taking over. Then she left Hugo and Nina in the kitchen eating untoasted

English muffins—one of Nina's passions—and went downstairs to her studio. She would have liked to go outside, maybe walk in the fading afternoon down to the pond to see if the Canada geese were still there. But it was a clammy, cold day. November. Good weather for staying in. She walked around the studio, covered a forgotten pot of glaze, admired the row of soup bowls waiting for firing, patted the kitten who lay curled up on Alex's old sweatshirt in the wicker chair. From upstairs, there was the sound of laughter, Nina's squeal. Rain ticked gently against the window.

She sat down at the wheel, wet her hands, took a lump of clay and centered it. She would have to get an early dinner to leave plenty of time to get to the airport, but there were still a couple of hours. The clay revolved between her palms, becoming smooth and sleek. What to make? Something new, something so beautiful that it would surprise even her. She leaned into it, feeling the rhythm in her fingers like music, and let the clay take over.